# FLIGHT
## OF THE
# RAVEN

**Ingrid Seymour** is a *USA Today* bestselling author. When she's not writing books, she spends her time cooking exotic recipes, hanging out with her family, and working out. She writes fiction in a variety of genres, including fantasy romance, urban fantasy, romance, paranormal, and sci-fi. Her favourite outings involve a trip to the library or bookstore. She's an avid reader and fangirl of many amazing books. She is a dreamer and a fighter who believes perseverance and hard work can make dreams come true. She lives in Birmingham, AL with her husband, two kids, and a cat named Ossie.

Instagram: **@ingrid_seymour**
X: **@Ingrid_Seymour**
TikTok: **@ ingridseymour**
Facebook: **/IngridSeymourAuthor**

# FLIGHT

## OF THE

## RAVEN

## INGRID SEYMOUR

HEADLINE
ETERNAL

Published by arrangement with PenDreams

First published in Great Britain in this paperback edition in 2025
by HEADLINE ETERNAL
An imprint of HEADLINE PUBLISHING GROUP

1

Cataloguing in Publication Data is available from the British Library

PAPERBACK ISBN 978 1 0354 2070 4

Internal artwork by Deposit Photos

Map © Ingrid Seymour 2024

Typeset in 11/16pt EB Garamond by Jouve (UK), Milton Keynes

Printed and bound in Great Britain by Clays Ltd, Elcograf S.p.A.

Headline's policy is to use papers that are natural, renewable and recyclable
products and made from wood grown in well-managed forests and other
controlled sources. The logging and manufacturing processes are expected
to conform to the environmental regulations of the country of origin.

Headline Publishing Group Limited
An Hachette UK Company
Carmelite House
50 Victoria Embankment
London EC4Y 0DZ

The authorised representative in the EEA is Hachette Ireland, 8 Castlecourt Centre,
Dublin 15, D15 XTP3, Ireland (email: info@hbgi.ie)

www.headline.co.uk
www.hachette.co.uk

To Alex
there's no hiding that big heart of yours
I see it

# Calendar Eras

**AV** – After the veil
**DV** – During the veil
**BV** – Before the veil

# I

## SAETHARA

*"Don't fail us, Saethara. We are counting on you."*

**Lirion Faolborn – Fae Shifter – 1980 DV**

*S*aethara straddled Korben, her movements careful to avoid waking him up. Positioning her knees to either side of his hips, she lifted her arms high above her head, dagger clenched tightly in both hands. The blade glinted in the candlelight, and The Eldrystone seemed to wink in response.

She licked her lips, anticipating the moment.

The amulet rested on his smooth chest, right over his breastbone. She would have to make sure it did not get in her way.

A nervous thrill traveled through her. She doubted so many times, thought she would never get this far. Yet, here she was, the most powerful object in existence well within her reach.

He slept peacefully, the fool. There was even a slight smile stretching his lips. He was handsome. She had to admit that much, but she was never attracted to him. It was someone else entirely who claimed that honor.

1

It hadn't been easy to lay with Korben—the naïve and undeserving Fae King—but that was a small price to pay for what she was about to gain.

Securing her grip around the hilt, Saethara plunged the weapon downward. It hit its mark right above the amulet, between the "V" of its chain that snaked through its clasp.

The dagger was sharp, crafted by an expert and imbued with magic. It cut through bone and sinew as easily as a needle piercing fabric.

Korben reared up, gasping in pain and surprise, hands wrapping around her hands over the hilt of the dagger. His black eyes met hers, pupils blown, threatening to swallow her whole. His mouth opened, and he tried to speak, but only a dribble of red came out. Choking on his own blood, he fell back down on the pillow, his gaze never leaving hers. There was a question in his expression, a begging plea.

Why? he seemed to ask, even as his eyes flicked toward the answer: The Eldrystone.

His grip over her hands slackened, then his arms fell limply to the sides. Blood flowed freely, sliding over his ribs to their nuptial sheets, soaking them through. For good measure, she leaned into the weapon, using her entire weight and twisting the blade deeper and deeper.

Korben's eyes rolled into the back of his head. More blood gurgled from his mouth, and a moment later, he went absolutely still.

"The king is dead. Long live the queen," Saethara murmured as she unstraddled him and immediately set out to relieve him of the amulet.

It was crafted from a perfect opal, held within an intricate golden framework. The metalwork was a delicate array of swirling vines, the work of the finest fae craftfolk or perhaps Niamhara, the so-called Goddess of Radiance. Small runic symbols lined its underside, written in a script she did not understand.

*Her hand wrapped around it, causing a wave of elation to course through her body.*

Finally. Finally!

*It had been a long journey, and it was over at last. She had been nothing but a young girl when the task was thrust upon her. For a long time, she believed it impossible. How could a nobody from a small village ever become Queen of Tirnanog? And now . . .*

*It was easy, so easy, to slip the amulet over Korben's head and pull the chain free, his dead weight offering only a small obstacle.*

*And thus, The Eldrystone was hers. All hers.*

*Standing over her dead husband, naked and with the amulet in her hand, Saethara trembled. Years of yearning had come to an end. Niamhara's power was hers.*

*A shiver ran up her spine, making her scalp tingle. She was suddenly filled with fear as she caught sight of Korben's face, the color completely gone from his cheeks and lips.*

I killed the Fae King.

*She had been so focused on her task that she had barely stopped to contemplate how it would feel to kill someone or exactly what she would do once the years of planning had yielded fruit.*

*Her heart hammered, and her breaths grew sharp and shallow.*

*Unable to stand the sight of the gruesome display any longer, she turned away from the bed.*

I have to get out of here, away from . . . him.

*Her eyes wide and fixed on a faraway point, she put on a silken robe and tied it around her narrow waist. Hurrying out of the bedchamber, her steps guided her away. Her mind replayed the moment the dagger plunged into Korben's chest. There had been little to no resistance, and it*

3

had felt easy, but now a nauseous knot was building in the pit of her stomach.

She thought killing would be easy, and it had been, but all that blood. Gods! She glanced down at the amulet. It felt cold between her fingers, empty. Numbly, she lifted it and stared at it more closely, even as her steps continued guiding her . . . elsewhere.

On closer inspection, the amulet—which had looked dazzling around Korben's neck as he rode her, lost in the throes of his release—now seemed like a trinket from a cheap bazaar. Possessing it did not feel the way she had imagined. She had fancied it would fill her with a sense of power. Instead, a dire sensation crowded her chest.

She began to doubt herself, panic starting a loud ringing in her ears. Her steps changed direction, guiding her with purpose to Loreleia, her best friend, but when she found her bedchamber empty, Saethara started hyperventilating.

Korben's people were going to kill her. Once they found out what she had done, they would sentence her to death. They would not let her be queen. She had murdered Korben Theric, the forty-first king from a long dynasty.

Niamhara had entrusted her conduit to his family thousands of years ago, and they had kept Tirnanog prosperous ever since. Othano Theric, a young farmer, was one of Niamhara's faithful worshipers, and with the amulet, he brought the fae together, ushering them into progress and greatness, ending the squabbles that had plagued them since their creation.

The ringing in Saethara's ears mounted to a deafening level. She turned away from Loreleia's door and ran down the long corridor, heedless of the destination.

*Her bare feet slapped the cold marble, and when she crossed the threshold into a small courtyard, she came to an abrupt stop.*

*Loreleia was there, sitting on the lowest branch of an earthbinder tree. Pink blossoms hovered around her, swooping down from higher branches as if she were made of light and they needed to be near her.*

*Her friend was reading a book, her expression as sweet and calm as ever. Sensing her presence, Loreleia glanced up, an automatic smile stretching her lips. As soon as she laid eyes on Saethara, however, the smile faded. Loreleia set the book aside on the branch and ran to her. The blossoms retreated.*

*"What happened? You look . . ." Loreleia didn't finish her sentence. Instead, she scanned Saethara from head to toes, eventually pausing at the amulet clenched between her fingers and the blood staining them.*

*"I killed him," Saethara said, her tone even, void of all emotion.*

*Loreleia swallowed, blue eyes growing wide. "Who? Who did you kill?"*

*"Him."*

*"The . . . the king?"*

*Loreleia knew Saethara was supposed to be with her husband. They had just retired to consummate their marriage a mere thirty minutes ago, after all. They were supposed to be drowning in each other's arms, blissfully enjoying their first night as a mated couple. But then Korben had been so eager, like a boy, undressing her quickly and taking her in a rush of passion that did not last.*

*"I love you," he had whispered in her ear as he collapsed next to her, thinking he had satisfied her after she had made the right sounds for him.*

*"The king?" Loreleia repeated her question.*

*Saethara nodded.*

*"Oh, gods!" Her friend gasped, pressing a delicate hand to her mouth as horror filled her clear blue gaze. "Did he . . . did he hurt you?"*

*It took Saethara a moment to process the question.*

*Of course, innocent Loreleia, who had known Saethara since they were small girls growing up in Nilhalari, would not assume Saethara had done something so terrible, so hideous, without a justifiable reason. Of course, she would produce a perfect excuse for Saethara, one that she could use to explain away her actions. They would not harm her once she explained. She would tell everyone Korben had been rough and had—*

*The anxious thoughts stopped abruptly, and an unnatural calmness descended over Saethara, easing her agitated breaths and slowing down her heartbeat to a normal level.*

*Why had she panicked? There was no reason for that. She had The Eldrystone in her possession. The entire realm would bow down to her and the power she could now command.*

*Still, having an excuse was convenient. A little sympathy from her subjects was not unwarranted. It might even make things easier for her.*

*Conjuring tears to her eyes, Saethara nodded. "He . . . he was so . . ." Without finishing, she broke into sobs that wracked her body like physical blows.*

*"Oh, Saethara." Loreleia wrapped her in her arms and squeezed tightly. "I am so sorry. I thought he loved you, but he was a deceiver. I am so sorry."*

*Loreleia did not doubt her, not for an instant.*

*In the warmth of her friend's embrace, Saethara smiled with satisfaction. It seemed she was condemned to be surrounded by fools. Well, not* entirely. She had Lirion. He was a clever one. Saethara would have never gotten this far without him.

The sound of steps from within the palace tore their attention from each other. They pulled apart and glanced toward the archway that led out of the courtyard.

Saethara's heart stopped.

Korben stood with a sword in his hand, dry blood caked all over his bare chest.

He is not dead! Why is he not dead?

Her heart went back to pounding out of control. What was she to do now? She had failed.

The Fae King roared in anger, an animalistic utterance that made the pink earthbinder blossoms retreat far up into the trees.

As his gaze landed on her, he bellowed, "Saethara! You filthy liar. I will end you." He raised his sword and marched in her direction.

# 2

# VALERIA

*"I wish I knew if Amira or Valeria inherited my shifting abilities,
if they will be able to rely on them if the veil ever reopens."*

**Rey Simón Plumanegra (Casa Plumanegra) – Human King – 12 AV**

I'm breaking.

The sound of my fracturing bones translates to unbearable pain, and I scream.

*I'm dying.*

Korben is here, and Jago too. I sense them. Korben is talking, but his words make no sense. My ears roar with too many sounds, loud, overwhelming.

Something alien accompanies the pain. It festers across every inch of my body. My skin itches, prickles, burns. Bile rises up my throat. My mouth opens with the gag reflex, and a shrill sound comes out. My revulsion redoubles.

The pain stretches into agony. I forget who I am, only wishing for a swift death. No life is worth this horror. Oblivion is better than this.

*Gods, take me!*

After an eternity, I'm partially aware of the pain slowly diminishing, but I'm so lost in the aftermath that I miss the exact moment when it finally stops. The next thing I know, I'm lying on my side, enveloped by a myriad of sounds and a riot of colors almost as overwhelming as the pain.

I blink to clear my vision, but even that small motion feels foreign. I try to stand but fail. My body feels lopsided and . . . insubstantial. I kick my legs, and they move ineffectually, circling and circling without gaining any traction. I don't know how to stand. My arms are no help as I try to push off the ground.

I hear a croak, and then someone pushes me to my feet. Standing feels as odd as lying down. My toes are digging into the earth. I glance down at them.

*Gods!* No, not feet. Talons!

Panicked, I shriek, sounding like Cuervo.

That's when I realize he's standing right next to me. He was the one who helped me up. I stare at him. He's my size. No, I'm *his* size. I know it is Cuervo. I recognize his features. However, the colors on his feathers are nothing like I remember. Instead, they're a thousand different shades of purple, blue, green. Hues I never knew existed.

"Friend!" he croaks, head bobbing.

"Cuervo," I say, or at least I try. What comes out is an entirely different sound.

The logical part of my brain understands exactly what just happened. I've shifted into a raven. But understanding and accepting are two entirely different things.

*I'm not ready for this. I'm not! I'm not even sure I want it, no matter how much I used to think I did.*

I squeeze my eyes shut and wish for my human shape to return.

Nothing happens. I remain the same, a small creature with the world looming all around me. Korben's boots are larger than me. He stands facing away from me, ignoring me. Why? Why when I need him most?!

"Greetings," he's saying, his voice ringing with a deeper quality in my new ears.

"Hold it right there," someone responds, followed by the sound of a sword unsheathing, the *zing* of metal a melody of many tones. "You are hereby detained."

"Detained?" Korben echoes. "Under what grounds and authority?"

"You are under arrest for . . . breaching the veil. By decree of Queen Saethara, you are under arrest."

Memories rush back like an avalanche. For a small eternity, I was nothing but pain, followed by the sudden shattering realization that I *did* inherit my father's shifting abilities. Except now, I remember exactly where we are and why.

I reopened the veil to Tirnanog, and now we stand in my mother's realm, the place that saw her birth and that of half of my ancestors. Moreover, we're in Korben's kingdom. Twenty years after he disappeared. All that time, he was locked away in Castella while life went on without him here, and not entirely in the way he suspected.

Saethara . . . the female he married, the monster who tried to kill him on their wedding night, is still alive. Not only that, in his absence, she remains queen, and it seems she has been waiting for this day. Why else would people be here ready to arrest anyone crossing the newly reopened veil?

*Saints and feathers!* We have to get out of here.

# 3

# SAETHARA

*"Has anyone seen King Korben? Do not look at me with blank faces.*
*Answer me!"*

**Vonall Darawin – King's Adviser – 1999 DV**

*U*pon seeing the Fae King striding in her direction, Saethara's first instinct was to run. His sword gleamed, and it seemed to vibrate with a deafening zing, a cruel melody announcing her death.

It was at the verge of whirling around to escape that she remembered what she held in her hand. Like a breeze blowing away smoke, the thought cleared away her fear, leaving behind the thrilling desire to use the amulet for the first time and find out what it was capable of.

As Korben approached, his expression was unlike anything she had ever seen on his face. From the first moment they met, the Fae King had shown only solicitousness toward her. Now, she saw hatred.

When Saethara and Loreleia left their village, it had been in a flurry of nerves and uncertainty. Despite everyone's reassurances, Saethara was not so sure she would win the Royal Mate Rite. Females from all across Tirnanog were traveling to the capital to appear before

11

*the king and face his scrutiny. They were to go through a series of meet-ings and tests to determine whether or not they were worthy of becoming Korben Theric's wife and by extension Tirnanog's queen.*

*For the first time in her life, Saethara felt uncertain about her ability to ensnare a male with her innate beauty. Her hair was the color of the summer sky, matched by bright cerulean eyes. Her plump breasts and rounded hips always caused males to ogle. And at an early age, she learned the power of her allure and used it to her advantage. Yet, she feared failure.*

*Her nerves were the reason she enlisted Loreleia to accompany her, practically forcing her to leave their small village, Nilhalari. Loreleia was demure and plainly pretty, so Saethara was not worried about her friend becoming a rival during the contest. She did it because she wanted Loreleia's unconditional support and constant prattle about how won-derful Saethara was. Since they were little, Loreleia had tagged along like a house pet, the perfect acquiescent companion. This time it was no different. Despite having no interest in becoming queen, Loreleia agreed to accompany Saethara. The poor fool hardly had a thought of her own. Once Saethara became queen, she planned to keep Loreleia as her lady's maid. It would be helpful to have someone she trusted by her side, once Saethara accomplished her assigned task.*

*Saethara should have never doubted herself, however. The king was immediately taken with her. It was clear to her and everyone else that he had eyes for no other. Afterward, every meeting and test became a mere formality.*

*Now, Korben's dark eyes were fixed on Saethara, though void of the stupefied quality she'd grown accustomed to. Instead, in their depths, she saw only rancor, no evidence that mere moments ago there had been only love. His face wore the grimace of a predator, the scowl of an executioner. He meant to kill her, run her through the heart with his sword, just as she had done to him.*

"He may not die," *Lirion had said in one of her many lessons before she got to Elf-Dun, this magnificent palace.* "He is a shifter and has innate healing abilities. Though if he survives, it will not matter— not once you take the amulet from him."

"You never cared for me," *Korben said, walking closer.* "You only wanted The Eldrystone."

"You worked that out all on your own?" *Saethara asked, feeling untold satisfaction at having fooled him.*

*Next to her, Loreleia let out a quiet gasp. Her blue eyes wide, she regarded Saethara then Korben, a million questions seemingly rushing through her mind.*

"It does not belong to you," *Korben said, taking one more step.*

"I beg to disagree." *She dangled the amulet in front of him, its chain threaded through her long fingers.*

"What have you done, Saethara?" *Loreleia asked in a barely audible voice.*

*Saethara rolled her eyes. Sometimes her friend's dull-witted personality was too much.* "Did you actually think I came here to pine over this gullible male?"

*Loreleia's mouth opened and closed ineffectually.*

"You vile snake," *Korben hissed.* "I will destroy you and everyone you have ever loved, if you are even capable of such feelings. I will obliterate your village, and every wretched person who lives there. Nothing good can come from a place that spawns monsters such as you."

"No!" *Loreleia exclaimed.* "You cannot do that."

Korben ignored her and aimed his sword straight at Saethara's heart. A few more steps, and he would be upon her.

Taking a deep breath, Saethara lifted the amulet above her head, ready to wish for Korben's final demise. Then the unthinkable happened, Loreleia, her faithful pet, betrayed her, snatching The Eldrystone out of her hand at the very moment that Korben took one final step and ran Saethara through with his sword, plunging the blade down to the hilt and robbing her entirely of breath.

Knees buckling, Saethara crashed to the stone floor, trembling hands wrapping around the blade, attempting to pull it out and succeeding only in slicing her fingers and coating them with sticky blood.

Something warm bubbled up her throat and trickled out of the corner of her mouth. Lying on her side, she twitched and gasped in staccato bursts.

During her time of preparation, Lirion guaranteed her success.

"We have a powerful ally," he had said. "Someone who can defeat Niamhara."

Oh, how naïve Saethara had been. He had lied, and now she was dying, the future she had imagined quickly melting away, the path turning gloomy and promising purgatory as a destination.

"Korben, what . . . what are you doing?" a deep male voice suffused with shock called out from the edge of the courtyard.

Through blurry eyes, Saethara saw a pair of booted feet run past her. A physical struggle ensued. Someone else ran past, someone wearing dainty slippers and a heavy gown.

Loreleia!

Saethara reached out a bloody hand. The stupid woman was escaping with The Eldrystone while Korben fought whoever had decided to *intervene. The sound of swords clashing filled Saethara's ears, but it was faint. Everything was faint.*

*"Korben, stop! I beg. You have gone mad," the same male voice said.*

*Her vision went black, and she exhaled what she thought would be her final breath. Death was a certain thing. Saethara felt it, gripping her soul in its cold hand. She had failed.*

*Pressure on her chest, on the wound. The sword was removed. A flash of green light followed, and as she blinked and her eyes cleared, she saw Korben's friend—Vonall, was it?—hovering above her.*

*She began to sit up and scream.*

*"Easy, Your Majesty," the male said. "You are going to be all right."*

*Her scream came out as a weak whimper.*

*She looked around. Korben was nowhere to be seen. The trees in the courtyard appeared bare, with all the blooms retreated to safety. Her blood spread darkly beneath her, a large puddle with the shiny surface of a gruesome mirror.*

*"How do you feel?" the male asked.*

*She frowned up at him, scanning his face. Up close, she could see small lines starting to form around the corners of his eyes.*

He must be ancient. Over three hundred years old, most certainly, *she thought in a detached way.*

*He had a soft mouth with deep laugh lines that let her know he was one of those tenderhearted fools who thought everyone was their friend.*

*"I'm Vonall. Vonall Darawin," he said in a reassuring tone, as if he could tell she hardly remembered him.*

*She had met him during one of the many receptions they held throughout the Royal Mate Rite proceedings, and she had seen him in passing many times after that. He always seemed to hang around Korben, though in what capacity, she did not know.*

*"Allow me to help you sit on this bench." He lent her his strength, practically lifting her in his arms.*

*Saethara's robe was soaked in blood, sticking to her chest. It was half-opened, but Vonall kept his eyes on hers, the picture of propriety. Her bosoms, a sizable handful and plump with youth, were her strongest attribute, in her opinion. Few were ever able to resist even a furtive glance, but this male seemed immune, a sign that he must be attracted to his own sex.*

*"I know you are distressed," he said, his voice mellow and calming, "but I must know what happened? Did . . . did Korben do this to you?" He glanced at her chest now, but it was with a frown of concern and confusion.*

*She tried to speak, but her throat was parched. Besides, what could she tell him? That she had attempted to murder the king in order to steal his precious amulet? That she had failed miserably, and he had come looking for her, bent on revenge? That he had succeeded, running her through and through with his sword?*

*No, she could not answer his questions, so she shook her head, wrapping weak arms tightly around her middle and babbling incoherently.*

*"W-where . . . is he? And Loreleia. Oh, Loreleia!"*

You stupid cow! You ruined everything!

*"She . . . um . . . I bought her some time," Vonall said, believing Saethara was worried about her friend's safety, when in truth, she wanted to pick up Korben's sword and actually kill someone tonight. If that person could not be the Fae King, Loreleia would do.*

*"I could not stop him," Vonall went on. "I tried but he has always*

bested me with the sword. He went after her. Do you have any idea where she might have run to?"

Saethara shook her head.

"She . . . your friend . . . she had Korben's amulet? How did that happen? Korben never takes it off." He glanced down, suspicion creeping into his features.

Once more, she shook her head. It was a refusal to answer the question, but Vonall took it as something else. He thought Saethara was confused or didn't know what had happened.

"It is all right. I know you are in shock. You need to calm down and then maybe you will remember and will be able to tell us. I will fetch someone to help you. Forgive me for leaving you, but I must find the king. He is not in his right mind. I have never seen him act that way. He looked . . . deranged. I cannot think of any other way to describe it."

He left then, and soon after, several people came for her, including the royal healer. When they attempted to escort her to the bridal chamber, she grew agitated and insisted on going to the queen's quarters. She had never spent a single night there, but Korben had made sure to show her the grand chamber, a place with a four-poster bed, a fireplace, a bath chamber, and even a library, a place where she could retreat when she needed privacy.

No one questioned her request. She had to make sure they did not see the evidence of what had transpired in the bridal chamber. They might draw conclusions that would undoubtedly lead them to the truth.

She could only hope Loreleia would finish the job. Korben had threatened to destroy her precious Nilhalari, and the idiot was only fierce when it came to defending her own. With any luck, she would use The Eldrystone to make sure he never got the chance. If she did, it would be a stroke *of luck for Saethara. Not exactly what she had been after, but she would be queen. Vonall had called her* Your Majesty, *after all. And if no one found out what she had done, and Korben met his end at Loreleia's hand, then she could hunt that insipid female down and take the amulet back from her.*

*It was a lot of* ifs, *but it was her only hope. That, and keeping her mouth shut. They would all ask questions the same way Vonall had. She had to prepare the perfect answers.*

*Answers that would also satisfy Lirion. He would be furious, and he was terrifying when he was furious. Though his love-making got rough when he was angry, and she liked that.*

*As soon as the healer tended to her, she dismissed him and everyone else. Elf-Dún was in upheaval. She had seen people running to and fro on her way to her queenly chamber. But in this area of the palace, things were quiet.*

*Unseen, she hurried to the scene of the crime. The bed was soaked in dark blood, and the dagger she had used to stab Korben lay discarded on the floor. Securing the main entrance, she cautiously opened the double doors leading to a private garden. The sound of trickling water from the sorcerer-made grotto in the back reached her ears. Before coming into the chamber, Korben had taken her out there in some misguided attempt at romance. He had explained he had the area designed specially for her. She had been forced to admit it was a lovely place, but she would have rather Lirion had built it for her.*

*Holding her breath, she fiddled with the ring around her index finger, then lifted it toward her mouth and whispered the designated words.*

*"By the moon's silver glow, I call upon you, Servant of the true Goddess."*

*As she waited, her breath hung in the air, thick with anticipation. A few tense moments passed during which she imagined herself alone, Lirion never coming to her aid. But he had never deserted her. He would surely come now. Or would her failure change everything between them?*

Oh, gods, please do not allow that!

*The relief that washed over her as Lirion appeared in the garden—his round eyes glowing yellow as he pushed past a thick hedge—was like a tender caress on her agitated heart. He padded in her direction, long black claws clicking on the slate floor. His gray fur was thick around his neck and tapered down through the rest of his massive body.*

*He stopped in front of her. Saethara knelt and hugged his neck, enjoying the silky feel of his fur against her face.*

*Lirion took a step back, his yellow eyes locking with hers. She felt his unspoken question pass between them.*

*Swallowing thickly, she shook her head.*

*His black lips pulled back, and fierce canines gleamed with saliva as he growled in displeasure.*

*A shiver running through him, Lirion shifted from wolf to male in the blink of an eye. He towered over her, a wall of muscle and foul attitude. He wore a pair of black trousers that disappeared into tall boots. Other than that, the only thing he had on was a pair of silver cuffs around his wrists. That, and a swirling tattoo on his back.*

*Her face was leveled with his crotch. It bulged, betraying his size. The king had been just as powerful, but Saethara's hunger had never awakened in his presence, not the way it did when Lirion was around. Even though she feared his disapproval, she felt herself getting wet for him.*

*His nose twitched, likely scenting her desire. With a grunt, he grabbed her arm and pulled her to her feet.*

*"Why do you tarry?" he asked. "Kill him already."*

*"I did," she said, gesturing backward to point at the blood-soaked bed.*

*Lirion's thick gray eyebrows drew together. His hair color matched that of his wolf.*

*"He didn't stay dead," Saethara said. "He woke up and ran me through with his sword." She wished she still wore the bloody robe as proof.*

*He squeezed her arm. "Don't lie to me, Saethara."*

*"I am not lying." She told him then what had happened.*

*He grew increasingly angrier with every word, and when she was done, he grabbed her by the shoulders and shook her.*

*"It was a simple task. How could you fail so miserably?" Lirion demanded.*

*"It is not my fault. Besides, things might still work out."*

*"Not without The Eldrystone," he growled.*

*"It will not be hard taking it from Loreleia after she kills him."*

*"You're assuming too much. Theric will have no trouble taking it from her. I must find them before that happens."*

*"But how are you going to—?"*

*"Bring me something with his scent," he said, the last word nothing but a growl as he finished shifting back into his wolf form.*

*He nudged her with his snout, and she hurried inside. Eyes roving around the room, she found Korben's discarded clothes. She picked up his shirt and brought it outside for Lirion to smell. His black nose twitched once, twice, and then he was off, leaping over the hedges and disappearing into the night.*

*A moment after he was gone, Saethara let out a little whimper, cursing herself for forgetting to ask him to take care of the mess on the bed.*

*What would she do now? Despondently, she walked back into the room to discover that the bloodstains were gone. He had helped her with his magic, after all.*

*She breathed a sigh of relief, pressed a hand to her chest, and mouthed a thank you up at the ceiling.*

# 4

## KORBEN

*"I do not believe it—not for a pixie's breath. King Korben is not dead."*

**Gavalin Rossan – Riochtach Resident – 1 AV**

"By decree of Queen Saethara, you are under arrest."
Queen Saethara.

Queen Saethara.

Queen Saethara.

It cannot be. She is dead. I ran her through with my sword.

Three members of the Oakheart Brigade stand in front of me. The insignias on the left sleeve of their green uniforms reveal their affiliation. The one who appears to be their leader—a broad male with a shaved head and eyes the color of burnt wood—has unsheathed his broadsword, while two others have nocked arrows, fixing me in their sights.

They have appeared in our path with the worst possible news and at the worst possible moment. We have just crossed the veil, and Valeria needs me. She has just shifted for the first time, and I cannot imagine her disorientation.

I exchange glances with Jago and Galen who stand at my sides.

"Put down your weapons," I order. They must be rangers, given their post in this wilderness. It is not uncommon for members of this brigade to patrol forests.

The male and females exchange glances, appearing amused.

With my patience growing as brittle as dry leaves, I say, "I am King Korben Theric, and if you do not desist, you will pay dearly for your disrespect."

The archers pull their nocked arrows further back, their bows groaning. Their reaction to my words is pure hostility.

Their leader says, "King Korben Theric is dead. But you would not know that if you have been in . . . the human realm for the last twenty years." He glances warily toward the shimmering veil at my back.

*Dead?!* It is what Saethara would have liked, and apparently what she told everyone after I disappeared. There is a straightforward way to solve this problem, however. Niamhara made sure to give every Theric monarch the ability to prove their identity.

"Let the whispers t—" My words are cut off, as an invisible hand seems to wrap around my neck, choking me. I try again. "Let the whisp—"

*By the Goddess! What is happening?*

Since the day I became king—Father bestowing his crown and amulet upon me—I have been able to recite Niamhara's declaration.

*Let the whispers turn to screams if you dare defy me. My crown demands obedience. My blade demands respect. By the will of Niamhara and my people, I am your ruler.*

Only the true fae ruler can utter these words. They echo in my mind, but they refuse to move past my lips. I recited them with purpose for the first time only yesterday to stop Calierin from strangling me, and they flowed without impediment even though I was in Castella.

Why do they fail me now in my homeland?

The rangers scoff, their eyes filling with contempt. By my failed attempt to utter the sacred words, I have, in their eyes, become a worthless impostor, unworthy of our Goddess's respect.

Galen, my newly reappointed Master of Magic, joins my side. Out of the corner of his mouth, he murmurs, "What's the matter? Cat's got your tongue?"

The rangers frown at the expression, which the sorcerer surely learned during his exile in Castella, same as me.

I glower at him and attempt the pronouncement once more, this time failing at the first word.

The archer on the right pulls his bow tighter, arm shaking slightly with the effort. He is pointing the arrow straight at my chest. My thoughts race. I need to get us out of this situation without bloodshed.

I cast a sidelong glance toward the ground, where Valeria hops erratically in her raven shape. I cannot imagine how she must be feeling. She needs my help, and instead, I have to deal with this untimely threat. Jago and Cuervo hover near her, both appearing wary.

Focusing on the rangers once more, I realize there are two more ways I can prove who I am. The first one is The Eldrystone, though that alternative is also futile since Valeria has the amulet. When her shifting powers manifested, the amulet and her clothes were naturally swept away with the change. She would have to shift back in order for me to use The Eldrystone to prove my identity. Under these circumstances, however, she is safer as a raven. She represents a smaller target, one that may yet go unnoticed.

The overeager archer cracks his neck.

"Easy," the leader tells him.

"I do not like him," the archer replies.

"I know, but we cannot hurt them. We have clear instructions."

"And what might those instructions be?" Galen asks in his irritating, casual tone. He strolls forward, cocky as ever.

"Stay put!" the leader orders him, changing the angle of his drawn sword.

"Now, there's no need for all of that," Galen says. "Why don't we focus on what's important here, like for instance," he makes a demonstrative gesture toward the curtain of light extended behind us, "the veil has been reopened. After twenty years of exile, all the fae trapped on the other side can finally come home." He sounds like a salesman trying to peddle sawdust to a carpenter.

"And did *you* do that?" the leader asks. "Did you reopen the veil?"

"Of course we did," Galen answers before I can stop him.

*Damn sorcerer!* Will he ever learn to keep his mouth shut? How about assessing the situation before acting like a fool?

"Galen," I say, "please leave this to me."

"The veil was closed for a reason," the leader says between clenched teeth, "and tampering with it is against the law. Close it again."

"We cannot," I say. I will not take the chance of leaving Valeria trapped in Tirnanog.

He sneers. "I will not say this again . . . you are under arrest by the

authority of Queen Saethara. Submit yourselves or face the consequences. You will come to Riochtach and stand trial."

Galen glances at me over his shoulder. "Who in all the hells is
Queen Saethara?"

"This is quite enough disrespect." A ranger on the left—a blond
male with a face tattoo—quickly sets aside his bow, steps forward,
and raises a hand to strike the sorcerer.

Fast as always, Galen turns to face the threat, hands moving to
create a spell.

*Of course it would come to this*, I think, expecting the ranger to fly
backward from the impact of Galen's magic. Instead, the male lands
a punch across Galen's jaw, dropping him to the ground with its
force. I stare in confusion. Was Galen too slow? I have never seen him
be too slow, but I have not been around him in a long time.

"Ouch," Jago says, calling attention to himself.

The rangers take a moment to examine Jago closer, noticing his
rounded ears for the first time.

I put both hands up in a pacifying gesture, attempting to keep
their focus on me. "Forgive our ignorance," I say. "We have come
from Castella and do not know how things have changed since the
veil collapsed. We do not mean to cause any trouble."

The second way I can show these rangers who I am is by shifting.
There are few raven shifters in the realm, and they all have Theric
blood. Moreover, none of them can acquire Dreadwing form. I am
the only one who can do that.

I must assume Loreleia's curse is lifted. She condemned me to live
without love and to never come back home. Those two things have
now come to pass, and beyond all expectations, my feet are now

firmly planted in Tirnanog. I can only assume this means I have my magic back. I have not sensed a change within me, do not feel that vast power thrumming under my skin, ready to burst forth at the slightest invitation. But I have been without magic for twenty years, so perhaps it is only due to lack of use.

Tentatively, I reach within me, searching for that small spark that always ignited my veins with the power of thunder. I search and search and find nothing but empty space, a silent void that once thrived and roiled like water left over a fire.

My fists clench in frustration. No magic. Does Loreleia's curse persist? What now? How do I make these rangers understand who I am and what a big mistake they are making?

"What do we do, Korben?" Jago asks.

"You are part of this too, human?" the leader asks. "Did you help these two breach the veil? Are you an accomplice to this crime?"

Jago shakes his head. "It's . . . not a crime," he says, sounding uncertain.

"And do you think that by calling him Korben, we will believe your ruse? This is not our King. If he made you believe that, he has deceived you."

Jago glances at me uncertainly. Only a few days ago, I was Rífíor to him, a liar who had tricked his cousin and caused chaos in his home. He has no reason to stand by me and support my claims.

To my surprise, he straightens his shoulders and speaks in a reasonable tone. "We did not breach anything. The veil remained open for two millennia and closed for only two decades. I argue that we merely returned things to their original state. Our goal was to reestablish passage between Castella and Tirnanog, so your kin *and* mine can finally return home."

The leader huffs. "It is not for the likes of you to decide what is normal and what is not. Nor to determine who gets passage into our realm. We have seen and heard enough. You are coming with us and will face punishment for your crime. This is the last warning. Submit or be forced into submission."

Galen groans and blinks up at the sky, regaining consciousness.

"Restrain him," the leader orders.

The ranger who hit Galen jumps on top of the sorcerer, rolls him onto his back, and proceeds to bind his hands with a strip of thick rope.

"Please, stop," I say, unwilling to let this get more physical than it already has.

Galen fights, clearly attempting to tap into his magic, but like me, he is a dry well. *Why?* He had magic in Castella. Here, where Niamhara's power flows from the ground, infusing the entire land and all its inhabitants, he should only be more powerful. Instead, he is helpless.

"What is happening?" he asks in a fit of panic. "Why can't I use my magic?"

"A sorcerer then," the ranger holding him sneers, "and an out-of-favor one at that. More reason to take you with us, *Fuadach*."

Fuadach? From my studies, I know the word comes from our old language and means someone who is empty.

On the ground, Galen turns his head and looks up at me. His brow is split by several worry lines. His nostrils flare. He looks as terrified and confused as I felt when I discovered I was stranded in Castella without my skills and without The Eldrystone. For someone who has relied on magic their entire life, it is no easy matter to find oneself stripped of the very essence of their being.

Galen kicks frantically. "Let me go. Let me go back to Castella. I will close the veil again. I swear."

It is a desperate plea that reveals the terror this new situation arouses in the sorcerer. His identity is magic, his entire personality built on the knowledge that no matter the circumstances, no matter what asinine thing comes out of his mouth, he will always come out ahead with the help of a spell. If it weren't because I share in the awful nature of his situation, I am sure I would enjoy his plight. If there is anyone who deserves to be taught a lesson, it is Galen. This is terrible timing, however.

Putting their bows and arrows away, the other rangers start creeping forward, approaching Jago. We are unarmed, our weapons on the other side. In our eagerness to cross the veil, we left everything behind: horses, packs, swords. If we fight, we will have to do so with our bare hands.

Jago grabs my shoulder. "Let's get back."

"Oh, no, you will remain and answer for this," the leader says, rushing at me with a raised sword.

The rangers attack at the same time. I step aside, easily avoiding my attacker. However, Jago is not that fortunate, his human speed no match for a well-trained Oakheart Brigade member. With one quick maneuver from his opponent, Jago finds himself on the ground, face pushed into the earth.

Jago makes a valiant effort, swinging an arm and striking the side of the ranger's face, but he only succeeds in making him angrier.

Cursing, the male smashes his fist against the back of Jago's neck, who groans and goes still.

Seeing this, Valeria clumsily hops around the ranger and tries to peck his leg. In solidarity, Cuervo joins her.

*No!* I had hoped for Valeria to remain unnoticed, but she has jumped right into the fray.

Taking advantage of my opponent's distraction by the ruckus birds, I lunge, grab his wrist, relieve him of his sword, and turn it on him.

"I want to resolve this peacefully," I say, "but if you insist, I will gladly cut your head off."

Feigning an attack, I raise my sword and make a slashing motion mere inches from the leader's neck, leaving no doubt that if I want to, I can relieve him of that precious appendage.

Putting both hands up, he backs away. I take a step to the side and start toward Jago's attacker. He does not notice me, too intent on kicking at Valeria and batting at Cuervo to notice I bested his partner. Rage boiling over, I lean down, wrap a hand around his neck, and squeeze.

"Get up," I order him, fingers digging into his skin until I feel his windpipe in my grasp.

He makes a rasping sound, eyes wide with panic. I could tear his throat out of his neck and throw it to the ground. I want to do it in repayment for his attempt to hurt Valeria, but I curb my anger and, instead, let him go, shoving him toward his companions. He staggers back, bending over, coughing.

The leader glares at me, seething with hatred.

I think of what to do and quickly realize The Eldrystone is the only thing that can get this situation under control.

Against my better judgment, I say, "Valeria, can you shift back?"

I do not take my eyes off the rangers and notice their startled expressions at the news. These are not simple birds, they are thinking. These are shifters: raven shifters.

The call of a hawk flying overhead pierces the silence as I wait for Valeria to regain her human form, but the moment stretches and stretches, making it clear she is unable to control her new magic.

"You are a clever one," the ranger leader mocks. "But you will not fool us. You are not King Korben, and those birds are not of Theric blood either. They are plain ravens. Nothing more. Nothing less."

"It matters not what you believe, ranger," I say. "When the truth is revealed, you will regret your actions. Now, explain what has happened here or I swear I will make you rue the moment you were born."

I tighten my grip on the sword, the leather-wrapped hilt creaking under the pressure. With a speed matched by few, I spin the blade in a dazzling display, meant to unnerve them. The weapon sings as it cuts through the air, forcing the rangers to back up a step.

"What do you believe happened to King Korben Theric?" I demand.

"We believe nothing," the leader responds. "We *know* he is dead."

"Did you see his body?"

His mouth opens and closes a few times, but in the end, he produces a response. "Perhaps I did not, but I know his face was not marred by such a horrid scar."

31

"Much can happen in two decades, ranger."

He shrugs.

"And how did he die, according to your knowledge?"

"He was killed by the humans who closed the veil and stole magic."

"You cannot be serious! A human could never best me. Not even *you* could."

The rangers shift uncomfortably from foot to foot. It is clear they have wondered about this before. I was the most powerful shifter of my generation and had The Eldrystone besides. I doubt anyone could have bested me . . . except someone who blinded me to her treachery with beauty and promises of unending love.

"They say it was the Plumanegras," the leader says. "They have magic. They are shifters too and could have . . . and *killed* the king." He seems to have enough doubts, which manage to slip into his narrative.

Clever Saethara. This must have been the lie she concocted after I left Riochtach in pursuit of Loreleia. I swiftly try to imagine what happened after I left: Vonall using his healing powers to save Saethara's life, a slew of lies to disguise what she did, the veil conveniently collapsing and making her the luckiest female in history and allowing her to invent more lies to allow her to remain on the throne as a newly minted queen, an aggrieved widow who lost her mate on her wedding night.

*The horrid harpy!* When I get my hands on her I will make sure my blade goes through her heart, then I will repair whatever damage she—

"Captain, is everything all right?" an approaching voice calls.

The leader smiles, relaxing visibly. Cursing inwardly, I realize I have let down my guard. Humans tread heavily, and their steps are impossible to miss even when they attempt stealth. My kin, on the other hand, can cross a field covered in eggshells without making a sound. That is why I should have kept all my senses alert. If I had, I would not have missed the slight change of scent in the air.

Others are coming. More than I would be able to handle on my own.

Without taking my eyes off the rangers, I cut the ropes that bind Galen, then press the sole of my boot to his shoulder and shake him. It takes a moment, but he comes to, blinking, eyes out of focus.

"Get up! We need to get out of here," I order.

He clambers to his feet.

"Jago, pick up Valeria," I order.

Swaying, he pushes to his hands and knees and does as I instruct, gently cradling Valeria in his arms.

I brandish the sword to keep the rangers at bay. "Come close and I will gut you."

Their expressions tell me they believe me.

"Hurry!" the captain shouts. "Intruders!"

"Run!" I urge, turning toward the veil.

Galen and Jago are ahead of me, moving as fast as their legs allow. Cuervo takes to the air and swoops over our heads, cawing in alarm.

I glance over my shoulder just to find at least six more rangers joining the others.

"Stop them!" the captain orders.

They will not stop us. We have a fair advantage. At least that is what I think until one of the new rangers lifts his hands and blasts a dark wave of magic in our direction.

"Sorcerer!" I cry out in warning, for all the good it does.

# 5

# VALERIA

*"Anyone who harms the prisoners will answer to me."*

**Drothgar Nelyn – Oakheart Brigade Captain**

J ago holds me too tightly as he runs. My hollow bones feel frail under his heavy grip, and I fear he will break me.

I understand half of what's happening. Either my bird brain is slow, or the violent change took too much out of me. I suspect the latter because I do know our current predicament boils down to hostiles barring our passage and Korben's inability to prove he's Tirnanog's rightful king.

When he urged me to shift back into my human form, I tried. I wished it with all my strength, but nothing happened. I also tried to use The Eldrystone to help us, but nothing. It didn't respond. Instead, it only seemed to throb weakly, like a second heart inside my chest. I sense it within me, and the feeling is comforting.

Everything around me jostles. My mouth—no, my beak—clacks, opening and shutting. I clamp it down. Cuervo flies overhead, cawing. My ears instantly pinpoint his exact location.

We're only a few steps away from the shimmering veil.

"Sorcerer!" Korben shouts.

*Oh, gods!*

My heart beats so fast it's incomprehensible. I fear it will leap into my gullet.

"Save yourself, Val," Jago shouts, then pitches me forward, propelling me into the veil.

My beak opens as I cry a desperate *no*. A shrill caw comes out instead. Beak first, I pass into that iridescent curtain, piercing it like an arrow. Pure instinct urges me to fling my wings open. My plummeting descent stops, and it feels as if I'm being lifted by an invisible force.

When I first crossed the veil into Tirnanog a moment ago, I seemed to get lost in an in-between limbo, but this time it takes only an instant to appear on the other side.

Castella.

I barely register the change in scenery—the trees smaller, without luminescent vines twisting around them—when I feel a sudden, jarring sensation that begins at my head and travels down to my feet. I let out a scream of pain as my body shifts back to its human shape, then plummets toward the ground, my arms flailing helplessly.

Just before impact, I tuck my chin and turn sideways. My shoulder absorbs the brunt of the fall, and I roll to break the impact. After two spins, I regain my footing and stand up. Facing the veil, I watch Cuervo emerge, cawing frantically in distress.

Eyes roving over the ground, I spot La Matadora, my father's sword, reclining against a tree. Before I reopened the veil, we were resting here, taking a break after hours of failure upon failure. Korben sat with his back against a tree, eating dry bread, and trying not to appear disappointed in my botched attempts. Then Cuervo spotted a shining spot in midair, alerting us to a tear in the fabric of the veil. We were all too mesmerized and reanimated by the discovery to worry about potential dangers or the need for weapons on the other side.

Now, I pick up the sword and charge back into Tirnanog, the point of the blade leading the way. When I cross to the other side, I find my companions lying on the ground, unconscious, struck by espiritu.

I stand in front of them, ice slipping into my veins. At least a dozen fae face me, all wearing green uniforms and deep scowls. They seem startled as I appear but recover quickly.

"That is your king, you fools," I shout, holding La Matadora so that the blade protects my torso from hip to left shoulder.

If their sorcerer flings espiritu in my direction, the fae-made weapon will protect me. The voice of logic screams inside my head that no matter how fae-made the sword, there is absolutely no way I can defeat all of these opponents. But logic has nothing to do with this. There is no way in all the hells I will abandon my people.

"I can prove he's your king if you just . . ."

The sorcerer takes a step forward. I know he's the sorcerer because his hands move through the air in a circular pattern as if he were building a snowball. A sphere of what looks like black smoke forms between his fingers. Pulling a hand back, he throws the orb directly at my legs.

I crouch and swing the sword downward, blocking the attack, but a second one follows right away, and then a third and a fourth, and it's all I can do to wield the blade and block every attack.

The sorcerer and the others slowly press forward. I'm able to block every espiritu attack, but for how long? Suddenly, my stomach roils, and a nauseous feeling shakes me. Cold sweat breaks across my forehead as my skin begins to itch. Deflecting another volley from the sorcerer, I realize what's happening. I'm about to shift again.

But I can't. I can't.

I have to help Jago, Korben, and Galen . . . Yes, even that irritating sorcerer.

*Don't shift. Don't.*

I need my hands, my arms. I try to think about everything that makes me human, but the nausea and the itching only intensify. I'm going to shift, and there is nothing I can do to stop it.

*Gods, help me! Niamhara, help me!*

I reach for the power of The Eldrystone to stop the change, to stop the approaching fae, but the Goddess is silent again, abandoning us to this fate.

If they take us, there's a strong possibility they'll kill us. I doubt Saethara will receive Korben with open arms—not that he would run into her embrace after she stabbed him and left him for dead on their wedding night. If they take us, no one will know what happened. No one will even care. Amira might just be glad to be rid of me.

Part of me wants to stay and fight, even if it will mean my capture. The other part knows that if I slip from their grasp, hope will remain alive. I could follow my companions and find a way to free them.

I glance down at Korben. His expression is set in a grimace of pain and so is Jago's.

*I'm sorry. I'm not strong enough, but I'll find a way. I promise.*

The closest fae is only a few steps away from me now, and his gaze flicks warily toward the veil. The sorcerer prepares another attack.

Heavy with a mixture of anger and desolation, I take a step back and leave Tirnanog behind. An instant later, I stand on Castellan soil, holding my breath. La Matadora vibrates in my hand as I wait for the sorcerer's espiritu to come flying through the veil. Nothing happens.

"Friend!" Cuervo calls behind me.

I stare at the curtain of shifting colors that separates me from my companions, my heart aching.

I'm their only hope.

They're but a few steps away and yet so far. I widen the distance between the veil and me, expecting the fae to cross and come after me. They don't. Perhaps they're afraid. Perhaps they have orders not to cross if the veil were to reopen. Whatever the case, I stand alone.

No. Not alone. Cuervo is with me. He's standing by my side, intent on the veil, also expecting an attack.

Several tense moments pass, and we don't move. I watch him closely for the slightest change in demeanor. His senses are sharper than mine. I have always known this, but now . . . I *KNOW*.

Cautiously, I glance around, half of my attention still on the veil. Our horses eat grass placidly, none the wiser to our plight.

"Cuervo, watch for me, please." I point at my eye, then at the veil.

He bobs his head in understanding.

Still holding La Matadora, I gather the things we left strewn on the ground. Jago's saddlebag, full of dry bread, nuts, and jerky. Galen's olive-green cloak, hanging on a tree branch. The rapiers discarded on the ground.

Galen and I had been at the brink of engaging in a duel when Cuervo noticed the tear in the veil. We dropped everything and heedlessly ripped the barrier wide open. That was stupid, so stupid. We should have been more cautious. We should have—

I abandon that line of thought. Dwelling on it will do no good. What's done is done. Now, I have to focus on freeing my companions.

After loading all of our belongings onto the horses, I gather their reins and guide the animals away from the veil.

"Stay here and watch, Cuervo. I'll be right back."

He seems uneasy, but remains in place, beady eyes set on the veil.

Gently, I guide the horses through the trees, making my way back onto the path Galen cleared for us through the overgrown brush on our way here.

Eventually, I leave the path and push through the thick wilderness, finding passage with some difficulty. I stop at a small clearing and glance around. The vegetation is thick, and no one coming from Tirnanog would be able to spot the beasts here.

I still don't know what I'm going to do, but the horses and the food are important. I have to protect them. After tying their reins securely to a narrow trunk, I head back, my steps silent, my eyes swiveling from side to side.

Cuervo is not where I left him, and I almost panic, but I spot him on a tree branch, a better and safer vantage point to keep watch.

"Any changes?"

He whips his beak to one side, his way of saying *no*.

"Good."

Hopping from talon to talon, he peers at me, seeming to ask *what now?*

"I don't know, Cuervo. I'm thinking."

I run my free hand through my hair, tugging at it in frustration. I'm still gripping Father's sword, the urge to plunge it into one of those bastardos who ruined everything growing stronger by the second.

"What can I do to free them?" I ask out loud.

Cuervo caws.

"I'm just me, and there were so many of them." I shake my head. "I can't fight them." Even if they didn't have a sorcerer, I would be no match for them.

Once more, I turn my attention to The Eldrystone. "You helped me fight Calierin. Why won't you help me now?" I defeated the Tuathacath warrior, blocking all the espiritu she flung my way, my speed unmatched by hers. "I could defeat them if you lend me a hand."

Of course, there is no answer. Why this erratic behavior? I don't understand. All along, Niamhara's influence has been present, guiding us here. And now that we've done her will, what? She abandons us?

She wasn't only guiding us here, though. There was more. She also seemed to be doing everything within her power to drive Korben and me together. The Goddess succeeded in that, too. And for what? So we could be torn apart like this?

I shake my head, driving all those thoughts away and concentrating on the now.

"So if I can't fight them," I say, glancing up at Cuervo, "I need to come at them sideways. Unseen." I nod, an idea taking root. "I . . . I can free them when their captors are distracted. If I free Galen first, he can use his espiritu . . ."

I trail off. No. Galen can't use his powers. He tried and failed. Why? No answer occurs to me, so I abandon this train of thought as well.

"I'll free Korben first, then, and I'll give him La Matadora." I nod repeatedly.

As great as the idea seems, there's a nagging itch in the back of my head that I can't ignore. The fae, with their sharp senses, will spot me from miles away.

Cuervo caws again, snapping me out of my thoughts.

He lifts his beak toward the veil, as if to remind me it's there and our friends are waiting on the other side. At least they were ten minutes ago. Time is ticking by. Panic sizzles in my veins.

The male in charge said they couldn't hurt any hostages, that they had clear instructions to . . . to what? Take them to Riochtach, the capital? Yes, that's what he said. My thoughts are slow, impaired by the confusion of shifting, but they are coming back.

"They're going to take them to *her*," I say in a whisper, the thought becoming almost a certainty as the words ride on my shaky breath.

*Oh, gods!*

"Cuervo!" I approach the tree where he's perched, crouch down, and pat the ground. He dives down, the wind produced by his wings ruffling my hair as he lands.

I glance warily between him and the veil. "I need your help, friend." My voice trembles as I say this. I pet the side of his neck. "I'm sorry. I keep asking so much of you, but I don't know what else to do. I'm terrified something bad will happen to our friends."

He lets out a reassuring warble, as if saying, *Don't worry. I understand.*

"I need you to *spy* on Jago."

His eyes cut toward the veil with clear concern.

I'm tempted to reassure him, but I clamp my lips together. I will not cajole him with lies. I have no idea what risks he might face on the other side. The fae have a sorcerer. He might have wards and be alerted to Cuervo's presence right away.

"Spy?" Cuervo repeats after a moment.

I nod. He has done this for me before in the safety of Nido. He never shied away from the task as he seems to be doing now.

"Not too close," I say. "Just find him and tell me where he is."

He seems to consider. I don't think I've ever seen Cuervo frightened of any task I've assigned him. On the contrary, he's always eager to help. But now, he seems truly scared. Why? He faced Orys without hesitation, so I have a feeling he's not afraid of our fae foes, but of something else. Does he sense something beyond the obvious?

A chill runs through me, and I have to tense my muscles to avoid trembling with its intensity.

I'm starting to doubt Cuervo's willingness to return to Tirnanog when he suddenly soars upward, gaining altitude until he's barely visible through the thick canopy. Once he reaches a sufficient height, he turns toward the veil and disappears from sight. I can't see him cross due to the dense foliage, but I must assume he did.

"Clever bird!" I think, grateful for his wits. Hopefully, he'll be able to use his sharp sight to spy on our friends from a distance and report back.

In the meantime, there is something I need to do, something that could be the difference between freeing my friends or losing them forever.

# 6

# KORBEN

*"I am certain those birds can be trained. They are cleverer than any thieving street urchin."*

**Ralo Eliqen – Fae Trader – 1536 DV**

When I come to, my first thought is of Valeria. Dread threatens to cloud my thoughts, but that won't help anyone. Instead, I force myself to remain calm by taking a deep breath and thinking of her unharmed, near me.

I do not open my eyes and let my other senses take in my situation.

The rhythmic sound of booted feet and hooves surround me. The scent of smoke rides the air, accompanied by the musk from many people.

An undertone of pearl lilies tries to cut through the other strong scents. Pearl lilies were my mother's favorite flowers, and I must push back the memories that come rushing in at their sweetness. I had not caught that scent in decades, but I remember it, nonetheless.

I am sitting on the ground, Jago and Galen behind me. I recognize their scents. We are tied together, back to back, in a circle. The restraining force that binds us, a wide band that spans my entire torso, emits a slight hum, letting me know its nature: magic.

Slowly, I open my eyes.

The first thing I notice is the dark force that wraps around my chest. It looks like a girdle made of smoke. No thicker than a finger, its width covers my torso from clavicles to hips bones. I have never seen magic like this. The color is off, and so is its smoke-like state. Maybe Galen knows something about it.

I look up to inspect our surroundings and find a ranger watching us from a distance, a long spear in hand. It is the same male who struck Galen, the blond with the face tattoo. He meets my gaze for a brief instant, then looks away. All around, there is much activity. Males and females moving to and fro. They are preparing for departure, judging by the hitching of horses to a wagon and the packing of provisions.

The camp seems to be of medium size, occupied by some thirty Oakheart Brigade members.

Inspecting every inch of the camp, I search for Valeria, but I don't see her. I bite my tongue to contain my unfolding rage. The taste of metal fills my mouth.

"Jago," I manage in a low growl.

No response.

"JAGO!"

He moans as he stirs.

"Where is Valeria?" I demand.

He grunts. I imagine he's trying to clear his addled mind, so I give him a moment. No easy task.

At last, he answers, "In . . . Castella."

"What?"

"I sent her through the veil before we were hit."

The ranger observes us with care. Easily within earshot, he listens to every word we are saying.

"Did you go after her?" I ask, looking straight into the ranger's eyes.

His nostrils flare, and his chin goes up an inch, but he does not answer.

"You did not," I say, trying to sound certain, though I feel anything but. I am only testing his reaction to my words. If they went after Valeria, they clearly have not caught her as she is not here. At least that is what I choose to believe.

The tight expression around the ranger's eyes tells me he is afraid, but of what? Clearly not of us, pathetically restrained as we are.

"You are afraid of the veil's reappearance, are you not?"

His upper lip curls, and he avoids my gaze. I am right, which means they did not go after Valeria.

"She is safe," I whisper.

The pressure around my chest diminishes somewhat, making me realize it was caused by more than the restraining magic.

*She is safe. She is safe. She is safe.*

"How do you know?" Jago asks.

"They are afraid to cross the veil." I keep eye contact with the ranger, and the way he quickly glances away reaffirms my guess.

"Thank you for sending her back to Castella, Jago," I say without thinking.

He huffs. "Don't thank me, asshole. That's my cousin. I would do

45

anything for her. In fact, I've been doing just that long before you showed up."

My simmering anger is now colored with annoyance. I have broken more than one jaw for half this amount of disrespect. He should be glad we are tied up. Not that he is wrong. Not that I am not still grateful to him. He is certainly loyal to her, but it is going to take some time to learn how to tolerate him. He shares a casual disposition with Galen.

With a grunt, I turn my attention to the sorcerer. "Wake up, you useless *Master of Magic*."

He does not deserve the title. He forced me to give it back in exchange for The Eldrystone after he stole it back from Don Justo. Galen held the post before he betrayed me, and I exiled him. But what good is he without magic?

I try to jostle him, but the smoke-like force that binds us makes it impossible to move in the slightest.

"Galen!" I insist.

Still nothing.

I am about to call out the sorcerer's name again when I notice a black shape landing on a nearby tree.

*Cuervo!*

My thoughts race. What does this mean? Did Valeria send him? Has she crossed back into Tirnanog?

*No, Valeria. Stay in Castella. Stay safe, please!*

I know her too well, however. She will not abandon us. She will try to free us, even if the odds are stacked against her.

Galen lets out a moan, sounding as if he is just waking up from a nap.

"Oh, shit!" he exclaims, realizing it was not a nap after all.

"*Oh, shit* is right. Can you set us free?" I ask.

Out of the corner of my eye, I notice the ranger straighten further, sharpening his attention.

Galen is quiet for a moment, then he says, "I can't."

"Why not?"

I sense him shake his head. "I don't know. I feel entirely dry."

The ranger relaxes, a satisfied smile on his mouth. He has very thin lips that look like a slash across his face as they press together.

"Earlier," Jago says, "they called you something, said you were out of favor. What was it?"

"Fuadach," I say, recalling the word.

"What does it mean?" Jago asks.

"It means empty," Galen responds. "Exactly how I feel." He is quiet for a moment, then asks, "Korben, who's Saethara? Did she do this?"

Galen will find out one way or another, so there is no point in hiding it. "She was . . . is . . . my wife."

"What?!" He takes a moment to process that, then adds, "Of course! You turned two hundred and had to do that stupid Mate Rite. What kind of gem did you end up choosing? Do tell."

"This is not the time, Galen," I sneer. "We need to figure out what is happening, and before that, we have to get free."

"You are married?!" Jago demands. "Does Valeria know that? I swear I'm going to kill you if you've been lying to her."

"She knows," I say.

Jago sputters, then says, "I'm going to kill you anyway, as soon as I get free, I'll strangle you."

"Be my guest."

I would deserve it, if only for the stupidity of falling for the harpy.

My eyes cut in the direction of Cuervo. However, he is not there anymore. Surreptitiously, I inspect the nearby trees, but I don't see him. I want to tell Jago. He knows the bird better and could explain his behavior, but I cannot risk the ranger overhearing me. As it is, he seems extremely interested in our conversation. In that case, maybe he can join it.

"Why not tell us what happened during the last twenty years?" I say.

"Because I don't fucking know," Galen responds.

"Not you. The ranger watching us."

"Oh." Galen cannot see him from his vantage point.

"Go fuck yourself, *King Korben*." That slash across his face appears again. "You put on a good act, but I am not stupid. You will be brought to the queen, and she will decide your punishment. She will know how to seal that accursed veil again."

"So is that why everyone is in a hurry, packing? You are taking us to Riochtach?"

He clenches his jaw, as if determined to ignore us.

"Why did you call my friend Fuadach?" I ask. "What does that mean?"

Galen makes a sound in the back of his throat. "Friend, huh?"

"Shut up." Can he not see how precarious our situation is?

I wait for an answer from the ranger, but he is staring straight ahead, acting as if he is suddenly oblivious to our presence. It does not seem like I will be able to get much else out of him.

"What could have done this, Galen?" I ask. "What could have

dried up your magic? And . . . mine? I had hoped to be able to shift again once I reentered Tirnanog, but I also feel dry like you."

"How should I know?"

I open my mouth to respond, but Jago cuts me off. "I'd expect someone with the title of *Master of Magic* to have a comprehensive understanding of their supposed expertise. Or was the title just another empty boast you obtained through intimidation and extortion?"

I blow air through my nose. "Well, Jago, I could not have put it better myself."

"That is total shit!" Galen protests. "You know well that is not how I became Master of Magic the first time around. I earned the title in good right. None of the other candidates were able to best me."

"You are surely bested now." Jago does not mince words.

"I thought you and I were going to be friends, but I see I was wrong," Galen says with mock regret.

"Sorry, but being tied up puts me in a very bad mood." Jago exhales. "Unless the tying up is happening in the bedchamber by someone extremely attractive."

Galen laughs. "I take that back. You and I *will be* good friends."

I sigh in frustration. "Lucky me! I had to end up with two people who think everything is a joke."

"Better than having a stick up my ass," Jago puts in.

Galen laughs again, while all I can do is sit there, marinating in my own vexation. It seems I will have to try to figure this out without their help.

Closing my eyes, I search my mind for a possible explanation. I had a vast education, and magic was one of the subjects my tutors forced me to learn. Perhaps not as extensively as others, but maybe there's something in my memories that I can draw upon to help me understand what happened during my absence because humans did not take magic. That is a lie from Saethara.

"Something is wrong with Niamhara," Galen's quiet voice cuts through my thoughts. He does not sound like he is joking anymore. He sounds quite serious. It may take him some time to sober up, but he is certainly capable of doing it. He would have never become Master of Magic if weaving spells and turning everything into a jest were his only qualities.

My eyes spring open.

"That is the only explanation," he adds.

I glance up at the ranger, assessing his reaction. A slight frown creases his forehead, as if he's hearing about this possibility for the first time.

"The *only* explanation?" I press.

"All right then, the *best* explanation," Galen corrects.

"But you were fine in Castella."

"Yes, I already caught on to that notion, and my guess is that I was fine because the veil was closed. If we went back now . . ." he trails off.

What he is saying makes sense, but it does not explain everything.

"Valeria, she was able to . . ." I stop, the answer coming to me before I can finish the question. There is only one way to explain her ability to shift: The Eldrystone.

"Yes, Dear King Korben," Galen says. "That is exactly why."

The ranger's frown has intensified. His mind seems to be racing, but I doubt he has any clue about the true significance of our conversation.

I do not know if even Jago has grasped what Galen and I just realized. One way or another, he is blessedly quiet, giving nothing away. Instead, he jumps back to Galen's original statement.

"But what could possibly be wrong with Niamhara?" Jago asks. "She's a goddess. Or what? Do your gods get sick? Die?"

He seems as confused as I am. Niamhara has never wavered. Since the dawn of time, she has been revered as our creator. All ancient sacred texts portray her as the most powerful of all deities, perhaps even their creator too. As the fae population grew, and she witnessed the dark twist the innate magic took in some of her children, she came to our rescue. The Eldrystone was the solution to our conflict, and the unforeseen consequences of her creation. She gave us a way to defend ourselves from those who misuse magic.

The idea that she could get sick or die sounds ridiculous, but what do we know of gods and their powers? What if her life is finite, like ours?

"Hey!" I call to the ranger. "What do you think? Is Niamhara dead?"

He glares at me, obviously displeased by our conversation, which means we are either close to something he knows or . . . entirely far off. Most likely, he only thinks we are heretics for daring to suggest our Goddess is dead. Either way, he is no help, the arsehole.

With a shake of my head, I remind myself he is my subject, my responsibility, same as all the fae here and in Castella. He is only one more victim of Saethara's actions and lies.

I still need an answer to my question, however. Niamhara cannot be dead. If she were, The Eldrystone would be dead too, would it not?

*Gods!* What are we to do? If they bring us to Saethara, I see only one outcome: death.

As much as I hate to admit it, Valeria is our only hope. I would rather she not come, but there is no avoiding it. She is not the type of person to abandon her friends.

*Please be careful, Ravógin.*

I do not care if Saethara kills me as long as Valeria is safe. In fact—forgive me, Goddess—I don't care if this entire kingdom burns as long as Valeria is out of harm's way.

# 7

# VALERIA

*"Saints bless her! My cousin makes life an adventure worth living."*

**Jago Plumanegra (Casa Plumanegra) – 3rd in line to Plumanegra throne**

I sit cross-legged on the ground, hands resting on knees, taking deep breaths. The veil shimmers beyond the trees where I hide from potential fae scouts infiltrating Castella to find me. I try to quiet my thundering heart, but every small sound in the forest sends it back into a wild rhythm, forcing me to start the concentration process anew.

During one of my dozen attempts so far, it felt as if I got close to generating that awful tingling that raked all over my body when I shifted. Beyond that, I've felt nothing, no matter how tightly I hold on to The Eldrystone, no matter how fiercely I pray to the Goddess to help me shift.

I pound my fists into the ground. I can't shift. Not here in my realm, anyway. The veil continues shimmering, as if mocking me. Only a few steps past it, and I would shift without even trying. But if I cross, will those fae still be waiting? The answer is no mystery. Of course they will be. They were there when the veil was closed, watching, waiting. Now that it's open . . . only the gods know what will come next.

Saethara had to have known that Korben was caught on the other side when the veil collapsed. No doubt, she has lived in fear of his return all along. No doubt, she has made plans for such an eventuality. I shudder to think what those plans might be. Anyone capable of the kind of subterfuge she employed to get to Korben—of stabbing someone in cold blood as they sleep—is undoubtedly capable of anything.

Raking stiff fingers into my hair, I sink my nails into my scalp, trying to feel something other than the awful dread that gnaws away at my sanity.

I opened the veil.

I caused this.

That awful female will hear of this—if she hasn't already by some espiritu-infused method—and her full attention will turn toward the veil, toward Castella. And then what? It's not hard to imagine. First, she'll want to know where Korben is. She'll want to make sure he remains *dead*, for if her lies are exposed, her entire scheme will unravel, and I doubt anyone will show mercy to a murderess.

I caused this.

What if she manages to kill Korben? Will her treachery turn to Castella? Will she scour my realm to root out anyone who might know the truth about the Fae King? Will she want revenge for her people's mistreatment? Or will she feign loyalty, only to strike when we're most vulnerable?

I caused this.

The threat that now seems to hang over Castella . . . I unleashed it.

Amira won't forgive me if my actions bring suffering to our people. If that happens, she will never see what I did as anything but a betrayal. There will be nothing I can say to convince her otherwise.

I wanted to fix things, not make them worse, but I have single-handedly opened our realm to what might end up being our doom.

Legs trembling, I rise to my feet, a vile thought creeping into my mind. Glittering dust seems to rain down from the heavens to form the thin layer that separates me from Tirnanog. From Jago and Korben.

Just an hour ago, a small tear was all there was, a hole through which only a bug could pass, then I reached in and blew it wide open with a single thought. No, not one thought.

With The Eldrystone.

What would it take now to reverse my actions? To do what Mother did and wish the veil closed? Would one more wish suffice? It seems I will have to try. I have no other choice. Right now, the fae we encountered have stayed behind, but I have a feeling that could change with one flick of Saethara's fingers. I can't leave this door open. It is my duty to close it and protect my people.

So many times I fantasized about this day, and now I find that it was all a misguided dream, a mistake that could destroy everything Father and all my Plumanegra ancestors worked so hard to build.

I can't allow that. I can't.

Except I can't leave Jago behind. He came along to help me, not to get condemned to exile in Tirnanog. How can I make that choice for him? Yet, he's only one person, and his suffering can't compare to that of the thousands in Castella—many more than the fae Amira has consigned to the Haderia, the fae prison in the old Monasterio de San Corvus de la Corona.

Jago will hate me, but unlike Amira, he will understand my reasons. I'll make sure of that because he won't be trapped in Tirnanog alone. I'll be there to plead for his forgiveness, to beg him to absolve me for getting him tangled up in this fate of mine.

With that decision made, a measure of relief unfurls in my chest. I'll enter Tirnanog and close the veil.

My heart aches at the thought of never seeing Castella and my sister again. Yet, another part of me, the part that I inherited from Mother, relishes the thought of spending the rest of my days in her realm, learning about this other side of me. I can't deny it excites me, especially knowing that I also inherited the fae espiritu from my Plumanegra ancestors.

With a million thoughts swirling inside my head, I pace between two trees, impatient for Cuervo's return. What if the captors are taking my friends away from the veil? What if they get too far out of reach and I'm unable to track them? I can always rely on Cuervo's keen senses to guide me, but it's not him I'm worried about. It's my own inability to control my shifting. What kind of help can I be as a small raven? I don't even know if I will be able to fly to keep up with Cuervo.

At last, I hear the flap of wings high above. I peer up as Cuervo flies through a hole in the thick canopy and gracefully lands on a low branch where he stands at eye level.

"Did you find them?" I ask as soon as he settles.

He bobs his head up and down.

"Thank the gods!"

Relieved, I catch my breath, calming my racing heart. Getting more information from Cuervo will be challenging. In Nido, I had familiar landmarks I could reference to coax details out of him. Here, I have nothing.

"Are they far?" I ask.

Cuervo blinks.

"Not far?" I whisper to myself, unsure. "Are they nearby?"

He blinks again, staring at me as if I'm an idiot.

Frustrated, I scrub at my face. "Um . . . is Jago near?"

Cuervo bobs his head once.

I let out a *whoosh* of air, allowing my shoulders to relax. I think about asking him about their captors, but I'm afraid it will only confuse him.

"All right, all right." I'm pacing again, head down as I think about what to do next. "We're going to walk in that direction along the veil, away from here." I point north. "Then we'll cross."

I'm not going to reenter Tirnanog from this location. They undoubtedly left guards behind. In fact, I suspect there may be guards posted throughout the area. But I have to find a safe way to cross. Luckily, I have Cuervo. He'll help me. What would I do without him?

"Friend," I say, tapping my shoulder. "Come with me."

He flies off the branch and lands gently on my shoulder. I incline my head toward him, and he does the same, rubbing up and down.

"Good bird."

We walked Castellina's streets like this many times. He is curious and used to enjoy observing the world from my vantage point. That seems like so long ago now. A simpler time that I entangled with my childish thoughts. I used to believe I had troubles. Now, I understand I had it all.

I begin walking parallel to the veil, keeping a safe distance.

Trampling through the thick brush is no easy matter, and before long, Cuervo flies off my shoulder, jostled by my need to use La Matadora to clear a path. Circumventing all the obstacles would take too long, not to mention it would lead me away from the veil, so the sword it is.

After fifteen minutes of intensely moving onward, I stop and, wiping sweat from my brow, inspect my position. The veil keeps stretching north, seemingly forever. I wonder if it reaches the Eireno Ocean, if it goes all around the world, allowing fish to pass from one realm to another.

Shaking the whimsical idea away, I face the veil. It's impossible to see through to the other side. A million shimmering colors undulate as if stirred by a phantom wind, making me think of an iridescent sea turned on its side.

I reach a hand out, letting it hover close to the veil's surface. Energy tickles my palm despite the lack of contact. Taking a deep breath, I hold La Matadora in front of me and gather my courage to confront anything I might encounter on the other side.

Cuervo, who has found a branch to perch on, caws in complaint, startling me.

"What is it?" I ask. Can he sense something on the other side?

He shakes his entire body, feathers ruffling—his way of emphatically saying *no*.

"All right, so what then? Walk a little further?"

He makes a sound much like a huff, then flies upward and crosses the veil high above my head. It's evident he's not scared of going across like he was at first. Maybe things on the other side aren't as precarious as I'm imagining them. I hesitate for a moment, wondering if I should follow, then realize he doesn't want me to cross until he's had a chance to assess the area. A warm feeling spreads over my chest. Clever bird, indeed.

When he reappears, he does so at my feet, hopping a few times before he comes to a stop. I crouch, smiling.

"My dear friend," I pet the side of his neck, "Thank you." He does a little bow, lowering his head and stretching his wings outward. "So proper," I tease him. "You're quite the gentleman. Or should I say gentlebird?" I stand and take a deep breath. "Well, no time to waste."

Stowing away my apprehension and trusting Cuervo, I take a step forward, shivering as the veil's energy cascades over my skin like a sheet of rain.

Once on the other side, my eyes sweep around in a semicircle, ensuring no one is there. I trust Cuervo, but I can't be too careful. Once more, I'm struck by the strangeness of my surroundings.

Those towering, twisted trees reach for the heavens, their bark pulsing with inner lights of emerald green, sapphire blue, and violet. Thick vines writhe and glow while others bristle with wicked thorns. Underfoot, vibrant green moss ripples beneath my boots. Massive leaves obscure much of the sky, allowing only brief glimpses of iridescent clouds swirling in a multi-colored twilight unlike anything I've ever witnessed.

Cuervo crosses too and quickly finds a branch where to perch. I glance up at him and nod my thanks. He nods back.

"All right," I whisper to avoid oversensitive ears, "before I turn into a *you*, I need you to spy on Jago again."

There is a slight tightening of his wings, pressing closer to his body. I know this means he's displeased with my request. He doesn't want to leave my side.

"I'll be all right, Cuervo. Spy on Jago, then come back. I really need your help on this."

He lifts a talon and sets it back down, and I could swear it looks like he's stomping his foot in frustration.

"Please," I beg, sticking La Matadora into the earth and pressing my hands together in prayer. "Spy on Jago."

Cuervo makes that huffing sound again, but in the end, he flies off to do as I beg.

"Thank you," I mouth.

And just in time because that awful tingling is starting to climb up my spine. I clench my teeth to hold down the nausea, though it doesn't seem to be as violent as the last time.

The familiar weight of my clothes vanishes, replaced by the prickly coolness of air brushing against my naked skin. The world stretches, blurs, and condenses as feathers erupt from my skin. My legs twist and compress, rearranging themselves into talons. My arms, always strong for wielding a sword, morph into sleek, feathered wings. The world seems to tilt on its axis as I find myself balanced on spindly new appendages.

A guttural squawk escapes my beak, the sound strange and foreign on my own tongue. My vision sharpens, rainbows of color exploding before me. My ears and nose are also overwhelmed by a symphony of noise and smells I never knew existed.

A surge of instinct guides my movements, and I tentatively flex my wings. As they unfurl, a stray ray of sunlight strikes them, causing them to shimmer. I crane my neck for a better look, marveling at how they stretch further than I'd imagined they would. Each raven feather is a masterpiece of obsidian, some glistening with a touch of iridescent green along the edges, catching the light like scattered emeralds. As they taper toward the base, the feathers transition into a soft, downy blend of blue, purple, and black. They are simply beautiful.

A primal urge to test their power assaults me. With a tentative beat, air whips through them, and my talons come off the ground. My heart jumps to my throat, fear gripping me. I can't deny that the thought of flying hasn't been on my mind since I can remember. More than once, Father told me how it felt to jump off Nido's ramparts and soar through the sky, warm currents caressing his underside, Castella a faraway, toy-like world that felt much easier to protect than the vast reality he faced in his human form.

I tuck my wings close to my body, surprised by the ease of movement. It still feels strange when I think about it, but if I let the motions unfold as they're supposed to, they seem as natural as breathing.

Chiding myself, I focus on my surroundings. I didn't cross the veil to marvel at my raven shape or get used to it. I crossed because I need to learn how *not* to shift into a form that makes me clumsy and useless. I have no time for this. If I'm to free my friends, I need to be able to remain in my human form.

So now . . . how do I lose all these damn feathers?

# 8

# KORBEN

*"He is the best candidate we have seen in many decades. Galen Síocháin will make an excellent Master of Magic, if he can learn to control his irreverent behavior."*

*Vonall Darawin – King's Adviser – 1902 DV*

I scan the edge of the forest for the hundredth time, grateful to find no trace of Valeria's presence. If she's anywhere near the camp, she is staying out of sight and out of earshot.

Would it be too much to ask if she were on her way back to Nido? Yes, it would.

She's as stubborn as I am and would risk everything for those she loves—not that I count myself among them. I should be so lucky. But I'm certain she loves her cousin and would never abandon him.

We have been sitting quietly for the past twenty minutes, that strap of magic still wrapped tightly around us. During this time, the preparations for our departure have been completed. I do not know why we are not on the road already, but I am not complaining. When Valeria comes—because she *will* come—I want to still be close to the veil and as far from Riochtach as possible.

The ranger guarding us seems less alert than before. He was interested in our conversation, but since we've been silent for some time, he appears almost bored now.

I try to shift positions, testing our magical restraints, but my torso feels frozen. I can move my head and legs freely. I can also move my hands from the wrist down, but my arms are pressed firmly to my sides, so they are of no use.

Once more, I search my mind for ideas that might allow us to escape, but I have none. The only possibility seems to be Valeria's arrival with The Eldrystone. I must confess that—

Something bumps the back of my head, and I realize it's Jago, head butting me. I turn my head and glare at him from the corner of my eye. He meets my gaze with a similar sidelong glance. As our eyes lock, he jerks his chin, directing my attention to something. I follow his gesture and spot Cuervo standing on the ground at the base of a nearby tree.

He peers at us with small round eyes, well hidden from our guard's view since our bodies block the male's line of sight. That bird is indeed clever, as Valeria likes to remark.

Jago and I exchange another look. His expression tells me he feels exactly the way I do. He knows Valeria will not abandon us, but he is concerned about her safety.

Galen stirs on my left, also seeming to notice Cuervo. He gestures with several jerks of his head for the bird to approach. What in the hells?! I headbutt him the way Jago did to me. The sorcerer lets out a frustrated sigh, but mostly ignores me, continuing to urge the bird closer.

I dare not utter a word. The ranger will hear me even if I whisper.

To my great vexation, Cuervo hops closer, head cocked to one side as he focuses on Galen.

The mood is tense. If anyone notices Cuervo, the relative calm our captors have regained since they brought us here will vanish.

Cursing inwardly, I headbutt Galen again to no avail.

A few more hops, and Cuervo vanishes from view, hidden by Galen's body. The ranger's head swivels as he shifts his focus from the camp back to us. I quickly adopt a blank expression, silently pleading with the gods that Cuervo remains unseen. After a tense moment, the ranger turns his attention away. I exhale in relief.

Several seconds pass, and at last, Cuervo hops back toward the tree, then keeps hopping until he disappears completely through the foliage.

*Thank Niamhara!*

I headbutt Galen a third time. He cranes his head to glare at me. He mouths something. Shaking my head, I let him know I have no idea what he is trying to tell me. He mouths the same thing again.

Still nothing. I frown.

Galen rolls his eyes, then starts drawing something on the ground with his index finger. I know right away what it is: a rune, part of a written language used for quick messaging.

Cuervo is a Runescribe Raven, so Galen was giving the bird a message to deliver, but to whom? I doubt Valeria has knowledge of this particular system. Galen finishes tracing the rune and lets me look at it. It says *idiot*. I headbutt him again, for good measure. He grunts a complaint.

The ranger's head snaps in our direction. Brow furrowed, he approaches, inspecting us and our surroundings. I grind my teeth. I endured many humiliations in Castella, but I thought they would be over once I returned to my rightful home. I was wrong. And some-how, this feels worse than anything the humans put me through. I am a Theric. Blessed by the Goddess. I should not be sitting on the ground, bound like a pig by my own kin.

Except, it has been a long time since the Goddess blessed me, has it not? I thought that would be different after crossing the veil, but it seems I was wrong to hope.

"What is it with you three?" the ranger snaps.

"This *idiot* headbutted me," Galen replies. "If you don't separate us, he's gonna bust my head open."

"The way you talk . . . you sound like a human," the ranger tells Galen, his mouth twisting in disgust.

"Well, I've spent over fifty years in Castella. That might explain it, don't you think?"

"Fifty years? The veil has only been closed for twenty." The ranger frowns.

"There were extenuating circumstances."

The fact that the ranger is using the wrong tense does not escape me. It seems he still cannot wrap his head around the idea that the veil has been reopened.

"How old are you, ranger?" I ask.

"That is not your concern," he says.

At his words, I bristle in anger. It was my most common emotion in Castella, and it rises, uninvited. Before my exile, before Saethara, I was patient and tolerant, but I forgot myself. Valeria reminded me of who I am, her feelings for me a doorway to a past self I learned to despise for being naïve and easily fooled. She opened my eyes to new possibilities, to hope. I must not forget.

"Every one of my subjects is my concern," I say, attempting to channel my old self.

The ranger throws his head back and huffs. "You are either incredibly determined or delusional. I am not your subject, and you are not my king, so stop with all that nonsense. It makes me want to hit you."

"Then hit him," Galen says. "I won't mind."

"Some king you are," the ranger huffs. "Even your *Master of Magic* disrespects you." He shakes his head, walks away, and retakes his previous spot.

"Always so helpful," I tell Galen from the corner of my mouth.

"Happy to oblige."

"Galen is hardheaded," Jago says. "Just like my cousin."

Our eyes meet, and a common thought passes between us. He also knows Valeria is coming despite the risk. This banal comment is his way of telling me that.

"Indeed, she is," I agree.

"She'd better be all right," he says, and it sounds like a little prayer to his saints.

"Keep your mouths shut," the ranger warns, lifting his spear and jamming the butt downward in a threatening motion, as if to indicate he will break our teeth if we keep talking.

We fall into uneasy silence once more. That is until the captain appears with four others, including the sorcerer and two more rangers.

"Throw them in the wagon," the captain orders, his bald head dripping with sweat.

We cannot allow them to take us further away from the veil. We must do something.

# 9

## VALERIA

*"At last, my happiness is within reach."*

**Kadewyn Zinceran – Veilfallen**

Sweat pours down my forehead and back in small rivulets. Hands on knees, I hunch over, trying to catch my breath. I'm back on the Castellan side of the veil, recovering from hopping across the border and trying *not* to shift and shifting anyway.

Cuervo has been gone much longer than last time, and I'm starting to worry. Have the captors taken my friends far from the veil already? Is that the reason for Cuervo's delay? Did he have to fly a greater distance to find them? Because he found them. I'll consider no other alternative.

My chest still pumps from my previous exertion. I don't feel ready for another bout, but I must get a handle on this. I don't have another choice.

For the fifth time, I move through the veil. The change ripples over my body almost immediately, the speed increasing with every crossing. I try to stop the change by focusing on my hands, willing them not to morph into wings.

*Stay. Stay. Stay.*

Pain ripples through my bones, as if tiny axes were hacking away at them, breaking and grinding them down to be compacted into far smaller versions of themselves. Yet, the agony isn't as intense as it was the first few times. It seems my body is becoming more malleable, more accustomed to the transformation.

*Stay.*

*Stay.*

*Stay.*

I flex my fingers, stare at my nail beds and the pale half-moons at their base. Despite the pain in my bones, I still stand on booted feet. I still have elbows and . . . boobs. Sweat stings my eyes. My teeth grind.

Tiny quill-like tips sprout along the length of my forearms.

"Dammit!" I growl, air hissing through my clenched teeth.

*Go back!* I command.

My skin clears, and a surge of elation rushes over me. *I did it!* My focus breaks, and the transformation surges back, mercilessly ripping through me, grinding my body down to a pulp to reshape me into a small raven. I fall to the ground as shifting energy ravages my human shape. The transformation takes only a fraction of the time it took the first time, and the pain is almost bearable.

When it's over, I hop to my feet. The urge to spread my wings returns with a vengeance, and it takes everything in me to resist it. The flap of wings catches my attention, and I glance up. A riot of color fills my vision, but after shifting five times, I've learned not to overthink my avian abilities.

Instead of wondering at all the different shades of green and blue that I didn't know existed, I search for Cuervo in the dense foliage. He's coming, and I need to hear the news he brings. I need to know that he found Jago, Korben, and Galen, and that they're all right.

I spot Cuervo a couple of minutes later, and I marvel at the reach of my hearing. With my human ears, I wouldn't have heard him until now. He cuts through a gap in the leaves, diving downward like a plummeting rock. A few feet from the ground, he spreads his wings wide, slowing himself and alighting gently next to me, without a sound.

My mind catalogs his movements of its own accord, storing them like a lesson to be reviewed later, safekeeping them in a part of me that feels brand new and not entirely human.

I open my mouth to ask if he found our friends, and a caw comes out. I shake my head, feeling like an idiot. Cuervo hops closer, his round eyes examining me up and down. After getting a good look, he hops away, putting some distance between us. He seems disconcerted. The way he's looking at me makes me self-conscious and hyper aware of the *wrongness* of this body. I don't belong in this shape. Its skin is too small, its appendages wrong.

*I'm trapped. Trapped!*

Irrational panic builds inside of me, and a buzzing sound fills my head. My heart speeds up to an incredible speed, hammering in my tiny chest. I hop backward, head swiveling as I search for the veil: my escape. It's right behind me, but my vision blurs. I'm not getting enough air.

I stumble toward the veil, the feel of supple ground against naked flesh adding to the wrongness. The shimmering curtain seems to stretch away from me with every step I take. Then my vision goes blank, and I lose consciousness.

When I come to, I lie on my stomach, face pressed to the ground as I stare at Cuervo. I blink a few times, and realize I'm in Castella, in my human shape. He looks concerned, not disconcerted like before.

I sit up and instantly realize that half of my legs are still on the Tirnanog side. Panic surges through me, and I scramble backward on my bottom. A primal fear suddenly strikes me—that my feet will be talons, that I'll be a chimera, trapped in that form for the rest of my life. I hold my breath, bracing for the horror, but to my immense relief, every bit of me is human.

"Thank the gods!" I say in a rush of breath.

Hugging my legs, I take several deep breaths that get my heartbeat under control. What was that? A panic attack? It felt awful.

"I'm glad no one saw me."

Cuervo squawks as if saying, *I did*.

"Well, you don't count." I shake my head. "Gods! That was embarrassing." I've never been overtaken by panic in this way. Trying to forget about it, I turn to Cuervo. "Did you find them?"

He bobs his head.

My shoulders slump as relief washes over me.

*They're alive. They're alive.*

However, my relief is short-lived because I still haven't learned how to control the shift, and I will be of no help to anyone in the shape of an untried raven. I rub my temples, fear growing in my heart, creeping like a shadow, ready to obscure all hope.

Abruptly, I stand and pace, trying to figure out what to do. If I'm unable to stay in my human form, I still have to follow them. They won't be able to escape from a sorcerer—not without espiritu of their own.

Worse yet, as I stand here, they could be moving further away from me, and once they leave this area, I may never find them again. They could vanish in a thousand different directions, headed to inevitable doom. Even if they travel toward Riochtach, a place I could probably find since I'm familiar with maps of Tirnanog, there may be different routes. What if I take the wrong one? What if I'm delayed? Regardless, I can't allow them to reach the capital. That bitch, Saethara, will have them killed as soon as she lays eyes on them. I know that as well as I know night will soon be here.

I can't tarry anymore. I have to go after them *now* . . . as a raven, which means I have to learn to fly. My chest tightens at the thought of being hundreds of feet above the ground. What if I shift back to my human form mid-flight and plummet to my death?

No, I can't worry about that. I need to—

Cuervo paws at the ground, trying to catch my attention.

I crouch. "What is it, friend?"

Carefully, one claw outstretched, he traces a shape on the ground. I frown, remembering he used to do that in the very beginning when I first found him in the crystal ruins of the Realta Observatory. He only did it a couple of times, then promptly gave up. I had forgotten about it. Why is he doing it again now?

I examine the shape. It is deliberate and looks like some sort of character.

"What is that, Cuervo?"

He hops a distance away and carves the same shape once more. He looks from me to the glyph expecting me to decipher it.

"I'm sorry, I don't know what it means."

Suddenly, I remember something Galen said.

*"He is a perfectly normal Runescribe Raven. My family used to raise them. They're counted amongst the smartest animals in Tirnanog."*

Runescribe Raven.

I glance back at the *rune*. That's what he has drawn on the dirt: a rune. And it means something, and I have no idea what.

*Godsdammit!*

"I'm really sorry, Cuervo," I say, tears pooling in my eyes as the impossibility of my situation hits me anew. There is no way I will be able to save them.

Sinking to the ground, I start crying, biting my tongue to repress the sobs that threaten to shatter me. I bury my face into my hands, biting hard on the inside of my cheek, trying to feel something other than this hopelessness.

*Please, Niamhara, help me! This can't be the reason you brought us here. Please!*

Through a crack in my fingers, I see Cuervo's head jerk and cock to one side as if listening.

Swallowing thickly, I wipe my face with the back of my arms, quieting my agitated breaths.

"What is it?" I whisper. "Is someone coming?"

He bobs his head once.

*Shit!*

I remain perfectly still, crouched and ready to pounce. When I finally hear what Cuervo sensed, I quickly pinpoint its location, then move as silently as possible in the opposite direction. Rounding a bush, I find cover behind it.

"I thought I heard something," a voice says. "This way."

"There is nothing here," a second voice replies. "I have indulged you long enough. I must cross now."

Is that . . .? I recognize that voice.

Trying to peek through the bush, I find no gap between the packed leaves. I start to lean forward when Cuervo caws a warning. There is a *zing*: a sword drawn. Someone rounds the bush, and I leap back, crashing on my bottom.

"Who do we have here?" a voice I despise asks. Her violet eyes gleaming with satisfaction, Calierin points her sword at my chest. "If it isn't Little Princess Valeria Plumanegra."

# 10

# KORBEN

*"The new magic is most unnatural. Where does it come from?"*

***Zylsa Bromin – Fuadach Fae Sorceress – 7 AV***

The sorcerer weaves his hands, fingers flexing in a complex motion. I have not seen anyone do that in a long time, and I cannot help but stare. Weavings grant control and precision, leaving nothing to chance. I imagine that is why the magical strap that clamps my arms to my sides and keeps me anchored to Jago and Galen feels flawless and has not debilitated with time. This sorcerer's movements are slow compared to Galen's, but other than that he seems to have considerable skill. These bindings are something he has practiced, even perfected.

When the spell is done, I float to an upright position along with my companions. The sorcerer performs one more gesture, and I stagger forward, my connection to the others broken, though the band remains, constricting my arms.

"Walk," the captain orders, pointing at the wagon.

The rangers aim swords and spears at us. Their expressions

are determined, angry. They look at us as if we are the worst imaginable foe.

"May I ask where you are taking us, captain?" I already know the answer, so my question is simply a delaying tactic.

"That is none of your concern. Move!" he shouts, releasing a wave of bad breath.

"I suspect we are going to Riochtach. Is that correct?" Without waiting for his answer, I add, "I look forward to seeing Elf-Dún. I have missed my home greatly. Many will recognize me there, so I doubt you will march us in through the main door. If fact, if I were to venture a guess, I would say you will not take us straight to the palace for that very reason. Where are you taking us instead?"

"Shut up and walk!" The captain gestures to one of the rangers, who digs the butt of his spear into my back and shoves me.

Thrown off balance, I stumble forward but manage to regain my footing. Reining in my anger, I straighten up, meeting the captain's gaze with unwavering resolve. My chin lifts confidently, bolstered by the certainty that my words are true and that I fully understand how this is going to unfold.

"Who do you take orders from?" I ask.

I suspect he is not in direct contact with Saethara. For her to pull this off, there have to be others helping her. I can guess who some of them might be. A leader always has enemies. I am no exception. I had my share of political foes while I was still on the throne, but I would like to know exactly who I am dealing with.

With a growl that shows his teeth, he gestures again for the ranger to put me in my place, but this time I am ready. More than that, I am bent on repaying their kindness.

Avoiding the spear aimed at my ribs, I charge the captain. With a burst of energy, I leap off the ground, body twisting in mid air as I propel myself feet-first toward my target. My legs snap open in a scissor-like motion, locking around the male's neck. Using the momentum, I rotate my hips sharply, then squeeze with my thighs, pulling him off balance and bringing him crashing down with me. The captain groans, as I squeeze my legs further, choking him. I want to snap his neck, but it may not be to my advantage. He wants to keep us alive to take us to Riochtach. He undoubtedly has orders from someone to watch the veil, seemingly awaiting my return. I've begun to suspect they knew we were coming. The veil is too vast for our encounter to be a coincidence.

Our gazes lock. He is properly terrified as he struggles in vain to get free, bucking and trying to pry my legs apart.

In the next instant, two of the rangers come at me, the butt of their spears smashing into my back, my sides, my head. I try to throw my arms up to protect my face as they pelt me with vicious jabs, but my arms are still immobile. One of the spears strikes my temple. White spots appear in my vision. I release the captain and try to stand, but it is no easy matter. I only manage to get to my knees, turtling down to protect my face and middle while they continue hitting me.

"Stop, bastardos!" Jago shouts.

"What did you call us?" One of my attackers turns and jabs Jago in the stomach.

Jago doubles over, gasping for air.

"That's enough," the captain shouts.

Rubbing his neck, he's back on his feet, trying to appear in control, though I can see from his expression that he is addled and likely hoping he will be able to pay me back *after* he brings me to his leader. Whoever sent him gave orders not to harm me, and that is more concerning than reassuring.

My head throbs as they yank me to my feet. My vision blurs and a nauseous feeling whirls in my stomach. I sway on my feet, and I am surprised when Galen steps closer to steady me.

"You all right?" he asks with true concern etched on his features.

I grunt my assent and do my best to carry my own weight, but I would be lying if I said Galen's support is not of help.

They guide us toward the wagon, which has wooden walls on three sides and a curved roof on top. Before I duck inside, I surreptitiously glance around for signs of Valeria or Cuervo. I see none.

My chest clenches, and it takes me a moment to identify the sensation for what it is: apprehension. For so long, I have not cared about anyone. Not in this way. If anything were to happen to Valeria . . . I would not be able to go on, and I would not be responsible for anyone I take down with me.

*Protect her, Niamhara. Do not fail me in this.*

Jago climbs in before me, slightly bent over at the waist and taking deep, careful breaths. We sit across from each other, Galen at my side.

The wagon starts rolling a moment later. None of the rangers climb in with us, but they take their mounts and follow close behind, easily watching us as there is no door.

"You don't think they're taking us to your wife, the queen," Galen says.

I lean my head back, eyes closed, willing the nausea to go away. "No," I answer, even though it was not a question.

"Where then?"

"I have no idea."

"I'm going to assume," Jago says a little out of breath, "your *wife* wants you to remain dead, and she has allies who are helping her make sure you don't perform a resurrection. You got stranded in Castella when the veil fell," he pauses, scratching his head, making up a story that makes sense to him, "and since then she's grown used to being queen without a pesky king by her side."

A noble attempt, but in essence, far from the truth.

Galen's mouth draws downward as he nods. "That or she married another bloke . . . *or* . . . Korben pissed her off. What did you do to her, mate?"

"It is nothing like that." I shake my head and immediately regret it. The wagon's interior seems to spin, Jago and Galen gaining twin images and flipping sideways. The blow to my temple is almost more than I can handle. I inhale deeply, my breath shuddering as I let it out.

"You may have a concussion," Jago points out. "Don't fall asleep."

"Thank you for jumping to my defense . . . out there," I say, slurring the last of the sentence.

"Valeria would kill me if I let anything happen to you." He nudges my boot with his.

My eyes blink open.

"Don't fall asleep," he reminds me.

"She would . . . kill *me* if something happens to *you*," I reply.

I am sure of that, though not so sure if she would go as far as killing for my sake. The attraction between us is undeniable, and my feelings for her . . . Well, I have told her all about them. I am in love with her, and I am beginning to understand that what I once felt for

Saethara was a mere infatuation. I barely knew her when I married her. The Mate Rite was just that: a rite. A set of steps that I had to follow, that I trusted because my mother and father followed them as well as many others before them. But they were not meant to work for me.

Saethara came into my life with a purpose. She never felt anything for me, and I was too blind to see it. She broke something inside me, and I swore to never allow anyone in again.

But Valeria found the crack through the door I had sealed shut, and she wormed her way in deep, down to the root of my being, where she repaired what I believed to be destroyed forever. I tried to flush her out, told myself I hated her because she only cared about The Eldrystone. Except I knew that was not true. I doubted her many times, but deep in my soul I understood she was different.

So I fell.

I am wiser now, however, and I know I must not assume my feelings are reciprocated. In the end, when all of this is said and done, Valeria may go her own way, and I will be one experience in her arsenal.

She is young, so young.

"Are you awake, Korben?" Jago nudges my foot again.

"I am. Just let me rest my eyes." I cannot stand the light. It makes my head pulse harder.

"All right, but just for a moment."

I have pondered Valeria's youth before and more than ever I find myself hoping she inherited Loreleia's fae longevity. If I were human, my body would be withered and wasted, and she would consider me ancient—not that I would still be alive at the age of two hundred and twenty. But I am fae, and I age differently, more slowly, both in body and mind. Yet, life leaves its marks, and I was not immune to those. Time dulled my curiosity, my willingness, my excitement for the quotidian, and Valeria brought it back. Her vivacity and drive reawakened my hunger for life.

She is the sunshine after a century of darkness. I did not even know how arid my existence was until I met her.

Saethara never made me feel that way. If she had not tried to kill me, I am certain I would be terribly unhappy with her, ready to cross into the Glimmer, sure that life had nothing else to offer me.

Now, I want to live more than ever. With Valeria by my side.

I can only hope she wants me this badly too.

*Protect her, Niamhara. Protect her.*

# II

# VALERIA

*"I'm going, Gaspar. I don't care about the risks. You will not stop me."*

**Esmeralda Malla – Romani Healer**

Calierin's sword hovers a handspan from my nose. She hates me. She has tried to kill me more than once and, for days, derived endless enjoyment from torturing me. I despise her too and trust her not at all. So being glad to see her qualifies as the strangest and most uninvited emotion I've ever felt.

She's smirking, looking at me down the length of her weapon as I hide behind a bush like a frightened hare.

The last time I saw her, she was trapped in Galen's espiritu in the middle of Don Justo's camp after the awful man took The Eldrystone from us and tied us to a tree. And if I'm being honest, after we escaped, I didn't worry about her. Not one bit.

After Galen brought back The Eldrystone, we left town, intent on opening the veil, and neither Korben nor I mentioned trying to free the Tuathacath warrior.

And now, she's here.

*"Forgive me, my king. Never in my wildest dreams could I have guessed who you truly are. I wish to atone for my mistake. Please accept me as your humble servant. I am a Tuathacath warrior, and my order has always served our realm proudly. From today till the day I die, you have my loyalty and my sword."*

The words she offered Korben after she tried to kill him ring inside my head. She uttered them vehemently after he pronounced the declaration that only a Fae King can.

*Saints and feathers!* Is Calierin Niamhara's answer to my prayers? It can't be.

Glancing past the female and her very sharp sword, I spot Kadewyn. His pale silver hair hangs limply at either side of his face, and his bow and quiver peek out at the top of his head.

Or maybe the Goddess sent Kadewyn to help me. Another veil-fallen. The irony doesn't escape me. He wasn't with Calierin last we saw her, but he must have tracked her down. Maybe he was the one who helped her escape Don Justo.

Calierin opens her mouth to say something, but a voice and the sounds of trampling feet cut her off.

"No matter how hard you try, you're not gonna leave me behind." Past Kadewyn, pushing a branch out of the way, Esmeralda appears, looking sweaty and worn-down. Her mass of dark curls is held down by a colorful kerchief, and her normally long skirts are torn at the knees—something that seems to have been done on purpose. A satchel rests across her torso.

My jaw falls open.

*By all the gods, what is she doing here and in the company of these two?*

"Valeria!" Her eyes widen.

She runs in my direction, her bracelets tinkling. Rounding Calierin, she falls to her knees at my side. At first, it appears as if she's going to hug me. I start to lift my arms, but in the last instant, she stops herself. We peer at the ground awkwardly.

Esmeralda has an aloof personality and always acts as if everything is above her. I never figured her for the hugging kind. Or maybe she cut herself short because I'm Princess Valeria Plumanegra, and she suddenly got the notion that it's inappropriate to take such liberties. Many would feel that way. Not me. I'd welcome a hug, but since I don't understand her hesitation, all I can do is fidget.

"Um . . ." she glances around. "Where's Jago?"

Understanding dawns on me. When Korben and I got separated from the Romani troop on our way here, Jago remained with them. As my cousin joined us in Badajos, he showed signs of a certain attachment to Esmeralda. I never suspected it went deep enough to warrant the Romani woman leaving her troop to come after him.

*Gods!* I had been afraid Esmeralda, shrewd as she is, would teach Jago a painful lesson and cure him of his flirtatious ways, possibly breaking his heart. I never imagined it might be the other way around.

Calierin pushes Esmeralda out of the way, gruff as ever.

"Who cares about that nitwit!" the Tuathacath warrior barks. "Where is King Korben?"

"Go to hell, you ugly lamppost!" Esmeralda spits.

"Jago's not a nitwit," I protest at the same time.

Kadewyn comes forth. "I have wasted enough time already. I don't need any more delays. I must go to my family." He turns to the veil and starts toward it.

"I would be careful if I were you," I warn. "There are . . . hostiles on the other side. From the looks of it, they have instructions to arrest anyone who crosses."

"What?!" he and Calierin exclaim at the same time.

"They got Jago, Korben, and Galen," I say, answering Calierin's and Esmeralda's questions. "I was able to escape. With Cuervo." I point upward, where he perches on a high branch.

He caws in acknowledgment.

"Why would they arrest him? He is the king." Calierin shakes her head, confused.

"I can explain everything, but first . . ." I turn my attention to Cuervo.

His talons march in place on the branch as he gives me his full attention.

"Spy on Jago. Please," I say.

Without hesitation, he lunges into the air and disappears through the shimmering veil.

"*Kham!*" Esmeralda exclaims, then spits on the ground, a gesture that the Romani believe wards off evil.

Like me, she was born after the veil collapsed. She's never seen such a thing.

Calierin, sword still in her grip, says, "You had better explain quickly and tell me where to find King Korben. I am sworn to him and must protect him. If he has been arrested as you claim, I will free him right away."

She is full of bolstering and arrogance, but right now, I don't hate her nearly as much as usual.

Knowing time is of the essence, I stand, dust myself off, and explain everything that happened from the moment we opened the veil, to my transformation, to running into the hostile fae and the fight that ensued. I tell them I'm still free only because of Jago and explain how Cuervo has been keeping track of their location.

"I was starting to lose hope," I confess. "But can you help me free them?"

Calierin narrows her eyes. "Help *you*?" Her tone indicates she could never be *the help* to someone as useless as me. "Just tell me where he is, and I will take care of it."

"You did hear me, didn't you?" I demand. "There were at least ten of them, and they had a sorcerer. You can't take all of them on your own."

Calierin huffs. "And what? You will wave your little rapier about? Or use your little raven claws and beak to lighten the load for me?"

The heat of anger burns in my cheeks. She's insufferable. Not that she's wrong, which makes my anger worse. I didn't even tell them I can't shift back to my human shape, or that I don't know how to be a raven. Yet, Calierin needs me. I'm the only one who can tell her where her king is. She doesn't care about Jago as she clearly stated, so I have to make sure my cousin is also rescued. Nobody seems to give a damn about Galen, but he did help us, and even if Korben feigns indifference toward the sorcerer, I can tell he cares about him.

"Or maybe this Romani woman can throw bracelets at the enemy," Calierin mocks, giving Esmeralda a sideways glance.

"You're an unhappy bitch," Esmeralda shoots back. "How can you stand her, Kade?"

Kadewyn observes quietly, as is his manner. His expression is troubled, and he seems more preoccupied about the veil—throwing glances in its direction—than our argument.

Calierin literally bares her teeth and leans into Esmeralda.

"Hey!" I warn. "We're not the enemy here. We can all help. Kadewyn can fight, and Cuervo and I can cause a diversion."

Unable to fly, I can't really do anything, but she doesn't need to know the specifics of how utterly useless I'll be once we cross.

"Hey, what about me?!" Esmeralda demands. "I can help, too."

"Maybe it would be safer if you stay here and go back to your troop," I suggest.

She adamantly shakes her head. "I came to find Jago, and I'm not leaving without him."

Her words are firm, sincere. They warm my heart. Anyone who cares about Jago is my friend, no matter what.

I nod. "As long as you're aware it will be dangerous. Also, Jago may prefer it if you remain safe."

"If that's true, I'll have to teach him I always do whatever the hell I please."

Calierin shakes her head. "Idiots."

I ignore her and go on, "There's one more thing. When we cross, I'm going to try to close the veil again, so we might never be able to return home?"

"What?! I . . . why would you do that?"

"You can't!" Calierin exclaims at the same time. "King Korben would not want to leave our people behind—not only trapped but imprisoned."

"I have to protect Castella," I say. "That female, Saethara, she's . . . not a good person. She's not the kind of neighbor my realm needs."

This is all I'm going to say on the subject. What I know about Saethara isn't for me to divulge.

"I do not give a fuck about that," Calierin growls. "Closing the veil without freeing our people is wrong."

Esmeralda and Kadewyn say nothing, but I can see there's conflict in their eyes. They understand my concern better than Calierin ever could.

"I hold The Eldrystone, Calierin. It's *my* decision." I slowly pull The Eldrystone from under my tunic. "You may not think you should respect me, but I already taught you otherwise." I wish for the amulet to glow to punctuate my words, and I'm relieved when it does, even if it's only for an instant.

Her mouth works, and her hand flexes near her sword.

Soon after we left Castellina, I fought Calierin. The Eldrystone aided me, and I beat her with ease. I don't know if the amulet would help me now. It seems somehow weaker after opening the veil, but that's something else she doesn't need to be made aware of. All she needs to do is remember the humiliation of a Tuathacath warrior being bested by a human. I am half-fae, though, but she'll never see me as such.

Her eyes narrow as she regards the amulet. Perhaps I shouldn't show it to her as she also tried to steal it from me, but I have to gain some semblance of control over this situation.

I place The Eldrystone back under my tunic.

Calierin's nostrils flare, her expression hardening into a sneer. Oh, she hates me just as much as I hate her, but we need each other.

"You could open the veil again, right?" Esmeralda asks. "You did it once."

I nod. "It's a logical assumption, but still no more than that. I wouldn't count on it."

"Fair enough." Esmeralda sighs. "I'll take my chances."

My gaze shifts to Calierin.

"Fine, then," she snaps.

I nod, doing my best not to show my relief.

"I hate to spoil your plans," Kadewyn says, "but I am going my own way."

Slowly, Calierin turns sideways, making sure to keep an eye on me. "What is one more day if you can help your King, Kadewyn?"

He doesn't respond. Kadewyn is the quiet sort. All I know about him is what Korben told me, that Kadewyn has a wife and daughter in Tirnanog, and his only desire is to get back to them.

"My king," he says, pronouncing the words with skepticism. "I do not know if Rífíor is truly King Korben Theric, but the male I know would understand my decision."

"Something is not right across that veil." Calierin points in the direction of Tirnanog. "This *Queen Saethara* has been ruling in King Korben's stead for over twenty years, usurping his throne."

"Or so *she* says." Kadewyn turns his skepticism toward me this time. "She did not quite explain how this Saethara got there in the first place, and I think she knows."

"It's not my story to tell," I say firmly. "Korben confided in me, and it wasn't easy for him. I know for a fact he wouldn't want me to divulge his secrets to the entire realm."

He blows air through his nose. "Either way. My family is my priority."

"From the way she described the assailants and their uniforms,"

Calierin says, "I think they belong to the Oakheart Brigade. Their purpose is to patrol the wilderness for bandits and that sort of thing. They are not soldiers meant to protect a border. Since the king cannot prove his identity, they must think he is some sort of criminal trying to stir trouble by claiming to be Korben Theric. Per procedure, they will take him to the capital for trial, but if this Saethara hears of his capture, I have a feeling he will never stand in front of a judge. Something is terribly wrong. I feel it in my bones. Mark my words, ensuring that King Korben regains his rightful place as soon as possible would be in your and your family's best interest."

Kadewyn thinks for a long moment, and at last, he asks, "Are they far?"

I shake my head. "Shouldn't be. The last time Cuervo returned quickly."

That isn't quite true, but my job right now seems to be mincing information. It occurs to me that Cuervo was delayed by something to do with that rune he traced on the ground. Reminded of it, I search for it quickly, but it seems to have been trampled by Calierin's boots.

"All right, I will help," Kadewyn says, though he doesn't seem happy about it.

Calierin whirls and faces the veil. "Let's go then."

"We'll wait for Cuervo, then he can guide us," I say. "Besides, I have your horse, Calierin. Also, three others and some supplies. We may need them. I hid them that way." I hook a thumb over my shoulder.

She seems to like the news. "Let's fetch them then. This morning, after someone forgot to tie down our mounts, they got spooked and ran off." The look of disdain she shoots at Esmeralda makes the Romani woman shrink a little. I don't think I've ever seen Esmeralda blush, but there seems to be a first time for everything.

Quickly, I guide Calierin toward the animals. We retrieve them, accompanied by an awkward silence, there and back. We wait impatiently for Cuervo's return.

"I thought you said they were not far," Kadewyn huffs ten minutes later.

"Um . . ." I shrug. What else can I do?

When Calierin starts pacing and exhaling loudly, I start to worry.

"What if something happened to the bird?" Esmeralda asks.

"Nothing happened to him," I snap.

"I don't mean to—"

Cuervo reappears and lands on the same branch as before.

*Thank the gods!*

His little chest pumps fast, as if he flew as hard as he could.

"Hello, friend," I greet him and pat my horse's saddle. He flies down and lands on it. "Did you find them?"

He bobs his head.

"Good. Are they near?"

"Wagon," he says.

I startle at this. "They are on a wagon?"

He bobs his head again.

"Moving?"

Another head bob.

"We had better follow. Now!" Calierin offers one of the horses' reins to Kadewyn, and they quickly mount.

I pull Esmeralda close and lean in closer to whisper in her ear, words streaming out in a hurry. "When we cross the veil, I'm going to shift into a raven."

"Yes, you said that." She tries to pull away to look at me, but I hold her arm tightly.

"I will be unable to shift back, and I will be useless. I don't know how to do anything in that form, and you—"

Calierin glances over her shoulder, and I step away from Esmeralda, smile, and hand over the reins to the fourth horse to the Romani woman.

"Jago was riding this one," I tell her, causing Calierin to roll her eyes.

"You have to help me," I mouth at Esmeralda. "Please."

She nods uncertainly, and I nod back in thanks.

I don't want Calierin to learn of my impediments. Not yet anyway. It's bad enough as it is. Having Esmeralda on my side makes me feel better, though. If she cares for Jago, the feeling might transfer to me, if only for his sake. My relationship with Esmeralda might have had a friendly beginning, but after she sold me out to Bastien things took a wrong turn. We haven't had time to patch the damage of her betrayal and my subsequent order to throw her into a dungeon cell. She did forgive Jago for imprisoning her at my request, so maybe she will forgive me, too.

"We can cross here," I say. "No one was on the other side last I checked, but let's be careful."

I pull my horse all the way to the veil.

Calierin and Kadewyn stare at the shimmering curtain with both anticipation and apprehension. Kadewyn's eyes waver, tears pooling. His breathing is labored, and it's clear he's fighting back tears. I can only imagine how difficult it has been for him to be away from his family. He'll finally get to see his wife and daughter again, though the time he missed with them will never be replaced. At least, he can look forward to many years with them, his fae longevity grants him that. The same cannot be said about the humans who got trapped in Tirnanog. Twenty years is a long time for the likes of us.

As harsh as Calierin is, I can still see the warring emotions on her face. Did she leave family behind? A husband? Children? It's hard to imagine her doing anything besides wielding a sword and lopping off heads, but she didn't just pop out of the air, so at least she has parents. Does she miss them? Maybe she misses grunting and yelling at them.

Esmeralda for her part only looks scared. She just barely met Jago, so abandoning her troop and own realm for him seems rash. She has a sick mother in Castellina. Is she not worried about her well-being? Maybe not. She is a Romani, after all, used to a transient life, always visiting new places. Perhaps searching for adventure is in her blood.

The moment gets awkwardly long, so I turn to Cuervo.

"Safe?" I say, pointing at the veil.

He goes across to check and comes back with a positive answer.

"Thank you. Now, take me to Jago, all right?"

He bobs his head.

I inhale a deep breath, and without waiting for the others, I cross, telling myself we'll soon find our friends, and everything will be fine.

# 12

# VALERIA

*"I do not trust her. She is not telling us the entire truth."*

**Calierin Kelraek – Tuathacath Warrior and Veilfallen**

As we cross into Tirnanog, I fight the shift with all my strength. Regardless, it comes, reducing me to an ungainly, useless creature.

The horses' hooves look enormous, and I jump back, afraid of being trampled. As Esmeralda crosses the glimmering divide, her boot lands on my talon. I squawk in pain, wings beating fast.

She lets out a little squeal and steps back. Free of her foot's hold, I involuntarily fly up and, in an instant, find myself a few feet off the ground. Panic seizes me, and I become conscious of every wing beat. I falter and start to fall.

*Gods, it will hurt!*

Esmeralda snatches me out of the air, her hands gentle around me. My first instinct is to fight, but I'm able to prevail over it. Instead, I tuck my wings, a motion that's beginning to feel familiar.

"I got you." Esmeralda's green eyes rove over me, her expression full of amazement. "So you truly are a Plumanegra, huh? My ma has told me stories of your grandpa and pa flying over Castellina when she was little. I guess she wasn't pulling my leg."

She sets me down next to Cuervo on the horse's saddle.

"Friend," Cuervo croaks, still looking nervously at me.

I can't imagine how confused he must feel.

"Saints be damned!" Esmeralda exclaims as she takes in the forest. "This can't be real." She reaches a hand to touch the iridescent bark of one of the trees.

Calierin and Kadewyn cross the veil at the same time, horses trailing behind them. The way their faces transform as they lay eyes on their homeland is something I'd like to capture in an image and keep forever. There are so many emotions in their eyes that it's impossible to name them all.

I'm glad for their distraction because they don't notice me, but I'm also reminded that I'm leaving Castella and everything I know behind. My sister. My home, Nido. Castellina with its bustle of merchants and performers, and its familiar streets that I traversed with Mother and Father. What if I'm never able to return again?

*Gods, what a terrible risk!*

And yet, if I stay and go back now, what would I encounter? Not the city I used to know—not if my sister has turned it into a place full of hatred for anyone who is different.

*That's why you're here, Valeria. To save Amira from the biggest mistake of her life.*

Things aren't going exactly as I'd hoped. It's going to take much longer than I anticipated, and there are unforeseen complications, but that doesn't mean my goal has changed.

*It only got much, much, MUCH harder. That's all*, the sly side of me puts in.

Hating that part of myself, I sigh, which apparently is a thing birds can also do. It's undeniable that it'll be harder to save Amira from herself now. I first have to save Jago, Korben, and Galen. And then what? Save Tirnanog, too? It looks that way.

I can't let that overwhelm me, however.

*One step at a time.* The next one is closing the veil.

Focusing on the amulet, which I feel within me like a warm touch, I wish for the veil to close. I wait, breath held in expectation. Nothing happens. The massive dividing curtain continues to shimmer, indifferent to my desires.

Esmeralda looks back, following my gaze. "Are you going to close it?" she asks.

I shake my head.

"You changed your mind?"

Another shake of my head.

"You tried, but you can't."

I nod once.

Calierin huffs with satisfaction. "Good. Serves you right." She pauses, frowning at me. "Why did you shift?"

I stare at her, holding her gaze.

She pushes a burst of air through her lips and turns away, annoyed. Clearly, she's had enough of me. Good. I've had enough of her, too. For a lifetime.

Turning to Cuervo, I look to the almost-dark sky. He catches my meaning and takes to the air, heading further west. Riochtach is one day's ride from the border if I remember correctly. I'm grateful for its proximity. Though, if we're lucky, we won't need to go that far.

The others mount and begin to follow Cuervo. He stops on a tree branch ahead, making sure he's well within sight. Many times he guided me through Nido's grounds just like this, taking me to Father, Amira, Jago, or whoever I'd asked him to find for me. It's not a skill I taught him. He already knew how to do that when I met him.

Runescribe Raven . . . I've always known he's clever, but it's clear there is more to Cuervo than I imagined. It seems perhaps he was properly trained, and I may not even know half of what he can do, including his ability to write messages.

Cuervo keeps flying ahead and stopping until we catch up. Calierin leads the way, followed by Kadewyn, and then Esmeralda, who pulls my horse. I stand on the saddle, finding it surprisingly easy to balance as we sway from side to side. My surroundings enthrall me, many sights and sounds in ranges of color and pitch I've never experienced.

About fifteen minutes in, Calierin glances back and notices my small shape. Frowning, she stops her horse and waits until we catch up.

"What is she doing?" she asks Esmeralda.

"I don't know. Practicing?" Esmeralda replies.

"Why ride a horse like that? It is strange . . . a raven acting like a person. Why not fly with Cuervo?"

*Because I'm a sorry raven and have no idea how to do any raven things.*

"She *is* a person," Esmeralda says. "Maybe she's tired. That must be it."

Calierin sneers. "It is the stupidest thing I have ever seen."

"Is it? At least her horse won't be as tired when we get wherever it is we're going, unlike *your* horse with your fat ass on it." Esmeralda's green eyes sparkle with amusement.

I let out a series of caws that sounds like a laugh, then clamp my beak shut, taken aback by the sound.

With a huff, Calierin urges her horse forward. "Strange and stupid, like I said."

"There's something wrong with that one," Esmeralda whispers in my direction.

If she only knew.

Calierin is bitter and ruthless, but she also seems to be loyal and determined. She vowed to serve Korben and seems bound to stick to that promise.

Esmeralda thinks for a moment, then asks over her shoulder, "Can you understand me fully?"

I nod once.

"Good. Do not want to waste my breath." She pauses as she maneuvers my mount forward until it walks next to hers. "That's better. I can see you now. So you can't shift back?"

I shake my head.

"You were you before we crossed the veil." She ponders. "But as soon as we entered Tirnanog you changed, so something here is doing that. Right?"

With a slight movement of my wings, I mimic a shrug.

"And you said you were useless in this shape," she continues musing, "so . . . you can't fly."

I shake my head.

"But you're a bird, and your wings seem fine. Why don't you try? Fly up to that branch, then back down to the horse." She points at a nearby tree.

*I can't. I can't. I can't,* that's the chant that repeats endlessly inside my head. I'm too old to learn. Father once told Amira and me that he didn't remember learning how to fly. He just knew he'd been doing it most of his life.

If I try, I know I will overthink everything, and I'll plummet to the ground. I don't know how to *not* overthink. It would be like telling someone not to think of food when they're starving. It'd be the first and only thing they would do! My only hope is to learn how to shift back to my human shape. With that in mind, I start trying again.

After another fifteen minutes of riding, I'm exhausted. I want to slump down on the saddle, but if I do that I'll slide to the ground and be trampled by the horse. I tried everything I could think of to shift back, starting with imagining every limb in a human shape and ending with recalling the most human things imaginable, like playing the violin, reciting poetry, and braiding my hair.

Nothing worked.

Esmeralda rears up, craning her neck. "There's something ahead."

From my vantage point all I see is my horse's long neck. It isn't until we pass right in front of a trodden section of land that I see what she's talking about.

Calierin and Kadewyn dismount and inspect the area. The former spends some time crouching over different patches of ground, features pinched in concentration. She pokes at a circle of rocks where someone built a fire. She scents the air and counts foot and hoof prints. She places hands on hips and ponders.

When she's done, she climbs onto her horse again. "I would say about thirty rangers on horseback. There are still traces of Korben's scent, so they left recently. There are wheel marks heading west. I suspect they loaded him onto a wagon, so their progress will be slow. We can catch up. Maybe one hour or two at most." She looks up at the sky. "Night is nearly here. I suspect they will ride on to wherever they are going. Otherwise, why leave so late? Regardless, we can use the cover of darkness to our advantage."

Calierin shakes her reins, and the horse starts forward. Now that we have more definite information, she speeds up, confident.

"Thank the saints!" Esmeralda exclaims. "We're coming, Jago." Her eyes lift to the heavens as she says this. It sounds like a promise, one she hopes reaches his ears.

If only I could fly ahead and deliver the message myself.

*We're coming. Don't do anything stupid before we get there.*

# 13

# KORBEN

*"Will we ever be rid of the Theric curse?"*

**Glandell Shanan – Fae Noble – 1857 DV**

"Wake up, Korben! Wake up!" Jago's voice is insistent.

My eyelids are heavy. I look at Jago and Galen through blurry vision.

"I told you he was all right," Galen says. "His head is harder than a petroclaw's carapace."

Jago frowns. "A what?"

"A petroclaw's carapace. It's a type of large crustacean that lives in the Giantran Sea, near my home. They're vicious and hard to kill. Like this one." He points at me.

"Fuck you, Galen," I say.

"Like I told you . . . as enchanted as a fairy tale."

The nausea I felt earlier has passed, but I still have a pounding headache.

"How long have I been out? Did I miss anything?" I squint, peering outside. It is dark now.

Jago shakes his head. "No, we've just been riding in the same direction."

I attempt to lift an arm to rub my head to be reminded of the magical restraint around my torso. It is infuriating to be thus hindered. This is a first for me. Of course, I experienced plenty of firsts in Castella, but magic was so scarce there, this sort of humiliation was not one of them.

Now, we are back in Tirnanog, and it seems there are more *firsts* to be discovered. No matter. Everything I've been through has only made me stronger and more resilient. I have also learned much, among those things a fair amount of humility. Others may not agree with this assessment, but they did not know me before.

I take deep breaths, willing the headache to go away. I need to be awake and ready for when Valeria comes. Maybe she will take out the sorcerer, and we will be free to fight. That is the sort of action I expect from her. She is smart . . . and can be shrewd if she needs to be.

Suddenly, a small door folds back at the front of the wagon's roof, and a ray of moonlight shines through. We all glance up, surprised. The driver's head appears within the square. He is checking on us. It is the same male who was guarding us before.

I do not expect him to speak. I imagine he is only doing his job and keeping a close eye on his charges, but after glancing all around, he whispers something unexpected.

"You really are Korben Theric." It is not a question, but a statement.

Still, I nod once, trying to figure out if being believed is good or bad at this point.

"I overheard Drothgar, the captain, saying it to his . . . friend." A long silence follows. He looks ahead a few times, likely to make sure we do not deviate from the path. "He believes you?" Strangely, *this* comes back as a question.

I exchanged glances with Galen.

"Drothgar believes he's the king?" Galen rolls the words in his mouth. "Not an easy claim to make after the way he treated us." He pauses. "Perhaps he knows Korben *is* the king . . . somehow."

The male grimaces at this. He does not like that train of thought one bit.

My mind is addled from the blow, but I manage to get my head around the situation. If Drothgar *knows* who I am, it means he is committing treason. Moreover, the driver's reaction tells me that Drothgar's knowledge of events is not necessarily unusual. Perhaps there have been other times when his leader seemed to know things he shouldn't have, like our presence at the veil. That is the sort of behavior that does not sit well with many people. Divination is not a common skill, not even among the best fae sorcerers and sorceresses, and oftentimes involves the use of dark forces.

It is the reason why Gaspar's ability surprised me. For someone who claims to be only a quarter fae, his skill to sense the future is remarkable.

What is to happen to our kind is decided by Niamhara. Sometimes low gods and goddesses might have a glimpse into her desires, but rarely the fae. Moreover, it is believed that her influence on future matters is only minor. Holy scripture teaches us that she may use her power to influence events, to nudge people in a certain direction, but in the end, we have freewill to decide our own path.

So it is indeed strange for Drothgar to know with any certainty who I am. Moreover to have been waiting for me at the very moment and the very location where I came back through the veil.

"Drothgar is no diviner," the male says with a huff. "But . . ." he trails off, shaking his head.

"What is your name?" I ask.

He frowns, a groove appearing across his forehead as the corners of his mouth draw down. He thinks for a moment, then closes the door, shutting us out.

"What is going on here?" I ask no one in particular.

"More than meets the eye, for sure." Galen cocks his head to one side. "I think they were specifically waiting for you at the veil, right there where we appeared."

"That is exactly what I was thinking," I reply.

"So what you're saying," Jago puts in, "is that this *Queen Saethara* knew you were coming and sent this lot to intercept you because . . . well, she is a cheat, and it's in her best interest if no one finds out she ousted you somehow." His expression strains as he appears to think hard on the matter. He really wants to figure out what happened between Saethara and me. It is almost entertaining seeing him try.

One of Galen's eyebrows goes up. "Why don't you just tell us what happened, Korben."

"It is a long story," I say.

I appreciate that Valeria did not share my story with her cousin. I have kept that secret for a long time, and even sharing it with Valeria was difficult. Still, I would not have blamed her if she had confided in Jago.

The sorcerer kicks back and folds one foot over the other. "We seem to have nothing but time, so I'm all ears."

"Are you? Must be why you are so ugly."

"How mature!"

"You bring out the best in me, dear Master of Magic."

He rolls his eyes, but lets it go. "This wife of yours . . . she must have powerful allies."

I grunt, making a mental list of all the royals who opposed me while I still sat on the throne. It is not a short list, but how many of them would Saethara have trusted with the truth? And how many of them would have willingly allowed her to assume her position as queen knowing that I was still alive? Legally, she has all the rights. We were married in front of the entire court, after all. But what she did to me—her husband, the king—should have barred her from presiding over anything other than a dungeon cell or the executioner's block.

I do not think most of those conceited royals would support her, anyway—not when they could have easily challenged her to take the throne for themselves had they known the truth.

Once more, I find myself wondering about Vonall, my dear friend. He was a captain in my father's guard when he was young. He is several decades older than me, but that did not impede our friendship. He became my adviser when I took the throne and never minced words when I needed it most.

Vonall witnessed some of what happened. He knows I went after Loreleia. Was he not there to ask questions? Without knowledge of what led me to action, what he *did* witness must have appeared terrible to him, yet he knew me better than anyone. He would have suspected something.

While in Castella, I often imagined Vonall getting down to the bottom of things and punishing Saethara. I thought a steward would take my place to guard the throne until my return. It seemed obvious that they would eventually figure out I was trapped on the other side of the veil. I even hoped my loyal subjects would devise a way to remove the barrier that kept me from returning home. The hope only lasted a few months, then I realized it was wishful thinking and that The Eldrystone was the only tool capable of helping me.

But all my conjectures were wrong. Instead, everyone in Tirnanog thinks I am dead, which leads me to believe that Vonall, who knows the truth, met an unfortunate end.

*Oh, dear friend. I am so sorry.*

The question remains: who is aiding Saethara? Did she have allies from the beginning? Did she plan my murder with the help of someone who surpasses her coldblooded nature? What if she is only that person's puppet?

"What are you thinking about, Korben?" Galen asks, noting my frown.

"Just wondering who we are up against."

"Any luck?"

I shake my head.

"It's been some time since I left Elf-Dún. I'm not sure who still graces its halls, but I might put Glandell, Vrinox, and . . . Crooner on your list."

"Vrinox crossed into the Glimmer. Glandell and Crooner are likely candidates. But to be honest, I have a feeling something else is afoot."

"Whatever that is, it doesn't bode well for us."

"Exactly."

"Your beloved better hurry up then," he says in barely more than a whisper. He has also figured out that Valeria is coming.

As if his thoughts have conjured her, a commotion starts outside. My entire body goes tense with apprehension. She is here!

# 14

## KORBEN

*"What do I do? I am only a lowly officer. Why must this decision lie with me?"*

**Pharinor Elphyratra – Oakheart Brigade Officer**

Someone shouts a warning. *"Something is following us."*

A shrill cry rents the night.

Moving awkwardly, I scoot along the bench, closer to the back of the wagon. Eyes roving over the path, I try to spot the source of the commotion. Our wagon comes to a stop.

I spot two rangers sprawled on the ground, arrows sprouting from their backs. Their horses are riderless, spooked, and trotting away with wide eyes.

*This cannot be Valeria's doing, can it?*

An arrow flies by and hits another ranger. It embeds itself in her neck. She crashes to the ground, lifeless.

*No, it's not Valeria. She's a sword fighter, not an archer. Besides, we weren't carrying arrows.*

Is this highway robbery? Something else entirely?

Drothgar urges his mount closer to the wagon and jumps off, his

106

sorcerer right behind him. Drawing his broadsword, the captain glares at us, a warning not to try anything.

His rangers scramble around, trying to hide behind trees, taking cover from the arrows. One of their archers leaps from his horse and takes a knee. He fires one of his projectiles toward the source of the attack. The arrow *thwacks*. Did he hit his mark? There is no cry of pain or any other indication that he did.

Another ranger falls, screaming in pain, the arrow lodged in his calf. He had been hiding behind his horse, but the arrow found him through the animal's legs. This attack came from a different direction, but I suspect it's the same archer since the assaults were not simultaneous. When the third arrow hits, flying from yet another direction and impaling itself in a sturdy ranger's chest, I'm certain it's the same archer, a damn good one and fast.

"This isn't Val," Jago says. "What's happening?"

I open my mouth to say I have no idea, when I spot a figure running from the cover of one tree to another.

*No, it cannot be.*

The figure carrying a sword dashes across the path, cutting a ranger down, then disappears behind the line of trees on the other side.

Another arrow flies from the opposite side. Another dead.

Calierin and Kadewyn are here! I have no idea how they found us, but I am damn glad they did. I begin to hope we will get out of this in one piece, and with no risk to Valeria's life.

"There!" Drothgar shouts as Calierin appears once more, this time closer to the wagon.

"It's Calierin!" Jago exclaims, able to spot her now that she's nearer. "But where's Val?"

That is the same question I am asking myself. Is she with them? Or did they find us on their own? It seems too much of a coincidence to be true.

Rangers falls to the ground right and left as my veilfallen attack like phantoms out of a lower hell. They are not veilfallen anymore. They are home! Yet, I cannot help but use that moniker to describe them.

Calierin and Kadewyn are fast and effective, real warriors, far better than our captors.

"Friends of yours, I assume?" Galen asks.

I nod once, never taking my eyes off the road.

The rangers are falling fast, their bigger numbers making no difference—not against Calierin's and Kadewyn's furtive skills, tactics learned while fighting humans who always outnumbered them.

It does not escape me that Calierin is not using magic. Is she—like Galen and me—dry? That is the only explanation. She enjoys using her magical powers too much to forsake them now.

Drothgar growls in frustration as he stands in the middle of the path, sword raised, head swiveling from side to side as he tries to figure out where the next attack will come from.

"Do something!" Drothgar yells at his sorcerer.

"I have to be able to see them," he protests.

"Who the fuck cares?! Blast them!"

The sorcerer sends a volley of his strange dark magic toward the general area where Calierin was last seen. When it strikes the bushes, they burst into flames, releasing a wave of heat that radiates toward the wagon and makes me recoil.

I hold my breath, expecting Calierin to stumble into the path, her body aflame. Everything is quiet as we stare at the conflagration.

"There!" Drothgar points as a shadow dashes behind a set of trees a moment later.

Aiming at the spot, the sorcerer sends another surge of magic, setting that spot on fire, too.

Silence ensues once more.

Drothgar's head swivels all around.

"A little terrified, are you?" Galen asks him in a quiet, mocking tone.

"Shut your fucking mouth, Fuadach, or I will slit your throat. No one cares if you make it to Riochtach alive." He clamps his lips together, realizing he said something he should not have.

Bushes rustle to the right. Drothgar whirls. "There!"

The sorcerer begins to turn, but he is too slow. Calierin darts out from behind a thick tree and runs at him, sword held high. He barely has time to raise his hand before she slashes her weapon from left to right, lopping his head clean off. Blood gushes as the body falls, spraying Drothgar's face. The captain leaps back, wiping his eyes and barely parrying a vicious blow from Calierin.

Galen grunts, straining against his restraints. "Dammit! His magic still holds."

The sorcerer is dead. We should be free of his hold, but the invisible band around my torso is just as tight as before.

"What in the hells kind of magic is this?!" Galen demands.

On the ground, the sorcerer's body turns black, his skin becoming as dark and shiny as an oil puddle. Gray smoke slowly wafts upward from his exposed skin, looking like fog over a field.

Galen stares in disgust. "Faoloir's bollocks. I've never seen anything like that before."

"Drive, Pharinor! Drive!" Drothgar orders, hitting the back of the wagon with the pommel of his sword. That done, he attacks Calierin, responding with a stab toward her chest. He slices only air as Calierin sidesteps and twirls her weapon in a smug demonstration of skill.

"Go! Go!" the driver shouts. The crack of a whip reverberates in the air.

The wagon lurches forward.

We pitch to one side, and then the other, nearly spilling onto the floorboards.

"I am the King's Protector, Calierin Kelraek of the Tuathacath clan," I hear her say, over the pounding of horse hooves. "You will pay for your disrespect."

Swords clash and *zing* as we ride away. Calierin and Drothgar become smaller and smaller.

"No! Stop, you bastardo!" Jago screams, but he is wasting his breath.

The wagon is going fast now as the driver continues to crack his whip. Galen stomps his feet, still struggling against the restraining magic around him.

"This shouldn't be. It's unnatural. Mallachtdorch!" he curses.

"Let's jump." I try to stand, but the violent rocking of the wagon over the uneven path tosses me back down.

"What? Are you fucking mad?" Jago shakes his head. "I'll break every bone in my body."

True, he is a fragile human, but I cannot be driven away like this—not when Valeria may be back there with the others.

"You two can stay," I say, trying to stand again.

This time, I manage to do it. Slowly, I move closer toward the back, but as I prepare to leap, the wagon goes off the path, traveling over rocky terrain. We lurch from side to side as if inside a boat in a tempest. I lose my balance and fall on Galen's lap.

"Well, well," he says, "I always suspected you had a thing for me."

"Fuck off, arsehole."

I manage to move and land on the bench at his side. We knock into each other as the wagon continues to travel over what feels like a rock-slide. We are on a downward trajectory, going too fast. Did the driver lose control of the horses? Did he abandon his post figuring it would be safer to get as far away from this mess as quickly as possible?

My teeth rattle with every roll of the wheels. We all end up on the floorboards, piled against the front of the wagon, jumping a foot into the air with every bump.

Wood cracks with the sound of a thunderbolt. My stomach lurches as we drop. The wagon scrapes the ground, the axle surely broken. Everything groans around us, wood splintering. The roof collapses, partially falling on top of us.

At last, we come to a stop.

"Is everyone all right?" I ask.

Galen grumbles an affirmative.

"Jago?" I press when he does not respond. My chest tightens. Valeria will kill me if—

He makes spitting sounds as if something got in his mouth. "I-I'm . . . fine."

"Are you sure?"

"Yes."

I start pushing the broken roof out of the way, and the motion makes me realize my arms are finally free. The magical hold is gone.

"Oh, thank fucking Bodhránghealach!" Galen exclaims as he realizes the same thing.

"Help me get this off."

We all start pushing on the roof, but some of the planks are stuck.

"This is fucking ridiculous," Galen grumbles in frustration as we keep pushing.

Something tugs at the largest piece from outside, and then it is off. I am so turned around I do not know which way is up. It takes me a moment to see our driver, Pharinor, looming over us.

"I'm going to kill you!" Galen makes as if to chase the guard but cannot stand. There is a piece of roof across his lap. I do not have the same problem, however, and with one push and a jump, I am up and reaching for him.

Pharinor backs up, hands in the air. "Please, King Theric." He bows his head. "I drove us off the road to hide you from Drothgar. We just need to—"

My hands are around his neck, cutting his words off. He does not try to fight. He only looks resigned to whatever fate I choose for him. His expression is contrite. I try to detect the lie, the deception, but he appears truly remorseful. Slowly, I ease my chokehold. He has a dagger in his belt and has made no attempt to draw it.

"Uh, w-we can . . . ga-gather some branches," he starts hesitantly, and when I do not stop him, he gains confidence, "and cover the area where we went off the path. Without Kalines, the sorcerer, they will not realize we are not on our way to Riochtach."

I relieve him of his weapon. His eyes widen in fear. I let him go, pushing him away in disgust. He breathes a sigh of relief. I glance back. Jago and Galen are already out of the wrecked wagon. Miraculously, the horses are in one piece, no broken limbs, though they do appear terrified.

Using Pharinor's dagger, I cut the animals free of their harness, leaving only the leads. I hand Jago the reins to one of the horses and keep the other.

"I am going back and killing that bastard Drothgar," I say, pulling the horse up the slope toward the path.

Galen glares at the driver as if he still wants to kill him.

"He is not worth it," I say over my shoulder.

"Exactly," Galen replies, taking a step toward the male.

"Let him be. That is an order."

Galen stops, muttering something under his breath.

Jago huffs. "*I'll* kill him. Korben isn't *my* king."

"We have no time to waste. We need to get back," I say.

We exchange glances.

"Fine!" he grumbles, following me, his horse trailing behind.

"Your Ma-Majesty," Pharinor says, "you should not go back. You should . . . hide."

"The rightful Fae King does not hide," Galen blurts out. "What in the hells is the matter with you?"

"A lot has changed since you have been gone," Pharinor adds in a heavy tone that makes me reevaluate him.

But I cannot listen to anything this male says. He is untrustworthy, nothing more than a thug. Ignoring him, I continue up the slope. Broken branches and trampled bushes mark our bumpy descent.

"You must be suicidal," Galen tells the male. "Who drives a wagon down a slope like this?"

"Not my best decision, I admit, but I was looking out for you." Pharinor is following us, gathering fallen branches as we go and dragging them over the rough ground with a scraping sound.

When we make it back onto the path, he arranges the branches in such a way that they effectively hide our altered course.

"Useless," Galen sneers, examining the male's job. "Who cares about hiding the wagon when we're headed right back the way we came?"

The male shrugs and scratches his head as if that had not occurred to him.

Holding the reins, I leap onto the horse's back. He is big, an Ironmane. His powerful legs will take me back more quickly than I can run.

Jago mounts too, Galen settling himself behind him without an argument.

I throw one glance over my shoulder and meet Pharinor's gaze.

"Drothgar works for someone powerful, Your Majesty. If you want your throne back, you'll need to gather an army," he says.

As I urge my mount forward, I have a feeling he is speaking the truth.

# 15
## VALERIA

*"Let us expedite the wedding, shall we, Sara?"*

**Don Justo Ramiro Medrano – Master Mason**

S tanding on top of my horse, I watch helplessly from the back of the line, a safe distance from the battle.

"What's happening?" Esmeralda whispers, rising on tiptoes to peer over her saddle. "I can't see a thing."

For my part, my sharp raven eyes miss no detail—not even Kadewyn's arrows as they fly loose and hit their target. I also see Jago, Korben, and Galen sitting inside the wagon, watching the chaos unfold.

So far, Calierin's and Kadewyn's evasive tactics are more than the kidnappers can handle.

My hope soars as it seems the battle will be short-lived. That is until the sorcerer lets his espiritu fly, setting a patch of forest on fire. At first, I think Calierin's been hit, but then she reappears, the sorcerer her next target. Without batting an eye, she strikes. The sorcerer's head drops to the ground before his body. Blood sprays everywhere.

"Drive, Pharinor! Drive!" someone yells.

A whip cracks. The cry of horses follows, and the wagon lurches forward and speeds down the path.

*No!*

Without thinking, I jump off the horse, wings beating.

Esmeralda yelps.

When I realize what I've done, I begin to drop, my small body leaden. Then Cuervo sweeps down from a nearby branch, flies next to me, and caws as if in encouragement.

His presence sharpens a set of instincts that hide under the surface of my mind, instincts that were awakened during my first shift. Pushing all conscious thought aside, I let those instincts swell and grow stronger. To my utter astonishment, I find that ignoring my human consciousness isn't as hard as I'd feared, and there are . . .

Wing beats matching my friend's.

Air buffering feathers.

The ground falling behind.

Everything becoming smaller as I rise higher and higher.

The dark sky is a glorious expanse, ripe for the taking. There's nothing in front of me but a million destinations, all of them welcoming, all of them mine.

Below there are oceans of leaves and trees and rocks—obstacles that don't exist in this grandness and I can easily leave behind.

A caw from my side. I glance over and see a friend flying next to me, matching my every wingbeat.

He banks to the right, and the tilt of my wings matches his. We lose altitude, the wind ruffling our feathers. The feeling is exultant.

A sense of betrayal rears its head trying to taint the moment. Why was I robbed of this experience for so long?

But none of that matters. I'm here now.

Moonlight bathes my obsidian feathers, and they reflect back a million colors.

We fly closer to the ground, over a path that winds through an espiritu-filled forest. A few trees glow and are surrounded by a white aura. On closer inspection I realize the trees are a haven to small creatures made of ethereal light. I want to eat one of them. I start my descent toward one of the trees. My friend caws, but I ignore him. I want to know what the little creatures taste like. I have a feeling they'll be delicious.

My talons skim over the leaves of several dark trees, but my keen eyes are set on the biggest glowing tree of all.

One more caw from my friend.

Another.

And another.

I glance toward him, annoyed.

He veers toward the path as if to entice me to follow, but nothing is as enticing as the thought of tearing one of the little creature's limbs and swallowing them whole.

More caws and more and more.

Abruptly, the guttural caws morph, unfurling from a sharp, gravelly sound to a softer sound. The shrill call takes the shape of syllables.

"Spy. Jago," my friend says.

A jolt of recognition hits me.

*Jago! My cousin!*

As the thought cuts through me, slicing the animal instincts that have taken over, my wingbeats become a series of frantic bursts. One wing dips lower than the other, throwing me off balance. I move upward in a ragged spiral, then begin plummeting with a sickening lurch. Panic fills me. I think I'm going to die until the sight of Cuervo reminds me I've already been up here, gracefully conquering the currents.

I can do this.

As soon as I make the decision, my erratic movements even out, and I fly smoothly once more. I follow Cuervo, who seems to know exactly where to go. I thank Niamhara for his presence because I've already lost track of my location, and there's no way I'd be able to find my way back.

Cuervo backtracks the way we came, and I follow.

Trees rush past.

*I'm flying. I'M FLYING!*

*Oh, Father, it's every bit as wonderful as you described it. If only you could be here with me.*

I miss him more than ever, wishing I could share this moment with him.

Many wingbeats later, Cuervo swoops down and caws. Right underneath us, a wagon lies broken at the bottom of a rocky slope. My heart pounds as we circle over it. I detect no signs of life. Is it the same wagon? Maybe it isn't. The horses would've surely collapsed traveling down such jagged terrain. Only a miracle could have saved them. Niamhara's intervention?

We rise and soon fly over the path.

Another caw from Cuervo alerts me to the presence of a male sitting at the edge of the road. He's rubbing his neck as if it hurts. Throwing his head back, he looks at us. Cuervo and I fly on.

In the distance, I see a cloud of dust.

Cuervo sees it too and beats his wings faster. I match him easily, and it's a wondrous thing that fills my heart with untold emotions.

Soon, the cloud resolves into two horses. The animals gallop at full pelt, their riders leaning forward. Korben leads the way while Jago follows close behind, Galen as his riding companion.

Cuervo dips low and glides alongside my cousin's galloping horse, matching its frantic pace.

Jago glances over, then does a double-take as he realizes Cuervo is there.

"Cuervo!" The raven's name an exclamation. "Where's Valeria?"

As easily as he dipped down, Cuervo swoops upward to my side. Jago strains his neck and catches sight of me.

"Stop!" he shouts. "Stop! It's Valeria."

Ahead of him, Korben glances over his shoulder.

Jago repeats his call. "Valeria! It's Valeria!"

Korben follows Jago's gaze and spots Cuervo and me. He pulls on the reins and brings his horse to a full stop. He dismounts in one fluid motion, twisting in midair so that he lands facing Jago. My cousin veers his horse to the left to avoid a crash and also comes to a stop.

"Valeria!" Korben exclaims, a huge smile stretching his lips, a combination of relief and true joy to see me.

Cuervo circles once, then lands on Korben's saddle.

"Thank you, friend." Korben bows respectfully, and Cuervo does the same in return.

Jago joins Korben's side, also craning his neck and grinning. "Well, all the saints be damned! Look who finally decided to show up. Come down here so I can give you a proper hug."

I fly in circles over their heads, my heart pounding faster even though I'm as relieved as they are. I have no idea how to land, and I'm afraid I'll break every bone in my body if I try.

They wait, watching me.

Jago's smile slowly disappears. "Um, yes, I can see you're flying, Princess Plumanegra. Quit showing off and come down here."

Cuervo sweeps upward and lands on the saddle once more, as eager a teacher as Maestro Elizondo.

An image of my broken body on the ground flashes before my eyes. A little shudder goes through me, making the feathers on my neck stand on end.

Korben seems to recognize this for what it is and speaks in a soothing tone. "You have never landed before, so it is understandable if you are nervous. But you can do this."

"Oh, fuck," Jago mutters.

*Very helpful, cousin!*

"Come down," Korben says encouragingly. "Don't fight the landing, feel the ground rise to meet you and the air guiding you down."

Easy for him to say. He's probably done it a thousand times. I hesitate, circling wider, the wind tugging at me.

"Stop flapping your wings, then tilt them forward, like you are cupping the wind. It will slow your descent."

I do as he instructs.

"Good. Use your tail feathers against any crosswind to balance yourself, small flicks left and right to adjust your direction. You want to touch down with your talons first, strong and balanced."

"Who would've thought? Korben Theric can be gentle!" Galen chimes in.

"Shut the fuck up, Galen," Korben growls in response, not gentle at all.

"Never mind. It must be an anomaly," Galen sneers.

"You are distracting her, arsehole."

Galen puts his hands up.

Korben repeats his instructions. Doing as he says, I begin a slow descent.

"You're doing great, cousin." Jago twists his hands together, clearly worried.

Even though I'm gradually slowing down, I feel like the ground is rushing up to smack me. I'm tempted to forget about landing and simply soar through the sky forever and ever, but I force myself to resist the urge to flap my wings and escape.

My body wavers from side to side, and I'm anything but steady. Moving parallel with the path, I fly past my awaiting friends. They turn, following my trajectory. I leave them behind, following a steep downward line. I try to adjust, to reduce the sharpness of my decline, but instead, I do the opposite.

My talons scrape the ground. I decide to abort, but it's too late, and the next thing I know I'm tumbling over the ground, head over tail, wings flapping all over the place.

"Valeria!" Korben and Jago cry out in unison.

There is a snap. Crippling pain follows, and I shriek. I take a few more tumbles and finally come to a stop, seeing red from the pain. I twitch on the ground, one wing tucked in, the other outstretched, its bottom half bent at an unnatural angle.

Someone skids to a stop next to me, then gentle hands pick me up.

I blink up at Korben. I'm so relieved to see his fierce, dark eyes again. But the pain coursing through my small body is more than I can bear, and I start to lose consciousness.

"Hey, look at me!" Korben says.

My eyes snap open.

Jago is there now, honey-colored gaze wide, blond hair matted to his forehead with sweat. "Oh, saints! Can you fix her wing?"

Korben shakes his head. "I cannot, but Valeria can. She needs to shift."

*Oh, shit!*

My eyes close again.

Korben shakes me slightly. "Shift, Valeria."

I shake my head and say, "I can't." No words come out, only a weak caw.

What a pathetic raven shifter I make, incapable of even the most basic things.

"Valeria, please. Shift!" Jago begs.

"She is unable to do it," Korben says.

"What? Are you joking?"

"She does not know how."

"Can't you instruct her like you did before?"

Through blurry eyes, I see Korben's frown. He looks as if he's trying to figure out how to explain something obvious but can't quite find the right words.

"Something's wrong with magic in the realm." Galen's voice comes from somewhere off to the side. He sounds like he's inside a tunnel.

I feel very tired, and all I want to do is sleep. My body has been through a thousand hells and back in one day, my bones taking the brunt of every shift and finally this horrible, horrible landing. My eyes drift closed once more.

"Valeria, try to focus on—"

"Someone's coming," Galen cuts Korben off.

I hear it, too, the distant sound of hoofbeats, but I'm too tired to care.

"Take her, Jago." Korben hands me off as if I'm a packet that needs minding. "Get off the path and hide behind those trees. Protect her with your life."

"You don't have to tell me what to do," Jago replies angrily. "I know how to take care of my family."

Their voices sound far away, and whatever they say next is lost to me as I drift off into darkness.

# 16

## KORBEN

*"He is the king, Jaws, and it is not to our advantage to allow his return."*

**Drothgar Nelyn – Oakheart Brigade Captain**

Jago disappears behind the trees, taking Valeria with him. A broken wing . . . she must be in terrible pain. Shifting is the foolproof way to heal herself. The transformation would set her bones right, remolding them to accommodate her human shape. Trying to repair the fragile, porous bones of a wing is no easy task.

She *has* to shift.

But why can she not? Why has it not come naturally to her? Is it because she is too old to easily learn? Or does it have to do with the strange way magic is behaving here?

Reluctantly, I set those thoughts aside. The hoofbeats are closer now, enough that I can see the shape of the riders in the distance.

Out of the corner of my eye, I notice Galen edging away from me and heading toward Jago.

"Where are you going, Master of Magic?" I ask, without turning to look at him.

"Um, I can't be a Master of Magic if I have no magic, so I doubt I'll be of much use. I'm just going to . . ." He hooks a finger over his shoulder.

"You are staying right where you are."

"I'm no fighter, Korben—not without my powers anyway. Do you want me to get killed?"

"I never figured you for a coward."

Galen stops mid-step. I can feel his anger radiating in my direction. *Good*. Let him be mad. It might help him fight whoever is coming.

A few more hoofbeats and I am able to discern two riders. One of them is Drothgar.

"I will take the leader," I say. "You take the other one."

Galen grunts but comes closer. He shakes his hands, the way he always does when he is about to weave a spell. But today, there is no magic here to aid him. In the past, that might have worried me. For a long time, I relied too heavily on The Eldrystone, and before that, on my shifter abilities. My time in Castella taught me a different way.

Briefly, I wonder where Calierin and Kadewyn are? I trust they are all right, finishing off the rangers these two cowards abandoned. I hate that innocent people have to die. Considering what Pharinor told us, Drothgar was misleading the rangers, lying to them when he knew the truth all too well.

I tighten my grip on the dagger I took from the poor devil. This small weapon is more than I need to take care of this bastard. He will pay for the way he treated us, for deceiving those under his command.

Feet planted firmly in the middle of the path, I wait. Drothgar's face twists in a furious grimace when he recognizes me. Still several lengths away, he pulls his horse to a stop. His companion, a man twice Drothgar's size, stops next to him. He wears only his green uniform trousers stuffed into boots and a crown made of the mandibles (teeth still attached) of some large animal. Three slashes of black paint streak his cheekbones. Where in all the hells did he come from? I did not see him earlier. Perhaps he had time for a costume change. Some warriors are superstitious about this sort of thing.

Galen swallows thickly at the sight of the male. "This is a joke, right?"

I say nothing.

"What do you want me to do?" Galen asks from the corner of his mouth. "Charm him with my good looks? I have no weapon, Korben."

I toss him the dagger. "Now you do."

He tries to catch it, but it falls and embeds itself in the ground. With a sigh, he picks it up. "For all the good it'll do against that mountain."

The painted warrior lets out a scathing laugh.

"Who sent you?" I demand. "And do not lie. I know you are perfectly aware of who I am."

Drothgar narrows his eyes. "You do not know my master, but you will. Soon."

"It will be my pleasure. Tell me where to find this person. Tell me their name."

Drothgar leaps off the horse, landing in a crouch and drawing his broadsword. "Do not fret. I will take you to him."

A male then—not Saethara.

The large warrior leaps off his horse, too. "Do your best with your little knife," he tells Galen, spreading out his hands to indicate he will not draw a weapon.

"Why don't we let the king and your captain settle things first?" Galen suggests. "Wouldn't you rather fight this strapping male?" He points at me with the dagger. "Your leader is going to lose. I bet you ten gold crowns. Against you on the other hand, it's a toss up. If you win, you could boast you bested the Fae King himself."

"Your Master of Magic is a loyal subject indeed." Drothgar laughs. "But enough talk."

Drothgar, all bluster and bad breath, lumbers toward me, his broadsword held high, a pathetic attempt to intimidate. The stench of sweat and fear waft off him in waves. His male companion stays in place, making no attempt to go after Galen. He does not come at me either. Instead, he crosses his thick arms over his chest. Interesting. Perhaps he has what Drothgar lacks in spades: honor.

Moonlight filters through the leaves of the towering trees lining the path, casting an eerie dance of shadows that writhes with every gust of wind. Drothgar's sword catches the moonlight in a deadly glint. His stench hangs heavy in the cool night air.

With a hand gesture, I invite him to attack.

He lunges, predictable and slow as a human guard. A sidestep, a flick of my wrist, and steel screams, the tip of his blade scraping the ground. Drothgar roars, the sound echoing through the silent woods, frustration rather than fury boiling out of him.

Sweat slicks his brow. A grin spreads across my face as he twirls his sword, circling me. His challenge falls flat, an amateur's attempt to rattle me, but I see right through it.

He lunges again, another predictable attack aimed at my chest. I twist aside effortlessly. The blade cuts through the air. His heavy boots churn the dirt path as he spins to face me again. He fights with a brute strength that lacks the finesse of a true swordsman.

Drothgar swings in a wide arc aimed for my head this time. I duck, air whistling in my ears. As he lumbers past, I slam my elbow against his knee. He roars, a sound of surprised pain, his momentum faltering. The sword hangs loose in his grip, and in one quick motion, I disarm him, the weight of the broadsword settling comfortably in my hand as I pull back and stab him.

The corrupt captain stares at me, his face a mask of disbelief. He looks down at the sword sticking to the hilt right through his side. He makes a choking sound as he drops to his knees, then falls dead.

Turning calmly, I glance toward the remaining male. He stands impassive, arms still crossed.

"You owe me ten gold crowns." Galen smiles, smug. "Maybe you should pay me before . . . you know."

He ignores Galen, never taking his eyes off me. "Are you really the king?"

"I am."

"And he knew?" He pushes his wide chin toward his fallen leader.

"You be the judge of that."

He blows air through his nose.

"What is your name?" I ask.

"They call me Jaws."

"Oh, because of your crown. Right. Right." Galen uses a sarcastic tone meant to sound as if it took a big leap to understand such a clever moniker.

"Galen," I snap in warning.

"Sorry. My apologies, Jaws. It's been a long day." Galen walks off and sits on a fallen log, scaring away the sprites that hover around its decaying bark. He scrubs a hand down his face.

"I was trapped on the other side of the veil, Jaws," I say calmly, hoping the male will be reasonable, though I still keep within reach of the sword protruding from Drothgar's stomach. "I am not surprised things have changed. I expected it, but it seems even my most daring supposition falls short of what I have witnessed thus far. I would appreciate it if you enlightened me and gave me a brief run down of the last twenty years."

Jaws throws his head back and laughs with true merriment.

Galen and I exchange a glance.

"That's an understatement if I have ever heard one." Jaws places an enormous hand on his stomach as he continues to laugh.

Straightening, he abruptly sobers up and glances over his shoulder. He huffs, then climbs onto his horse, a mount bigger than any I have ever seen. His head is nearly as long as my arms, and his hooves could easily crush a male's head.

"This day," I tell him, "I will let you go."

He lets out a curt laugh as if to say he is the one letting *me* go. But we both know that is not the case.

"Tell your master what you have seen," I say, "tell him I will meet him whenever, wherever," I continue. "And next time you and I see each other, be prepared to meet your maker."

"Big words for a little male."

I tilt my head to one side. "I am not the one running away."

His large, heavy-lidded eyes burn with anger. He makes no excuse for his departure as he nudges his mount forward. Instead, he delivers his own threat. "My maker is on my side, weak king, but is yours? I look forward to slicing your throat and carving out your entrails."

The animal's hooves pound the dirt, leaving huge imprints and kicking back dust as Jaws rides away.

"Pleasant fellow," Galen says, standing behind me. "And here come more."

We turn to face the other direction. Calierin, Kadewyn, and to my utter surprise, Esmeralda, are riding toward us. She pulls a riderless horse behind her.

Leading the way, Calierin scans me up and down with wide violet eyes. Once she is close, she jumps off her horse, the same one we took from her some days back, and falls to one knee in front of me.

"My king! It pleases me to see you are all right." She bows her head, gaze locked on the ground.

Kadewyn dismounts next, his silver hair glowing in the moonlight. He approaches with soft, cautious steps, and starts to kneel.

"No need for that, my friend," I say.

He remains standing, but he bows. "King Korben."

"Korben will do. You too, Calierin. Stand." She continues kneeling.

Esmeralda watches from the top of her saddle in disbelief.

"Stand, Calierin," I repeat, this time with a hint of command. "Let me thank you and Kadewyn for freeing us."

She finally climbs to her feet but continues to stare at the ground.

"Thank you once more, my veilfallen," I say. "Without your help, I fear we would have met our end. There are strange things afoot in Tirnanog, and it seems I am not welcome."

"Where's Jago?" Esmeralda blurts out, the words spilling out in a rush.

"Esmeralda?" Jago steps out from behind the trees, cradling Valeria in his hands. Cuervo perches on his shoulder, intent on his injured friend.

Jago walks onto the path, gaping. Esmeralda dismounts, and I take Valeria from Jago before they crush each other in a desperate embrace, Cuervo flying off to perch on a branch. They share a passionate kiss, and we all turn our attention elsewhere to offer them privacy.

My concern is for Valeria, however, even if Jago and Esmeralda's attachment comes as a surprise.

"Galen," I say, "how can we help her?"

He approaches, brow furrowed. His family owned Runescribe Ravens like Cuervo. Maybe he knows how to repair a broken wing.

Gingerly, he feels Valeria's wing, fingers traveling up and down its length. He closes his eyes as he palpates the bones. Everything is silent but for Jago's and Esmeralda's murmured words and the chirping of insects.

"It's a clean break," Galen says at last. "I think I can set it, but it will be painful. Shifting would be best."

I nod in understanding, peering down at her limp shape. She is still unconscious, and the sight of her fragility terrifies me.

When she first transformed, I felt strangely glad to learn she was like me: a raven shifter. For a brief instant, I imagined us soaring through the sky together, masters of the wind. Free and with no boundaries to hold us back. I did not think of her inexperience and the risks she might face.

I glance up, feeling lost. Everyone is looking at me, even Jago and Esmeralda, who lean into each other's embrace.

For a moment, I do not know what to do. Without Valeria, the edge of despair she drove away would return and cut me anew. But she is still here. She still breathes, and I will let no harm come to her again. I will protect her with my own life.

"All right," I say, "let's help her."

# 17

## VALERIA

*"I fear the worst, Faolan. They need to hurry."*

**Shara Theric – Fae Queen**

S omething drips into my mouth. Water! I lap at it, grateful for the refreshing taste.

I open my eyes and stare at a glowing bush. Blinking several times, I attempt to dispel the strange image, until I remember I'm in Tirnanog and glowing bushes are apparently commonplace.

"She's awake," Korben says.

I try to move, and a stab of pain travels up my arm. No, not my arm. My wing. I broke it, trying to land, and—

"*Shh*, do not move, Ravógín. You are injured."

Inspecting my surroundings, I realize I'm resting on Korben's lap as he sits on a log. Others are nearby, appearing upside down from my vantage point. Their faces are blurry, and I don't have the presence of mind to focus on them. The pain seems to consume me, stealing all my attention.

"You need to shift," Korben says. "It is the best way to repair your wing with no ill effects. Can you try?"

*I have tried*, I would say if I could.

I lost track of how many times I attempted it, and it was all for naught. As long as Tirnanog's magic flows through me, I'm stuck in this shape.

And now, I can't even fly. I'm useless.

Korben regards me expectantly.

For his sake, I attempt to shift. Compared to my earlier efforts, this one is far from worthy. I barely have any strength, and the pain drives me to distraction—not to mention I don't expect to succeed.

*"Always believe you can,"* Father used to say. *"If you don't believe in yourself, who will?"*

So no, I am never going to shift back into my human form. I gave it my best effort already, and it wasn't good enough. At least Jago, Korben, and Galen are safe now. Not that I had anything to do with their rescue. Cuervo did much more than me while I only served as a liability.

"You are trying?" Korben asks in a careful tone.

I nod once, which makes pain shoot down the length of my wing.

He glances up and shakes his head at someone. Galen appears in my line of sight.

"I examined your wing, Princess Valeria," he says. "The good news is that you have a simple fracture, and I can fix it. The bad news is that it's going to hurt. Um . . . hurt more, I mean. We want to act now because we don't want it to heal the wrong way. As a shifter, you have accelerated healing, so . . ."

"Do you understand, Ravógín?" Korben asks.

I nod weakly, my consciousness hanging by a thread.

"I'm going to set your bone now," Galen says. "You're going to feel me grab your wing." His voice is a distant drone, a calm counterpoint to the storm of emotions and pain raging inside me.

His fingers wrap around my upper arm, upper wing . . . whatever it's called. The searing pain from the break itself has dulled, but with each press of his fingers, a fresh wave of agony crashes against me. I clench my beak, a silent scream trapped in my throat.

"I'm just locating the—"

*Crack!*

The world shrinks to the pinpoint of the white-hot agony in my wing. The bones grind, a sickening plunge within my stomach. My eyes water, not just from the pain, but from the utter helplessness. I feel like a broken toy that has been forced back into shape.

"There you go." Galen pulls away, releasing his hold.

The pain doesn't vanish, but a strange sense of relief washes over me. It's a new kind of pain, a throbbing ache that feels oddly manageable compared to the bone-grinding agony of moments ago. My wing feels alien, heavy and numb, but maybe it will be all right. Eventually, I force myself to breathe, slow and measured, but I feel defeated, drained. I fight to keep my eyes open.

"Rest now, Ravógín," Korben says. "You did well. Your strength astounds me."

I don't feel strong. I want to sob, but I don't know how to do that in this body, so instead, I tuck my wings, though not without a flash of pain, and let oblivion take me.

I fly from one tree to another. Swaying leaves and pine needles tickle the underside of clouds. Soaring through the sky is the most amazing thing I've ever done. I never want to stop.

A large pink cloud looms ahead. I veer in its direction, navigating the currents, easily gliding without a single wingbeat. I pierce through the cloud and find myself inside it. Other ravens fly within, while some perch in white, fluffy turrets.

I hover before a sight that steals the air from my lungs. Sun illuminates the expansive cloud from the outside, creating the most dazzling array of color to ever grace the sky. As if carved from pure sunlight and stardust, spires reach like grasping fingers toward infinity. Gossamer clouds swirl around their base, flowing like water in a moat. Luminescent flowers bloom on the battlements, their petals casting an ethereal glow upon the entire structure.

A castle lives within the cloud. A castle of dreams.

The wind seems to whisper a song, the melody at times soothing and at times distressing. The air crackles with tenuous energy, a tangible magic that dances upon my feathers.

The other birds greet me, their thoughts resonating inside my head. There aren't any words, but I know they are welcoming me. They say they've been waiting for me. But how is that possible? I settle on one of the turrets to ponder.

*Why have they been waiting for me?*

Ravens enter and leave the downy confines. They all seem content and in no hurry. I like this place. I never knew ravens had such homes among the clouds. I wish to stay. I wonder if they would let me.

Something tells me they won't.

—*No, you cannot stay,* an androgynous voice says.

Though it isn't exactly a voice forming words that I can hear. It's like the ravens—a thought that permeates into my mind, and I simply *know*. In truth, it's much more than that. It's a symphony of shapes and concepts, a cacophony that somehow becomes a single idea. It tumbles like a thousand waves crashing, yet holds the delicate touch of a gentle breeze. It's a mountain collapsing and a leaf drifting to the ground, all at once.

*Hello?* I ask tentatively, trembling with fear and expectation.

Looking around, I search for the source, but I'm alone. All the ravens are gone, though I never saw them leave. They just disappeared.

—*You have much to do, Valeria Plumanegra.*

The thought pierces through me with chilling clarity and authority. Each pulse inside my mind carries the weight of ages and resonates deep within my bones.

*Who is this?*

—*You know who I am.*

*This is a dream. That's all I know.*

There is no reply, and somehow, I realize there will continue to be no reply until I speak the truth. I consider for a long moment. Is this a dream? Yes . . . well, I'm not really inside a cloud, so this is definitely happening inside my mind. Yet, it's real. As real as any waking thought, as any conversation I've ever had.

Someone is actually speaking into my mind, and it's not birds. This is no mere dream fortress. I'm inside a living entity, and the song riding in the wing is its heartbeat. Awe washes over me, a tidal wave of wonder that threatens to pull me under.

*Niamhara!*

*—I took great effort to bring you here.*

This ushers a dozen questions into my mind, but I can only ask one.

*Why?*

*—Because I am weak.*

I wanted to know why she needed to bring me here, not why it took great effort but now that she has provided this answer, the original questions are erased, and new ones take their place.

*How can a goddess be weak?*

*—I do not have time to explain everything right now. Being here also takes great effort. I need to conserve whatever energy I can. You must find me, and you* must *bring me The Eldrystone.*

Find a goddess? How does one do that?

*Goddess of Radiance, I will gladly do as you request. Please, tell me, where do I need to go?*

No answer.

*Goddess?*

*—I do not remember.*

What?! I want to repeat my question, but the answer would be the same. The truth of everything she says is like the air in my lungs, real and essential. Moreover, I sense she has little time.

*Is there anyone who can help me?*

*—Korben.*

*Why not talk to him?*

*—Because* you *have The Eldrystone.*

This answer feels dimmer, almost like an afterthought. She's fading.

*—Come quickly.*

She sounds dimmer still.

*How can I help if I can't shift back?*

*—You can.*

*I've tried, but I can't stop being a raven!*

*—Take off the amulet.*

How?! It's not around my neck. I have no idea where it went. All I know is that it was swallowed by my shifting espiritu.

*How do I do that, Goddess?*

No answer. Or maybe there is one, but it's faint, as if spoken from thousands of miles away, and I'm unable to discern the words.

By degrees, the castle frays at the edges, the gossamer clouds melting and hanging listlessly. The flowers on the battlements wither, their ethereal glow replaced by a dull, spectral gray. The spires tumble, and the song sputters and fades to be replaced by an unsettling silence. With a final, shuddering gasp, the entire structure dissolves into shimmering dust, leaving behind only tendrils of mist swirling in the vast emptiness.

Niamhara is gone.

# 18

## VALERIA

*"Where is my sister? I don't even know if she's dead or alive."*

**Reina Amira Plumanegra (Casa Plumanegra) – Queen of Castella**

My eyes spring open, echoes of the heavenly castle imprinted in my vision like glowing phantoms.

It takes several beats for the afterimages to clear, and the background to resolve into a night sky swimming with constellations and much more. Light unfurls, a slow, majestic dance of color. Emerald ribbons streak across the velvet darkness, their edges shimmering like spun gold. A deep violet throbs beneath them, and the stars seem to dim, overwhelmed by the breathtaking rivers of light.

I have awakened into another dream. At least that is what I think until Korben appears above me.

"You are awake, Ravógín. How do you feel?" He has one knee on the ground while he rests an arm on the opposite bent leg.

It seems I'm lying on my back, an unusual and helpless position for a bird. I try to stand, but I only manage to rock awkwardly like a boat at sea.

Korben offers me a gentle smile, then picks me up and sets me on my talons. I blink at a fire. Logs glow and crackle. Several bundles lie beyond it, the others sleeping. Only Korben is awake, watching over me, though he must be as tired as everyone else. We've had a long journey, and not an easy one at that.

*I was dreaming*, I want to say to him.

Except I can't remember what the dream was about. Everything is slipping away so quickly. I blink up at the sky, trying to decide if I'm still asleep. The display mesmerizes me. I have never seen anything like it in Castella, but like the glowing bushes . . . maybe rivers of light are commonplace in Tirnanog, too.

Korben sits next to me and cranes his neck, too. "It is a phenomenon like your aurora borealis," he offers in explanation, sensing my wonder. "It does not occur in Castella, but I have heard travelers in your realm say that it happens further north. Here, it's nearly a nightly occurrence. I missed it so. We call it *etherglow*."

He sounds so sad, it makes my heart constrict, imagining all the nights he spent in Castella longing for his home, wondering if he would ever see it again.

"I was so worried about you," Korben says. "And I must confess, I still am. I have been thinking as you rested. You did rest? Did you not? You did not seem at ease. Mayhap a bad dream? I hope not. Anyway, like I said, I was thinking."

He pauses and looks down at me. Another smile grazes his chiseled lips. In the past, it was a rare thing to witness, and at the moment, he seems to be all smiles. It's not a good sign.

"Something is not right in the realm," he continues. "Leaving aside the revelation that Saethara has implanted herself as queen, which is shocking enough, from what little else we have been able to observe, it seems that magic is . . . not behaving as it should."

He's giving me more smiles and words in one go than in days at a time. I'm confounded and genuinely concerned now. He's doing this to ease my worries, but why?

Korben goes on. "I cannot shift. Galen and Calierin cannot cast any spells. Yet, the rangers had a sorcerer who could do it all. His magic was strong and went on for some time even after Calierin beheaded him. That is unheard of. Only the most powerful sorcerers' and sorceresses' magic can hold over distances and as they sleep. But after death? Never.

"And when he went down his death was most . . . unnatural. He withered and strange smoke emanated from his body, like a cloud of evil. To add to all of these disturbing facts, they knew we were coming. They were waiting for us at the exact time and place. Their captain pretended not to know me and denied my rightful claim as Fae King. Yet, later, we discovered he knew exactly who I was, and that he was charged with taking me to his *master*. I suspect they are linked to Saethara. If you hadn't come, they would have, no doubt, killed me to prevent me from exposing her for what she truly is, a liar and a murderer."

His quiet words slip away on the breeze, leaving a chill hanging over me like the hand of a corpse. We sit quietly for a long time. The light from the etherglow reflects on his dark eyes, giving them an eerie purple and teal shimmer.

"At any rate," he says at last, peering at me sidelong, "I was thinking that . . . you should go back to Castella."

*What? No!* I shake my head adamantly. My wing smarts with pain.

"Esmeralda said they found you there in your human form," he goes on, ignoring my determined refusal to his foolish proposal. "Being as you are, I am afraid for you. It will take you time to heal, and for all the unknowns, I am certain of one thing . . . today's battle was only the beginning. Danger lies ahead, Valeria."

I shake my head once more. *I'm* not *leaving you.*

"You want to stay, I understand, but you must understand me, too. I have to be able to focus. I cannot be worried about you and your safety. You may not want to hear this, but I am not one to mince words . . . you are a liability, injured and in this shape."

Anger boils in my veins, searing everything in its path. He wants me gone because he thinks I'm useless, and my departure will ease his mind.

*But you are a burden, Valeria*, a part of me says.

He's only echoing the same thoughts I had earlier.

"I want to escort you back to the veil," he says. "I know it is not what we planned, but Castella needs you, the fae there need you. I cannot do anything for them until I repair what is wrong here."

*What would I be able to do against Amira and her armies?* I want to stomp and rage and scream, but all I do is tremble with my fury, my feathers lifting and shivering.

Korben recognizes this for what it is. "I know you are angry. I know you are impotent, but it is for the best. I will find you as soon as I can. I promise you that." After a pause, he adds, "We leave at dawn. Get some rest." He stands in one fluid motion and towers over me, a giant to my tiny form.

Turning his back on me, he walks toward the nearby trees, sits with his back to the trunk, and closes his eyes. It feels as if he's putting me out of his mind, turning his focus to what really matters to him. Suddenly, I'm a child again, reminded of all the times Father made a decision for me, giving me no choice in the matter.

*It's for your own good*, he would say, and that would be that.

I always fought him and, one way or another, found a way to do what I thought best for myself. There was a difference then, however. I was capable, not a broken thing that needed to be carried around and stored away when things got rough. And of course, I understand Korben. I would do the same for Castella.

Regardless, I can't help but feel hurt, slighted.

I glance down at my broken wing. If only it would heal quickly. Taking a deep breath, I try to stretch it, but I have to retract it right away as pain explodes at the site of the fracture, trembling its way over the rest of my bones.

It's futile. Like this, I can't be of help to anyone, only a damn hindrance.

# 19

## VALERIA

*"They got away. How?! Damn all the gods. Send the hob."*

**Lirion Faolborn – Fae Shifter**

Galen throws dirt on the fire, extinguishing it. The sun peeks over the horizon, igniting a riot of color that seems to be part of an extended dream but is quite real.

Korben talks quietly to Jago, out of earshot. It isn't hard to imagine what he's telling him.

*Go with Valeria. Protect her.*

Back in Castella, I won't need protection. I will shift back. My bones will heal, and then . . . what? Go back to Castellina to be arrested and possibly executed by my own sister? Remain hidden to escape death? It seems that no matter where I go, I'm bound to be worthless.

Jago leaves Korben, pulling his horse behind him.

"Good morning, cousin." Gently, Jago picks me up and settles me on the saddled horse.

I like it much better up here, where I can look everyone in the eyes.

"I hear we're going back to Castella," he whispers, glancing back over his shoulder at Korben, who is now talking to Galen, Calierin, and Kadewyn. "I'm fairly certain you're . . . not happy about that—the big fae bloke telling you what to do." He pauses as if mulling over his next words. "You'll hate me for this, but I think he's right, I have to admit. He's doing it because he cares about you. A lot. You know that, right?"

He waits for acknowledgement, but I turn my head and glance away, not giving him the satisfaction.

Jago sighs. "I'm sure I'll get an earful once we cross the veil."

Bracelets jangling and dark curls swinging in the breeze, Esmeralda saunters in our direction. "Do we really have to leave? We just got here, and everything is so . . . different." Her green eyes glint with wonder as they rove over the land. "I would like to see more."

"We'll come back." Jago wraps an arm around her waist and pulls her close. "I promise."

I'm surprised by their familiarity, and his warm display of affection. The Jago I know is more of a one-night-stand kind of man.

He caresses her check. "As soon as Valeria learns how to stop being a raven all the time, we'll cross the veil again."

*Stop being a raven?!*

Something quivers in the back of my mind, a forgotten thought attempting to awaken.

Korben approaches. "The others will remain here to wait for me. Except for Kadewyn, he is going back to his wife and daughter." This seems to please Korben.

My cousin frowns. "Shouldn't you ask him to stay and help you? I'm sure you'll need his archery skills sooner rather than later."

I listen with half an ear as, in the back of my mind, whispered words fight for my attention.

*How can I help if I can't shift back?*

Suddenly, the memory of my dream hits me like a lightning strike.

*—You can.*

*I've tried, but I can't stop being a raven!*

*—Take off the amulet.*

*—Take off the amulet.*

*—Take off the amulet.*

"What is it, Val?" Jago stares at me, frowning in concern.

I'm hopping from leg to leg excitedly, energy vibrating throughout my body.

*How do I take it off? How?!* I scream, but only shrill caws come out.

"Is your wing hurting?" Esmeralda asks.

I shake my head.

Jago scratches his head. "Um, you need to use the privy?"

*No, you idiot!*

Korben comes close. His eyes are leveled with mine despite the horse's height. "I know you want to stay, but I need you to be safe. If something happened to you, I do not—"

My entire body shakes in a negative answer.

"Maybe she's afflicted by *bird brain*," Jago suggests.

Korben narrows his eyes at Jago as he seems to consider whether or not my cousin deserves to be smacked for his clever, though obnoxious quip. Jago is an acquired taste, one that I terribly enjoy. However, right now isn't the time. If he keeps it up, I'm going to have to remember to kill him when I finally shift.

*Saints and feathers!* If I could only figure out how to take off the stupid amulet. I can't touch it. I can't even see it, for all the gods' sakes. Maybe I'll just use my imaginary hands to take off my imaginary amulet. I freeze, considering the idea.

"All right," Jago cocks his head, regarding me. "She stopped. It was not an avian seizure. She's unharmed, I think."

Closing my eyes, I do exactly that . . . I imagine lifting my hands in front of me. I turn them to examine my palms, then flex my fingers several times, making fists until they feel almost real, almost there. Slowly, I reach toward my neck and imagine pinching the amulet's chain between my thumbs and forefingers. Once I take hold of it, I roll it between my fingers, feeling its texture, its interconnected links.

*Yes, it's real. It's there!*

Fearing the feeling will pass, I quickly pull The Eldrystone over my head and release my hold.

As I blink my eyes open, I watch the amulet fall to the ground.

Jago, Korben, and Esmeralda gasp in unison.

My vision flickers, the colors of the realm dimming, the sounds growing muffled. My body stretches, and for an instant, I teeter atop the saddle. Quickly, I turn to face the front, and as my legs elongate, they drape over the horse's sides. When the transformation is over, I'm staring at Galen, Calierin, and Kadewyn, the horse's ears framing them. They stare back.

"Valeria!" Korben exclaims, taking me by the waist and hoisting me down. He wraps me in a tight hug and twirls me around in a burst of happiness such as I've never seen from him.

I pull away, pushing on his shoulders. His dark eyes sparkle. His smile makes his face look many years younger. Drinking him in, I can't help the joyous feeling that warms my chest. Taking his strong jaw between my hands, I plant a kiss on his lips, our teeth smashing together as we both grin like idiots.

As his grip loosens, I slide down, my chest sliding against his, my breasts sensing every bit of his sculpted torso, ridges and valleys I've explored a few times, though not as thoroughly as I would like.

Our kiss deepens, his tongue sliding into my mouth. An electric thrill spirals to my core, and I suddenly want him inside me, rocking his hips and shattering my world.

Jago clears his throat.

"Do you know this male?" Galen asks Kadewyn, elbowing him. "He resembles the Fae King, but he acts nothing like him."

Kadewyn only shrugs, looking abashed. It's Calierin who responds.

"That is certainly not the male I know."

Pressing his forehead to mine, Korben sighs and lets me go. Remembering my injury, I flex my arm and marvel at the complete absence of pain.

"How . . . did you do that?" Korben looks at The Eldrystone, which still lies on the ground.

Pushing away the rush caused by Korben's passionate kiss, I pick up the amulet, a feeling of awe descending over me. As my fingers wrap around it, that infernal itching attacks my skin, a sensation I've started to associate with shifting. Quickly, I hand the amulet to Korben, who takes it in confusion.

"Something wrong?" he asks.

"I shouldn't touch it," I say. "The amulet is the reason I couldn't shift back. That's why I had to take it off."

Korben frowns. "Strange. I wore it all the time, no matter which shape I took. It was never an impediment. It must be another change in the way magic is behaving. What do you think, Galen?"

The sorcerer approaches, rubbing his chin. "Must be," he replies absently, still considering. "Maybe Niamhara's magic is stronger within the stone. Put it on, Korben," he adds abruptly. "Maybe you'll be able to shift if you do."

Korben shakes his head. "I am already touching it, and I feel no difference. I am still dry."

Galen shrugs one shoulder as if to indicate nothing will be lost by trying.

With a shrug of his own, Korben slips the chain over his head. Everyone seems to tense in anticipation.

One beat. Two beats. Korben shakes his head.

Galen extends a hand toward Korben. "May I?"

Korben lets out a curt laugh. "You know I cannot trust you with it. Besides, it belongs to Valeria."

"It really does?" Calierin asks.

Apparently, she hadn't believed me.

"Yes." Korben offers me the amulet.

I hesitate, not wanting to touch it, but in the end, I pull the sleeve of my tunic over my hand and take it, avoiding skin contact.

Reaching inside the folds of her skirt, Esmeralda pulls out a colorful kerchief. "Here."

I notice the initials *E.M.* lovingly stitched in one corner. "Are you sure?"

"Of course."

I take it, wrap it around the amulet, then store it in the pouch that hangs from the belt at my waist.

"How did you know to take it off?" Galen asks.

I frown at him, unsure of how to explain.

"How did you know to take off the amulet in order to return to your human shape?" he clarifies.

"I . . . I had a dream, except I don't think it was a dream."

Korben takes my hand and leads me toward a fallen log. He invites me to sit. As I do, the others gather around me, sitting on the grass and looking intrigued. Only Korben remains standing.

"Can you tell us about it?" Korben asks.

Telling them about a castle made of clouds sounds ridiculous, so I avoid that part and get straight to the point. "This will sound crazy, but I think I . . . talked to Niamhara."

My eyes rove around the group. I expect them to laugh, but instead, their expressions range from intrigued to awed.

Encouraged, I go on. "She said that it took great effort to bring me here."

Korben looks as if he wants to start pacing. There's nowhere to go, though, so he just shuffles his feet on the spot. "From the beginning," he says, "it has seemed to me as if she were *guiding* things. The way The Eldrystone worked sometimes and not others . . . it appeared to have a purpose."

I nod. "I thought the same. However, she also told me she was weak. She could only talk to me for a brief time. She said she had to conserve energy, so maybe that's another reason the amulet has been erratic and why espiritu is acting strange."

"Weak?" Galen echoes. "The *Goddess of Radiance* is weak?"

"That's what she said." I rub nervous hands over my knees. "She told me I should take the amulet off in order to shift back, and . . ."

I glance at Korben, "most importantly, she said we had to find her and bring her The Eldrystone."

Galen shoots to his feet. "That makes no sense. How can *the* Goddess be weak? She created all of this." He throws his hands up and turns in a circle. "And how in all the hells are we supposed to find her? Isn't she everywhere and nowhere at the same time?"

"She said Korben would know how." I glance up at Korben and so do the others.

We wait expectantly, as if hoping he'll pull out a map and show us a specific set of coordinates, pinpointing the celestial home of the Fae Goddess, creator of all. Instead, he sits on the log next to me and runs stiff fingers through his black hair.

"What is it?" I place a hand on his knee.

He smiles, takes my hand, and squeezes it.

"Do you *know* where to find her?" Galen asks.

Korben responds in a near whisper. "There is an old legend, or at least that is what I thought it was. My father told it to me when he passed down The Eldrystone. In turn, my grandfather told it to him, and my great grandfather told it to my grandfather, and so on, all the way back to Othano Theric, my original ancestor who first received The Eldrystone from Niamhara. The legend says there is a moor known as . . ." He trails off, frowning. He seems not to remember.

Abruptly, Kadewyn jumps to a standing position, drawing an arrow from his quiver, nocking it, and letting it loose. The arrow flies over my head and strikes someone behind us. A loud cry of pain follows, like the baying of a gutted donkey.

Korben, who jumped into action at the same time as Kadewyn, has already pounced on the interloper. He's on top of a midsize creature, dagger poised to kill. I'm unable to discern what or who he has captured.

"Who are you?" Korben demands.

"Gah, let go me, you beast," the creature screeches. "My leg. My leg. Oh, pain. Horrible. Dreadful."

I stand and move closer for a better look. Korben hoists the being by the throat and slams it against a tree trunk. I'm confounded by what I see.

He—it's a male, for sure—is about half of Korben's size, but nearly as wide. He has leathery skin and short, thick legs that ineffectually kick in the air. His blocky feet are bare. They each have four toes of equal size, tipped with black claws. He wears a knee-length skirt made of a collection of items threaded together with twine. The items—hollow branches, seashells, rocks, feathers, bones, coins, silverware, keys, beads, fruit pits, vines, and more—knock together as he kicks, sounding like some sort of eclectic wind chime. His torso is naked, his chest sprouting with coarse, dark hair. Atop his trunk-like neck sits a perfectly round bald head with large, pointed ears, tufted with hairs. Strangely, his face is completely hairless, without even eyebrows or lashes.

"Little eavesdropper." Kadewyn plucks the arrow from the creature's leg, though not before giving it a twist. Dark green blood oozes out.

More shrieks ensue, but they're a waste of breath. No one cares.

Except . . . me.

"Is all of this really necessary?" I ask. "Maybe he was just . . . passing by."

"Ay, passing by. Me. Toad passes by. Always," the creature says.

"If you open your mouth to lie one more time, I will gut you, *Toad*." Korben digs the dagger under his ribs.

"Gah! Gah!"

"Or if you scream again."

Toad's screams cease immediately as he seals his lips together, his wide eyes growing to three times the size of mine.

"Allow me to enlighten you, Valeria." Galen saunters in front of me, wearing a professorial air. "This creature here is a trinket hob. He is by nature cunning and resourceful, and due to his kind's ability to manipulate objects and create illusions, they are widely used as spies."

"A spy? With that skirt?" Esmeralda asks. "It would be like *me* trying to spy." She lifts an arm and shakes her many bracelets, making them clink.

"Yet, you didn't hear him approaching, did you?" Galen offers.

I move closer, meeting the creature's gaze. "So you were spying on us?"

"Ay." He shakes his head, realizing his slip. "Naaaaah."

"For a spy, you are a poor liar. Who is your master?" Korben demands, giving him a shake.

"Saying the name means death to Toad," he answers, sounding terrified.

"Silence means death to Toad as well." Korben puts pressure on the dagger, drawing more green blood.

Toad has a full-body shiver that causes him to make a *beeheehee* sound.

Suddenly, I feel terribly sorry for him. He seems legitimately scared.

"Let him go, Korben," I say.

"Ay. Please. The nice lady. Listen to her."

"Do not let him fool you, Valeria. It is all an act." Korben digs his blade deeper still.

"Toad speaks. Toad speaks. Gah, the pain. Dreadful."

Korben pulls back the dagger. "I am waiting."

"The name of my master is . . ." He hesitates.

Korben growls deep in his throat.

"His name is Lirion Faolborn."

"And what does Lirion Faolborn want?"

"To know what the king plans."

"And where can I find him?"

"Toad knows not."

The dagger returns to Toad's side.

"Toad knows not. Toad knows not!"

With a grunt of disgust, Korben lets him go and takes a step back. The creature plummets to the ground. His skirt clanks and jingles as accompaniment to his cries of pain.

Without thinking, I reach out to help him.

"No!" Korben warns.

In a heartbeat, Toad's face morphs, twisting into a terrifying grimace. His eyes turn entirely red and hundreds of needle-like teeth spring into his mouth. With the speed of a snake, he strikes, biting my forearm and clamping his jaws around it.

I growl and punch him as hard as I can in the eye. He shrieks with the same helpless quality as before and attempts to retreat, but it's too late for him. Korben dispatches him efficiently, one swift swipe of his dagger and the creature falls lifeless to the ground.

He stands over it, watching the hob with a frown.

"Nasty creature," he spits. Once he's sure Toad is dead, Korben turns his attention to me. "Ravógín, I'm sorry this happened." He peers at my arm. "Let's get the amulet to help you shift and take care of that arm."

# 20

## KORBEN

*"Please, Goddess of Radiance, intervene so the king allows me to return to Radina and Valya."*

### Kadewyn Zinceran – Veilfallen

The rage that seared through me as the hideous creature caused Valeria pain still burns in my veins.

I force myself to take a deep breath and calm down. Taking her hand, I guide her away from the hob and step off to the side.

Hundreds of punctures mark her forearm, blood seeping from each. The creature's saliva is caustic, so I know it must be causing Valeria much pain. Yet, besides a slight tightening of her features, she barely shows any sign of discomfort.

She is fierce, and though I admire her for it and know she can withstand much, I cannot absolve anyone who causes her harm.

Reaching for the pouch at her belt, I retrieve The Eldrystone and hang the chain around her neck. The shift is swift, unlike the first time. I am surprised by how smoothly it happens. Watching her makes me long for that feeling, the exuberant transformation into a creature of flight and distinct skills from those of my fae shape.

In a short moment, the amulet detaches from her raven shape, and I catch it in midair before it falls to the ground. Once more, Valeria stands in front of me with her lustrous brown hair and flawless olive skin. I suddenly want the entire realm to disappear, so I can have her all to myself. Instead, I offer back The Eldrystone, resisting the urge to wrap her in my arms like I did before.

She frowns at the amulet, then examines her now-healed arm. "So strange."

"Not strange. It is as it should be, as it should have always been."

"I suppose you're right." She pulls the kerchief from her pouch, takes the amulet, starts to put it away, but stops halfway. "You should have it back, Korben. It's yours, and you're back in your realm. Niamhara needs *you*."

"Yet, she talked to you."

"Only because I had this." She proffers the opal back.

I shake my head. "*You* got us this far. Besides, you are still the strongest against its corrupting force."

"You gave it to me because I didn't trust you."

The feelings these words release in my chest are like cold shards. She thinks I gave her the amulet to coerce her. I cannot let her believe that.

"I did not give you The Eldrystone to gain your trust, Ravógín. I gave it to you because I realized my time with it was done, and someone else, someone like you, should be in charge of that sort of power."

She looks up at the sky and takes a deep breath. "It should be someone else," she says with difficulty as if the words choke her. "Now that we're here, it should be someone else. I'm not fae. I—"

"But you are. You are Loreleia Elhice's daughter. Your mother knew that neither Saethara nor I should hold The Eldrystone. Instead, she let you keep it."

"She let me play with it, and then she died."

"Do you honestly think she would have let you *play* with it, if she did not know your heart?"

My question stumps her, but after a moment's thought, she comes up with another argument. "No one here will like it, a human carrying Niamhara's conduit."

"A half-fae and more . . . a raven shifter, which means you inherited our ancestors' blood."

"And what about this?" she gestures to one of her well-rounded ears.

"What?" I rest my fingers on the side of her neck, then gently caress her earlobe with my thumb. "Your beautiful ears."

"They instantly give away my human blood."

"Are you ashamed of it?"

"Of course not!"

"Then why worry?"

She looks at the ground. "Because . . . I'm afraid they'll hate me."

"My dear Valeria, if people wish to hate you, they will find a reason, even if you look exactly like them. A dark heart knows no other way."

She shakes her head, gaze meeting mine. "Is this really you? The *real* you?"

I sniff and thumb my nose, feeling stupid and sentimental. "I suppose. In Castella, I spent a lot of time being one of those hateful people I was just referring to. Before that, I was someone else entirely. A male raised in privilege, used to comfort and deference, someone who crumbled at the first sign of strife. Not very strong of me." I huff derisively. "My time in your realm—not to mention you—taught me a lot."

"And now, you're sappy, my friend." Galen comes behind me and slaps a hand on my shoulder.

I shrug him off, angry at his interruption. "What do you want, Galen?"

He dusts his hands, rubbing them against each other. "Nothing, it's your friend over there." He gestures toward Kadewyn. "He's leaving, taking one of the horses."

"That he is," I grunt, then take Valeria's hand and guide her toward Kadewyn.

"My king." Kadewyn bows.

"I told you to forget that nonsense."

"Forgive me, but I find it difficult."

"You should not. We shared gruel and earthen beds and battles. We are brothers." I put out my arm.

He hesitates for a moment, his pale eyes wavering. At last, he clasps my forearm, and I clasp his.

"We need all the help we can get, Korben," Galen says. "You should make him stay."

Kadewyn swallows thickly, dread entering his features.

I let go of his arm and turn to face the sorcerer. "You forget your place, Galen. I will ask your opinion when I need it. Otherwise, keep it to yourself. And if you do not like it, you are welcome to leave."

I am growing tired of his quips. He bullied his way into our group through extortion. He demanded I let him be Master of Magic using The Eldrystone as leverage. If he thinks I have forgiven him for that and for his previous betrayal, he is sorely mistaken.

The sorcerer clenches his teeth, a muscle jumping in his jaw. I have a feeling he would blast me if his magic were not dry. Instead, he steps back, turns around, and walks away.

I return my attention to Kadewyn. "Go back to your family, Kade."

He clears his throat. "I . . . I would stay if you asked me, my king."

"I know, but I want you to go. Radina and Valya are waiting for you."

He smiles, his entire face lighting up at the idea of rejoining his wife and daughter.

Kadewyn deserves his peaceful trader's life. He is a quiet man, but whenever he talked about returning to Tirnanog, he always referred to the simple joys of his past life: traveling to exchange goods, returning home with gifts for his family, hunting for game in the woods around his property, sitting quietly with his wife by a warm fire while their daughter slept nearby. Yes, he deserves to never again raise his bow to kill anything but prey. He has faithfully fought for me long enough.

"Farewell, Kade."

"Farewell, my king."

He mounts his horse and rides west. He lives close to the ocean, and I have a feeling he will exhaust the poor beast in order to get there as soon as possible.

When I face the others, I am surprised to find Calierin following Kadewyn's progress with a forlorn expression, as if she is sad to see him go. She quickly composes her features into an indifferent mask and pretends to check her saddle straps. She and Kadewyn were together in Castellina before I arrived there. They were part of a disorganized veilfallen force in need of strong leadership. Without them, I would not be here.

"I would bid you go home as well, Calierin," I say, "but I am afraid I will have need of a Tuathacath warrior many times before this is all over."

She lowers her head and holds the bow. "I promised you my sword and my loyalty, My Liege. I do not intend to leave your side."

"I thank you."

"There is no need."

I glance toward the hob's body, thinking of the male who sent him.

*Lirion Faolborn, who are you?*

"What do we do now?" Valeria asks. "You still don't expect me to go back to Castella, I hope."

I would still want her to be safe and away from the dangers that seem to assail us at every turn, but in her human form, she is a capable warrior. Besides, she is used to being independent and beholden to no one, except herself. Going against her wishes would mean nothing but trouble.

"Of course not," I say. "You have to bring the amulet to Niamhara, and I have to help you find her."

She raises one eyebrow as if surprised by my decision, then nods.

"Let us ride away from here," I add. "We have stayed too long, and the hob may have reported our location already."

"How?" Jago asks.

"Hobs have magic that lets them communicate through long distances. It is one more reason they are used as spies."

Valeria approaches her cousin, wearing a frown. "You and Esmeralda should go back. Things here, they seem . . . treacherous."

"The more reason to stay with you, Val." Jago mock-punches her in the arm.

"And I ain't leaving," Esmeralda says. "I'm here for adventure."

"Hey!" Jago appears injured. "I thought you were here for me."

"Sorry to disappoint you, Chavé." She winks. "You're not as exciting as Tirnanog is turning out to be."

"Isn't that an understatement?" Galen says.

"Hush, lame sorcerer," Jago snaps back. "No one asked for your opinion."

I stifle a wince. By chastising him, I meant to put Galen in his place, but not for him to lose everyone's respect. Though, I suppose he should earn that on his own.

With Kadewyn gone, there are five horses and six of us.

"Would you like to ride with me?" I ask Valeria.

A slight blush colors her cheeks before she nods.

I never feel happier than when I can hold her between my arms, where I know she is safe, and I can protect her.

Calierin is the first to mount her horse. "So . . . where does one find a goddess?"

"We will talk about it later," I reply. "For now, we ride."

Cuervo caws as he takes flight and leads the way.

# 21

# KORBEN

*"Find a way to seal all those passages."*

**Saethara Orenthal – Queen of Tirnanog – 1 AV**

"*In the hushed twilight of the Whispering Wilds, where reality bends and magic hums, dwells Niamhara, the Goddess of Creation and Radiance. There, the air shimmers with a thousand hues, spun from moonlight and starlight. Gossamer flowers bloom in impossible shades, their petals catching whispers on the breeze and morphing into tiny sentient creatures with iridescent wings. Towering trees, older than time, hold the secrets of forgotten eras within their gnarled roots. Dragons, their scales like gemstones, glide through the opalescent sky, leaving in their wake trails of stardust, ice, and fire.*

*This wondrous realm, unseen by the fae, exists behind a veil, a door from Tirnanog into her domain. To find Niamhara, one must embark on a perilous journey, for the Whispering Wilds guard their secrets fiercely. First, you must seek the place where the wicked witches once lived. The air there thrums with hushed, evil secrets, carried on the wind to anyone who dares enter.*

*Danger lurks. Ready yourself.*

*Ignore the calls. Carve your own path until you reach a lonely rock mound, where no grave was ever dug. Here, you must search for a wink of light, and beyond it the Whispering Wilds will be revealed.*

*If the Goddess and her conduit favor you, the light will give way, revealing what you seek. Enter, heart pounding, for you do not know what you will find. The path may lead you to a jade cave, deposit you in a field of fireflies, or even transport you to a grove guarded by watchful griffins.*

*Finally, you will arrive at the heart of the Whispering Wilds, a palace so grand, an entire universe. Its entrance is always open to let in the sunlight and moonlight. Step into the palace, behold its walls glittering with a million captured rainbows. Jewels of every color imaginable, mined from the dreams of fallen stars, pave the floor. In the center, bathed in a soft, ethereal glow, sits Niamhara, the Goddess of Radiance. Her hair is a cascade of living starlight, her eyes pools of liquid light. She once spun tales into entire realms, her every breath creating rivers, valleys, mountains, and a myriad of creatures to inhabit her creations.*

*Approach with reverence, for even a goddess can be lost in thought. If your cause is just, your voice will carry through the palace, reaching her ears. But be warned, Niamhara judges all who seek her. Only those of pure heart and noble deeds will find solace in the Whispering Wilds. For the Goddess of Radiance is not one to be trifled with. Her power is vast and boundless as the ethereal realm she calls home."*

We have traveled all day, and now we sit around a modest fire after an equally modest supper of roasted rabbit and wild potatoes. The horses munch on grass, snorting gently and stomping the ground.

The moon hangs low, looking as if it could fall from the sky and flatten us. It never looks that big in Castella.

The etherglow flows ceaselessly, moving in serpentine patterns that go nowhere and everywhere.

My companions' mood is heavy and pensive after my story.

"Another realm then?" Valeria says at last. "Through another veil?"

Galen scratches his chin, green eyes reflecting the firelight. "I've often pondered if there could be other realms. It seems I was right."

Esmeralda frowns. "I thought gods were supposed to live in heaven or something."

"Right!" Jago nods. "If Niamhara's just in another realm, then does that mean she's . . . like us? I don't mean human or fae, but like us. A realm . . . dweller, just one of a different kind."

Galen nods. "That's an interesting thought. We, fae, have magic. We can create spells of fire, wind, light. What if Niamhara simply has more magic, enough to create another realm full of people?"

"Which in turn," Valeria says, "could mean that, in yet another realm, there are beings more powerful than Niamhara, a being who . . ." She trails off, as if afraid to finish the thought.

I finish it for her. "A being that can create gods."

"And so on and so forth," Galen adds. "Realm after realm with increasingly more powerful beings capable of creating . . . universes."

Jago makes a face and presses a hand to his middle. "The thought makes me feel sick for some reason."

"Perhaps because your kind is at the bottom of this lovely hierarchy," Calierin offers, her wit always cutting and ill-timed.

Valeria crosses her arms. "This is simply conjecture, and who is to say espiritu is the measuring stick. For all we know it's a degenerative quality. Look at all the trouble it causes."

Calierin opens her mouth to respond, surely some biting retort, but she checks herself after a quick glance in my direction. She has vowed to honor me. Disrespecting the woman I love only breaks that promise. I am glad she realizes that. I know it cannot be easy for her to defer to Valeria, but it is crucial that she does. Otherwise, her vow would be useless, and I would have to dismiss her.

Instead, she switches the conversation to more practical matters. "So how do we get there? Where do we find the *land where the wicked witches once lived*? That is not a helpful clue."

"It sure isn't," Galen agrees.

"The legend is complemented by a large codex," I say. "It contains the details necessary to find Niamhara."

Valeria lets out a frustrated sigh. "Are you saying you don't know the exact location of this other veil?"

I nod.

"You haven't read the entire codex?"

I shake my head. "Never got around to it."

Confessing this makes me feel callous. This is something I should have memorized as well as I memorized the legend. I did try, but it has been a hundred years since I studied the subject, and in that time, most of what I learned has been erased from my mind by other, more pressing, information.

"So that means we need the codex?" Galen asks.

"Correct."

"And, let me guess, it's in Riochtach?"

"Correct again," I say. "I have been giving it some thought.

Niamhara seems to need The Eldrystone to regain her strength. But why did she lose it in the first place?" I do not offer my opinion. I want to learn what they think and see if we draw the same conclusion.

"Um, maybe because . . ." Valeria starts tentatively, "because the amulet was locked away in Castella."

This was exactly my thought.

Galen agrees with a grunt, then adds, "It makes sense. The Eldrystone was in Tirnanog for thousands of years, and nothing like this ever happened."

He rubs a thumb over the knuckles of his opposite hand, a movement that I know creates a light to illuminate his path. I have seen him do that gesture a thousand times, except now it is nothing but an empty spell.

"Twenty years in Castella," Galen adds, "and the *Goddess of Radiance* is now quite dull."

"I'd be careful with my words if I were you, Galen," Jago says. "If we find Niamhara and give back The Eldrystone, she might want to teach you a lesson or two about respect."

I expect Galen to issue another mocking comment. Instead, he appears thoughtful. He has always been blasphemous, no matter how sacred the topic, but it seems that the possibility of actually facing Niamhara gives him pause.

"But if that's the reason," Esmeralda says, frowning, "shouldn't she be fine now that the amulet is back?"

"I have considered this," I say, "and mayhap Niamhara's loss of strength took place slowly, which means her recovery might take time as well. Unless . . . we're too late. Valeria and I saw Niamhara's hand at work several times in Castella, but her influence grew more erratic and weaker every day. Valeria's dream confirms that. At any rate, I agree with Valeria, it appears as if the veil's collapse is to blame for the Goddess's weakness, which brings me to another possible conclusion."

"What is that?" Valeria asks, her brown eyes sparkling with moonlight.

"I think The Eldrystone cannot be responsible for the collapse of the veil between Tirnanog and Castella."

Everyone takes the idea in and ponders. After a moment, they all nod in unison.

Calierin is the first one to speak. "Niamhara would not have allowed the veil to collapse—not if it meant losing contact with the amulet."

"Exactly," I say.

"That means someone else was responsible," Valeria says, her gaze meeting mine, and I know she is thinking of her mother. It was Loreleia, after all, who issued the curse.

"It wasn't my mother," Valeria protests immediately. "She didn't have that kind of power. Her only skill was communicating with plants."

"I agree," I say, "but if Niamhara's power—through The Eldrystone—was not what caused the veil to fall, mayhap the one truly responsible made it look that way."

Valeria's thoughts leap and reach the only possible destination. "Saethara then? She must have known that using the veil to separate Niamhara from the conduit would weaken the Goddess."

"Wait!" Esmeralda puts a hand up. "I thought you said Saethara isn't a sorceress. So where would she get the power to close the veil? Oh, this is so confusing."

"It sure is," Jago agrees.

"She could've . . . lied about not having magic," Galen offers. "That, or she has allies who do. Allies like this Lirion Faolborn."

"That is what I have come to believe after much pondering," I say. "He must have been helping Saethara from the beginning. I do not believe she could have staged a coup of this magnitude all by herself."

"Lirion Faolborn," Galen repeats the name under his breath.

Valeria pokes at the fire with a stick. "For all we know, he's just Saethara's muscle, a crony she employs to do her dirty work."

"Or he could be the mastermind," Galen says, postulating an inverse possibility.

"Either way," Jago says, "it doesn't matter, right? We bring The Eldrystone to Niamhara, and she'll fix everything, won't she?"

"Things are never that easy." Galen takes a sip of water from a waterskin, then adds, "We have to go to Riochtach and get our hands on that codex Korben is talking about."

"Where is the codex, Korben?" Valeria asks. "In Elf-Dún?"

I nod. "Yes."

"What if Saethara has it? What if she destroyed it?!" Her tone is panicked, her eyes wide.

"I trust the codex is safe. Well hidden," I say.

"Oh, fuck!" Galen's hand flies to the side of his head as his own panic takes hold. "If Saethara and Lirion knew that trapping the conduit in Castella would weaken Niamhara, they could easily have other information like the location of the codex. Valeria's fear isn't unfounded."

I understand their panic, but they are wrong. "There are things such as the Whispering Wilds story that only the Theric kings know. The existence of that codex is one of those things. I assure you, it is well hidden. Not only that, to gain access to its location one must possess Theric blood. It is a common failsafe in Elf-Dún."

"Well, that's a relief, I guess," Galen says sarcastically. "Now we only need to infiltrate the most secure place in all of Tirnanog."

"That shouldn't be a problem for this one." Jago hooks a finger in my direction. "He infiltrated Nido and made himself so comfortable that he seduced one of the princesses. I don't think he'll find it difficult to infiltrate his own home." He laughs heartily.

Valeria glares at her cousin as if she wishes her eyes could shoot daggers. This sends Esmeralda into a fit of laughter, which seems to amuse the others. Even if they only half smile, the overall mood lightens somewhat.

"I do have an idea of how to get in," I say. "It is my home after all, as Jago pointed out. Let us get some rest, and I will tell you all about it tomorrow. I'll take the first watch unless someone else wants it."

No one volunteers. Everyone is tired and wishes to get some sleep right away.

"I'll take the second one," Valeria says, without meeting my eyes. Her shy expression gives me an idea of what she has in mind for us during that shift change. I have to turn away and hide my body's reaction.

This woman! I am at her complete mercy.

# 22

# VALERIA

*"Tell them to keep chanting and praying. It gives her strength."*

**Faolan Theric – King of Tirnanog**

"Wake up, Ravógín," Korben's deep voice whispers in my ear.

I turn and lie on my back, blinking to chase away my heavy sleep.

He smiles down at me, his dark eyes full of burning desire. I'm suddenly reminded that this was my idea. I wanted a moment to ourselves, and Korben seems quite willing to give it to me.

As a jolt spirals down to my core, my sleepiness dissolves like ink in water.

Carefully, he slides behind me, his body pressed to mine.

"The others are sleeping, but you will have to be extremely quiet not to wake them," he says.

Heat builds in my cheeks. "Maybe this is a bad idea."

"I disagree. I think it is a wonderful idea."

Korben kisses my cheek, his mouth gentle and warm. Slowly, his hand slips down between my thighs. His kisses travel along my jaw as he cups me through my leggings. My breaths sharpen at the sensations that settle in my middle. He nibbles my ear. My chest grows heavy.

"Do you like it?" he whispers in my ear.

I can't answer. I'm afraid to make a sound.

"Do you like it?" he insists.

My voice quivers as I speak. "I do."

He pulls me more tightly toward him. My rear fits against his hips. A sound like a storm rumbles deep in his throat. I rub against him, enjoying his hardness.

His fingers begin rubbing me, tracing the seam of my leggings, which feel as thin as silk, yet too thick for my taste. Damp heat rushes to my core. He continues kissing me and rubbing with the right amount of maddening pressure, his tongue lapping at the same rhythm of his fingers.

"I want to be inside you," he says. "I bet you are wet and ready for me. I want to know."

His hand moves up, slides under the waistband, and travels farther south. His long fingers part me, and I take a sharp inhalation of pleasure. They start circling against my most sensitive spot, the wetness there nulling all friction.

"I knew you would be wet," his voice rumbles. "So delicious."

Circling and circling in the most maddening rhythm, he drives me to the edge of madness.

"Open wider," he orders.

I obey.

One of his fingers slips inside me, and every part of my body feels the thrill. My pulse pounds. My hips rock against his hand and against *him*.

"You are tight," he says, "and so hot." He slips a second finger, going in and out. I shudder, so lost in the sensations he unleashes within me.

Low, repressed moans escape my lips, my body going tense.

His hand shifts and his thumb moves over my swollen bud. Now, he pumps in and out at the same time that his thumb circles me. Hot kisses travel the length of my throat, and the intense combination of sensations makes the pressure and tension build within me.

"I want to fuck you," he growls.

The tension breaks. Pleasure washes over me with the force of a tempest. Waves crash inside me. My nipples harden in response. My core throbs exquisitely, while Korben holds my body through its uncontrollable quaking, waiting for the storm to pass. When it does, he whispers in my ear.

"Valeria, you are my everything."

# 23

## VALERIA

*"He really seems to love her. Maybe I have nothing to worry about."*

*Jago Plumanegra (Casa Plumanegra) – 3rd in line to Plumanegra throne*

The next morning, we avoid the main road to Riochtach and, instead, travel through wooded areas, the horses gingerly weaving past bushes and heavy roots, some as thick as two men. At this rate, it will take us twice as long to get there, but we hope to remain unseen. Korben says the many creatures and their espiritu can interfere with location spells others may cast.

Korben and I ride together, his solid body behind me a wonderful comfort.

I'm reminded of our approach to the veil on Castella's side, where we had to cut through overgrown vegetation as we traveled, though Galen had espiritu to clear our path then.

Now, we only have swords. However, we're not allowed to use them. Even the suggestion made Korben, Galen, and even Calierin blanch. The plants are living creatures they would never hurt.

"So for you it's easier to run a person through with your blade than this bush?" Jago asked Calierin when she told us not to dare harm anything in the forest.

"Yes," was her dry response.

However, the further we go, the more I understand their reasons. The forest is alive in a way that forests in the human realm are not. Undisturbed, some of the bushes glow even in daylight. But when we brush against them, they flash in and out as if in warning. Small creatures of different shapes and sizes fly at us, shaking tiny fists and spewing what sounds like gibberish in their high-pitched voices. They are harmless though, their wings a work of art in gossamer. Pixies.

Mother always called me her *little pixie*, and finally seeing one of the small creatures I understand why. To her, I was small, beautiful, and fragile. My heart aches.

"Are you all right, little raven?" Korben asks, noticing my forlorn expression.

I pat our horse's neck, putting on a smile. "I'm all right."

Korben pushes my hair aside and leans closer to whisper in my ear. "Everything will work out. I promise."

I want to believe that, but entering Elf-Dún sounds even more daunting than gaining access to Nido. True, Korben was able to infiltrate my home posing as a Guardia Real, but he had a year to plan his incursion. We don't have that luxury this time.

He hasn't told us how we'll accomplish stealing into the fae palace, retrieving the codex, and leaving without detection. He has been quiet for hours, lost in thought. I haven't dared say a word for fear of breaking his concentration at a crucial moment.

"Does that mean you have a plan now?" I ask.

"I am still mulling over a few ideas."

"Are they promising?"

"It depends. I will need to assess the situation first, but they could be."

"Know that I'm willing to help. I'll do anything you ask me to do."

His arm slips around my waist. "I know."

"I don't want to sit uselessly waiting while you risk everything."

"I know."

"Dammit, Korben! Don't just say *I know*. I'm serious."

"I know," he replies, a hint of a smile in his voice. I glance back over my shoulder, and sure enough, he's grinning from ear to ear.

I glare at him.

He sobers up. "Much is at stake for both my kin and yours. Trust me when I say you *and* I will do everything within our power to set things right."

It's a satisfactory answer, I suppose.

Until he adds, "We will not take unnecessary risks, however."

He winks at me as I glare at him sidelong.

I don't argue further. I worry about him, too. I'm not familiar with Elf-Dún, so it makes sense for him to be at the forefront and take all the risks. But if I could, I would put him away and keep him safe. If something happened to him, I would . . .

I would what? I'm not sure, but I don't like the way my chest tightens at the thought. He told me he loves me—not in that many words, but close.

*"What are you worried about then? That you'll fall in love with me?"* I asked him the day he relinquished The Eldrystone to me.

*"No, princess, that already happened,"* he replied.

177

My attraction to him has been undeniable since the beginning, but do I love him? I'm not surprised to find that the answer is *no*. I care. That's why I was worried about him when the rangers took him. That's why the thought of something happening to him as we undertake this task makes my chest feel like a load of stones is sitting on it.

But love . . . that is something else entirely. Love is built on trust, and we had a rocky start in that respect. Though, the male I'm discovering under all the heavy protective layers he built up around him . . . well, that male is certainly worth getting to know. Maybe even loving.

Besides, there is one more thing that wears heavily upon me. I have no license falling in love with someone who will outlive me, while I get old and lackluster.

"May I ask what you are thinking about, Ravógín?" Korben kisses the back of my neck, inhaling my scent and humming as if I'm something delicious he plans to devour.

"Nothing."

"Oh, it is definitely something. You can talk to me about it."

"Can I?"

"Always."

"Hmm, I'm still trying to reconcile Korben with Rífíor *and* Bastien."

He stiffens behind me, his hand falling from my waist. "I . . . cannot blame you for that."

"There's so little I know about you," I admit, glad to be facing away from those fierce black eyes. It's easier to say what's on my mind.

"I have already told you. There is nothing to reconcile. I am the same male. But I admit, you are correct. I . . . hid behind my worst traits for a long time, and you know next to nothing about my charm and wit."

I laugh at his attempt to lighten the mood, but quickly press my lips together. If this is his way to evade me, it won't work. "You won't get off so easily."

"I do not intend to, princess. Ask me anything you want to know. I want nothing more than to open myself to you."

I notice the others have fallen behind, keeping their distance from us. Jago and Esmeralda bring up the rear, likely attempting to find some privacy of their own.

"You said your father passed into the Glimmer, what about your mother?" I ask.

"My mother," he says in a faraway voice that seems to take him to a dark place.

It seems I started with entirely the wrong question. "You don't have to answer if—"

"It is all right. The subject is not an easy one, but if I cannot talk to you about it, then who else?"

He lets the question hang, and behind it I hear the unspoken truth. If he can't talk about the difficult things with the woman he claims to love, then who else can he trust?

Korben clears his throat. "She died when I was ten years old."

Died. Not passed into the Glimmer, but died. That means she didn't live a full life, that she didn't depart on her own terms. When fae reach a certain age, Mother explained, they grow tired and yearn for rest. It is then that they decide their time to cross into oblivion has come. Normally, the decision arrives when there are no regrets left and all accounts have been settled.

Korben is quiet for a long time, and I fear he will be unable to tell me more, but eventually, he continues. "It happened during childbirth. Father did not tell me the details right away, but I overheard others talking about it. My sibling, a girl . . . there was something wrong with her. She inherited our shifting abilities and erratically transformed during labor. Mother battled for hours. They both suffered and eventually died."

I press a hand to my chest, wishing I hadn't asked the question. There's so much desolation in Korben's voice that I feel it like a gloomy shroud falling over us.

"Korben, I don't know what to say." No words seem appropriate.

"She was a wonderful mother," he goes on. "Where Father was always stern, she was gentle and encouraging. She made me believe I could do anything I wanted. Though my memories of her are distant, I still miss her."

"It sounds a lot like my parents. My father was always strict, while Mother got us to do what she needed through games and tender cajoling."

"We have that in common then."

"Yes." I smile through the sadness that hangs around us. "Having things in common is good, though I hope we can find happier instances."

"I am sure we will. We have shared much strife since we met, but I will be damned if I cannot bring you the happiness you deserve."

He nuzzles me, pressing his lips to my neck and wrapping both arms around my waist. It's a tight, sort of desperate embrace, as if he means to hold me and never let me go.

I can't help but imagine him as a little boy, crying over his mother's unexpected death, exactly the way I did. I know the desolation he felt. I know it's the sort of thing one never truly recovers from.

When he married Saethara, did he imagine she would be a tender mother to his children? He must have. It was what he knew. What a terrible, terrible blow it must have been to discover she was only interested in The Eldrystone.

I can't blame him for being guarded and bitter when I first met him, and I can't ignore the courage it must take for him to make himself vulnerable to me the way he just did.

*Saints and feathers!* If falling in love requires a leap, I believe I stand at the edge.

# 24

## VALERIA

*"Why would the king give a human The Eldrystone? I do not understand."*

*Calierin Kelraek – Tuathacath Warrior and Veilfallen*

Korben and I talk in hushed tones for hours, our horse leading the way and moving at an easy pace through the woods. When it's time to stop for the night, I want to keep conversing with him and feel like a child who has found their favorite game and never wants to stop playing.

So far, I have learned about his favorite tutor; the time he broke his leg trying to fly without shifting; his first kiss with a pretty Riochtach fruit seller who had no idea he was the prince; the way his father used to drag him along to every official event as soon as he turned thirteen; his best friend—Vonall—who Korben is definitely worried about and hopes to meet again soon.

He is indeed charming and witty and rather good at making me smile *and* even laugh out loud. It's clear he paid attention and got to know me all those days he stood by my side as a stern-faced Guardia Real. I'm reminded of his dark eyes on me. He stood tall in his black uniform, rapier at his side, expression unreadable. He appeared so stiff and corpse-like that I came to believe he didn't care. Then as Ríftor, there was so much hatred in him, along with a single-minded determination for retribution. How could I have ever suspected that all along he was learning *everything* about me? And to my astonishment, falling in love with me?

*Ludicrous!*

Our physical attraction is easy to explain. Our instincts and passion are strong. He's a powerful, virile male, and I'm a young, very curious woman. My surrender to him was inevitable that first night we were together and when he came to me in El Gran Místico's wagon. But during that time, I never had the chance to fall for him. I was too busy denying our attraction and hating him for what he did to Amira and me. And now, as our mutual attraction grows stronger and I finally begin to discover who he really is, I can't help but wonder if letting myself fall for the Fae King is a good idea. Or instead, the biggest blunder I could ever commit.

Perhaps I should stop riding with him, sever this one-horse closeness that is so delicious. Perhaps I should stop asking questions and deny him the chance to make me smile, laugh, blush, and want more and more of him.

*Gods!* What should I do?

Korben brings our mount to a stop inside the circle of a small clearing. Twilight is here. Yet, there's still enough light to see our surroundings.

Our companions arrive a minute apart from each other. Galen comes second, looking bored to the marrow of his bones. Next comes Calierin, alert and on edge. She seems to be expecting monsters to jump out from behind every tree. Her attitude makes me realize how careless I've been, more worried about Korben than searching for the danger that's sure to come our way sooner or later.

Korben jumps off the horse, then offers me a hand and helps me get down, his touch and eye contact lingering in a way that makes me smolder inside.

"We will make camp here, let the horses rest," he says. "They have had a rough trek through these gnarly woods."

"*I've* had a rough trek through these gnarly woods," Galen complains, sighing deeply. "My backside is in agony. How do you ride these beasts without magic offering a cushion?"

Calierin makes a face. "You use magic to pad your arse while you ride? Who raised you, fluttering pixies?"

"I'm a male of class!" Galen sounds offended. "Not a savage Tuathacath warrior from a backwoods village."

Calierin's fists tighten. "You are a soft, good-for-nothing milksop, who turns into a useless waste of space the moment he cannot use magic. I have lost my magic, too. Do you hear me whining?"

Galen opens his mouth to respond, but Korben steps between them, bringing their argument short. "We should reserve our energy to fight our enemies, not each other."

"Yes, my king." Calierin bows her head. Though she sends a glare in Galen's direction that promises untold suffering.

With a careless shrug, Galen begins to step aside. Korben clears his throat and raises an eyebrow.

"Um . . . yes, my king," the sorcerer replies under his breath.

Galen doesn't seem to have a deferential bone in his body, but

Korben is slowly taming his insolence. He seems to be a king who demands respect, though not without offering it back.

We make camp, efficiently and quickly. Esmeralda forages for violet-colored swiftberries after Calierin points out they're safe to eat. Jago sets traps and catches a few birds that look like chickens, except they have no wings, despite being covered in feathers.

Once roasted, I find the meat is fattier with a stronger taste than chicken meat. It's not bad, but far from my favorite.

I refill our waterskins in a nearby stream that teems with translucent fish the size of my smallest finger. They have what appear to be antennae with tiny lanterns hanging from their ends. They dart in and out of holes, skittish of the slightest movement.

"They are called twinklefish," Korben says, appearing behind me.

I stand and feel a blush heating my cheeks.

He frowns, looking amused. "What is it? Something in that mind of yours?"

"Well, yes." I pause. "Could we . . . take our shifts next to each other again?"

Leaning close, he brings his mouth close to mine and speaks. "I would not have it any other way, princess."

"I . . . want to try something."

"Oh?" He pulls back to regard me better.

I can't possibly utter the words, so instead, I glance down toward his manhood. Or should it be *malehood*? He's not a man, after all. That's a human term. He's fae.

He cocks his head to one side, appearing slightly confused. "Exactly what are you referring to?"

I push to the tips of my toes and kiss him softly, my tongue gliding over his bottom lip, then suggestively, my gaze drops low again.

His chest rumbles, his eyelids at half-mast as a wave of desire seems to wash over him. Abruptly, he snakes an arm around my waist and roughly pulls me to him. I can feel the immediate effect my words have had on him as my stomach presses against his hard and ready shaft.

"That's what one little word from you does to me." He pauses. "You know you do not have to, right?"

"I *want* to."

"Oh, fuck!" He inhales deeply, throws his head back as if imploring the heavens, then takes a step back. "I should stay away from you for now. Else I will take you right here, right now."

I shrug and bite my lower lip as if it's all the same to me.

He chuckles deep in his chest. "Do not tempt me."

His onyx gaze turns predatory. A jolt of excitement cuts through me, but it dies quickly when Galen appears from the side, removing his shirt.

"Excuse me," he says, "but I'm overdue for a bath."

When he starts removing his pants, I pick up the waterskins and walk back to the camp. Korben stays behind, admonishing the sorcerer about common decency.

Some time later, we all sit around a small fire, which is just enough to curb the chill that comes over when the sun goes down. We all look expectantly at Korben, waiting for him to explain how he plans to infiltrate Elf-Dún. He's been mulling over different possibilities. Hopefully, he has decided at least one of them is viable.

"Just like in Nido," Korben begins, looking from Jago to me, "there are secret passages that lead in and out of Elf-Dún. They are known to few. Members of the Theric family for the most part, though there are others. To be honest, I am not hopeful they will be accessible. I suspect our enemies have had them sealed. However, this would be the easiest way to get inside undetected, so it will be our first target. If that fails, there is only one other way we will make it inside, and that is through the front gate."

Galen huffs. "Then let's pray those passages are open. By the way, I made a mental note of the fact you didn't tell *me* of their existence."

"Try being a Plumanegra and not knowing about the secret passages in Nido," Jago pipes in. "No one told *me* about them." He glares at me.

"Sorry," I say. "I already apologized about that many times."

He blows air through his nose.

"You had no right to know. You are not even close to a Theric. Or are you?" Calierin asks Galen in a fake solicitous tone.

"Korben and I were the best of friends once," Galen says with a hint of regret he tries to hide.

Calierin waits for Korben to say something, and when he doesn't, she adds, "*Were* being the operative word. As Master of Magic you should not expect friendship. Your only concern should be to serve."

"Is that so?" Galen sneers. "That leads me to believe you count your friends with your fingers curled in like this." He puts a fist out and turns it in all directions, searching for digits to count. There are none.

"You think yourself clever, but you are tiresome."

Korben sighs. "You are both tiresome."

Calierin turns red from embarrassment, which comes as a shock to me. I never knew she was capable of such an emotion. But clearly, she takes her vow to her king very seriously.

"Apologies, my king," Calierin says. "I will endeavor to ignore any arising nuances."

"The front gate," I say, trying to get the conversation back on track. "What do you mean exactly? Wear a disguise? Find an ally to help us through? Fight our way in?"

Korben is quiet for several beats before he responds, "No, I mean announce my presence."

"What?!" Calierin and I exclaim in unison.

I frown at the sorceress, feeling awkward that we share the same concern.

"Korben, are you sure that's a good idea?" I ask. "Are you hoping there are people in Elf-Dún who will recognize you and are still loyal to you? Because I wouldn't count on that."

He shakes his head. "I am not. In fact, I expect she has surrounded herself solely with traitors to the crown. I would expect nothing less from that harpy."

"So what then?" I demand, not liking this plan at all. "You give her exactly what she wants? You surrender?"

"Yes and no. I give her what she wants, but I don't surrender."

Calierin pushes to the edge of the rock she's using as a seat and hones in all her attention on Korben. "I look forward to hearing the entirety of your plan, my king."

They exchange a glance, giving me a glimpse of how things went as the veilfallen planned attacks in Castellina.

Korben leans in closer too and explains what he has in mind. My stomach drops. I don't like it at all.

This time, I take the first shift. The entire time I feel distracted, imagining undoing his pants and putting him in my mouth. Why is that such a tempting idea? And why has it invaded my mind?

*Tonight, I'm going to find out why.*

I fidget until it's time to awaken Korben. When my shift is finally over, I jump up and pad to where he lies next to a tree away from the others. I watch him for a moment, my gaze roving down the length of his body. He rests on his back, right arm folded, hand under his head. His huge biceps bulges under this shirt, and his firm chest moves gently.

*Gods! He's so handsome.*

Everything about him is chiseled perfection, especially that strong jaw. Suddenly, his lips stretch in a cocky grin.

"Like what you see, princess?" he asks in a whisper.

"How conceited are you, king?" I straddle him, my legs settling snuggly around his hips. "I believe you need to be taught a lesson."

One of his dark eyebrows goes up. "Should I be afraid?"

"Very."

Propping my hands on either side of his head, I lower my mouth close to his, without kissing him. My hair falls like a curtain around us.

"You're not allowed to move," I say. "If you do, I will leave."

"Leave? After you have," he thrusts his hips, pressing his length to my core, "teased me so."

"Precisely."

"You are cruel, woman."

"You're about to find out just how cruel."

My tongue flicks over his lips, tasting him. He moans and starts to rear up.

I shake a finger at him. "Nah-ah. No moving allowed. This is your first and only warning. Understood?"

He nods, swallowing thickly.

I begin kissing the length of his perfect jaw, stopping to tease his earlobe and whisper something I think will drive him crazy.

"I've been thinking about this all night, king, and my undergarments are wet from imagining your cock in my mouth."

He groans, jaw clenching. "Those are dirty words for a little princess."

"So why do you like them?"

"Why, indeed?"

My mouth makes its way down the column of his neck, licking and sucking. I want to take his shirt off, but I content myself with pulling it up as high as it will go to reveal his glorious torso. I plant kisses on his pecs and the ridges of his abdomen, savoring his taste.

At the waistband, I stop to tease the trail of dark hairs that travels from his navel and disappears under the intrusive fabric.

Wiggling my hips, I move farther down, getting my face parallel to the impressive bulge tenting his pants. The string that serves as a tie strains precariously.

"Careful or you might ruin your pants, Your Majesty." I smirk as

I lower my mouth to his covered length and pretend to take a bite, my gaze locked with Korben's. His eyes close, and a little moan escapes him.

I pull at the string with my teeth, undoing it slowly. I want to rip it off all at once, but I promised to teach him a lesson. His hands squeeze handfuls of his sleeping mat. He's not supposed to move at all, but I guess I can forgive this lapse.

When the string is, at last, undone, I pull the closure wide open. His shaft breaks free, and I gasp. I've never taken a close look like this. It's splendid, thick and with a large head. Veins travel the underside, flush and throbbing, begging to be licked. A bead of moisture sits at the slit at the top. I lick my lips and make eye contact. He bites his lower lip and stares at me accusingly.

"After the way you tortured me last night, the least I can do is repay the favor." As I speak, I let my breath caress his length.

He purrs deep inside his chest.

I lap at the clear bead at the head. "Hmm."

Korben shudders.

Warm wetness flowing between my legs, I lick around the head of his shaft, making him hiss. Opening wider, I wrap my mouth around the tip and suck. Korben seems to melt into the ground.

*Oh, gods!* I want to take off my clothes and take him in, but I also want to keep doing this. It's intoxicating. Moving up and down, I suck and lick his considerable girth.

A delicious ache starts in my jaw as I attempt to take him all the way in, but it's a daunting task. He's too big. Yet, I do all I can, putting my best effort forward. Teasing, I take him out for a brief moment to lick the bulging veins, following the paths they cut along his length. Quickly, I bestow my attention to his tip, taking him into my mouth, then wrapping a hand around the base. In awe, I wonder at the way he feels . . . like steel wrapped in the most delicate material. My hands glide freely up and down while I suck eagerly at the tip.

Korben growls, body trembling. Unable to help himself, he begins to move back and forth, fucking my mouth. He broke the rules. I'm supposed to leave, but I can't. I'm enraptured by the task, enjoying the waves of desire rolling off me, and the way I've dismantled this male, making him utterly mine.

Moving my hand down, I explore another part of him, his sizable testicles. Surprising myself, I moan, a pang of pleasure electrifying my core. *Gods! This is exhilarating.*

My hands move faster as I keep sucking. Korben tenses further, just as I fear my jaw will unhinge. Then his body quakes, and I taste him hungrily, savoring his shuddering helplessness.

*You're mine. So mine!*

# 25

## VALERIA

*"Stop complaining and use the bellows. Magic may never come back, so you had better strengthen those spindly arms."*

**Qilan Rava – Fae Blacksmith – 2 AV**

Many times, I tried to imagine how Tirnanog would be different from Castella. I assembled all the stories Mother told me along with all the texts I read in Nido's libraries and set my imagination to work.

But now that I'm here, I know I fell short.

There is a vibrant undercurrent of colors, sounds, and smells that is unlike anything found in Castella. There are animals—mammals, fish, insects—such as I have never seen, not to mention pixies, hobs, and other creatures I've not yet encountered. Plants glow and move, the night sky shivers with a multitude of colors, and the moon hangs so close I feel I can almost touch it.

Magic seems to thrum underground, like a never-ending tiny earthquake, though Korben says it's much weaker than it used to be, which seems to worry him as well as all the other things that are wrong in the realm.

Once more, as we approach Riochtach from the east, I'm made aware of the utter deficiency of my imagination. Mother never talked about the fae capital. She never even mentioned visiting it. She only told me stories of her hometown, Nilhalari. I thought she never visited the capital, so I took it upon myself to read as much as I could about Castellina's counterpart across the veil. I thought I'd created a good mental image of what Riochtach must look like, but *saints and feathers*, was I wrong.

The city that spreads before me, glinting like a jewel in the valley below, is nothing short of majestic.

My breath hitches in my throat as we finish cresting the hill, dismount, and the capital's full splendor is revealed. The city sprawls far and wide, and I can't determine where it ends or where it begins. Buildings, impossibly tall and slender, rise from the ground like crystallized dreams. Their walls shimmer with inner light, pulsing with hues of amethyst, rose quartz, and emerald, offering me a glimpse of what the Realta Observatory must have looked like before it came crumbling down the day the veil collapsed.

Some of the structures twist skyward, their balconies adorned with torrents of multicolor flowers. One is shaped like a giant butterfly, wings outstretched in frozen flight. Another one resembles a blossoming lily, its petals forming a roof with stamen-shaped towers protruding from the center.

A wide river snakes through the city's heart, its water teeming with bioluminescent life. It branches into a network of canals that weave in and out, blending seamlessly with the buildings and the abundant trees. Greenery climbs over every structure and completely carpets the ground. The only exception is the cobble paths, which appear to be paved in distinct patterns and colors.

Dominating the cityscape is Elf-Dún, the fae palace. Unlike the other structures, Elf-Dún has no walls of stone or crystal. Instead, it rises from the ground in an imposing fortress of vines, their branches forming a series of interconnected towers that spiral upward and glow with emerald threads of protective espiritu. Within the walls, at the center, more vines intertwine to form a tower shaped like a crown, the highest point of the structure. It's difficult to see all the details from this distance, but I'm certain the edifice will be spellbinding when we get closer.

I tear my eyes from the sight to look at Korben.

My heart stutters, caught unawares by his striking figure . . . the sunlight painting his face a pale gold, his onyx hair shining, and his dark eyes full of emotion.

He hasn't set foot in Riochtach in twenty years, not since his wedding night and the most awful betrayal from the female he loved. As I watch him, worry lines form around his eyes and a deep crease appears between his brows. There's a weariness in his posture, a slump to his broad shoulders. I thought he would rejoice to see his home again, but being here seems to pain him.

There's something else, too. Regret? Longing? Whatever it is, I feel it in the air around him. Riochtach must be a bittersweet sight to him. Returning should have guaranteed him a warm welcome, yet he traveled here like a thief in the night, afraid of spies and persecution.

Sensing the mix of emotions raging through him, I think I understand. This city, this vibrant tapestry of espiritu and life, is his heart.

He missed it desperately. His absence haunted him for years. Did everyone here feel it as deeply? A pang of sympathy shoots through me. Whatever wrongs he may have committed, his love for his people is undeniable.

"*Kham!*" Esmeralda curses, her green eyes dancing over the capital, nearly popping out of their sockets. "Now I've seen it all. I'd say this was worth every bump in the road."

"It sure was," Jago says, standing behind her.

Galen and Calierin say nothing. They only peer down at the city, almost as affected as Korben. Cuervo flies overhead, looking quite at home in Tirnanog's sky—not surprising since this is also his homeland.

I intertwine my fingers with Korben's, offering what little support I can. I wish I could ease this homecoming for him, but I'm afraid the unresolved emotions he still carries are something he will have to face on his own. He squeezes my hand back and smiles tenderly. When I see him like this, vulnerable, I ask myself how he can be the same male I first met. And how that awful woman could have hurt him so.

Esmeralda scratches her head. "This may be a stupid question, but if espiritu is wonky in the realm, how come none of those buildings have collapsed."

"Gods! I didn't think of that," I exclaim. "Why, indeed?"

I glance between Korben and Galen, but they only shake their heads in confusion.

"What is happening here?" Korben grumbles.

Calierin breaks the prolonged silence. "What is the safest route to get down there?"

"There's a path further south that is less traveled," Korben answers. "It leads to the more residential parts of the city, away from commerce and official buildings. It will take us farther away from Elf-Dún, but we will encounter far fewer people."

"Do we head there now? Or do we wait until tomorrow?" Calierin asks.

"We should go now. We will search for an inn or two where to settle—we should not all shelter in the same place. When night falls, we will inspect the palace."

We mount our horses again and make our way south. We find the path without trouble, and though we run into a few people who give us assessing glances, they cause us no trouble. Unaware of how humans have fared stranded here during the past two decades, Jago, Esmeralda, and I pull our cloaks over our heads to hide our ears. If the people we pass notice anything odd about our group, they don't show it.

Once we get closer, Calierin travels ahead, finds four different inns, and pays for four rooms. She returns with keys and directions to each place, which we decide to approach separately.

From up close, the city is as magnificent as from above, if not more. All the greenery resolves into individual plants, some resembling giant ferns, their fronds pulsing with a soft, rhythmic light. Others are bushes with leaves of irregular sizes and shapes, no leaf the same in any one bush, while other plants bloom luminously and fragrantly, tickling my senses with a combination of sweet nectar and something strangely sharp that makes my nose sting a little.

All over, roots of ancient trees intertwine, creating steps, benches, and tables. Strange creatures flit between the buildings, and I swear I see a band of cats with shimmering fur and pixie-like wings fly above us. Riochtach is a city of wonder, a place where nature and architecture coexist in breathtaking harmony. It makes Castellina feel drab and savage in comparison.

The cobble paths have names such as Butterfly Lane, Acorn Track, Dragonscale Way and such, and the patterns I saw from above suddenly make sense. The cobbles are of different shades of gray and arranged in repeating figures that are suggestive of their namesakes. Stones of the right shade and shape are placed strategically to form the wings of butterflies or the scales of dragons. The artistry is breathtaking, and something tells me espiritu wasn't used to create the designs. This is all craft.

"One would have to be an idiot to get lost in Riochtach, eh cousin?" Jago jabs my side before we go our separate ways. "What with the paths' names practically spelled out on the cobbles."

"No one will believe me when I tell them," Esmeralda says, stopping her horse to admire the design of a coiled snake on Slither Road.

Calierin and Galen lead our mounts to two separate stables several paths over, hoping to confuse anyone trying to locate a group of six riders.

Before we head to our inn, I give Cuervo clear instructions to follow us. I lead the way on foot, walking on Moon Street, which displays designs of all the moon phases. A hush falls over me as I approach the inn. It isn't a building at all, but a massive willow tree, its ancient trunk hollowed out. Moss crawls up the bark of the intricately carved wooden entrance.

With a deep breath, I push the door open. The sound echoes softly in the stillness. Inside, the air smells of earth after a heavy rain. The hollowed-out trunk has been transformed into a cozy haven. Walls, polished smooth by time, curve with the natural shape of the tree. Floorboards, seemingly woven from living roots, creak slightly beneath my boots. The ceiling, high above, is a breathtaking expanse of sky speckled with leaves and stars.

*But what if it rains?*

I presume espiritu would keep the water out. Or perhaps, the sky is only an illusion. Soft lights, nestled in nooks and crannies, cast a warm glow. The relaxing sound of trickling water revolves all around me, though I can't find the source.

My gaze drifts to the far end where a massive branch, thick enough to be a table, stretches out. Its surface is smooth and adorned with flower petals pressed into the wood. Around it, smaller branches, each a comfortable size, have been carved into stools, their bark intricately etched with designs that seem to move in the dim light.

My mouth hangs open. I don't know if it's the ingenuity of the construction or the otherworldly beauty, but I feel as if the place is not only alive but sentient.

A portly female greets me by bowing and pressing her hands together as if in prayer. "Welcome to Willow's Bend, weary traveler. May I take your cloak?"

I try not to stare at her overly large ears. They are pointed as is to be expected, but they stick out and prolong three times more than what I'm used to.

"Uh, I am all right. Thank you for your hospitality." I speak formally, making no use of contractions as we normally do in Castella. "I have a room already." I show her the key.

Korben walks in then, greeting the female the same way she greeted me. "Good evening to you."

"Um, *we* have a room already," I say, suddenly needing an explanation since I'll be sharing said room with Korben. "Me and . . . my husband."

There is a slight glint in Korben's eye, but he falls smoothly into the lie. He moves closer and places an arm around my waist. "Ah, yes. We sent a friend ahead to secure a room. We are so very weary and in need of food and rest."

"You can call me Branwen." The innkeeper presses her hands together and bows again. "I am at your service if you need anything."

"Could we have a hearty supper delivered to our room?" Korben asks.

"Certainly. Anything in particular?"

"I leave it to your discretion, Branwen." Korben bows again.

I stare at the interaction, dumbfounded. I thought things in Nido and its court were formal. If this is everyday interaction here, I'd hate to see how things are inside the fae palace when conducting official business. I may need to polish my maestros' manners lessons.

We find our room without trouble on the second floor.

Pushing open the intricately carved door, I'm met with a fantastic bedroom. In fact, the room isn't quite a room but more of a whimsical cocoon, woven from the living willow. Walls—formed by the smooth, pale interior of the trunk—curve gently, their surface dappled with soft light emanating from the moss-covered ceiling. The wooden floorboards are surprisingly springy underfoot and feel like walking on clouds.

My gaze drifts to the back wall and a mesmerizing mosaic of

translucent leaves that appear as if they've captured sunlight within them. To complete the space, a massive, hollowed-out branch serves as a plush bed, its surface appearing as inviting as fluffy cotton. Smaller branches act as tables, holding glowing grass-like tendrils that serve as lamps.

"Wow," I whisper.

Korben, pensive by the door, shakes his head and moves closer. "Uh, do you like it?" The question seems like an afterthought; more important things are on his mind.

"Yes," I answer. "It's lovely."

"My bedchamber in Elf-Dún is adorned more simply, but when I am back in charge, I will make sure it is exactly to your taste."

I blink up at him in surprise. Did he just say that? He seems to realize his blunder. Distracted as he is, it seems he didn't notice exactly what he was saying.

"I am sorry," he hurries to add. "That is quite presumptuous of me." An awkward smile stretches his lips as he walks toward a corner of the room and turns his back on me.

I feel it's something we must talk about, but right now it's entirely the wrong time for such a conversation. We cannot get ahead of ourselves. The priority is to get him back on the throne, so we can return to Castella and undo this awful thing my sister has done.

We are saved from the awkwardness by a knock at the door. For a moment, I tense up, realizing someone hostile could be on the other side. But when Branwen announces she has our meals, I relax. Only to grow tense again when I realize that it's too soon for anyone to have put our food together.

"I will open." Korben hurries to stand between me and the door.

He peeps through a small hole carved in the middle of the door right at his height. There are others set at lower heights, while others are even higher. At first, I'm confused about what he's doing, then I realize the hole allows him to see who's outside. A clever idea, but can't others look in on us? Odd.

Once he's satisfied with our visitor, he opens the door. Indeed, Branwen is here, carrying a large tray topped with several covered dishes.

"I hope the food is to your liking," she says, then quickly retreats, walking backward in short steps, head bowed. Before she exits, however, she gives Korben a strange look.

He closes the door, and we exchange a glance.

"What was that about?" I ask.

Korben frowns and walks to the tray. Uncovering the food, he looks at it closely, then smells it.

*Oh, gods!* Does he suspect poison? Did his enemies already find us?

He narrows his eyes at the food, then says, "She knows you are human."

"What?! Why do you say that?"

I approach and look at what the innkeeper brought. There are two large plates and four small ones. One of the large ones contains a fragrant meat stew with what appear to be star-shaped mushrooms. They swim in the creamy sauce, dotted with green garnish and red and yellow flowers. The second large plate contains something completely different, though ten times more delicious-looking than the first one: a lovely lamb chop over a bed of rice seasoned with saffron and vegetables. The smaller plates also contain different offerings. Two look foreign, and two look familiar—things I would eat at home.

"I see what you mean," I say. "Is this a good thing? Or a bad thing?"

"I lean toward the former. I am rather encouraged by this."

"How come?"

"It indicates humans have found a place in Tirnanog."

When I appear confused at his assessment, he goes on, "If recipes from your realm can be found at an inn such as this, I am inclined to believe their patronage is welcome. Establishments such as this would not waste their time learning to cook food for people they don't wish to entice."

He speaks the truth. No one ever bothered to learn how to cook fae food in Castella—not that many of the ingredients are available, as our vegetation and wildlife are so different, but still. This realization embarrasses me, revealing the stark possibility that my kin possess less exalted sensibilities, an inability to embrace others and a preference for hate.

"Eat," Korben says. "It looks and smells rather good, don't you think?"

"Is it . . . safe?"

He nods, tapping his nose. "I am trained in detecting all deadly poisons as well as any who might just cause you to . . . run for the privy."

I snicker like a child.

He winks and walks to the door.

"Where are you going?"

"To talk to Branwen. She may enlighten me a little. That look she gave me before she left . . . it has made me curious. I believe we are safe here, but lock the door while I am gone."

I bite the inside of my cheek, not quite comfortable with being left alone. What if the floorboards spring to life and suck me underground? This inn is *too* alive.

"I will return promptly. I promise. You may also enjoy a bath." He points toward a door in the back.

Now, a bath sounds like the best thing in all the realms.

I smile. "Fine, but hurry up."

## KORBEN

Back in the waiting area by the entrance, Branwen sits with a large ledger on her lap. She looks up as soon as she senses me and welcomes me with a smile.

"Thank you for the wonderful meal," I say, joining my hands and bowing.

She sets the book aside on one of the low tables. Standing, she returns my bow.

Many questions brim inside my mind, but it is hard to know which one to ask first. It seems I must lie in order not to give away our ignorance of . . . well, everything.

"I have been away from Riochtach for some time," I say. "What news would you share with me that may be helpful during my stay here?"

"The weather has been nice," she replies. "Some heavy rains, but no more than is to be expected this time of the year. A delegation from Caernamara arrived a few days ago. Taverns and inns in the city center are bustling. Not so much here. There's a bit of tension between the bakers' guild and the millers' guild. Seems there is a disagreement over the price of flour. Hopefully, they will settle it soon."

I do not know what to say or what I was expecting, but this is not helpful.

She seems to notice something in my expression because she asks, "When you say *away for some time*, how long do you mean exactly?"

I consider her astute question for a moment, then decide on a number of years greater than the fall of the veil. "Nearly twenty-five years."

"Dear Achnamhair, you should have started with that. What has *not* changed since then?" She taps her chin thoughtfully. "King Korben was murdered by humans the same day the veil separated us from their realm. But I am sure you know all about that." She raises her eyebrows, seeming to ask whether this information is too commonplace.

"It is fine. Go on." I put on a nonchalant air to indicate I do not mind a reminder. She seems the kind who likes to talk, and she started right where it matters most to me, so she is more than welcome to continue.

"Queen Saethara was left a widow also on that same day, her very own wedding night. They did not find the king's body, so the poor dear had no one to bury. She has been our ruler since, which brought about some changes as is to be expected. She was not raised to be a ruler. She grew up in a small village. King Korben selected her during his Mate Rite, so she is doing her best. I am sure. There are many who are willing to help, as you might expect. Some better than others." She bobs her head from side to side, then shrugs. "Too much has happened in that time. More than ever happened in my first hundred and ten, I would say."

She is careful with her words, but I sense an undercurrent of disapproval and skepticism in everything she shared. The fact that she is not willing to openly discuss the state of things makes me wonder if she fears repercussions.

I am cautious with my next question, hoping not to discourage her. I wish to ask her what people think of *Queen Saethara*. Do they like her? That is too subjective, however, so I try to stick to questions for which she can offer factual answers.

"A new ruler certainly means changes," I say. "Have there been many?"

"That would be an understatement." She does not elaborate.

"For the better?" This question can also lead to subjective opinions, but I am eager to learn all I can. Unfortunately, Branwen does not look as willing to talk as she did at first.

She purses her lips, as if trying to repress her next words. In the end, she loses the battle and blurts out, "Who are you?"

"My name is Ríffor Vothinal," I say. "I just married that lovely human girl, and I thought to show her our magnificent capital. She had never visited."

Branwen huffs, looking as if she does not believe a word I have said.

"It is not smart to speak ill of the queen," she offers. "I will tell you that much. Be careful who and what you ask. You never know who might take offense. Understand?"

"I do. Thank you for the warning. Anything else you would like to share with me?"

"Not unless you have a question about a gift for your pretty lady. Or any such matters. I thought that was what you needed."

I can tell she is done with me, so I pull out a coin from my pouch and offer it to her. It is Castellan currency. Regardless, she takes it with a gracious bow.

I walk back, my worries heightened by her covert answers. It is clear she has lost her liberty to speak her mind. Instead, what should be her indisputable right has been replaced by fear.

# 26

## VALERIA

*"This is not peace. This is fear mongering. We have lost our freedom."*

*Lantan Ratiner – Pleasure Guild – 10 AV*

Korben doesn't sleep. Instead, he sits by the window, staring into the darkness through a crack in the shutters, cocking his head to better listen to sounds that don't exist.

Worry sets in the line of his jaw and the spot right between his eyebrows, giving him an angry look. I peer at him from the bed, lying on my side, hands between my face and the pillow. My eyelids are heavy, and I drift in and out of sleep, always coming to Korben sitting in the same position, wearing the same expression.

When it's time to leave, he wakes me with a gentle touch on my arm. He doesn't speak a word. He only nods, and I quickly don my clothes, strap on my rapier, and follow him out of the bedchamber.

Silently, we make it to the front door. The mushroom lights in the corners shine dimly, a subdued glow more appropriate for the early hour. We are to meet the others an hour after midnight, in a spot we passed on our way here.

Korben is about to open the front door when Branwen comes into view behind the counter, looking as if she materialized from thin air. His hand flies to the hilt of La Matadora at his back. The innkeeper shakes her head as if to say, "*Not necessary. I'm not a threat.*"

"You'd best leave through the back door," she says, hooking a thumb over her shoulder.

Korben and I exchange a worried glance.

The innkeeper smiles. "I have a feeling you are not who you say you are. I also have a feeling you are here for reasons I approve of. You can trust me."

Her movements are calm as she picks up one of the mushroom lights and guides the way. Past the threshold, she glances back as we stand there, unmoving. Her dim light illuminates a narrow passage, no other doors in sight where someone could be hiding, waiting to ambush us.

Korben nods once and goes after her. He moves like a predator, crouching slightly, ready for anything. A couple of minutes later, we make it to the back exit. She opens the door and steps aside.

"You are welcome back anytime," the innkeeper says. "As long as you don't bring trouble with you."

"Thank you, Branwen." Korben bows once and exits the building with care, making sure no one is in the alley outside.

When the innkeeper closes the door behind us, I breathe a sigh of relief. The narrow alley where we stand is deserted, not a soul in sight except for Cuervo, who appears as soon as he hears us.

Like a cat prowling the night, Korben finds shadowed paths that keep us hidden from streetlights and potential prying eyes. The lithe way he moves leaves me in awe. I try to imitate him, stepping where he steps, walking as if I weigh no more than a feather. I'm surprised by how right it feels to move this way. I truly feel more agile, more . . . fae. I wonder if it's due to the espiritu that permeates Tirnanog. Or perhaps The Eldrystone.

Half an hour later, we arrive at the prescribed location. It's a large tree in the middle of a wooded area, no buildings around. We both hold our breaths for the couple of minutes it takes the others to arrive. I'm relieved to see Jago, walking hand in hand with Esmeralda. I'm also glad to see Calierin hasn't killed Galen.

"Everyone all right?" Jago asks.

I welcome him with a hug and nod. "You?"

"Heard a few interesting things at a tavern," he replies.

"Tavern? You went to a tavern? You were supposed to stay out of sight." I want to slap him. Why is he always so brazen?

"Calm down, cousin. We shouldn't have worried about rounded ears. There is no ill will toward humans. They like us because we work hard and don't complain about having no espiritu anymore, like many fae workers do."

Korben doesn't seem pleased about Jago's behavior, but he chooses to focus on the *interesting things* instead. Perhaps because he could not get much out of our innkeeper.

"What did you hear?" Korben asks.

"People seem unhappy with Saethara," Jago says. "They are careful when they talk about her, going in a roundabout way to complain. They hate the curfew. Everyone left the tavern grumbling when 10:00 PM came around."

"Curfew," Korben echoes. "That explains why we didn't see anyone on our way here."

Jago goes on. "There was another human there. I asked him a few questions. He acted as if I'd been hiding under a rock and refused to answer even after I paid for his feyglen. By the way, what do you put in that stuff? Two sips, and I started feeling drunk."

Calierin wipes her mouth with the back of her hand as if the simple mention of fae wine has made her thirsty.

"Anything else?" Korben asks.

Jago shakes his head with a sigh. This isn't much more than what we learned from Branwen.

"And you?" He turns to Calierin and Galen.

"Much of the same," Calierin replies with a shrug.

"It was much the same for me. Except . . ." Galen pauses and seems to think for a moment.

"Except what?"

"Something I found strange. Ever since I left Tirnanog, questions about the war in my land have plagued me. I wanted to know about it, so it was the first thing I asked my server at the tavern where I found supper. The male, he was young, knew nothing about it, but he asked the owner and came back with an answer. He said the war ended twenty years ago, said after everyone lost their magic, the troops retreated to work out how to continue the fight without one of their main weapons. And after that, the fighting never resumed."

Korben frowns, his dark eyes dancing over the ground as he considers.

"I would think that's . . . a good thing," Jago says dubiously.

"A good thing," Korben replies, "but strange, indeed. We tried long and hard to end that war. Every effort, every plea for peace, every treaty, failed."

"I don't believe the loss of magic alone would have stopped Qfaren and Eamon," Galen says. "They both fiercely wanted revenge. Something else must have prompted them to stop. After I finished my supper, I asked to talk to the owner. He seemed unsettled by my lack of knowledge on the matter. I told him I'd been away at sea, and he reluctantly elaborated. He said it was the same everywhere, that as soon as Queen Saethara sat on the throne all skirmishes everywhere stopped. He said Her Majesty had brought peace to the realm, and even Morwen the Mistwraith hasn't been heard from in over twenty years. He was careful to frame his words in a positive light, but I could tell he didn't seem convinced Saethara had anything to do with any of it. That or, despite the peace, he doesn't approve of her for some reason."

"Who is Morwen the Mistwraith?" Jago asks.

Korben explains. "Someone who caused a lot of problems for a long time. She seemed to come out of nowhere to stoke old rivalries between neighbors. She caused accidents, terrorized villages, stole food, burnt crops, and more. I had the entire army looking for her, but she eluded us with ease. She was responsible for starting a war in Caernamara, Galen's homeland."

"Do you think this person might somehow work for Saethara?" I ask.

"Or the other way around," Galen says. "It's clear Saethara's not working alone. We know Lirion Faolborn is helping her. Morwen the Mistwraith could be another one of her allies."

Korben seems unsure. "Morwen started causing trouble in the realm some fifty years ago."

"Someone would have to be playing a very long game," Jago suggests.

"Exactly," Korben says. "Saethara is young. Barely twenty-three years old when we married. If Morwen is involved, then Saethara would be nothing more than a pawn in Morwen's scheme."

Galen rubs his chin. "Not a far-fetched concept."

Korben grunts in agreement, then says, "Let us get started. We will not find out more by standing here. Jago and Galen, stay with Esmeralda and protect her."

"What?!" Esmeralda protests. "I thought I was going with you."

"That was before we found out about the curfew. It would be safer if you stay here."

"But what if we have to go with plan B?" Jago asks. "How will we be able to help if we don't become familiar with the area around the palace?" He doesn't like the idea of staying either. Only Galen looks pleased about the decision.

"We can take care of that tomorrow," Korben says in that commanding tone that brooks no argument.

I have a feeling he would leave me here too if he could, but I'm integral to his plan to get into Elf-Dún, so he has no other alternative but to take me with him. As for Calierin, she's a fiend in a fight, even without her espiritu. He's not worried about her. Cuervo comes along as I gesture for him to follow. He needs to become familiar with the palace as well as he's part of our backup plan.

Korben unstraps La Matadora from his back. "You take this, Valeria. I do not wish to appear like a threat." I strap it to my waist, giving my rapier to Jago for safekeeping.

We leave the same way we came, hiding under shadows and stepping as lightly as floating feathers. Silence hangs eerily over the cobble paths, seeming unnatural even to me. I have the feeling Riochtach was vibrant and alive at all hours of the day before Saethara stole the throne.

My gaze roves around, trying to catch a glimpse of Elf-Dún at every turn, but since we're sticking closely to the buildings and their shadows, it's impossible. It isn't until we reach a row of taverns that I first set my eyes on the fae palace's outer walls. I stare, jaw falling open.

Vines intertwine, forming an impenetrable barrier. They glow with emerald espiritu all the way to the towers on top. Past the walls, in the middle of the compound, the spire with the crown as its pinnacle takes center stage. It's a massive structure with curved branches intricately braided to form a sturdy frame. A balcony surrounds its base, flowers growing in crevices to mimic encrusted jewels. Vibrant strands of ivy twine all over, their leaves contrasting beautifully with the rich brown of the wood. The crown stands proudly, a mighty symbol of the monarchs who have ruled Riochtach for millennia.

"This is the east side of Elf-Dún," Korben whispers, snapping me back into the moment. "You two, stay here."

I grab his hand and hold him in place, my pleading gaze meeting his dark eyes. *Please, be careful!*

"I will be all right, Ravógín."

Calierin looks worried, too. When we discussed the plan earlier, she offered to check the secret entrances herself, but Korben explained it must be him since their espiritu would only respond to him.

"I . . ." I don't know what I'm trying to say.

He caresses my cheek with the back of his hand, smiles, then ducks into the shadows that lead to the palace. Calierin and I peer into the darkness, following his progress. Eventually, he disappears from view, and we retreat, pressing our backs to the building behind us. I put my restless hands against it and focus on the wall's rugged texture.

I become aware that the building isn't made of stone, brick, or even wooden planks. Instead, it is a live tree with rough bark and interwoven branches, heavy leaves acting as a roof. I glance up to the canopy above, trying to distract myself from the fact that Korben is in danger and Calierin is standing right next to me. I can do nothing more than tolerate her presence, and I have no doubt it's the same for her.

A thought enters my mind. I frown. When Korben disappeared into the darkness, Calierin and I both pulled back in unison, as if we stopped seeing his progress at the same time. Is that possible? Has my eyesight improved in Tirnanog? The Eldrystone helped me improve my speed when I fought Calierin, but it never improved my senses. Curious.

"I would do it again," Calierin says, her quiet voice making me jump.

I have no idea what she's talking about, so I say nothing. I don't look at her. I don't feel I owe her even that much.

Instead of taking my silence as a lack of invitation—I want only what is absolutely necessary to pass between us—she takes it upon herself to clarify what she meant.

"I would torture you again."

"Saints and feathers! You're such a conversationalist. Has anyone ever told you that?"

I quickly push away the memories her words bring to the surface.

What *Rífíor* and Calierin did to me in those catacombs almost destroyed me. The nightmares while I slept and the festering memories while I was awake nearly drove me mad, keeping me locked in my bedchamber with a pillow over my head as I decidedly wished to spend the rest of my life sleeping. Only Jago's help and insistence pulled me out of my stupor.

Now, there is nothing else I can do but keep those memories buried as deeply as possible. If I don't, I fear I will grow bitter toward Korben.

"The Eldrystone belongs to the Fae King, not to a *human*," Calierin adds, sending another unsettling jolt into the cemetery of my mind, that place where I bury all the things I would rather forget, except nothing ever seems to remain where I put it, like the broken image of my father's body after I failed to save him with the amulet in question.

"*Human* is an excellent term for me," I say. "I don't mind it at all. If I were you, however, I would think of me as *half-fae*, instead. It might help you deal with the fact that *I* wear the amulet. Though," I add thoughtfully, "I doubt it will help since it seems Tuathacath warriors are trained to be obstinate."

She inhales deeply, and I swear I can hear her fingers as they fold into tight fists. Interesting! Has my hearing also improved?

"You have no right," she growls between clenched teeth.

"I have all the right. He *gave* it to me."

"Only because you are a hopeless shifter."

I force air through my nose, trying to act amused. "You know well he gave it to me while we were still in Castella, but go ahead and tell yourself whatever you want, if that makes you happy."

Putting on a crooked smile, I glance at her sidelong, touching the pouch at my belt.

"Would you still like it for yourself?" I ask, even though I know it's a bad idea to taunt her.

She nearly strangled me before, trying to steal it. I wonder if she still wants to take it, if she would tell herself it's for Korben's sake. Or if she would simply put it around *her* neck, forgetting the oath to her Fae King.

A cry in the night interrupts our *lovely* conversation. Immediately, we're both on high alert, weapons in hand. We come away from the building, crouching, peering into the darkness. My heart slams into my rib cage, a thrill of panic coursing through my body.

Before we even know what's happening, Calierin takes off into the darkness.

"*Wait!*" I hiss.

She doesn't listen and goes after Korben, moving fast.

*Damn Tuathacath warrior!* Act first, ask questions later. I realize I used to be that way, but all I've been through since Father died seems to have taught me a little restraint.

Reaching for the pouch, I clasp my hand around it, sensing the shape of The Eldrystone beneath. I now know why its espiritu is so erratic. Niamhara is weak, needing to save her energy for when it matters most. Is this one of those moments? I feel no heat spreading through my body. No help is to come from her tonight. I hope she still has more to give us, however. Otherwise, I fear we'll never reach her. Maybe I should start praying to the saints to keep her alive.

Sweat makes my hold of La Matadora slippery. I want to run after Korben too, but he warned me several times that he could take care of himself, and that my job was to take care of The Eldrystone. If they capture me wearing the amulet . . .

I shake my head, feeling stupid. I don't have to stand here doing nothing. I can look for Korben. *Saints!* I long for the day the knowledge of my shifting powers becomes second nature. As of now, I'm still surprised every time I remember I can transform into a raven.

Sheathing my weapon, I take Esmeralda's handkerchief out of my pocket and unwrap the amulet. The transformation is smooth and instantaneous.

Fear for Korben spurs me forward, and after one thoughtless leap into the air, I'm flying, wings beating frantically, taking me higher and higher until I soar above Elf-Dún's perimeter. I'm careful to stay away from its walls, remembering Korben's words of caution. There's an invisible dome made of espiritu hanging over the palace. It will kill me if I touch it. Cuervo joins me, flying by my side, his presence a relief. On our way into the city, we practiced what he needs to do a couple of times. I hope he remembers.

My new keen eyes pierce the darkness outside the massive vines that form the wall. Up close, I realize they are thicker than I had imagined, and the way they intertwine—leaving absolutely no gaps and forming a barrier as thick as three of Nido's outer walls—makes me think the place must be impenetrable.

The cries resolve into words, which come from the west side of Elf-Dún. They warn that an intruder has been sighted. I bank in that direction, flapping my wings as fast as I can. Korben was supposed to scan the entire perimeter of the palace, and he seems to have made it halfway through before he was spotted.

Head down, eyes roving over the plant-strewn terrain, I search for him. Calierin took off in the wrong direction, so I don't expect to see her. What I do see are archers atop the walls, standing on parapets made of living branches. They shoot arrows, aiming downward, the projectiles flying one after the other.

*Oh, gods!*

My heart beats impossibly faster than before.

*If they're still shooting, it means he's still alive and moving*, I tell myself.

I continue searching for Korben, but he's nowhere to be seen. Instead, my attention is drawn to a section of the wall cracking open, thick vines bending impossibly to allow a host of brown-clad guards to flood out. There are three groups. One that carries bows and arrows, another one holding spears, and the last one brandishing swords.

*Shit!*

What now? How is Korben going to get away from all those flying arrows and the many guards quickly spreading in every direction, searching for a target to annihilate? Gods! Because clearly, he didn't manage to sneak into Elf-Dún through one of its espiritu-infused secret entrances—not if they're looking for him out here. What can I do from up here besides endanger our entire plan?

I rush toward the area where the archers seem to be concentrating. That is his most likely location. When I get there, I circle several times until I finally spot him, running away from the wall, zigzagging between falling arrows as if he knows exactly where they're going to land. They embed themselves in the ground, *thwacking*, miraculously missing their target.

"Over here," the guards shout from above, directing their comrades outside the wall.

Korben runs at a prodigious speed, arrows hitting the ground all around him. I stare in awe at the way he moves, his arms and legs pumping, his entire body dashing with the speed and grace of a feline. It seems his already amazing agility is even greater here than it ever was in Castella.

For a moment, I think he'll get away. He'll reach the adjacent ring of buildings and will disappear into the city before anyone can catch a glimpse of him.

However, that hope dies as a large figure pulls away from the group of chasing guards and runs at full pelt in Korben's direction.

The male is big, clearly as strong and fit as Korben. He moves at a diagonal, quickly gaining distance. When Korben notices him, he veers away from him. From above, the archers fire a thick volley of arrows, effectively cutting off that path of escape. Korben's pursuer gains on him even more.

With a new burst of energy, Korben heads toward the closest building, but his pursuer matches him step for step and takes a tremendous leap like some sort of starving predator, knocking Korben off his feet.

As they fall, the male wraps his arms around Korben's waist. They crash to the ground and tumble over one another. When they come to a stop, the pursuer ends up on top. Korben bucks, throwing him off balance. As the male tries to regain the upper hand, Korben elbows him in the gut. The male grunts and bends over at the same time that he reaches to grab Korben.

He seems desperate to touch him, and when there's finally skin to skin contact, I understand why. A blast of dark espiritu hits Korben. He screams, back arching. As his victim finally goes still, the male pulls away, holding his middle and struggling to catch his breath. Within moments, Korben is surrounded by guards pointing spears and swords down at him. It all happens so fast that I have no time to think whether or not I can help him somehow. Feeling utterly useless, I circle above the group, mind scrambling for something to do.

As I stare, wishing to swoop down and claw someone's eyes out, Korben slowly climbs to his feet and stands up. The tips of the weapons rise with him. He inhales deeply and cracks his neck, glancing around at the circle of guards, his aura giving nothing but poise and confidence as he assesses his foes.

"Greetings to all," he says with a slight bow and a wince of pain. "I was expecting a much better welcome after being away from home for so long."

He speaks in a louder tone than necessary, casually tipping his head back and flicking his gaze heavenward to look in my general direction. He knows I'm here. The small gesture is unnecessary, however. I recognize his words. Earlier today, he spoke them verbatim when we discussed our alternative plan if this one didn't work.

We weren't supposed to implement that particular scheme until tomorrow, but I suppose this is as good a time as any. I know exactly what to do, and I'm a step ahead since I'm already in my raven form.

"You are breaking the queen's curfew law, and you will pay for your infraction." A female with brown skin and braided hair steps forward, sheathing her sword.

"Curfew?" Korben sounds as if the word has a terrible smell to it. "We have never had a curfew in Riochtach or anywhere else in Tirnanog. Is my city not a safe place anymore?"

"Who in the hells are you?" the female demands.

Korben appraises her, examining her face with care. "I don't remember you, captain." The insignia in her uniform must tell him her rank. "You are undoubtedly new. Therefore, I can forgive your ignorance. In fact," he glances around the group, bestowing a few seconds to scan each face with the same care, "I forgive everyone's ignorance. You are all new."

"New?" The female huffs. "I've been in this post nearly twenty years, and so have many of us."

"Exactly." Korben smirks. "New, as I said."

"Such insolence! Arrest him!" the captain orders. When no one moves to obey the command, she points at two guards. "You and you, do as I command."

Looking wary, they make as if to move forward, but a simple arresting hand gesture from Korben stops them in their tracks. He's a king through and through. His entire personality exudes confidence and authority. He knows in his bones that they should obey *him* and not the captain. The guards sense it, too.

"What is your name, captain?"

"Captain Aisling Herendi, if you must know."

"I *must* know, and I also must ask you and your guards to stand down. I am King Korben Theric, and I have returned to reclaim my throne from my treacherous wife."

# 27

## KORBEN

*"I think it really is him. Niamhara, hear my prayers."*

**Branwen Lazanar – Fae Innkeeper**

"I *must* know," I say firmly, holding the captain's gaze, "and I also must ask you and your guards to stand down. I am King Korben Theric, and I have returned to reclaim my throne from my treacherous wife."

For a moment, there is an eerie silence, then the captain lets out a burst of laughter. A few of the other guards follow suit. The entire group seems to relax.

The captain sobers up. "Ah, so you are the lunatic who is traveling around Tirnanog telling all who will listen that you are King Korben. We were warned about you, poor devil."

Of course, it could not be that simple. Of course, Saethara and her allies would do something like this to undermine my credibility—not that I have much left when the corrupted magic flowing through the realm prevents me from declaring who I am.

"I almost feel sorry for you," the captain says, "but I have express orders to stop you from soiling our king's name."

"I am pleased to see that, at least, my name is still respected."

The captain rolls her eyes. "For a crazy person, your act is not half bad. Arrest him."

This time, the guards do not hesitate. They come forward, jaws set, determined to do their job.

I step back. "No need to use force. I will go quite willingly."

Holding my hands up, I begin to walk toward the gap in the wall. I go slowly, making no sudden movements.

I sense Valeria and Cuervo flying over me, and I am confident she knows what to do and will ensure Cuervo does his part. He is the only one that worries me, but he's a smart creature, so I must trust it will all work out.

Expectation builds within me. I have been gone for so long and have dreamed of this moment countless times. I grew up within those vine walls. I shared happy times with my family. I played with cousins, learned from teachers, got drunk on feyglen for the first time, spent quiet times with my parents.

I had a good life until Saethara came to ruin it all.

Except she was an anomaly in an otherwise privileged existence. I barely knew her before I married her. I was so blinded by her beauty and subterfuge that I hurried through the Mate Rite, giving myself no chance to get to know her. She is the only darkness I ever encountered in Elf-Dún, and now her taint has spread to the rest of the realm.

The death I once tried to dispense was too swift compared to what she really deserves.

"Are there no portraits of me or my family left in the palace, Captain Herendi?" I ask.

Saethara might have removed all of my portraits from every wall, but Father and I shared a great resemblance.

Captain Herendi frowns but offers no answer.

"No?" I press.

No answer still.

"I must assume the answer is *no*." I pause and let that sink it, giving her a chance to contradict me. "Don't you find that strange?"

Someone pushes me from behind, and I stagger forward. The captain flashes an angry look to whoever did it. I think I like her. She seems to think for herself and does not abuse her power. Perhaps that's the reason she carries a commendation medal pinned to her chest, a gold star with a bright ruby in the center.

I keep my steps steady as we approach the gap in the wall. I cannot cross too fast. I need to give Cuervo time to swoop in and alight on me. Treading lightly, I set foot past the threshold, make a slight pause, and pretend to scratch my shoulder.

*Please, Cuervo, do not fail us.*

Relief washes over me as I sense the raven's quick, but silent descent. The moment his talons clamp over my shoulder, I hurry inside.

The vine walls protest with a loud groan, their way of alerting the guards that an intruder has crossed the magical barrier that protects Elf-Dún—an ancient spell that has been in place for generations.

"Oi!" one of the guards exclaims. "Get that raven out of here."

As everyone's attention turns to Cuervo, Valeria flies in and veers toward one of the many perches located around the palace grounds. I fear she will have difficulty landing—we were supposed to practice that if our original plan failed—but she manages with only a minor misstep, which she quickly corrects with a flap of her wings.

*Good job, Ravógín.* She is learning at a rapid pace, as I knew she would.

On the perch, she blends in with the other palace ravens—beautiful, highly respected birds who are raised by and cared for by appointed ravenmasters. Among them, Valeria goes unnoticed, even if the other ravens start squawking in protest, as if warning everyone she does not belong.

A male with a shaved head in the manner of the Aoncarra tries to snatch Cuervo off my shoulder. The bird jumps off and, to my utter dismay, flies toward Valeria and takes a spot next to her.

A few guards rush toward the perch, but Captain Herendi orders them to stop. "All you will do is cause a ruckus. I will take care of that damnable bird."

The Elf-Dún Ravens are gentle and accustomed to the palace inhabitants. They were domesticated several hundred years ago, and to one versed in their care the creatures pose no challenges. It appears the captain is such a person.

I freeze, my gaze set on Valeria.

The captain stands below the perch and looks up. She appears confused, as if she does not know which of the ravens is the intruder. There is a way to tell. Elf-Dún Ravens have white streaks under their wings. I pray the need to take a closer look does not become necessary.

"It is the third one from the left," one of the guards says.

"Yes," another one echoes.

I curse inwardly. The third one from the left is Valeria. *Idiots!*

"I believe they are wrong," I dare intervene. "It is the fourth one from the left."

Captain Herendi gives me a narrow-eyed look that says, *You are the last one I would ever trust.*

The captain lifts her left arm, bent at the elbow. Clicking her tongue, she taps her forearm in invitation. Yes, she is definitely versed in the care of our ravens.

Valeria's wings twitch. I sense her indecision. Obey? Or flee?

*Do not fly away. Do not fly away!*

If she does, they will not be so gentle. They might even suspect she is a shifter, one unaffected by their chokehold on magic, in which case they would not rest until they capture her and Saethara would obtain what she wants most: The Eldrystone. We knew this was a terrible risk, bringing the amulet here, but it was the only feasible plan we were able to devise. Niamhara has brought us this far. We must trust she will help us in critical times despite her weakness.

*Goddess, if you can hear me . . . this may be one of those times!*

The captain taps her arm again, a calculating expression settling over her features. She is clearly preparing to snatch Valeria if she does not come down.

For her part, Valeria seems to make a decision, and I fear it is the wrong one. She hops as if to fly away, but instead, she scoots closer to Cuervo and nudges him, directing a pointed glance toward the captain's chest.

Cuervo's eyes widen.

Excitedly, he hops off the perch and, talons extended, swoops down to snatch the captain's jeweled medal. There is a tearing sound as he digs his claws into the jacket and pulls, ripping off the shiny object.

"Treasure," he squawks as he attempts to fly away.

But he never has a chance. The captain, quick as a serpent and practiced in handling ravens—clamps her hands around him and snatches him out of the air before he can escape. He struggles for only a moment, then wisely goes still.

The medal shines in Cuervo's black claws.

"I told you that was the one," I say with a smirk of satisfaction.

"I have never heard a raven talk," one of the guards says, scratching his head.

"I have," I say, making it sound as if it's the most normal thing in the realm, even though Cuervo is the only one I have ever encountered. "I saw this in Castella, where I have been stranded this past twenty years," I add, leaving it at that, knowing it will spark curiosity in the guards.

Holding Cuervo in both hands, his beak and claws pointing away from her, the captain approaches. She stops in front of me, her expression fierce. One of the guards opens his mouth, getting ready to speak, but after a pointed glare from the captain, he presses his lips together.

"This bird is going in a cage," she announces, watching carefully for my reaction. "Fetch one for me," she instructs one of her guards, who runs in the direction of the aviary.

I school my features into a mask of indifference. Out of the corner of my eye, I see Valeria hop from talon to talon, worry for Cuervo evident in her restlessness. I am sure she feels awful for getting him captured, but she has nothing to worry about. Cuervo will not be harmed.

The captain seems to expect a protest from me, and when it does not come, her fierceness dissolves.

"Captain Herendi," I say, "you have nothing to fear from me, on the contrary, it is Saethara you must be worried about."

"That is Queen Saethara to you, impostor."

"She is not the queen of anything, except mayhap queen of *lies*."

"If you were King Korben, you would admit you married her, and *that* makes her Queen of Tirnanog."

"I made a terrible mistake by marrying that female, captain. I have returned to correct it."

Her mouth works, but no words come out. I can tell she is dying to ask something but is doing her best to refrain. In the end, she loses the battle.

"Why would they have talking ravens in Castella?"

Her question is clever, indirect. The story goes I was murdered when the veil to Castella collapsed, so hearing that I was stranded in the human realm instead begs many questions besides this one. Questions that a loyal captain to the crown should never ask.

Smiling, I proceed to answer, aware of the captain's surreptitious curiosity. "That is a Runescribe Raven." I gesture toward Cuervo. "You may not be familiar with them since they are a breed most predominant in Caernamara. They are trained to deliver messages through runes."

"Yes, I have heard of them," the same talkative guard pipes in.

"Since these birds are used to communicating," I go on, "they must have felt rather frustrated trapped in Castella, so I imagine they learned to talk. This one must have crossed the veil around the same time I did."

It is my turn to watch the captain's reaction, and it delights me to see a flinch of surprise.

"The . . . the veil has reopened?" the chatting guard asks.

As I suspected, Saethara has kept the news to herself.

Another glare from the captain makes the guard retreat back a step.

I offer a single nod in response.

The guard returns with the cage and sets it on the ground, opening its door. Crouching, the captain deposits Cuervo inside, snatches the *treasure* from his claws, and closes the door, latching it securely.

Cuervo hops, turning as he examines the cage. "Treasure, treasure, treasure," he croaks in a panic, clearly upset about his imprisonment and not the medal.

I know Valeria must be screaming inside her head. She loves this bird as one loves family. I want to tell her that Cuervo will be all right. No one will harm him, especially once they confirm he is not a shifter. No one in Elf-Dún would ever harm a raven. I refuse to accept any other possibilities, even if things have changed dramatically around here.

Captain Herendi stretches to her full height, which is a head shorter than mine. She dusts her hands.

"Nothing this male says is to be taken seriously," she declares. "His lies are scored on his face. King Korben had no scar."

"I *have* been gone for over twenty years, captain, and they have *bears* in Castella."

"If you are a Theric king, declare it then," she challenges.

I imagine making this request from anyone who claims to be me is part of all guards' training now. Clever. This impediment is a perfect boon for Saethara. No fae would ever believe that Niamhara's magic would fail so spectacularly.

I huff. "Magic is broken in the realm, captain. Everyone knows it."

"How convenient," she says. "Show me The Eldrystone then."

I say nothing. I only hold her gaze, without flinching.

She sneers, her expression resolute once more. Any doubts that may have entered her mind during our conversation have been instantly erased.

"Throw him in a dungeon cell. I will inform General Faolborn of the lunatic's arrival." She marches away, her spine straight, her entire demeanor full of command.

*General Faolborn?!*

Is she referring to Lirion Faolborn? She must be. There was not a general by that name when I was in command.

I do not glance toward Valeria as they lead me away. I am tempted to, but I manage to refrain. She knows what to do next, so all I have left is a prayer to all the gods of Tirnanog and all the saints of Castella to keep her safe.

# 28

## VALERIA

*"You have your orders, captain. The male is mad and dangerous.
If he comes, capture him and inform me immediately."*

**Lirion Faolborn – Fae General**

Anger courses through my body, feeling like fire in my veins, an emotion too grand for this small raven body.

I imagine myself swooping down, casting off The Eldrystone, and landing in a crouch, La Matadora in hand. I want to strike the captain for putting Cuervo in a cage, for treating Korben as if he's a swindler, and not her king. But it's a ridiculous impulse. It would accomplish nothing. My bravado would be no match to the might of a well-trained group of fae guards.

Taking deep breaths, I do my best to calm down as they lead Korben away. I'm also tempted to follow him to see exactly where they're taking him, but there's no time for that. I have a task to accomplish before I can go to him.

I take a moment to orient myself, the captain's last words echoing inside my mind.

*General Faolborn.*

Could this be the male the trinket hob was referring to? I shake my head. I can't worry about that right now.

The crown tower looms above me, the intertwined column of branches that hold it up appearing too spindly for such a magnificent load. The position of the ornate balcony that faces Riochtach helps me pinpoint which way is north.

With one last glance toward Korben's and Cuervo's retreating figures, I take flight, headed toward the library. Gliding over the compound, the grandness of the palace takes shape. This place is nothing like Nido. It's more like a city within a city, consisting of separate buildings rather than being a single structure. I'm mesmerized by the intricate architecture. Structures, nestled among towering trees, blend seamlessly with their natural surroundings; and a network of winding paths connects the buildings, leading to a central plaza where a fountain stands tall.

Ahead, I spot my destination, an edifice with a moss-covered roof, adorned with delicate carvings and shimmering crystals. Impossible to miss. I descend and land on the steeple, where a large diamond serves as a beacon. There, I'm just another raven out of the many that live in the palace. I watch for a long moment, keen eyes piercing the dark. Everything is quiet, no one moving around at this hour, as we expected.

Next, I fly down to the ground and hop toward the door. My heart hammers as I stand on the stoop, listening for any sounds that might betray a patron inside or a prowling guard outside.

Nothing.

I don't want to shift. I would like to have the strength to open the door while I remain in this shape, but like Korben said, "*It would be far stranger to see a raven open the door to the library than a beautiful female.*" If not for my beak, I would smile at the memory of that comment.

After shifting, I wrap the amulet in Esmeralda's kerchief and pull the hood of my cloak over my head. Quickly, I reach out a hand for the door handle. Korben assured me it wouldn't be locked, but I still breathe a sigh of relief when it gives. He said most buildings inside Elf-Dún are never locked, especially places like the library, the apothecary, the bath houses, and the museums. Honestly, this palace makes Nido feel inadequate in its size and comforts.

Swift as a shadow, I step inside and ease the door behind me without a sound. Fairy lights flank the door on either side, their glow dim, appropriate for the hour. I stay there for several beats, listening.

From here, I can see the long counter that dominates the vestibule. Like most furniture in Tirnanog, it seems to grow from the ground, many branches intertwining into a base, then changing in texture to form a polished top as smooth and shiny as marble.

No one is in attendance, but there is a small bell to call for help if needed—like Korben said there would be.

It is hard not to skulk as I move further into the building. It is also hard not to rush, but I force myself to walk normally. If anyone is here, doing some late-night reading or studying, they'll ignore me as long as they think I belong.

My steps are light, producing no sound on the polished stone floor. I marvel at my ease of movement, questioning whether or not something in me has changed since crossing the veil. Well . . . something *has* changed. I can shift into a raven now, but is that it? I push these thoughts aside and focus on my task. I pass the statue of a female surrounded by fawns, a landmark Korben said I would encounter on my way to the secret chamber that holds the codex. There, I turn right and face the wall.

*"It will look like any other passage,"* Korben said. *"There will be no indentation on the wall—not until you get The Eldrystone near it. That is when the keyhole will appear."*

I know I'm alone, but I still look over my shoulder before unwrapping the amulet from the kerchief. I stare at the wall, waiting for a change, but nothing happens. Panic threatens to rise from my chest and choke me. I swallow thickly, forcing it down.

*Not until you get The Eldrystone near it.*

I take a step closer, holding the amulet an inch from the wall. There's a strange, subtle sound like rock crumbling, and I expect to see dust in the air, but when I glance at the indentation that has appeared on the wall, the air is clear. The depression that sits in front of me is shallow and in the exact shape of The Eldrystone.

Carefully, I fit the amulet into the hollow, holding my breath. Another subtle sound like crumbling rock ensues, and a section of the wall retreats. The space left behind is just the right size, only a little wider and taller to allow my passage. It stretches into darkness, seemingly forever.

My stomach twists. I don't want to go in. Besides, it's dark. How will I be able to see anything—not that I'd get lost inside a Valeria-shaped tube. Why didn't Korben suggest I bring a light? Cursing under my breath, I take a step forward. I stand at the threshold, hesitating.

*Don't be silly. Korben wouldn't send you into a dark passage that offered no return.*

The thought does nothing to ease my nerves. Korben hasn't been here long, and he has no idea what has or hasn't changed in the palace. What if the corrupt espiritu that now runs through Tirnanog has infiltrated this place without the help of The Eldrystone? What if the codex isn't here? What if Saethara, or whoever, has set a trap for the first idiot to enter this chamber?

I could be skewered by spikes the moment I move forward. Or I could—

*Oh, stop it, Val!*

*You didn't come all the way here to cower at the first sign of . . . pitch black.*

Gathering all my courage, I take another step.

The sound of crumbling rocks resumes, this time behind me. My heart knocks out of control as I fling a hand backward and find the wall has closed.

*Dammit! Now, how in all the hells do I get out of—*

A dim fairy light comes on right above me, illuminating the way ahead, though only for about five or so steps. It's still an improvement, so I take a third step forward. More lights come on ahead, while the ones behind me go off. Encouraged, I walk deeper and deeper. The lights follow my progress. After five minutes moving in the same direction, the passage becomes a steep slope that drives me underground. I cling to The Eldrystone, trying not to think about being encased in stone with many feet of dirt above my head.

At last, the passage ends, leading into a large perfectly round room, dominated by a circular table in the middle. The walls are made of gray stone, shaped into seamless bookshelves that hold hundreds of ancient-looking books, some with shimmering titles that seem to beckon me.

Right in the center of the table, there is another amulet-shaped indentation. Suddenly, I'm not worried about spikes or anyone appearing out of nowhere. This place feels abandoned. I don't know why, but it seems as if no one has been here for a long time, as if the room's stillness is saturated with reproach. Or maybe it's the books. Maybe they're angry no one has been here to read them.

Shaking my head to drive away my nonsensical reverie, I place the amulet in the center of the table. There is a slight *click* and a pulse of light as it settles in, fitting perfectly.

I bite my lower lip, recalling Korben's instructions.

"Retrieve the codex," I say, then quickly add, "please." That last word wasn't part of what I needed to say, but it felt necessary.

A sound behind me.

I turn to see a thick codex sliding out of one of the high stone shelves. As if carried by an invisible librarian, the book floats in my direction and gently settles itself down on the table. The codex is as large as my torso and must contain thousands of pages. I would have never been able to remove it from the shelf without it landing squarely on my head.

All right, all of Nido's libraries are officially declared obsolete. We need invisible librarians, too.

Reverently, I stand in front of the book and begin turning pages, searching for the section Korben instructed. The book is written in old fae script. I don't understand a word, but I'm mesmerized by the beauty of the characters, the tilting penmanship, the skillful illustrations, and the shimmering quality of the ink.

It takes me several moments to reach the illustration I'm looking for. It depicts a simple rock mound. I examine the following pages, which Korben said contain the instructions to find Niamhara's home.

"*It won't be easy for you to do,*" he said. "*I've seen how you handle books, but you will have to rip out the pages. It won't be possible for you to carry the codex out.*"

When he said it, I thought he was wrong. Ripping pages of a book didn't sound too hard a challenge compared to what is at stake, but now, looking at this work of art, I must admit that Korben knows me better than I thought.

"I'm sorry," I tell the book as if it can understand me. I'm not convinced it can't—not when I still feel as if the room is in a mood for not having been visited in a while.

Biting my lower lip, I rip out one page at a time until I've gathered all three. They are large, and when I fold them, they form a thick pack that I stuff into the waistband of my leggings, hiding it under my tunic. Apologizing again, I close the codex.

"Sorry. I promise I'll bring the pages back after we're done." My voice echoes and comes back to me like a dare. "I won't forget."

I'm sure that if . . . no, *when* we restore the balance, I'll be able to use The Eldrystone to repair the damage.

Reaching toward the center of the table, I retrieve the amulet and march toward the tunnel. I pause and when I glance back, the codex is floating back to its shelf. It makes me sad to leave, to see the table with all the empty chairs around it.

"I'll come back," I say, "if I don't die. Right now, I have to find Korben."

# 29

## KORBEN

*"No white feathers under his wings, no proper training. Indeed,*
*this bird does not belong here. He is a fine specimen, nonetheless.*
*Let us find out if he is a shifter."*

**Aimer Corvalur – Elf-Dún Ravenmaster**

I count the minutes, pacing the small dungeon cell. All the guards who live in Elf-Dún reside in the east wing of the palace, so it should take Captain Herendi approximately five minutes to reach Lirion. From there, I suspect the general will contact Saethara herself, which might take another five minutes. Add to that the time to reach the dungeons, and Valeria should have a total of fifteen minutes to retrieve the pages and find her way here.

This is a risky estimate at best. It could take far less time or a little more depending on the circumstances. Lirion might be the one truly in charge here, which means he might arrive in the next ten minutes, ready to dispense a swift death.

Still, I'm inclined to believe Saethara will want to see me, if only to rub her cleverness in my face. What few things I know about her were lies, an act. She presented to be gentle, thoughtful, and demure. But the female I encountered in the courtyard with Loreleia was none of those things. Instead, she appeared cruel and frosty—just the type of person who would enjoy boasting about her victory.

In my mind's eye, I imagine every step Valeria must take to retrieve the pages from the codex. Right now, she must be inside the chamber, wincing at the prospect of defiling the codex. My mouth tips in a smile as I imagine her biting her lower lip in order to gather enough courage to do it.

Interminable minutes go by. I stop pacing, deciding she must be near, ready to create a distraction that will draw the guards out of the garrison. When they brought me in, I counted five males. I was handed over to their care, and those who delivered me returned to their duties at the wall.

In her raven shape, Valeria will be able to fly in when the garrison door opens and then—

Shouts echo down the corridor. I rush to the bars and listen intently, trying to make out the words, but more than one person is shouting, so it is difficult. I hear rushing steps, presumably guards exiting the garrison.

"Come on, Valeria. Come on," I whisper, willing her to be safe.

"*Drocháin!* One of those bothersome birds got in. Catch it," a guard calls.

*She's here!*

I try to rattle the door, but it is firm and does not budge at all. So I pick up the piss bucket and slam it against the bars. A loud *clank* rings through the cells, announcing my exact location.

## VALERIA

I use flint and tinder to set a building near the garrison on fire. With that done, I shift into my raven shape and wait atop a branch. Promptly, the door opens, and three guards spill out, calling for the fire brigade. When the last one spills out, I jump from my perch and swoop toward the open door, afraid I won't make it.

Nerves make my blood *zing*, but as I glide in with time to spare before the door closes, I realize all my calculations of distance, time, and rate of survival are being estimated by a human brain, for a human shape. This body, this creature that I'm able to *become*, is capable of far more, and I need to reevaluate everything I know.

"Drocháin! One of those bothersome birds got in. Catch it," one of the two guards left inside calls as I fly past. Neither male attempts to come after me, however. They only appear annoyed by my presence—not alarmed at all.

Flying as fast as I can in the tight space, I head to the archway in the back. It leads to two corridors, one branching left and the other one right. *Gods!* I don't know which way to turn. Korben said I would know but . . .

A metallic *clank* comes from the right. That must be my cue! I have just enough time to bank in that direction, and as I turn, I notice one of the guards looking at me and frowning with unease. Perhaps a warning is ringing in the back of his head, telling him something isn't quite right. I beg Niamhara that he doesn't listen to it. At least not until I have enough time to make it to Korben.

I flap my wings with all my might. A moment later, I hear the guard's steps behind me. Heading straight for the source of the clanking, I ignore the many faces that peer at me through the bars of every cell I pass. This place seems to be packed full of bodies, but it's Korben I need to find.

When I spot his exact location, I don't think. Instead, I drop The Eldrystone. My body begins to shift mid air. For a panicked moment, I fear I will land on my face, but my feet hit the stone floor running, and amazingly, I have the presence of mind and agility to stick my hand under my tunic to catch the amulet as it falls. I wrap my hand around it, the fabric preventing skin contact.

As I take the next step, I unsheathe La Matadora.

"Intruder!" the pursuing guard shouts as he sees my transformation.

Quick as molten metal, I judge the distance I have left to reach Korben against the distance between me and the guard. *Dammit!* I won't make it.

Whatever Korben's using to make noise *clanks* to the floor, then he sticks a hand through the bars. Like me, he has realized I don't have time, so he comes up with a second option: he'll have to free himself.

I angle the sword to deposit it in his hand.

"Stop!" the guard yells, crashing into me just as Korben takes the weapon from my fingers and swiftly pulls it in through the bars.

The guard knocks the air from my lungs as he crashes into me and takes me down. I'm disoriented, blinking and trying to catch my breath.

*The Eldrystone! Where is The Eldrystone?*

I sense it under me, still hidden under my tunic even though it slipped my grip.

"Valeria!" Korben cries in warning at the same time that he begins to hack at the bars. La Matadora is a fae-made sword, capable of withstanding espiritu and cutting through the toughest materials.

Heeding the warning in his voice, I ignore the pain around my ribs and swing, trying to hit the guard. My arm collides with his as he raises a dagger, seemingly conjured out of thin air.

Taking advantage of his lapse, I buck and claw at the floor, pulling myself forward, managing to get my legs from under his weight. Gritting my teeth, I roll onto my back, kicking. My boot catches the male in the jaw, but after barely flinching, he raises the dagger again and leaps to stab me, aiming for the heart.

Crossing my arms, I raise them to block the blow. I prepare myself for impact, but instead of steel, I'm struck by a spray of warm blood as La Matadora pierces through the male's chest, killing him instantly.

Korben plants a foot on the guard's back, pulls out the sword, and whirls to face a second guard. My attacker's body collapses on top of me, and I push him away, scrambling, using the sleeve of my tunic to wipe away the blood sliding down my face. A set of hands reaches for me through the bars of the nearest cell. I push out of the way before they can get a hold of me. I glance back into the face of a crazed-looking male, with matted white hair and a face darkened by grime.

The Eldrystone starts sliding from under my tunic, so I quickly retrieve the kerchief, wrap it around the amulet, and secure it in my pouch.

"Stand down, guard," Korben orders. "I do not wish to kill you."

The guard does no such thing and hacks with his sword, intent on cutting Korben in two. With incredible ease, Korben parries the blow and sidesteps, causing his opponent to stagger forward. Seeing his opportunity, Korben uses the hilt of his sword to strike the guard in the back of the head. There is a sickening sound, followed by the guard's *thud* to the floor.

Turning, Korben helps me stand. I'm inhaling deeply, still trying to catch my breath.

"Are you all right?" He examines me from head to toe.

I nod.

"Did you get the pages?"

"Yes."

"Then let's get out of here." He takes my hand, and we run for the exit.

"Help us!" one of the prisoners calls.

Others echo the same plea as we run by.

Korben hesitates for only an instant, then shakes his head and keeps going. We don't have time to free these people. Our end goal is more important than any who might have been unjustly imprisoned. In the end, if we succeed, everyone will benefit, even these wretched souls.

No one is out in the garrison. Everyone's still outside dealing with the fire. Cautiously, Korben opens the door and peers out. After a quick perusal, he exits and guides me around the building and into the shadows. There, we wait for a few seconds, watching people haul buckets of water. The flames have grown larger than I anticipated.

When no one is looking in our direction, we run across open space to the shelter of a large tree. We pause again. We're about to keep going, when a group of people round the corner of a tall tower. We freeze.

At the head of the group, a woman dressed in a burgundy gown walks with confident steps. Next to her is a tall male in military garb, the general, I presume. A group of four guards walks behind them. They are large in height and girth, each at least seven feet tall, armed with broadswords, and wearing light armor.

Korben and I exchange glances. He nods when he notices the question stamped on my face, *Is that her?*

Saethara, Korben's wife.

She is tall and walks with her head held high, giving the impression of a proper queen even though she's a usurper. She has silky blue hair that flows down her front, reaching her full breasts. Her narrow waist gives way to curvaceous hips that sway with every step. Her skin is as smooth as white marble, and her lips are painted apple-red.

She is beautiful.

A nauseous feeling turns my stomach.

I look at Korben, his profile obscured by shadows. His eyes are narrowed, watching her, following her progress. I don't know what I'm trying to find in his expression, but whatever it is, I don't see it. Instead, his features are composed into that unreadable mask he used to wear as Bastien. In this moment, I would give anything to know what he's thinking, what the sight of her is making him feel.

My heart shies away from the possibilities. He was in love with her once. What if her presence unearths emotions he didn't know he still had? I suddenly realize this is something I have been afraid to confront. When Korben last saw Saethara, his actions were fueled by anger. She had just stabbed him in the chest, and he was hungry for revenge. Now, he's had time to think—two decades during which a lot has changed.

Next to her, the male I assume is General Faolborn looms almost as tall as the armored guards. He has yellow eyes that gleam strangely.

When Saethara and the others notice the fire, the retinue stops. The general sends one of the guards ahead to ask what's happening. I hear his words faintly, even though I know I shouldn't be able to. It does seem my hearing has improved. The fact barely seems worthy of notice now. My concerns have taken a different turn.

I never thought I was a jealous woman, but it appears I'm exactly that, and I find myself truly hating Saethara as I've never hated anyone.

The guard quickly returns with information for the general. "They do not know how the fire started, General Faolborn, but they have it under control. The prisoner awaits. The guards inside will show you to him."

The general frowns. Looking unsettled, he turns toward Saethara. "Perhaps you should wait here while I take a look, Your Majesty."

"No," she responds categorically. "I want to see him right away."

The general bows and extends a hand to show the way. Saethara resumes walking, her expression that of a spider stalking toward her prey.

Korben's gaze follows her progress, unblinking. Does he notice the evil intent that mars her demeanor? Or does he see something else?

After they pass in front of us and disappear into the garrison, Korben remains frozen, as if hypnotized by the ghost of her presence. When I put a hand on his shoulder, he startles and looks at me with a frown. Perhaps he thinks I just sprouted from the ground.

"We need to go," I whisper.

He nods and checks on the guards still tending the fire. Their focus wanders now that things seem under control, so it takes a moment before we have a chance to keep moving.

"Walk briskly," Korben whispers in my ear, pulling me onto the path. He holds La Matadora awkwardly in front of his body to keep it out of sight.

This time, we don't hide. The open path ahead is all we've got. My hands sweat, making me self-conscious. I want to both let go and continue holding Korben's hand. Our steps are quick, but the urge to go even faster is fierce. I'm tempted to glance back over my shoulder, but I also manage to control this urge. We're almost to the end of the path where we can disappear around the corner. Almost there.

"Hey, you two."

Korben stops and flicks his head to one side to indicate I should take care of this. *Shit!* I don't want to do it, but he probably fears they'll recognize him.

Slowly, I glance back.

"Did you see what caused this fire?" a guard asks with enough suspicion in her voice that the question sounds like an accusation.

"I did not." I turn, and we continue walking.

"Hold it. I have one more question."

I glance back to find her jogging toward us. "*Dammit!* She's coming."

"Run!" Korben lets go of my hand and propels me forward with a push at my lower back.

For a moment, I fear he intends to stay back and fight, but it seems he wants me leading the way, likely to keep an eye on me and make sure I'm not the target of a well-aimed arrow.

"Get back here!" the guard shouts. "Drek and Venmyar, with me!"

"Turn right," Korben instructs.

As I skid around the corner, I see three guards taking chase. They are fast, but so are we. My legs and arms pump at a prodigious speed. Korben pulls up next to me, his eyebrows up in surprise. We take a few more turns down narrow passages, then run across an open field. Three arrows *thunk* into the ground. Korben hisses and falters slightly, grazed by one of the arrows, but he continues running without any sign of injury.

I push my concern down as we zigzag through the field. More arrows hit the ground, missing us by mere inches. We finally make it to a line of buildings that runs along the north wall.

The arrows stop as soon as we enter a narrow passage flanked by two mushroom-shaped structures. Taking the lead, Korben heads straight ahead, then suddenly veers to the left when a group of guards appears in front of us.

*What?!*

Where did they come from? Are they the same guards we left behind? Either way, espiritu must be involved. The guards must have a way to send alerts to each other using spells or a charmed device. We'll never be able to evade them now.

"We are almost there," Korben says.

Another set of guards appears ahead. Korben curses and, this time, turns right. This passage dead ends in a building with many branch steps leading to a glass front door. Each step springs from the ground, a thick branch that bends at a ninety-degree angle then runs parallel to the ground.

Korben leaps onto the third step and keeps taking three at a time. I follow suit, praying I don't slip on the rounded trunks and fall through the space between the branches. Instead, my feet barely seem to touch the bark as I leap from one to the other. Never stopping, I run past the front door as Korben throws it open.

As we keep running, I realize we aren't really inside a building. Even though there are walls around us, the roof is nothing but the black open sky shimmering with the beautiful etherglow that always adorns the night.

Korben runs without pause. I follow, registering small details about our surroundings, part of me wishing I could stop to admire them. We seem to be in some sort of garden. Plants such as I've never seen grow from the ground, ornate containers, coarse sand, and even rocks. Mother would have loved this place.

Our pursuers crash through the entrance. I see no exit ahead, but I trust Korben knows where he's going. Ahead, he takes an abrupt left. I try to turn, but my momentum is too great. Just as I think I will lose my balance and fall to the ground, his strong arm hooks around my waist and pulls me.

I crash against him with a *humph*.

"The Eldrystone!" he says, letting me go.

Blood roaring in my ears, I quickly pull the amulet out of my pouch and hand it over. He unravels it from the kerchief and presses it to the surface of an enormous tree. My gaze follows the trunk upward. It rises in a perfectly straight line. I expect it to go on forever, but it ends abruptly at about twelve feet as if it's been cut, except broad blue leaves as wide as a man sprout from the top. Odd.

I'm so distracted by the strange tree that I nearly miss the moment Korben presses The Eldrystone to the indentation that has appeared on the trunk. This time, an arched passageway as tall and wide as

Korben opens up. Without hesitation, he turns to face me, takes a backward step inside, and pulls me in with him, still holding La Matadora in his hand since I have the scabbard.

Enveloping us in darkness, the trunk closes just as the guards round the corner.

"Where did they go?" a muffled voice asks on the other side.

I exhale in relief.

*Gods, that was close!*

The ground underneath trembles. I tense in Korben's arms.

"It is all right, Ravógín. We are getting out of here."

In the dark, it's hard to tell what's happening, but I think we're moving downward, the very ground we stand on descending, taking us underground.

*Not again.*

I press my cheek to Korben's firm chest. His heart *thuds* strongly. I find comfort in the sound and focus on it, ignoring the fact we're being buried under a tree.

When we stop moving, Korben walks out of the enclosure, lifting me slightly and easily carrying me with him.

"How are we going to find our way out? It's pitch dark," I say as I turn to face our would-be exit.

"Lights come on when you need them."

"Well, we need them."

"No, we do not. We can put a hand on the wall and simply follow the passage to the exit. Let us hurry before someone gets clever and realizes where to send a search party."

He takes my hand and presses it to the wall. It feels cool and damp.

"Guide us, princess."

"Don't call me that," I snap, starting to walk.

"I am sorry?" His words sound like a question, as if he has no idea why it suddenly bothers me.

"Bastien and Ríffor used to call me that," I say.

"I apologize. Does that mean you are starting to prefer Korben?"

I huff, feeling angry. I know it's due to the sudden jealousy that assaulted me when we ran into Saethara. It's petty of me, but I spoke without thinking.

"Is Cuervo going to be all right?" I ask.

"I believe so. The ravenmasters in Elf-Dún would never harm him. They revere the animals."

I nod, even though Korben can't see me. I hurry my steps, gaining confidence since the way appears straight forward.

"How long is this passage?" I ask.

"We are almost there."

I'm reminded of our escape from Nido, where we also traversed underground, narrow passages to reach the outside.

"Your ancestors must have been involved in the design and construction of Nido," I say. "No doubt they knew these secret passages were a necessity."

"They were your ancestors, too."

"Please don't bring that up. I don't really like the idea that we're related."

"Very distantly. Enough not to be discomforting."

"I suppose." It seems I'm trying to find any reason to be aggravated at Korben.

We walk quietly for a couple of minutes. A metallic scent enters my awareness, reminding me of the arrow that struck Korben.

"I smell blood," I say. "Are you all right?"

"Just a scrape in my leg." He pauses. "Your senses . . . they have changed, have they not?"

"Yes, I think so."

"And your speed as you ran . . . I stopped worrying you would not be able to keep up."

"You mean I'm not a liability anymore."

"No, little raven. That is not what I mean," he says in an adamant tone. "Is something wrong? You seem . . . angry at me."

I'm saved from answering when my foot hits something, and I'm forced to stop. I put out a hand and discover a wall. Korben runs into me.

"I think this is the end," I say. "I assume the amulet will let us out."

"Correct."

Korben hands me The Eldrystone wrapped in the kerchief. I bring the amulet close to the wall and, with my free hand, search for the indentation. When I find it, I carefully fit the opal into place.

The wall parts, and moonlight slips in, refracting from the surface of a sword.

### KORBEN

The glint of moonlight on a sword spurs me into action. I push Valeria down, out of the way.

In the tight space, it's impossible to wield La Matadora, so all I can do is turn my body sideways as the guard stabs his weapon into our space. The blade cuts through my shirt, the sharp edge slicing across my abdomen.

I clench my teeth against the pain, grab the attacker's arm, and slam it against the wall. He's a large male and holds on to the weapon, attempting to pull his arm back to strike again. At my feet where Valeria crouches, she leaps out of the alcove, slamming her shoulder against the guard's shins and knocking him off balance.

Charging out after her, I slam my fist against the male's jaw. Between Valeria and me, we send him crashing to the ground. We jump back and away from him, striking a defensive pose. I brandish La Matadora, a warning for him to stay down.

A dozen guards step out of the darkness and form a circle around us—Captain Herendi among them.

*Fuck!*

I meet her gaze. Her dark eyes dance between Valeria and me.

"How?" she asks.

"How did I know about the passage if I am a deranged pretender?" I say, smirking, pretending satisfaction, though I feel nothing but defeat. We are surrounded. "I bet there are a million other questions swimming in your mind right now. Are there not, captain?"

"Shut your mouth," she orders, anger thick in her voice—the kind that indicates she hates me for making her doubt. "Drop your weapon. You are surrounded."

It cannot end here, so I make my stand. I would rather die fighting.

"Run when I tell you, Valeria," I whisper.

"Never," she responds.

"Do not be stubborn."

"You know me too well to ask that of me." She pulls her dagger from her belt, letting the guards know a fight is coming their way.

Sidling close to her, I take the dagger and give her La Matadora.

"That is better," I say with a wink.

There is a chance we might make it out of here alive, *if* Niamhara helps us.

A battle cry rents the night, and two of the guards drop, their heads rolling to the ground. The bodies have no time to drop before Calierin attacks a third guard, knocking the sword off his grip as he tries to parry her blow.

Valeria and I jump into action, weapons raised.

The battle rages, a whirlwind of steel and desperation. My heart pounds as I dodge a spear thrust, the tip brushing my cheek. I parry a sword strike with the dagger, the metal singing against the other blade. My companions, their swords flashing in the moonlight, fight with a ferocity that matches my own. We are outnumbered, but our cause spurs us on. I feel a surge of energy as I disarm two guards at once, their swords clattering to the ground. They regard me in surprise, their eyes filled with a mix of doubt and respect. I know I must act quickly, so I aim my dagger at one of the male's legs and strike. He lets out a cry of pain and falls, holding the wound.

I turn to face another guard, and I see Calierin lop off another head.

"Refrain from killing, Calierin," I shout as Captain Herendi charges me.

Out of the corner of my eye, I notice Valeria drop to one knee, her sword crossed with her opponent's as he bears down on her.

The captain thrusts with her sword, aiming for my heart. She is fast, but I am faster and step out of the way just in time. I want to go to Valeria, but Captain Herendi comes at me again. I fight with a desperation I have never known before, my movements becoming purely instinctive. I must help Valeria.

With the agility that only years of sword training can bestow, Valeria bends her elbows and rolls to one side, causing her opponent to stagger forward. In one single motion, she comes up on one knee and pivots, slicing her rival's calf.

*Gods! She is good. Why was I worried about her?*

Instead, I should worry about myself. The captain is coming at me again, bent on making me pay for throwing her world into chaos. Sword raised, she hacks as if I am a log she means to split in two. I do not retreat and rather step forward, wrapping a hand around her wrist, stopping her progress. She growls, teeth bared.

"You fight your king, Captain Herendi," I say. "What about your oath to protect the crown?"

"You are not my king."

She fights to get free, but I am stronger and bend her wrist until she is forced to drop her weapon. It clatters to the ground, the sound marking the captain's defeat.

"I forgive you. This time," I say with a smile that she reciprocates with a growl. "You have grit, and I like that. Next time, however, I expect you will know better."

Her dark eyes never leave mine—not until I release her only to knock her unconscious with a right hook to the jaw. She drops like a rock.

Turning, I face the others. Bodies are strewn all around us, some dead, others moaning in pain and holding their incapacitating wounds. I can tell which ones succumbed to Calierin, which is the majority of them. A Tuathacath warrior is worth ten of us. Valeria and I could have never escaped on our own. I bow to her, though I wish she were not so ruthless with her own kin.

"Let us go before more guards come," I say.

"Wait." Calierin crouches and takes several weapons, including a bow and quiver strapped to the back of one of the fallen guards.

As we run away from the palace, I spare one last glance toward the captain. She will have a serious headache when she wakes up, but I hope that is the extent of it. Saethara could decide to punish her for failing to capture us, but I must hope Captain Herendi will be all right in the end.

# 30

## VALERIA

*"Saints! I can hardly breathe when I look at her."*

*Jago Plumanegra (Casa Plumanegra) – 3rd in line to Plumanegra throne*

We leave Riochtach, riding west as fast as we can. Korben ignores his wounds, claiming they're superficial. We run the horses ragged and stop only because the animals require rest. At every minor stop, Korben pores over the pages of the codex. He's the only one able to read the ancient language—part of his education as the conduit bearer, he says.

At the moment, he's bent over the pages, the light of a too-dim fire assisting his task. Everyone seems worried, especially Galen and Calierin. They can't sit still and pace like caged animals. The idea makes me think of Cuervo. He's used to being free, and I can only imagine what he must be feeling.

*I'll free you, Cuervo. I swear by all the gods and saints!*

"I wish he would say something." Jago gestures toward Korben as he picks debris from Esmeralda's hair. Her mass of black curls is the perfect resting place for small twigs and leaves carried by the wind.

257

We sit a good distance away from the fire, wrapped in our bedrolls, the shelter of a thick tree protecting us from the wind. The terrain around us has changed. The trees and other vegetation are sparse, and the ground under our feet is turning more and more arid the farther west we travel.

I glance at Korben, wishing the same as my cousin. Korben has been too pensive since we left Elf-Dún . . . since we ran into Saethara.

"We saw her," I whisper so quietly that even Jago and Esmeralda have difficulty hearing me.

Jago leans closer, eyes wide. "Her? *Her?*"

I nod.

He leans closer still, joined by Esmeralda, whose sharp green eyes seem to swallow all the light.

When I say nothing else, Jago presses me. "Well?"

I shrug. I don't know what else to say. I don't even know why I brought it up. "Um, she was on her way to the dungeons, likely to make sure it was really Korben they'd captured."

"What did she look like?" Esmeralda asks.

*Beautiful*, I think to myself.

"Ruthless," I say instead.

Jago narrows his eyes, cocking his head to one side. His expression seems to say *I know there is more, cousin. Out with it!* He doesn't press me, however. Instead, he goes back to picking bits of dry leaves from Esmeralda's hair.

"My backside hurts." Esmeralda shifts uncomfortably.

Thinking I can't hear him, Jago whispers in her ear. "I can massage it if you'd like."

Esmeralda shoves him away, though her gaze sparkles with mischief.

After everyone lies down to sleep, Korben continues examining the stolen pages—though now, he's spending more time reflecting and looking into the distance than actually reading.

Feeling stiff, I stand and pace the outer ring of our small camp. The etherglow stirs above us, marveling me anew and making me realize how much things have changed in a short time. My life is nearly unrecognizable. Visiting Tirnanog was a lifelong dream I never thought would come true.

Yet, as I stand here, I think of the adage: *Be careful what you wish for.*

Countless times, I imagined myself flying, inheriting Father's skill and unbound espiritu. In addition, I envisioned Castella and Tirnanog reconciling the differences they had before the veil collapsed and becoming allies once more. But if Korben doesn't retake the throne, I fear an allegiance, much less peace, will never be possible between our realms. I don't know much about Saethara, but something tells me she isn't the kind to make treaties. When I learned of her actions against Korben, I realized she was heartless, but after laying eyes on her, I can tell there's more.

She's not only cruel. She is determined. That look in her eyes . . . she's the kind of person who would willingly die for what she wants, whether or not it belongs to her.

Startled by Jago's sudden presence, I snap out of my thoughts. I was so lost in thought I didn't notice his approach.

Rubbing at his face, he sits on a log, facing away from the fire. His blond hair stands on end, and his honey-colored eyes are rimmed by the red of exhaustion. I realize that despite the lack of proper rest, I'm not as tired as I should be.

He yawns and cracks his neck. "How come you look as fresh as a newborn calf?"

Taking a seat next to him, I rest my head on his shoulder. "Do you see that purple flower over there?"

I point toward a solitary bush with wide leaves. The flower looks like a slumped figure, taking a nap while standing. I imagine its petals will open up when the sun comes out.

Jago squints at the darkness. "Purple flower?"

I let that sink in, knowing he'll grasp my meaning.

"Oh," he finally says. "So it is more than being able to shift?"

"Yes. I can also hear a lot better."

He huffs. "Lucky you. I bet you'll also live forever."

Sitting up straight, I meet his gaze. "I hadn't thought about longevity," I say, noticing his slight frown and wondering if that's bitterness I hear in his voice.

"I . . ." Words escape me. What does one say in a situation like this? I'm sorry you aren't one of *those* Plumanegras?

The traits we inherited from our fae ancestors never passed down consistently through the many generations of Plumanegras. My father inherited the ability to shift into a small raven, more precisely the Corvus form. His brother—Jago's father—inherited no espiritu at all. But it seems Jago still hoped, even if he never talked about it like I did. Maybe I blabbered enough for the both of us. I want to say *I'm sorry*, but I know it's not what he wants to hear.

"It's not your fault, cousin," he says, showing that he understands exactly what's on my mind. "I'm glad one of us is a proper Plumanegra."

"Hey, don't say that."

"I wonder if Amira has suddenly sprouted feathers on her arse?"

Thoughts of my sister pop into my mind all the time, but I've been pushing them aside, aware that focusing on our mission is the best way to help her. I hadn't considered she might be able to shift, too. Except . . . she wouldn't. Something is wrong with the flow of espiritu.

"I'm an idiot!" I sit up straighter and pull out The Eldrystone from the pouch, unwrapping it. "Here. Try it. I should have thought of it earlier. If you have the ability, it won't manifest unless you touch it."

He glares at the amulet.

"It's all right," I say encouragingly.

"It seemed to hurt like hell." His mouth twists, lips pursed, as he considers.

"If Cuervo were here, he'd call you a chicken."

Jago huffs. "I'm sorry he got captured, Val."

"Korben is sure they won't harm him."

Inhaling deeply, Jago takes The Eldrystone from me. We wait with bated breaths. Tension builds in the air, full of anticipation. Nothing happens. Jago shrugs and gives back the amulet. I put it back in the pouch, disappointed. I wish he could experience this with me.

"So tell me about Saethara," Jago says, quickly changing the subject.

I sigh and shake my head, aware that he hates to dwell on what he considers his shortcomings. Besides, I don't want to talk about my problems—not when I have been so insensitive and oblivious to what he's been feeling.

"Nah, why don't you tell me about Esmeralda?" I nudge his shoulder with mine.

A stupid grin stretches his lips.

"It's that good, huh?"

"She's different from all the women in court."

"I bet."

He's pensive for a moment, then asks, "Do you . . . disapprove?"

"What?! You can't be serious with that question. I slept with a guard."

"Who turned out to be a king."

"That's not the point." I glance back at said king. He's still sitting by the fire, looking increasingly troubled. "I didn't care about any of that when we . . . you know. Then I found out he was the leader of the veilfallen, and I could have killed him. Then I thought he slept with my mother. That was quite entertaining. And then . . . um, I found out he stabbed his wife through the chest."

"He did what?"

There's a weird twist in my stomach, the same I felt when Korben first confessed what he did. The idea of the rage that drove him to do something like that was incomprehensible. It made me realize the intensity with which he feels. It terrified me.

"Stabbed her, but not before she stabbed him first," I say. "On their wedding night, in order to steal The Eldrystone for herself."

"Saints be damned! Now, I understand." Jago rubs the back of his neck, looking flabbergasted.

"What if he still has feelings for her?" The question blurts out of my mouth before I can stop it.

"Ha, I knew there was something bothering you."

I stare at the ground, embarrassed, wishing I could take the words back.

"You should ask him," Jago says.

"What? No. I can't ask him that."

"Why not?"

"If he does, he will deny it."

Jago considers. "If you don't trust him, that's the first problem."

A bitter sense fills me as I accept the truth of his statement. I blow air through my nose. "How did you get so wise, oh, Maestro Jago?"

"I've always been wise. You just happen to get too caught up in your own affairs to notice." He brushes non-existent dust from his shoulder in a show of mock superiority.

Even though he acts like he's joking, I feel the barbs in this new quip. He doesn't mean to be hurtful, but he isn't wrong.

"I'm sorry, Jago. I'm terribly selfish, am I not?"

"I didn't—"

"I know you didn't mean anything by it. That doesn't make it a lie. I do think of you and Amira. A lot. I want the best for you, want you to be happy."

"Don't be foolish," he says. "You don't have to explain yourself. It's the realm—the realms, I should say—against you and me. It's always been like that. As long as we have each other's backs, we can face anything. Even . . . falling in love."

I raise an eyebrow. "Are you saying that you're . . .?" I glance toward Esmeralda, who lies on the ground, sleeping in a tight bundle of blankets.

He shrugs. "I honestly don't know. This is so new to me. Others I've been with . . . they only seemed to care about my last name, but I don't think she does. She came here for me." He appears incredulous. "Before we left Badajos, and I went to tell her goodbye, she offered to come with us. Gaspar helped me talk her out of it, but obviously, it didn't stick. She left Castella, her troop, to find me. Despite the danger, the unknown. I feel like," he pauses and thinks for a moment, "like life and all its twists and turns will be sweeter with her by my side."

Suddenly, my eyes are brimming with tears. I bite my lower lip and blink rapidly, gaze pointed at the sky. If Jago notices my reaction, he says nothing. Instead, he stands and pats my shoulder.

"Ask, cousin. Ask," he says, then goes back to Esmeralda's side.

As if Korben has been waiting for Jago to leave, he approaches, his shirt bloody from the wound he received in his abdomen.

"Hey," I say as he takes my cousin's place. His hands are empty, the pages he's been clinging to stowed away at last.

"How is that?" I point toward his stomach.

"Barely a scratch. I am fine."

For a moment, I panic, thinking he overheard my conversation with Jago, but as I examine his stern expression, I can tell he's concerned with far more important things than my insecurity.

"You should be sleeping, Ravógín," he says, interlacing his fingers with mine. His touch is warm, soothing.

"You, too."

"I could not if I tried."

"Did you . . . figure it out? The location of the Whispering Wilds?"

He nods, looking somber.

"It is far, then." That must be why he looks so worried.

"It is not. It is only a day's ride away."

"Oh!" That surprises me. "Then why do you look so . . . concerned?"

"Because it is in the Mourning Moor, a very dangerous place."

I frown. "The Mourning Moor." I search my mind, but I don't recall Mother or any of my books mentioning the place. It sounds awful enough. "Dangerous as in we'll get wounded or as in we'll die?"

"Dangerous as in we might lose our souls and never leave."

I swallow thickly, sure I don't want to know any more about the place, sure I only want to stay here, sitting quietly on this log, his warmth seeping into my body while the etherglow swims endlessly above us.

Wrapping an arm around my waist, he pulls me closer. We turn toward each other, and I rest my head on his firm chest.

"Ravógín?"

"Hmm."

"I love you."

My breath catches.

"Do not fear. What I feel for you is real. I now know I never felt any love toward her. I do not blame you for not trusting me." He presses his nose to the top of my head and takes a deep breath. "I was cruel to you and do not deserve moments like this. Not a day goes by that I do not ask for forgiveness, that I do not think of all the ways I could have broken you if you were not as strong as you are.

"You are all the things I never was, and I have learned so much from you. I dwelled in my pain. I indulged in it and used it to justify my every action and inaction. While you . . . well, you use your pain to rise above, to help others. You are made of something stronger than steel. I can only aspire to be like you. So, Ravógín, you may ask anything you want."

I'm on the verge of tears. How can I ask such a paltry question after what he has just told me.

"There's nothing I need to ask," I manage.

"Are you sure?"

"Yes, I am."

It may still take me a long time to fully trust Korben. But tonight, I trust him a little more, and I find myself teetering on that edge, not just ready to fall—but perhaps . . . to leap.

# 31

# KORBEN

*"Try harder. Do not tell me it is impossible. Find a way to seal the passages."*

**Saethara Orenthal – Queen of Tirnanog – 2 AV**

"The Mourning Moor?!" Galen exclaims. "The Mourning Moor?!" he repeats incredulously.

It is two hours before dawn. We cannot remain in any one place for long—not with Saethara's people surely scouring the realm to find us. We might have escaped unnoticed thus far, but I doubt things will remain so.

Everyone looks exhausted, especially Jago and Esmeralda. I'm surprised, however, by Valeria's endurance. Like me, she didn't sleep all night and doesn't seem any worse for wear.

"Fucking Niamhara!" Galen continues on his rant. "She might as well have hidden herself at the bottom of the Giantran Sea. We will never reach her. Never."

"Anyone care to explain what's so awful about this place," Jago demands.

I am yet to explain the nature of the Mourning Moor to our

human companions. Valeria chose not to ask me earlier, so I did not offer more details. She seems resigned to whatever fate awaits us, as if she would go to the end of all ends with me—no questions asked.

I love her all the more for it.

A love that's starting to grow so vast I fear I may lose myself in it.

A love that scares me more than the Mourning Moor.

"It's a graveyard," Calierin says, her tone low and ominous.

I have never known her to show fear, but right now, it is spelled clearly on her angular features. The sight is enough to properly scare the others. It seems they have gotten to know her, even in the short time spent together.

"So what is so terrible about this graveyard?" Esmeralda asks. "Um . . . the dead can't hurt you."

"These ones can," Galen huffs.

"A long time ago," I explain, "before Niamhara bequeathed her conduit to us, there was a coven of powerful witches that occupied the western lands. They were referred to as the Hexen Horde and had little magic, though they made up for it by the use of other . . . dark deeds."

I pause, examining each face in turn. I need to make sure they understand exactly what we are dealing with. They must make an informed decision about whether or not to come to the Mourning Moor with me. In fact, I hope to dissuade them, though it will not be an easy task to accomplish. At least I have their full attention.

"Lower gods drew strength from their dark deeds," I go on. "Blood oaths, soul binding, sacrifices . . . they did it all for power. However, what they wanted more than anything was eternal life. In this pursuit, they were deceived by one of the gods they worshiped.

A trickster, it is said. He gave them what they sought, but not without exacting a terrible cost.

"You see . . . they *did* gain the ability to live forever, though not in the way they intended. Instead, death still comes naturally to them, and it is not until someone steps on their graves that they are given the opportunity to rise and fight for a new body, a stolen vessel for their wicked souls."

"Fuck," Jago says under his breath. "You make that sound as fun as someone driving a nail into my eyeball. Fuck!" He curses again. "Can't we go around this *lovely* graveyard?"

Valeria's brown eyes hold mine. Her expression tells me she knows the answer already. If there was a way to avoid the danger, we would not be discussing this.

"No," I answer. "This is not your usual graveyard. The witches littered the moor with their graves—an area as expansive as your Eireno Ocean, the majority of its boundaries uncertain."

"But there has to be—"

Valeria interrupts Jago. "You said the witches must fight to claim a body. How hard are they to beat?"

Galen sneers. "Hard enough. They're not flesh and bone—not to mention some of them went willingly into mass graves, vowing to rise together. You step on one grave and release ten of them."

Esmeralda shakes as if assaulted by a chill. She spits on the ground to ward off evil.

"Not flesh and bones," Valeria echoes. "That means our weapons won't hurt them. How do you fight them then?"

"With your will," Calierin answers. She stands behind the group, reclined against a young tree, a blade of grass in her mouth. She seems amused rather than fearful now, as if the idea of this challenge has grown on her.

Jago opens his mouth, then shuts it, his teeth clicking together.

"Our will?" Valeria asks. "Is that really the answer? That's ridiculous. There has to be a . . . tried solution."

Calierin rolls her eyes. "Scholars aren't exactly lining up to devise a list of steps to repel these evil spirits, dear."

Valeria's eyes narrow, animosity aimed at the Tuathacath warrior. Despite our need to work together, they have not overcome their differences. In truth, I suspected it would take a miracle for that to happen.

"I . . . I can't go," Jago declares. "I'm no coward, but I have the will of a moth faced with candlelight. Put a fluffy bed in front of me, and I have to lie on it. A glass of wine, and I have to drink it. A nice backside, and I have to . . ." he trails off as Esmeralda crosses her arms and glares at him.

I nod in understanding. "Only Valeria and I need risk our lives. The rest can wait for us. There is a small wood near the eastern side of the moor. You can hide there, and hopefully remain undetected while you wait for our return."

Calierin throws down her blade of grass. "I will not hide like a coward. Besides, I am not going to miss the chance to fight the spirit of a Hexen Horde witch—much less the chance to meet Niamhara herself."

I nod. I had not expected anything less from her. Her oath to me binds her. Though I am sure she would come, oath or not.

"Fuck, fuck, fuck." Jago stomps the ground, pulling at his hair. "I have to go. I won't abandon Val."

Valeria shakes her head. "No, Jago. I'll be fine. You don't need to risk your life. Besides, it would be foolish for all of us to walk into danger when it's unnecessary."

"But Val, I promised Nana I would take care of you."

Valeria laughs. "And I promised her *I* would take care of *you*. Who do you think she trusts to do a better job?"

Jago presses a fist to his mouth, obviously frustrated and defeated by Valeria's question.

"We should leave." Calierin walks toward the already-saddled horses and mounts her own.

Everyone else does the same, the mood heavy under the still-dark sky. Valeria pats our horse's neck, her mind seemingly racing.

When I approach, she glances sidelong at me. "Earlier, you told me that we might never leave the Mourning Moor. Why is that?"

She misses nothing with that inquisitiveness of hers.

"Because," I say, "as a witch invades her host, she drives their spirit out and sends it into her grave, binding it to her old bones. That way, she does not have to worry about the rightful owner coming back to reclaim what is theirs."

"And the best part . . ." Galen chimes in from atop his horse, "Spirits bound to witch bones never die."

"Fucking saints and feathers!" Jago exclaims. "You're talking about eternal torture." He looks up at Valeria. "Is this quest really worth that risk, cousin?"

Valeria nods without hesitation. "Amira's terrible deeds may condemn her to a similar fate, Jago. I have to do all I can to save her."

Without another word, she mounts our horse and waits for me to do the same.

I admire Valeria's devotion to her loved ones, but I cannot help the pang of jealousy that assails me. Will Valeria ever love me that way? Or at least half as much? If she does, I will be the happiest male alive.

As I prepare to mount, Jago grabs my arm and pulls me aside.

"I don't like this, Korben," he hisses in a low whisper.

I open my mouth to reply, but he cuts me off.

"You have to promise me something."

"I will, if it is within my power."

"If something happens to me, promise you'll defend Valeria with your life."

"I promise, Jago," I say with absolutely no hesitation. "My life would be nothing without her. Of course, I would sacrifice it to save her."

He nods, looking satisfied.

Undoubtedly, we are both of the same mind. Valeria's life is a treasure.

# 32

# VALERIA

*"I would like to torture the bastard. If you can, bring him to me."*

**Saethara Orenthal – Queen of Tirnanog**

We ride across open land. It is unnerving. We're exposed for anyone to see. The only advantage is that we will see them, too.

A vast land stretches out before us, an unforgiving expanse of brown and green with thorny shrubs, coarse grass, and ragged rocks. Storm clouds, heavy and laden with rain, huddle on the horizon, their dark color promising a deluge. The wind whips across the open land, carrying the mournful cries of birds of prey overhead. Our horse shies at the sudden flash of lightning that illuminates the desolate landscape.

We move on, a silent party, each lost in their own grim thoughts. Our destination is a place of dread, a graveyard of witches who will possess us if we tread over their accursed ground. Fear, like a tangible presence, hangs heavy in the air. With every clop of hooves, I brace myself for what's to come, pushing away the dire images my imagination conjures.

Behind us, the distant thunder rumbles like an angry god, a reminder of the dangers that could be closing in. Even though we haven't seen signs of pursuit, I feel certain Saethara's people will come. With every creak of saddle leather, I expect to hear the familiar *whoosh* of arrows or the thunder of hooves bearing down on us.

Yet, greater than the fear of mortal enemies is the awful journey that awaits us in the heart of this desolate expanse. Will we find Niamhara? Or will this wasteland be our tomb and eternal jail to our souls?

"Hey, Korben," Jago calls from the side, peering at the ground with a frown. "How do you know we haven't entered the Mourning Moor yet? You said the boundaries are uncertain."

"I said the majority of the boundaries," Korben answers, riding with a straight back, his chin held high. He looks regal atop our mount, even if I crowd the saddle and the animal is a humble Castella beast of no special breed. "On this side, there is a clear marker. Enough people have inadvertently entered the area, and those who managed to survive have shared their stories with nearby residents. They have gradually established a clear border."

Jago's head swivels all around. "Nearby residents? You mean the hares and snakes?"

We haven't seen any settlements during our journey. I imagine Korben is keeping them at a distance. Still he humors Jago instead of pointing out the obvious.

"The hares, yes," he says. "Not the snakes. They have no hands to fashion such warnings."

"Did the Fae King just tell a joke?" Jago asks the gray clouds above.

A smirk stretches Korben's lips, and I can't help but wish I'd met him before Saethara entered his life.

Bringing up the rear, Calierin interrupts our small respite with the news we've been dreading. "Riders. Two leagues away."

We all turn on our mounts and look. She points past a conglomeration of spiked boulders. I spot our pursuers at the same time that Korben does.

"At least fifty soldiers," he says, his grip tightening around the reins.

"What do you want to do?" Calierin asks, as if the answer isn't obvious.

"There is nothing we can do but try to keep ahead of them." He turns the horse around, faces west once more, and digs his heels into the beast's sides.

My heart gallops as well as the horses. We weave through the rough terrain, avoiding rocks and leaping over thorny bushes. The animals are tired, and according to Korben's last update, we still have two hours before we reach the Mourning Moor.

After twenty minutes of hard riding, it becomes clear our pursuers are gaining on us.

"They're going to catch us," Galen says, followed by a string of curses. "If I weren't so fucking useless without my magic."

With my new hearing, his muttering is clear despite the thundering sound of hooves and the rumbling of the tempestuous sky.

"We can't let them." Korben shakes the reins. "Come on. Go!"

Our horse goes faster, even though the animal appears to be on the last dregs of its energy. The other horses respond to the challenge, also quickening their pace. Korben knows how to lead and is not afraid to do it.

An hour later, our pursuers are even closer, so close that when I glance over my shoulder, I can almost distinguish their features. Calierin, in a daring move that leaves me in awe, flips around on the saddle, nocks an arrow, and lets it loose. Her projectile flies true and hits one of the horses in the lead. The animal topples, crashing to the ground and causing others to do the same. The rest veer right and left, avoiding collision. Our enemies keep riding, undeterred by Calierin's arrows. I fear they will respond in kind, but no arrows come our way. Also . . . no espiritu.

*They want us alive.*

The thought sends a shiver over my body. I can only imagine what Saethara would do to us. Maybe, like Korben, she has been dreaming of revenge all these years.

*Niamhara, if you can hear me, help us!*

I'm tempted to reach for The Eldrystone, but if I touch it, I'll shift. Perhaps I should, anyway. Maybe the Goddess will speak to me again and tell me what to do. Except we're riding too fast, and I fear injuring myself.

"The marker," Korben shouts. "I see it. We can make it! They will not dare enter the moor."

I look into the distance, trying to pinpoint the location even as our horse leaps over a dead bush. It takes me a moment to spot the meager marker, two red-stained posts staked to the ground, and a trail of rocks over the ground.

To our right, there is a small wood, the one where Jago and the others were supposed to hide, but no more. I glance sidelong in my cousin's direction. His expression is intent on Esmeralda, who rides ahead of him. Jago is the best rider I know, and his horse seems to have some leagues left in him. He could be leading us all, but instead, he's protecting Esmeralda.

*Gods!* What if we awaken the spirits, and they come after him. He doesn't think he has the will to fight them, and that lack of confidence is the first problem. If any of us are to come out of the Mourning Moor unscathed, we need to believe in ourselves.

Calierin continues shooting, felling more soldiers. It isn't until she runs out of arrows that she flips back to face the front and leans forward, pushing her mount for more speed and getting right behind Korben, intent on protecting him.

"Halt or we'll shoot," one of our pursuers shouts.

We ride on, the marker only two hundred yards away now.

Arrows *zing* through the air, missing us by mere inches, bouncing off rocks or embedding themselves in bushes. The shots are clearly meant to scare us into heeding their command to stop.

The marker looms closer, the posts taller that I first thought. Bleached skulls circle them at the base, a dire sight that seems to warn death might be preferable to what awaits past the boundary.

Arrows rain down again. One of them flies so close to us that I feel the wind it displaces. These are not warning shots anymore. Korben urges the horse to the left. Another arrow strikes the ground where we would have been had he not changed course.

We're at the marker. Korben and I cross first, followed by Calierin, who is suddenly struck by an arrow and flies off her horse, landing with a bone-crashing *thud* and rolling several feet over the rough ground.

Noticing, Korben makes a wide turn, bringing our mount around. Without hesitation, he rides toward Calierin, leaps off the saddle, and lands next to her fallen shape, La Matadora in hand.

*Gods, we're dead!*

We won't even have to face the witches. This is where we make our stand.

I jump off and join Korben's side, rapier at the ready. Jago joins us a second later, and even Galen makes a show of strength, brandishing a sword he got from Calierin. Only Esmeralda stands back, though she holds a knife.

Our pursuers come to a halt on the other side of the marker. The soldiers arrange themselves next to General Lirion Faolborn. He wears a silver helm with plates that travel along his jawline. Perverse yellow eyes rove over our bedraggled group. A male wearing a crown made of mandible bones stops beside him. He stares at Korben and slides a finger across his throat.

"Surrender or we will kill every single one of you," Lirion says, his tone leaving no doubt in my mind that he means it.

"You will have to fight us." Korben holds the male's gaze, a personal challenge in his expression.

The male sneers. "No, we will not."

He puts a hand out, palm up, and slowly raises it. Several of the soldiers point loaded bows at us, while two others lift their hands, the threat of espiritu crackling at their fingertips.

*Dead or alive. Preferably alive.* Those must be his orders.

"Fight *me*, coward." Korben takes a step forward, blocking me, protecting me.

I start to move when heat flashes in my pocket.

*The Eldrystone!*

Dropping my rapier, I pull the amulet out, free it from the kerchief, and clench it between both hands. Espiritu courses through me, traveling with the speed of lightning, shooting up my arms, colliding in my chest, then zooming down to my feet. A scream tears out of my throat as my body seems to melt, arms and legs dripping black like wax from a candle.

Fluttering shapes peel away from me and take to the air. Ten, thirty, sixty, ninety . . . pairs of black wings beat in force. My consciousness splits a hundred, two hundred, three hundred times.

A swarm of ravens darkens the sky while I stand, still clenching the amulet. At first, I fear I'm losing my mind. There are too many sounds, too many eyes peering out in every direction, then Korben turns to face me and clamps his hands around mine, enveloping them along with The Eldrystone.

"You are all of them," he says. "Command them."

There's another burst of espiritu from the amulet—a last burst of help from Niamhara?—and my confusion vanishes, leaving behind the clarity of many minds acting as one.

*Help us!*

The thought echoes in the minds of a thousand ravens. Each one croaks in response, eyes lowering to our foes, who stare in astonishment, arms raised to release their assault, yet frozen.

The black swarm descends in one orchestrated move, effectively blotting the space between us and our enemies.

"Fire!" Lirion orders.

Arrows and espiritu issue forth. Panic tears through me.

*I'll die!*

"They are your shield and your sword," Korben says.

Flesh pierced. Feathers burned. I feel their deaths, each a stab of pain deep in my chest, a surge of agony and sadness that leaves me as quickly as it comes.

A dozen ravens plummet, but before they hit the ground, they disappear, leaving no trace of their existence.

*They are your shield* and *your sword*, Korben's words reverberate in my mind.

My shields! They died to protect us. Now, they will fight.

*Attack!*

Half of the swarm scatters, spreading over the line of soldiers, then swooping down like deadly arrows, beaks sharp, claws sharper.

Some of the archers loose their arrows while others duck, covering their faces, protecting their eyes. Screams fill the air. I have the sense of skin tearing under my fingernails, of strikes hitting me from all sides. I wince, shrinking, shoulders caving in.

"You are strong," Korben's reassuring voice rings in my ears, though I don't know where he is. All I see are the faces of the soldiers, blood oozing from empty eye sockets.

An image of Lirion flashes through my mind. He brandishes his sword with speed, while a hundred ravens dive in and out, pecking and tearing. That image is superimposed by several soldiers whirling their horses and fleeing, their mounts terrified in their own right.

When it's all said and done, half of the soldiers have fled while most of the others lie on the ground, huddled into tight balls. One crawls on all fours, palpating the ground aimlessly, blood streaking down both cheeks.

The espiritu coursing through my body slowly dies out, leaving me weak. Korben catches me as my legs falter. He holds me up, wrapping an arm around my waist, while I struggle to keep my head held high. I am spent, and I fear so is Niamhara. Another such swarm of ravens would be impossible, but our opponents don't need to know that, so I project strength.

Panting, I survey the damage with a single pair of eyes. There is no sign of the ravens—not even an errant black feather.

Bleeding from many cuts, Lirion stands alone. His breathing is heavy, and his sword hangs uselessly in his large hand. One of his pointed ears looks shorter than the other. He surveys what is left of his army, fallen figures who fared much worse than he did, horses scattered all around.

"Don't be so pleased by your little triumph, this means nothing," Lirion says bitterly. "You will die in that moor."

"I should have died a thousand times over since your so-called queen usurped the throne," Korben says. "Yet, here I am. And I dare say, this *little triumph* feels like fate. Remember me, soldier. Remember this face. If you encounter me again, do not stand in my way, for I am your king, and I will not be forgiving."

"I doubt we will ever meet again, but if we do, you will learn your fate is not so bright. I will delight in tearing you to pieces." Sheathing his sword, he climbs on his horse. Korben was right. Lirion will not brave the moor.

Those who can lick their wounds begin a retreat. We watch them gather their horses and their wounded. Soon, they march away, injured dogs with their tails between their legs.

As exhaustion descends on me, my body goes completely limp in Korben's arms, and the last thing I see is our foes' retreating figures.

# 33

## KORBEN

*"I do."*

**Don Justo Ramiro Medrano – Master Mason**

J ago rushes to my side as I deposit Valeria on the ground on the safe side of the marker. The Eldrystone falls from her hands, the opal looking dull.

"Is she all right?" he asks, concern etched on his forehead.

"She will be. She needs rest now."

He takes her hand and squeezes it. "What was that?"

"Scatter form. What she did . . . it takes practice to endure. I have never seen anything like it."

Which is to say, I have never been able to produce a swarm as mighty as what we just witnessed. A hundred was all I ever managed. But today, the sky was blotted by at least a thousand ravens. Every raven shifter I know can only conjure Corvus form. Up until today and for centuries, I was the only one able to achieve the other three forms.

I pick up the amulet. Esmeralda finds the kerchief and hands it over, her expression solemn as she regards a prone Valeria. I wrap the amulet and place it back in the pouch.

"I'll tend to her," Esmeralda says, retrieving her satchel and shooing Jago away. "I have a tonic that will help her regain some strength."

She pulls a green bottle with a cork stopper from the bag and tips it to Valeria's lips. I help hold Valeria's head. She swallows by reflex, and we repeat the motion a few more times until Esmeralda is satisfied.

"I made it," she explains. "I sell remedies with my troop." With confident hands, she checks her patient over, pressing her ear to Valeria's chest and peeling back her eyelids to inspect the pupils.

"She's going to be all right," she assures Jago, who has started pacing.

"Why is she always so reckless?" he mutters to himself. "And why am I so fucking useless?"

Gingerly, Galen steps over the line of stones, abandoning the *wrong* side of the marker. "It's a damn thing, isn't it, friend?" He pats Jago's shoulder. "Having nothing to hurl back at them." He gestures toward the retreating soldiers, who now look small in the distance.

Jago brushes Galen's hand away and goes back to pacing. I have a feeling he will only calm down once Valeria wakes up.

Still kneeling next to her, I smooth a lock of hair off her forehead. I know the exhaustion that comes after Scatter form, and this knowledge is the only reason I am not pacing alongside her cousin, cursing all my shortcomings.

"You did well, Ravógín. Without you . . ." I trail off, unwilling to contemplate what our state would be had she not defended us as she did.

Facing the moor, Calierin holds her bleeding shoulder where the arrow struck her. "Where exactly are we headed? How far?"

"Half a day's walk," I respond without looking. My main concern right now is Valeria. We're not going anywhere until I ensure she is truly unharmed.

Tearing part of her shirt with her teeth, Calierin devises a bandage and wraps her wound. With that done, she ties the horses to the marker posts. I have no idea if their hoofbeats can disturb the witches' graves, but it's best not to take chances.

Some thirty minutes later, Valeria opens her eyes. She is slow to get her bearings, blinking and swallowing thickly several times before talking in a hoarse voice.

"Did we win?" she asks.

"Thank the saints," Jago exclaims. "How do you feel, Val?"

I watch her closely, holding her hand.

"Um, strange," she replies.

"I bet. You . . . melted into a million ravens." Jago leans closer, eyes narrowed. "You could have given us a warning, you know? I thought I would have to glue you back together."

Valeria sits up, rubbing her forehead. She glances around and sighs in relief when she sees that the soldiers are long gone. We help her to her feet, Jago on her left, while I support her right arm. There is color in her cheeks. It seems Esmeralda's tonic did help.

Tentatively, she feels for the amulet in her pouch.

"Niamhara," she says. "She helped us. The Eldrystone grew warm and when I touched it . . ." She shakes her head, as if she still cannot believe what happened. "I can . . . I can do Scatter form?" she half asks. "Or maybe not. Maybe it was only because the Goddess helped me and—"

I intertwine my fingers with her. "Don't worry about it. You have plenty of time to figure it out. Just try to regain your strength now."

"I'm fine." She disentangles herself from me and walks to our horse, her steps steady.

I cannot help but wonder if she is pretending or truly recovered. She is strong. I do not doubt it, but what she just accomplished was no easy task. Perhaps Niamhara did most of the work? Should we get going? I glance over my shoulder toward the rock outcrop in the distance, our destination. The ground between here and there, as harmless as it appears, may hold our doom. Yet, what other choice do we have?

Valeria hangs her saddlebag over her shoulder. "We're leaving the horses, correct?"

I approach. "Yes. I do not know if animal steps can trigger the curse on the graves, but better to be cautious. It is only a few hours' walk, after all."

"Let's go then." She takes a few steps toward the marker line.

"Are you sure, Val?" Jago asks. "I *know* no one would object if you need to rest."

I am glad her cousin has voiced my own concern. She is more likely to listen to him.

Except she shakes her head. "If we leave now, we'll get there before nightfall. So let's not waste any more time."

I can tell there will be no changing her mind. "I thought about it, and we should form a line. I will lead the way, and you must step only where I step."

"*I'll* lead the way, my king." Calierin bows.

"No need," I reply.

She opens her mouth to protest and closes it when I glance at her sharply.

Jago approaches his horse and retrieves his saddlebag.

"What are you doing?" Valeria asks.

"I'm coming."

"I thought we agreed you would wait for us in the woods." She points toward the small group of trees.

"I changed my mind."

"Jago, please stay here."

He only stands with his chin held high, looking stubborn.

Esmeralda steps to Jago's side, her satchel already in tow.

Jago frowns down at her. "You're not—"

"*You're not* . . . about to tell me I need to hide in the woods, are you?" Esmeralda's gaze flashes fiercely in challenge.

Jago's mouth opens and closes, but no words come out.

The Romani woman makes a smug sound in the back of her throat. "That's what I thought."

"Fucking Faoloir!" Galen exclaims. "Now, if I don't go . . . I'll get deemed a coward."

"You shouldn't worry about that, Galen," I say. "No one will form a new opinion of you if you stay with the horses."

"Fuck you, Korben."

I laugh at his burst of anger. It is satisfying to see. Calierin's hand flies to the hilt of her sword. I shake my head to let her know she does not need to protect my honor. Not from Galen, anyway.

Galen growls in frustration and throws the hood of his cloak over his head. "Let's get this over with then."

We leave the horses tied to the marker posts. The merciful thing would be to set them free in case we don't return, but we can't afford to lose them if we do make it out alive. They should be fine for a day, which I hope is the most this part of our journey will take.

With the weight of La Matadora at my back, I cross over the boundary. The sword will be no help against wicked spirits, but it makes me feel better.

Looking out toward the distant outcrop, I wish I could plan a course that would help us avoid all the hidden graves and deliver us safely to our destination. But any patch of ground I step on is as dangerous as the other. There are no clues to help us avoid peril, so a straight line toward the outcrop is as good a path as any. With a silent prayer to Niamhara, I begin to walk. Valeria comes behind me, followed by Jago and Esmeralda, while Galen and Calierin bring up the rear.

*Guide my steps, Goddess. Do not let this be our end.*

# 34

## VALERIA

*"After all of this, I'd better get my magic back!"*

**Galen Síocháin – Fae Royal Master of Magic**

Korben's strides are longer than mine, so I must stretch uncomfortably to place my feet on his footprints. Esmeralda must be having the same issue, but neither one of us is complaining. We have been walking for thirty minutes now, my heart in my throat the entire time. I don't know exactly what will happen if we step on one of the witches' graves, but my imagination is having a time with it.

Maybe the ground will explode upward, giving way to a host of glowing monsters ready to plunge into our bodies. Or maybe the ground will give way, and we will fall into a pit where animated skeletons dressed in rags will stab us with their pointy bones to transfer their corrupted spirits into—

I shake my head to dismiss my increasingly morbid thoughts. A chilled wind blows across the moor. I think I hear voices, and I can almost tell what they're saying. I cock my head to listen, then decide that's a terrible idea.

"Galen," I say in an attempt to distract myself, "tell me about your family."

"What?" He sounds annoyed by my request.

"Do you have any brothers or sisters?" I insist.

"Um . . . a sister," he answers reluctantly.

"You do?" Korben asks, surprised. "You never said."

The sorcerer lets out a dismissive grunt.

"Where is she?" I ask.

"She lives in Caernamara, my homeland in the north." Galen sounds pensive now.

"Were you two . . . close?"

"Growing up, yes. Later, we lost touch. She married a male I disapproved of. He was of . . . low status." He sounds embarrassed by the admission, a sign that he doesn't think much of status anymore. What with having been in exile for decades, he might have learned a lesson or two about judging others based on riches.

He goes on. "I thought about her often during my time in Castella. More than I ever did after I left Caernamara and became Master of Magic." He clears his throat and adds, "But I'm sure she's better off without me."

"No doubt," Calierin says, as tactful as ever.

"I'm not surprised you feel that way, warrior," Esmeralda says. "I have a feeling you would behead your own mother if she spoke the wrong words."

Her tone is lighthearted, sounding like a joke, but I know better. Esmeralda's sharp wit and tongue are something I experienced on our trek from Alsur to Castellina when her troop helped me escape Don Justo. *Gods!* That feels like so long ago.

"Mother? What mother?" Calicrin says. "I sprouted from a leathery egg. I never met my mother."

Is she suggesting her mother was a snake? Is that supposed to be a joke? I can't tell. I glance over my shoulder. The Tuathacath warrior is focused on the ground, carefully positioning her foot in the spot Galen's just vacated. There is no hint of amusement in her expression.

The sorcerer laughs heartily. "I know some people who also think I'm a viper and sprouted from a leathery egg."

Calierin huffs. "Except in my case it is true. It's the Tuathacath warrior way."

For a moment, she has me believing she's some kind of fae that actually hatches. If cursed graves with ancient witches are possible, why not this? However, Korben's eye roll makes me realize Calierin is just trying to have fun at the expense of us humans.

"We are halfway there," Korben announces after some time. "I will take ten more steps and stop so everyone can take a drink."

At the mention of water, I suddenly realize how thirsty I am. After ten more careful steps, I open my waterskin and take a long swig. Water sloshes as Jago passes Esmeralda his container.

I wipe sweat from my forehead and examine the rocky outcrop in the distance. The terrain from here to there looks no different from the one we already traversed. So far so good. I'm even starting to wonder if this Hexen Horde legend is true, though I don't dare say that out loud, lest I cause us bad luck.

Everyone looks more relaxed, except for Korben. His shoulders are stiff. His every step has been careful and pronounced, as if he's trying to make the deepest imprint possible, so I don't miss my next target.

"We'll be all right, Korben," I say.

He seems startled by my words as his gaze snaps to mine. He was lost in his own thoughts. Perhaps weighing all the variables and all the risks the journey entails.

"I know," he says, without hesitation. His voice is firm, his gaze steady.

If my father hadn't been a king, Korben's performance might have convinced me, but I know well that portraying strength in the face of adversity is one of the most important jobs a leader has.

"What will we find when we get there? When we cross this other veil?" I ask. "A jade cave or a field of fireflies like the legend said?"

"I do not know. The codex did not explain that. It only described how to get here."

Behind us, Esmeralda yelps. A dull slapping sound follows. Heart hammering, I fear we've disturbed one of the graves. My head jerks in her direction. She's frozen, staring at Jago's waterskin on the ground, which she must have dropped.

"I'm sorry," she whispers.

Galen lets out a tired exhalation. "Really? Why don't you just—"

"Why don't you just shut your mouth before you regret it?" Jago cuts him off.

"Let us resume," Korben says in a commanding tone, cutting short the rising tension.

We continue walking. This time, there's no conversation. Our steps are the only sounds apart from the wind and the errant thunderclaps of the retreating storm that never materialized. Fortunately.

When, at last, the outcrop is only a few paces away, I feel like taking off at a run. My legs are restless, tired of overextending themselves, eager to move freely.

"Just a few more steps," Jago says under his breath. "Wouldn't it be ironic if—"

"I know what you're about to say," Esmeralda interrupts. "But bite your tongue, Chavé, before you bring on an ill omen."

"Amén," Galen says.

"Amén?" I echo. "Did the fae sorcerer learn to pray to our saints?"

"Nah. I just like the finality of the word."

"Oh, there's no finality to it. There are always more prayers."

"Indeed," Jago agrees. "In the last few hours, I've prayed to a hundred saints, and it looks like I'm going to have to pray to them a hundred more times just to thank them."

"Jagoooo," Esmeralda stretches out his name in warning. "Ill omens are real, and you're still inviting one by getting ahead of things. Wait till we get there before you start thanking anyone."

Up close, the outcrop is much larger than I first suspected. It's about twenty feet long and eight feet tall. It's made of gray stone, its face etched with the marks of time. Small plants take root in the crevices between the rocks, their green foliage providing a splash of color. The sun has almost disappeared in the horizon, and a beautiful sunset paints the sky with a palette of indescribable colors.

Korben stops in front of what looks like an accidental staircase built into the stone. "We have to climb these . . . steps. They are safe according to the codex."

"Let's get on with it then." Jago releases a big exhalation. "Thank you, San José, San Miguel, San Bernardo, San Pedro for not testing my will. Thank you, San Benedicto and San Rafael for getting us here safely. Thank you, San—"

"That's enough saints. Amén," Galen says, cutting Jago's prayer short.

A nervous laugh goes through the group, and even Jago joins in.

Korben climbs, and we follow. It's easy to find footing, easy to feel exultant in the light of the gorgeous sky and the safety of our spirits still rooted in our bodies. We crossed the Mourning Moor unscathed. I wonder briefly about the probability of what we just did, but I'm too relieved to do more than that.

*Unless the legend is all bolster and no substance*, a part of me says.

Regardless, we're here now, and there, just above Korben's head, I see the shimmering light of the torn veil.

*Saints and feathers!* We're about to meet a goddess.

# 35

## KORBEN

*"Let us go back, Jaws. I have an idea."*

**Lirion Faolborn – Fae General**

Valeria pulls The Eldrystone from her pouch and gingerly unwraps it from the kerchief.

"I'll shift if I touch it," she says, offering me the amulet. "I think you're meant to do this."

I shake my head slightly. I have not found favor with Niamhara in a long time, so I do not think Valeria is right. Still, she might find it difficult to widen the rip in the veil in her raven form, so I must try.

Holding the amulet tightly in my left hand, I reach overhead with my right hand. It disappears through the shimmering rip. At first, I feel nothing. I am about to pull out when a buzzing begins in my ears and a burst of light blinds me. I become overwhelmed, confused, my senses distorted.

*Open.*

I tighten my grip on The Eldrystone.

*Let us in, Goddess.*

Suddenly, the air shimmers, and I step through light, my chest tight with held breath. Millions of colors fill my vision. I blink to dispel them, and when they finally clear, I nearly jump back and draw my sword. It takes all my presence of mind to calm my instincts and look, really look.

A dozen people, positioned shoulder to shoulder, stand before me. The first thing I notice is their expressions. They are a combination of relief and gratitude. The second thing is their white flowing garments, held at the waist by a simple belt. The third is their pointed ears. They are fae, every single one of them. I am not sure what I was expecting, but it was not a group of my own kin.

"Welcome, Korben Theric," a female says, her voice shaking with emotion.

A knot forms in my throat at the sight of her beautiful face. Her dark eyes, so much like my own, regard me with more than relief and gratitude. They also brim with joy.

"Mother?" I whisper, sure that I somehow lost my mind when I crossed the veil.

"Son!" As if unable to help herself, she breaks from the line and envelops me in her arms.

At first, I am frozen, my arms tense at my sides. Then I realize it does not matter if I have gone mad. This is my mother. Overwhelmed by emotion, I return her embrace, coaxing a sob from her lips.

My companions appear behind me, crossing the veil one by one.

Valeria's eyes are wide, confusion shaping her expression. She regards my mother from head to toe, then scans the line of people who have turned to face her and bow reverently in welcome. It seems she sees the same thing I do, so perhaps I am not crazy.

"Korben, what's happening?" she asks, her words sharp with distrust.

I pull away from my mother. She lets me go reluctantly and takes a couple of steps back, a silver line of tears underlining her eyes.

"I am sure you have countless questions, my son," my mother says, "but first, we must take the conduit to Niamhara." Her eyes turn to Valeria as she says this.

If there was ever any doubt that I had lost the Goddess's favor, it is completely erased at that moment. I glance down at The Eldrystone still in my hand. Some time ago, this revelation would have hurt. Now, I know Valeria is a much better choice for this . . . privilege? Burden? Either way, I will be with her every step of the way to help her carry the load.

"Here." I offer her The Eldrystone.

She looks at it with a frown. "I'm not . . ." Her inquisitive brown eyes rove over my mother's face. "I'm only here to help Korben."

"And you have, child," my mother says.

*My mother!* How is she here? What is this place?

"Now, Niamhara needs you," she adds. "Take The Eldrystone and follow me."

Valeria hesitates.

"Take it, you will not shift," my mother reassures her, then turns. The line of people behind her parts to let her through, revealing a cave-like enclosure with curving walls that rise to a concave ceiling. The surface of the rock glows with jade-colored bioluminescence, casting the only light in the space.

Hesitantly, Valeria takes the amulet, and indeed, she does not shift. She looks up at me and shrugs.

As we follow, my mother enters a tunnel. Valeria goes in with hesitant steps, eying the people who continue to regard her with reverence.

"What in Faoloir's name is going on here?" Galen asks, leaning close to whisper in my ear.

I shake my head. "I am as confused as you are."

"Is that your mother?"

"She . . . looks like her."

I move to follow Valeria, half expecting to be told that I am not allowed, but no one says anything—not that I would have listened. There is no way in all the hells I would let her disappear through that tunnel by herself. Jago hurries after me, just as protective of his cousin. We nod to each other, a silent agreement passing between us.

We will protect Valeria with our lives.

Calierin is quick behind me. I am surprised she has managed to keep her sword sheathed. I can tell by the way her fingers keep flexing that it is no easy matter.

The tunnel is long and lined with the same bioluminescent creatures. My mother walks with hurried, yet graceful steps, her white robes billowing behind her. Valeria's steps match hers exactly, as if we are still walking over the Mourning Moor, and she is afraid to unleash evil on us.

After a ten-minute walk, we exit the tunnel and walk onto a long balcony, its railing seeming to grow from the floor, carved expertly from the stone itself. Beyond the balcony, an expanse of green forest stretches to meet the horizon and the bluest sky I have ever seen. Two suns shine above, one larger than the ones in Tirnanog and Castella, the other one smaller.

I lean close to the railing and look down. We are high above, perched on the side of what looks like a formidable peak. There is no way to tell how far from the ground we are, but the trees look massive, veritable giants that make even the tallest trees in my realm look like withered bushes.

We walk along the balcony, wind buffeting our hair. Esmeralda clings to Jago, clearly unsettled. Around a bend, on the side of the peak, steps lead further up. We climb at least a hundred of them before we enter the mountain once more and traverse up a steep tunnel.

Galen breathes raggedly.

"Exercise is good for the body, you know?" Jago says, his joking tone strained. "Or are you in the habit of bespelling rugs to get places?"

"So I'm not only a coward," Galen huffs. "I'm also lazy?"

"Your words, not mine."

When the tunnel ends, we exit onto a plateau surrounded by clouds and mist. The area is vast, nearly as big as Elf-Dún's grounds. In the middle, a palace with tall doors and windows rises majestically.

My gaze draws upward to the breathtaking sight that unfolds before me. The colossal building sparkles in the double sunlight, its walls and towers crafted from flawless jade. Intricate carvings and ornate details are etched into the stone, giving the walls the sense of movement. Surrounding the palace's base, formations of precious stones shine in vibrant hues, creating a dazzling spectacle. Spear-shaped ruby, emerald, and sapphire clusters gleam like stars against the backdrop of the jade, casting a magical aura over the entire scene.

"Now, I have seen it all," Esmeralda says in a rush of breath.

My mother guides us through the tall doors. Inside, everything is carved from precious stones or white marble. The floor shines, reflecting our shapes, leading us to a mezzanine that reveals hundreds of fae gathered below. They all glance in our direction, murmuring softly, their expressions hopeful.

We move further until we stand before a massive stone door.

"Niamhara's chamber," my mother says, her hand on a handle carved from the same slab as the door. She eases it open as if it weighs nothing.

A chamber entirely different from the rest of the palace is revealed. With walls, ceiling, and floor all crafted from rich, dark wood, the place radiates warmth and comfort. The light of two suns spills through a floor-to-ceiling window. Bookshelves line the walls, burdened with heavy volumes and countless scrolls. Colorful flowers adorn every corner, their sweet fragrance filling the air. This is a space to relax, read, and dream.

My mother guides Valeria deeper into the room toward a group of people who quietly retreat to the edges of the grand chamber, revealing what looks like a bed of scrolls where a towering female lies. It's difficult to tell, but she appears to be over seven feet tall, her long limbs wilting under a white gossamer dress. She has pointed ears and long hair the color of silver. She appears neither young nor old, only timeless. Her features contort in pain, a jarring contrast to a face that seems more suited to serenity and contemplation.

As I look closer, I notice her bronze skin appears translucent, giving the impression that she is fading away.

*Who is she? Where did she come from?*

"Approach, child." My mother invites Valeria with a hand gesture. "She has been waiting for you."

Valeria takes short steps, careful not to trample the edges of a long scroll that drapes like a sheet to the floor. The characters, though written in the same language as the codex, are illegible due to an unsteady hand.

"She is here, Niamhara," my mother says, using the Goddess's name with familiarity, the way one would talk to a friend and an equal, not a deity.

Slowly, the Goddess's eyes open. They match the color of her silver hair and remind me much of Kadewyn's pale gaze, except there is a hollow quality to Niamhara's wandering look. It takes her a moment to focus on Valeria. The Goddess opens her mouth, but only a breathy sound comes out despite her effort to form words.

"I . . . have your amulet," Valeria says, stretching The Eldrystone toward Niamhara's limp hand.

The Goddess's fingers twitch, but that is all. Valeria glances at my mother, who nods in encouragement. With her free hand, Valeria reaches for Niamhara and gently turns her palm up. Holding The Eldrystone by its chain, Valeria deposits it in the Goddess's hand. The opal looks small sitting there.

Expectantly, everyone stares at Niamhara's face, waiting for a change in her feeble appearance. There is none. My mother presses a fist to her mouth.

*Are we too late?*

Awkwardly reaching over the scrolls, Valeria rises to her tiptoes and folds Niamhara's long fingers over the amulet. When she lets go, they spring back open. Frustrated, she kicks the scrolls out of the way, stepping closer. Once more, she closes Niamhara's grip over the amulet, this time holding it in place.

We wait, frozen, watching for the smallest change in Niamhara's state.

Nothing.

"Is it too late?" Valeria glances at my mother, who shakes her head in despair, unable to provide an answer.

Valeria turns to the Goddess. "Please, stay. You can't leave. There's still much for you here. All of these people, they . . . they love you."

Yes, it is clear to see. They do love her . . . the way one loves a dear friend, someone who makes everything better only because they are there to listen, to offer a kind word. It is odd for me to simply know this, but it seems obvious.

Valeria's gaze returns to Niamhara. All hope in her expression disappears, despair taking its place. In her eyes I see the chaos that will engulf Tirnanog and Castella without the aid of the Goddess. We will fight, of course we will, but much unnecessary pain and death will follow. Saethara and her accomplices will be difficult to topple. It might take years to gather enough support to make any sort of difference. In the meantime—my kin still trapped in Castella, imprisoned by Amira's cruel decree—will continue to suffer unjustly.

Overcome by fear of that future, I step to Valeria's side and cover her hands with mine.

Valeria asked Niamhara to remain and enjoy all that is still here for her. I feel a different kind of entreaty is required.

"We need you, Goddess of Radiance," I say, squeezing hard, making the scrolls under Niamhara's wasted body crinkle. "Your children flounder without you. Some unknown evil has taken hold of Tirnanog. I feel it, rotting the magic that courses through the earth, filling us with something dark and wicked. We need you. That is why you have to stay."

A small moan escapes through Niamhara's quivering lips. With significant effort, she opens her eyes again. Her hand twitches slightly under our combined grips. She seems to focus all her strength on the slight pressure of her fingers around the amulet.

Suddenly, heat jumps from Valeria's hands to mine. It shoots up my arms and quickly suffuses me. In an instant, my blood quickens in my veins, traveling at a speed long forgotten, infusing every corner of my body with the energy to become something else. My heart gallops at a frantic rate. My skin prickles.

I feel reborn.

Through my own shock, I look at Valeria. She is glowing, her expression mirroring the way I feel. She begins to tremble, then her surprise morphs to pain—the same pain that abruptly tears through my muscles, threatening to shred them to bits.

The glow intensifies, and I realize it's coming from Niamhara, and we are trapped in it.

*Fuck!*

We need to let go or else . . .

I pull on Valeria's hands, but they seem glued to Niamhara's. I attempt to open my mouth to tell her to help me, but my jaw will not move. Instead, I search her gaze. Her eyes flash with a mixture of desperation and resignation. She seems willing to pay any price if it means the Goddess will be there to save our realms.

Except *I* am not!

For the past two decades, I have been miserable, full of nothing but hatred and desire for retribution, expecting nothing except further misery. But when I met Valeria, I found out more was still possible. She reshaped my life, and I am not willing to give that up.

*Help me, Valeria!*

My eyes jerk toward our joined hands as I silently entreat her. She blinks in acknowledgment and begins to pull. I feel the way her hands tense under mine. I heave with her as hard as I can.

We move not an inch.

The energy that first suffused me begins to flow in the opposite direction, back into The Eldrystone. Into Niamhara. It is as if the Goddess is absorbing it all back, even our life force.

"Hey, what's happening?!" Jago demands, his voice sounding like a distant echo. "Something's wrong. Will someone do something?"

When his request is met by inaction, he steps up to Valeria and tries to grab her shoulders. Before he makes contact, there is a burst of sparks, accompanied by a loud crackling sound, and he flies backward.

*Niamhara, please!* I beg.

As soon as the thought forms in my mind, the Goddess sits up with a jerk, and Valeria and I are thrown back as unceremoniously as Jago. We crash to the polished wooden floor and slide for several feet.

My head swims, but I manage to sit up and crawl to Valeria.

"Ravógín, are you all right?"

Her eyes are closed, her head lolling to one side. She had full contact with Niamhara. Valeria's energy was absorbed more directly, more fiercely than mine.

Her eyelashes are perfectly still. Her hair lies limp and lifeless around her face. Her mouth is slightly open. Is she breathing? *Oh, please!* A wave of despair washes over me, an icy, suffocating tide. She is deathly still, broken and discarded. And for what? I should have taken her with me, away from everything.

I take her face in my hands and turn it in my direction, looking for signs of life. I watch the stillness of her chest, a silent prayer on my lips. Her skin feels chilled and lacks her normal color.

"No, no, no. Valeria!"

My heart pounds in my ears. I trace the delicate lines of her face. She is so cold. Despair grips me, slowly turning to fury, a feeling I am well accustomed to.

*Someone will pay for this.*

A flicker of movement catches my eye. Her mouth trembles, then a small gasp escapes her lips, a sound as fragile as a newborn's cry. Her lids flutter, then open slowly. Tears fill my eyes.

"My love." I take her hand and press it to the side of my face. *Please be all right.*

Her chest heaves with each ragged breath. Her life hangs by a thread. If anything happens to her, the world will burn.

# 36

## VALERIA

*"Too late. It is too late."*

**Shara Theric – Fae Queen**

Darkness. A heavy, suffocating blanket smothers me. I try to move, to call out, but my body doesn't respond. Fear, cold and clammy, floods into the corners of my mind. I'm slipping away into a void of nothingness.

*"No, no, no. Valeria!"*

A spark ignites within the darkness. My lungs burn, a desperate plea for air. My muscles are on fire, every single one. Slowly, reluctantly, a shred of consciousness seeps in. Images flicker and fade, a disjointed puzzle trying to form. Where am I? What happened?

My eyes open. The world is a blur for a panicked moment. Sharp pain lances through my body. My head throbs, relentless drums beating against my skull. I try to sit up, but my body is weak, heavy. My gaze falls on a figure kneeling beside me, their face a mask of worry and relief. It's him. Korben. His eyes waver with unshed tears.

"My love," he says.

I groan weakly, feeling life slipping away.

He lets out a shaky breath. "You will be all right."

Uncertainty laces his tone. Maybe it's too late for me. I feel exhausted, my body hollowed out with nothing else to give.

"You will . . . help A-mira?" I ask, my words broken.

Korben shakes his head. His face looks strange, and I realize it's because the scar on his face is gone.

"*You* will help Amira," he says. "She needs her sister."

"I . . . I don't think I'm . . ."

Someone approaches. I don't hear them or see them, but I sense their aura. It's soothing, like a balm on all the injuries I've ever endured, and not just the physical ones. The relief is so great, I let out an involuntary whimper.

Korben looks up and up.

Niamhara stands nearby, her tall frame towering over us.

Wearing a gentle smile on her now-radiant face, she kneels and picks me up as if I'm nothing but a babe. Reluctantly, Korben lets go of my hand as she takes me to her bed. When she lays me down, the scrolls disappear into thin air.

The Goddess sits by my side, goodness radiating from her, like heat from a campfire. Shame washes over me as I think of all the terrible things I've done. I have been impatient, selfish, prideful. I have betrayed. I have hated.

I have murdered.

"Hello, Valeria," she says in the melodic voice of a lifetime friend. Leaning closer, she presses her index finger to my forehead and says, "You will be well."

Immediately, the pain in my muscles vanishes, and the fog over my mind clears, leaving me feeling as if I've just awakened from the most restful sleep of my life. I blink, perplexed, and look up at Niamhara in awe.

"I cannot have my chosen one feeling anything other than wonderful." She smiles with such openness and genuine happiness that I wonder if I've ever met anyone who is genuinely good.

Niamhara seems to be . . . pure.

I can't think of any other way to describe her.

Out of the corner of my eye, I notice Korben and Jago. Niamhara notices them, too, and gets up to allow them to come nearer. I push off the bed and hook one arm over Korben's neck, and the other over Jago's. They embrace me awkwardly but willingly, laughing and squeezing me tight.

When I pull away, I notice Esmeralda, Galen, and Calierin smiling, though Calierin's smile quickly disappears and she stares at the ceiling as if it's the most wondrous thing in the universe.

We turn to face the Goddess, craning our necks. I'm at a loss for words. What do you say to such an . . . awe-inspiring being?

She speaks first, extending her arms as if ready to embrace us all. "Welcome to the Whispering Wilds. I have looked forward to meeting each of you for a long time. I am sure you have many questions, and they will all be answered. But there is someone here who wishes to see you." She looks at Korben, who frowns in confusion.

"Faolan." She glances to the side and gestures with her hand. "Come."

Korben lets out a gasp and turns. A man of Korben's same height and build approaches. I know immediately who he is, the resemblance is uncanny.

Faolan Theric. Korben's father.

He's been standing there, hidden behind the attendants, waiting patiently. Arms wrapping tightly around Korben, he embraces him.

"Son!" he says, pouring so much emotion into that single word that goosebumps prickle up my arms.

"Father!"

They remain in each other's tight hold for a long moment. Korben's mother watches them, tears sliding down her cheeks as she smiles joyously.

How are they here? They're supposed to be . . . what? Dead? The fae don't talk about death the way we do. They depart, go to the Glimmer. Does that mean we're in . . . heaven? If so . . .

I glance around searching for Mother. She was fae. She . . .

Niamhara takes my hand, which looks like that of a child in her grip. "She is not here, dear. I am sorry. The veil was closed, and I could not bring her back to me. I have lost so many of my children." Sadness impregnates her voice, the ache of a mother's loss.

I clench my teeth to stop the tears that threaten to rise. Instead, I focus on Korben and his happiness.

He pulls away from his father. "How? How is this possible?"

"We're in the Glimmer," Galen says.

"What?" Calierin sounds panicked. "Does that mean we are dead?"

"No, Calierin," Niamhara responds, startling the Tuathacath warrior. "You are not dead. No one here is. We have much to discuss, but there is something else." She pads toward the stone door and walks out of the room. Now, I understand why all the doors and entryways are as tall as they are.

Outside, hundreds of voices rise in a mirthful chant. People cheer, clap, cry—their vigil rewarded by the only news they were willing to accept: their Goddess has been saved.

"It is all well, friends," she says, holding up The Eldrystone, which she has not let go of. "I am whole once more, and you will have to endure me forever."

Many laugh. Others bat their hands as if she just told a silly joke.

"Go home and know I thank you. Your thoughts for my well-being gave me the strength I needed to hold on. Everything will go back to normal now."

The crowd disperses reluctantly, though they talk excitedly, their moods turned around completely.

"This place is curious," Galen says under his breath. He doesn't seem comfortable for some reason.

"Indeed," Calierin says.

"The two of you in agreement?" Jago pipes in. "Of course it would happen the day we got to heaven. It's a miracle."

When I don't see Korben by our side, I scan the room and find him standing with his parents, the three of them forming a tight circle as they talk. Their expressions suggest tremendous eagerness to soak in every bit of each other's attention, and though I'm happy for him, I can't help the pang of sadness that assaults me once more.

What I wouldn't give to see my mother and father again.

"Loreleia was a fine person," Niamhara says, approaching me then guiding me toward an adjacent room—one that turns out to be some sort of waiting area to her bedchamber.

The space is vast and airy, bathed in a soft, ethereal light that filters through alabaster windows. The walls are adorned with scenes depicting gardens and forests made from multicolored jewels. They sparkle, making the scenes feel alive.

Galen whistles. "That's several fortunes on those walls."

He huffs as Calierin elbows him.

In the center of the room, a low platform is carved from what looks like a single slab of moonstone, its circular surface polished to a mirror sheen. Around it, a seating area is strewn with embroidered cushions and feather-soft throws. In the middle, instead of a fire pit, a cluster of amethysts—each the size of a child's head—emits a gentle warmth, casting a soothing purple hue over the room. The air is filled with the scent of jasmine and citrus. It's a lovely place meant for people to lounge in comfort.

Niamhara sits by the pit, closing her eyes to the warmth, enjoying it, as if glad to be alive. It seems like such an odd relief. Of course, I never imagined a goddess could die. In fact, I need to reassess my concept of what a deity is supposed to be.

We hesitate, and Niamhara encourages us to take seats around the pit. Everyone seems unsure of whether or not to sit close to her. Would it be disrespectful to do so? Or would it be rude not to?

"I will not bite," Niamhara says, sounding amused.

In the end, we find ourselves sitting at perfectly even intervals, as if we took a ruler and measured the distance to avoid offending anyone.

"Before I say anything else," Niamhara starts, "I must thank you for the risk you took coming here. You arrived with not a moment to spare." She seems sobered by the fact that she almost died. Spreading her arms out, she adds, "Now, I will answer anything you want to know."

My mind goes blank. I look at the others, sure they'll have questions of their own, but they seem as baffled as I am.

She smiles. "This is the typical reaction I get from everyone when they first arrive. Therefore, I am always prepared to commence with a little story that explains a lot and gets people comfortable to start asking questions, so now, hear my tale." She takes a deep breath, then begins.

"I am not a goddess, not any more than anyone who creates anything."

We all exchange confused glances. I feel my entire view of the universe is about to be completely remade.

"I came to the Whispering Wilds thousands of years ago, and I was not alone. My twin sister was with me. She wanted to travel, so we left our home together. We went from realm to realm, finding openings in the fabric between them. Some of the realms were dark and primitive, and others bright and advanced. Some were inhabited and others were not. Some were terribly dangerous, while others seemed lackadaisical in comparison.

"In short, we visited thousands upon thousands of worlds, many of them as different as a star from a dust mote. Others as similar as my sister and I are in appearance. We kept track of every place we visited, or so we thought. It turned out our record-keeping was wildly unsatisfactory, and we were never able to find our way back home."

I have the feeling she has told this story more times than she would care to count. Yet, the sadness in her expression seems as vivid as that of a first telling.

She goes on. "We tried. Oh, holy winds, did we try. But we were never able to return. I accepted our fate many years before my sister did. For her sake, however, I continued searching alongside her. During those futile centuries, try as I might to convince her to accept the truth, she never did and refused to stop looking.

"The day we arrived here, I was . . . tired. Searching, visiting realm after realm, only brought me deep disappointment. I fell ill—my mind turning dark and despondent. Seeing this, my sister acquiesced to make a temporary home here. She still continued searching while I recovered, mapping thousands of doors between this and other realms. She did not stray far, however. We learned our lesson well. We only had each other and would not run the risk of getting separated.

"She, inevitably, grew restless. As my mind improved, she began to insist it was time to leave, to continue the search for our home. Just the thought of returning to that futile task sent me back into despondency. My sister was understanding at first, but eventually, she came to believe that I was lying, that I was not truly ill.

"One day, I finally made a decision. You see, she was always the leader, the strongest of the two of us. It was her idea to leave home. She wanted adventure, and even though I was afraid to travel, I let her convince me. I thought it would be good for me, I thought it would make me brave. And I guess, in the end, it did, but not the way my sister would have hoped.

"Instead, I found the courage to stand up to her, to forge my own path."

She pauses and looks at everyone in turn. We are riveted by her story, eyes locked on her beautiful features, determined not to miss a single word.

"I told her I was staying here," she continues. "I told her I wanted to use my talent to create something good, to thrive in my own way.

She grew angry and left." Niamhara frowns, looking as if she's remembering that day.

She shakes her head. "Then I found Tirnanog. My sister had mentioned this realm when we first settled here, as a way to encourage me to keep searching." She looks at Korben. "It was enchanting, and I thought others should enjoy it, too.

"Yes, fae are my creation. It was imperfect, as creations often are. With time, I saw the trouble magic was causing among you, so I created The Eldrystone to help, placing part of my essence within the stone. I did not wish to intervene more than that. I wanted you to govern yourselves and learn. Othano Theric was full of goodness. He still is." She smiles fondly at the mention of the first Theric to ever hold The Eldrystone, Korben's ancestor. "For thousands of years, it worked." She sighs. "The Eldrystone allowed good leaders to control those who wanted to use magic for ill purposes. And it might have continued to work if not for . . . my sister's return."

*Her sister?!*

Niamhara glances at me, an expression of understanding stamped on her features. I'm suddenly reminded of Amira, and I can't help but think of all the trouble *she* has caused.

"You might have heard of her." Niamhara smiles sadly.

"Pardon me, Goddess," Korben says.

"Please, call me Niamhara."

"Sure, N-Niamhara. Um, I was not aware you had a sister. I have not heard of her." He searches Galen's and Calierin's faces, probably wondering if *they* have heard of such a thing.

They both shake their heads.

"Her name is Morwen."

Korben stiffens in surprise. "That is . . . you mean Morwen *the Mistwraith*?" he says, hardly able to put a full name to the revelation.

"Unfortunately, yes," Niamhara confirms. "She has been working against me for . . . what now?" She taps her forehead. "Time is difficult for me sometimes."

"Fifty years," Galen suggests. "That's around when the trouble began in Caernamara."

Niamhara nods. "I have not seen my sister since she left, before I first visited Tirnanog. I have tried to find her, to talk to her, but she eludes me. I imagine her continued search for our home was fruitless, so she eventually returned. It seems she didn't approve of what I'd done in Tirnanog, or perhaps she saw her interference as a way to get back at me for abandoning her."

"I'm sorry, but it looks to me as if *she* abandoned *you*," Esmeralda says in her usual bold, no-one-intimidates-me tone.

Niamhara shrugs. "It is a matter of perspective, I suppose."

"Is your sister behind Saethara's actions?" Korben asks, his gaze darkening.

At that moment, I can't help but wonder if he ever imagined a scenario where Saethara didn't betray him, where they met and remained happily married—no stabbing involved. Frowning, I stare at the glowing amethysts, feeling an unwelcome pang of jealousy again. The idea sounds stupid the more I think about it, but I'm yet to learn how to let my head prevail over my petty heart.

"I am afraid so, Korben," Niamhara replies, placing a hand atop his, her expression like that of a mother consoling her child. "Morwen first enlisted a male by the name of Lirion Faolborn, who in turn found Saethara and put her on the path to the Royal Mate

Rite. At first, they sought to steal The Eldrystone to simply cause chaos, but that changed. You see . . . when Aldryn Theric opened the veil between Tirnanog and Castella, the magic I injected into the fae realm was able to travel freely. It was a good thing, and I never imagined there could be devastating consequences for anyone, me included. But somehow, Morwen figured out that trapping The Eldrystone in Castella would weaken me, so she changed her plans."

She pauses, giving us a moment to process.

"One thing you should all know," she continues, "is that Morwen could have done all these things herself. We share the same skills. She did not need allies. However, she has always enjoyed games, and I am sure she has derived endless pleasure from using my children against me."

She seems distraught for a quick moment, but she expertly hides the emotion. Her sister's betrayal sounds horrible. It's far worse than anything Amira has ever done to me. In fact, Amira's decision to imprison the fae had nothing to do with me. She didn't do it to hurt me. If anything, she thinks she's protecting me from my own naïvety—not to mention she feels it's her responsibility as queen.

Galen grabs his head and pulls at his hair, stretching the skin around his eyes until they are only narrow slits. "I'm developing a headache."

"No, you are not," Niamhara says with a wide smile.

"All right, I'm not, but I'm . . . stunned. I could've never imagined any of this." He throws his arms out demonstratively. "What you are saying is that you come from a place where there are others like you? Others who can . . . *puff* . . ." he mimics an explosion with his hands, "create people. That's just incomprehensible." He seems disturbed by it all.

"We all have the power to create," Niamhara says.

"Yes, but people?!"

"You have the same power within you, Galen, but you have sworn never to have children."

"How do you know that I . . .?" He trails off, shaking his head. Instead, he asks a different question. "How did you do it? How did you create us?"

"I used my magic—to use a term you are familiar with."

Galen still seems displeased. "We're said to be made in your image, which is why we inherited magic, but I can't use it to create life."

"Do you wish you could?"

"No. I just want to understand how *you* made us." The way he says *you* makes it sound as if he's underwhelmed by his creator, as if upon seeing Niamhara he has found her lacking.

"Galen," Korben growls, "you are out of line."

"It is all right." Niamhara waves a hand at Korben. "These are valid questions, and it is not the first time someone has asked them." She thinks for a moment. "I have pondered this many times. I do not know why you did not inherit the entire spectrum of my abilities, but I do not think that is a bad thing."

"I don't either," Calierin says. "I would hate to see what kind of beings *this* one would create." She hooks a thumb in Galen's direction.

"Look who's talking," Galen bites back.

Deep in his throat, Korben growls in dissatisfaction, glaring at them. The two children—they're definitely acting like a couple of brats—look chagrined, while Niamhara smiles in amusement.

Nothing seems to affect her—at least not the way I expect. By all accounts, she's the mother of the fae. Yet, she doesn't act like any parent I've ever met. She strikes me more like an indulgent grandmother.

I like her. I like her a lot and find myself smiling. She sees it and returns the smile with a wink.

Unexpectedly, she rises to her feet. "I know there are more questions, but I also know you are hungry, tired, and dirty. There are chambers prepared for you where you can bathe, change, and rest. Afterwards, we shall enjoy a lavish supper. And do not worry, both Tirnanog and Castella will keep while you recover your strength, which you will need for what is to come."

She gestures toward an attendant by the entrance, who exits and immediately returns with a larger group of people dressed in the same white robes.

"They will guide you to your chambers and will fetch you when it is time for our supper. Now, I have a few things to attend to. Unfortunately, I have been . . . indisposed for quite some time."

She leaves, and we stand mute for several beats.

"With this palace, I thought I'd seen it all," Esmeralda pipes in, "but you lot really know how to keep things interesting."

We all smile if a bit stiffly. Interesting is one way to describe it.

# 37

## VALERIA

*"It was folly to think we could conquer the infinite realms."*

**Niamhara – Traveler**

Our bedchamber is as inviting as Niamhara's. The space is adorned in warm tones of brown and yellow, with soft tapestries hanging from the walls. There is an open balcony with a magnificent view of the forest we passed earlier. It stretches below us like a living carpet in every hue of green, while above, the azure sky shines with the dimming light of two suns.

"This is incredible," I say, my eyes roving over the awe-inspiring view. I can't help but think of Cuervo and how much he would enjoy perching on this balcony.

After inspecting the space, Korben stops behind me, wraps his arms around my waist, and pulls me to him. I melt into his solidity, unable to believe we're really here.

"We did it," I say.

"*You* did it."

"It was a team effort, and I will brook no argument about that."

"Yes, my love." The words, spoken as a whisper in my ear, send a shiver down my spine. "Anything you say. I seek only your happiness and . . . comfort."

Suddenly, he sweeps me off my feet and cradles me in his arms. I shriek in surprise.

"Comfort being the most important thing at this moment," he adds, walking toward a door in the back of the room.

The sound of running water registers in my ears for the first time.

"Quite the bath chamber, do you agree?" Korben says, setting me down on a stone floor radiating with warmth.

The room around us feels like the corner of a private forest rather than a bath chamber. Instead of a tub, an ever-flowing stream of water cascades into a crystalline pool. Around us, shelves made of twisting branches hold fluffy towels, robes, bars of fragrant soap, and bottles with liquids of every color.

"I agree," I say, then frown at him. His face has changed.

"What?"

"I noticed earlier . . . your scar is gone."

He touched his face. "Truly?"

I nod. "I kind of miss it."

"In that case . . ." The scar reappears.

I gasp. "How did you do that?"

He shrugs one shoulder. "My shifting magic is back."

"Oh."

Korben picks one of the bottles from the shelves and uncorks it. He tips it to his nose, then mine. "What do you think of this?"

"Umm." I don't recognize the scent, but it's wonderful.

Setting it back down, he takes hold of my tunic and pulls it over my head. "You are in terrible need of a bath."

"Really? Do I stink?" I try to smell myself.

"Nothing like that. It is just that your body needs my hands to soothe it."

I lift an eyebrow. "Is that so?"

He smirks, crouching to remove my boots, then proceeding with my leggings. Soon, I'm naked.

"I believe it's my turn." Sliding my hands under his shirt, I caress his muscular abdomen and chest.

He shudders.

"It seems I'm not the only one who needs to be *soothed*."

"Ravógín, your mere presence does that."

"You're such a charmer."

When I lower his trousers, his shaft falls heavily. He's hard, so hard, and I find my core growing instantly wet at the sight. Impatiently, he kicks off his boots and trousers, then lifts me slightly and walks me into the pool of water.

The temperature is perfect, and we both groan in satisfaction. He kisses me deeply, his length pressing against my navel. I run my fingers over his skin, trace the scar over his eye and the one across his chest. He lowers his head and gathers my nipple into his mouth, sucking and licking.

With a grunt of protest, he pulls away and spins me around. "You are too tempting, little raven. First, I must soothe you. Afterward, I will thoroughly fuck you."

He reaches for the bottle we smelled earlier and pours a heavy dose of pearlescent liquid into his palm. Gently, he proceeds to wash my hair, his fingers tracing relaxing circles into my scalp. My eyes close of their own accord, and I groan in pleasure.

"Hmm, can we stay here?" I ask.

"I would not object as long as this is one of my daily tasks." He comes closer, his shaft coming to rest directly over my rear.

He grips me suddenly, a hand flat on my abdomen, quickly descending to rub circles over my aching bud. I throw back my head, and Korben kisses my neck, his . . . cock—it's the word he uses, after all—pressing and pressing, going between my butt cheeks.

I gasp and look back questioningly.

He sobers a little, his hooded eyes clearing.

"Is that . . . something couples do?" I ask, feeling shy.

He nods. "Yes, but we don't ever have to, unless, of course, you want it."

I have no idea whether or not I want it, so I don't say anything.

"I did not intend to give you the impression it was what I wanted. It just felt good," he says.

"It . . . did," I agree demurely.

He smiles, then turns me around again, pushing me under the cascading stream to work the suds off my hair. I wash his hair next, the feel of the silky strands strangely erotic.

After we are thoroughly clean, we kiss under the waterfall, our hands exploring. He cradles my breasts, and I wrap a hand around his cock, pumping. He gets on his knees and parts me to flick his tongue over my . . . clit.

"I need to be inside you," he bursts, reaching for a towel and wrapping me in it.

Unceremoniously, he picks me up, takes me to the bed, deposits me in it. He promptly positions himself on top of me, parting my legs with his knees and regarding me with predatory hunger. Taking his cock in his hand, he guides it to my center and presses it to the entrance.

"Do you want it?" he demands.

"I do," I answer breathlessly.

"What exactly is it that you want, um?"

"I . . . I want you to . . ." I can't say it.

He pulls back his hips, eyebrows raised as if he'll punish me if I don't answer correctly.

"I want you to . . ." I add hurriedly.

He presses the tip of his cock to my core again. "To what?"

I swallow. "To fuck me."

He growls, aroused in a way I haven't seen before. Thrusting hard, he plunges his cock into me, making me scream in delight.

"You do not have to be quiet here. You can scream. You can moan. Let me hear you, Ravógín."

He rocks his hips, dipping his cock in and out, slamming it deep and hard, to the hilt. My hips match his movements even as tears of pleasure fill my eyes. He has never been rough, and I find it exhilarating.

Kissing me, he buries his face in my neck, and I hold him as he melts into me. He pushes and thrusts, driving me to the edge of ecstasy too quickly. Moaning, I arch my back, he starts moving his hips in circles, driving me crazy. As I scream in desperation, his mouth covers mine, and one of his hands fondles my breast. He's everywhere I want him to be. A well of sensations builds into a spire, growing higher and tighter. Reading my reaction, Korben increases his pace.

With a cry of pleasure, I rear up, intense spasms rocking my body. Korben cradles me in his arms as the raw climax courses through me, starting in my core, then expanding to the rest of my body.

His release comes immediately after mine, his muscular body shuddering in waves. I hold him the way he held me, and kiss him tenderly, in awe at the way he owns my body, coaxing exactly what he wants from it.

Spent, we lie in each other's embrace. As our breaths grow calm and our bodies relax, he whispers in my ear. "I love you."

He seems to expect an answer, and I want to give it, but I shy away from the feeling that seems to have been growing inside me too quickly for comfort.

Finally, I say, "I trust you more every day, Korben, but . . ."

"*Shh.*" He presses a finger to my lips. "You do not have to say anything."

Despite his words, I see the disappointment and fear in the depths of his black eyes. He's afraid I'll never feel for him the way he does for me.

# 38

## KORBEN

*"Incompetent creatures. Do I have to do it all?"*

**Morwen – Traveler**

I walk side by side with Valeria, following one of the white-robed attendants to the supper Niamhara promised us. I hate the tension that stretches between Valeria and me.

She does not love me.

I wish things had been different for us in the beginning, but I cannot change the past. I can only continue to make amends and hope to one day gain her full trust, and at last, her love. If only I could be certain she will come around. The thought of losing her terrifies me.

On the other hand, optimism for our realms fills me, a sensation that feels foreign. I do not remember the last time I believed things would be all right with my people.

With Niamhara's help and the return of my magic—I can feel it coursing through my veins again—I trust we will prevail over our enemies.

Bringing peace and stability to Tirnanog and Castella does not seem impossible anymore.

We return to the same space where we held our conversation earlier, except the room has been transformed. What was a serene space for contemplation is now a stage for opulence.

The moonstone platform is now laden with a feast fit for the gods. Golden platters are piled high with roasted peacock and venison, the meat glistening under the soft glow of the amethyst cluster. Exotic fruits, unknown to me, shimmer with iridescent hues, their sweet scent mingling with the savory aroma of roasting meats. Towering goblets of ruby-red wine stand at each place setting, their contents promising a taste of intoxication. In the center of the table, an extravagant cake, adorned with gold leaves and fresh flowers, seems to teeter precariously, defying all laws of physics—no doubt magic was involved in its creation. Attendants move with practiced grace, refilling goblets and offering delicacies.

Mother and Father are already here. I reach for Valeria's hand, hoping to break the tension. Her gaze flicks to mine. I offer her a smile.

"I would like to officially introduce you to my parents," I say.

She nods slowly, letting herself relax. "Of course. It would be an honor."

Hand in hand, we approach them. I cannot help the smile that stretches my lips. I feel proud of Valeria and have no doubt my parents will adore her. It strikes me that during the brief time I spent with Saethara, I never wished I could introduce her to them. Not once.

My parents smile broadly, too, waiting for us with eager expressions.

"Mother, Father." I bow to both in turn. "I want you to meet

Princess Valeria Plumanegra. Valeria, these are Faolan and Shara Theric."

"It is an honor to—" Valeria begins, but she cannot finish because my mother wraps her in a tight embrace, driving the air out of her lungs through sheer surprise.

"I am so happy to officially meet you," my mother says, pulling away, though she keeps her hands on Valeria's shoulders. "I cannot thank you enough for what you have done for our stubborn son."

"Indeed," Father agrees, nodding furiously, stroking his chin. "And for our realm," he adds.

I open my mouth but do not know what to say. I was not expecting this reaction. In truth, it is embarrassing. Still, they are not wrong, so I force a stream of words out.

"Yes, she is amazing. We would not be here without her help. I find myself in great debt as well as in love with her."

Valeria blushes fiercely. I do not think I have ever seen such a flush of color on her beautiful skin. However, she swiftly finds her composure.

"There is no debt," she assures us. "Korben has promised to help me set things straight in Castella once he retakes Tirnanog's throne. I could not ask for more."

"The male we raised knows how to keep his promises." My father sounds proud of me, despite the terrible way I failed.

"I do not think you should be, Father," I mutter. "I allowed lust and rage to blind me, and in doing so, I failed our people."

"Nonsense." My mother bats a hand in the air. "None of what happened is your fault. Morwen is to blame. She is wicked, misguided. She brought her woes upon herself and blames her sister for them. She manipulated countless people and situations in order to usurp your throne and steal The Eldrystone. What she did to you . . ." She shakes her head, sadness filling her eyes. "You must have been brokenhearted. I cannot fathom the pain you went through. In the end, our kin are paying for the consequences of Morwen's actions. Not yours."

My father nods in agreement, but their kind words cannot erase my errors. Valeria's distrust is proof of that. She squeezes my hand, surprising me. There is sympathy in her expression. Perhaps my mother's words will act like a salve on Valeria's doubts, bringing her closer to forgiving me.

"I still cannot believe you are here," I say.

"It is an incredible place, is it not?" my father says.

I nod. "Everyone is here? Every fae who ever lived?"

"Almost." My mother smiles tenderly at Valeria, whose mother could not make it here because of the veil's collapse.

"What about our grandparents?" I say. They would be a poor substitute for Valeria's mother, but they are still her kin.

"Yes, they are in Slatewater," my father responds. "Unfortunately, the settlement is not nearby. This is a big realm. Much bigger than our own. But there is no time. You must return and do your duty."

"Of course." I nod once. "Mayhap, we could come back . . ." I trail off.

Both my mother and father shake their heads.

"It is not allowed," my mother explains, sadness lacing her tone. "This was a special circumstance."

Disappointment washes over me. That means I will not be able to see them again, not for a long time—unless I die before I tire of my existence.

For the first time, a terrible question occurs to me.

Will Valeria come here too? Will she and I—?

A sudden commotion interrupts my thoughts, a crash and shouts coming from the next room. People run into our area, escaping whatever caused the disturbance.

"What in all the realms?!" my father exclaims, then starts fighting his way through the escaping crowd. "Stay there," he tells my mother.

I follow after him, and though I wish Valeria would stay too, I am not surprised when she joins me. Before we make it into the next room, the problem becomes evident. A towering figure, a perfect duplicate of Niamhara, looms ahead, confronting the Goddess.

Morwen the Mistwraith.

We stop past the threshold that leads to Niamhara's chamber as the last few people trickle out of the room. Watching the twins standing in front of each other is an eerie sight. Their features are identical, yet I am able to tell them apart. While Niamhara exudes kindness and good nature, Morwen's entire demeanor oozes contempt and hatred instead.

One of the tall bookshelves lies broken on the floor, volumes and scrolls strewn all over. A person lies under all the books. Galen! I nearly run toward him, but my father stops me. Others are already helping the sorcerer out. He seems shaken, but unharmed.

Morwen's eyes slide in his direction, giving him an odd look. After a moment, they rove in our direction. Niamhara moves and stands between us protectively. She seems afraid her sister will hurt us. Is there death in the Whispering Wilds? From the way everyone ran scared, I suspect there is.

"It has been a long time," Niamhara says. "It is good to see you."

Despite the hateful way her sister regards her, there is no animosity in Niamhara's voice. She sounds sincere.

Morwen sneers.

"Have you come to reconcile?" Niamhara asks.

"You are the same fool you have always been."

"I *have* changed, sister, and I am ready to go with you in search of our home."

"You think me an idiot?"

Niamhara shakes her head. "I want you to be happy."

Morwen jerks a hand upward. The books strewn on the floor rise, then dash toward Niamhara, who with a sweep of her own hand makes them vanish into thin air. Morwen lets out an annoyed grunt. I expect her to attack again, but she makes a dismissive gesture instead.

"Bah, there has never been any joy in fighting with you."

I imagine the similarity of their skills makes any magic-based conflict a futile endeavor. From the looks of it, they can simply cancel each other out.

"Why do you want to fight?" Niamhara asks. "There is no need. I will do whatever you want me to do."

"Only because you love them more than you ever loved me," Morwen shouts, leaning forward, her teeth bared. "Your little, useless creation."

"That is not true. I love you, Morwen."

She thrusts a hand in Niamhara's face. "Spare me."

"What else can I do to fix this?"

"I do not want anything from you. For now, there is only this game, and I am enjoying it greatly." Morwen smirks, eyes glinting.

"To think you almost died without that stupid amulet." She sounds thrilled by the thought, like a scientist whose experiment was producing unexpected, yet promising results. "And for them." She throws a hateful revolted glance in our direction.

"Have you given up on finding our home?" Niamhara asks.

Morwen's head jerks toward her sister. It seems Niamhara has touched on a sensitive matter.

Niamhara nods sagely. "Ah, that is it. Like me, you have come to believe we are lost forever."

"I have not given up, and never shall. Do not mistake me for a weakling like you."

Her words do not ring true, but Niamhara does not point that out. Instead, she speaks calmly.

"I am leaving the Whispering Wilds, sister," she says.

*What?!* I exchange a glance with Valeria.

*Will our realms be all right if she leaves?* she seems to ask.

I shake my head, uncertain.

"No, you are not," Morwen barks, the same surprise I feel etched in her features.

"If you will not continue the search, I will." Niamhara turns her back on her sister and faces the large window, which now displays a full moon the color of spun gold.

"Ah! You think I will lose interest in your little pets if you are not here. Well, you are wrong."

Niamhara remains still, her gaze locked on the moon, before she responds. "Your actions have caused me much distress, Morwen. I do not have the inclination to endure your . . . willful temperament and twisted games."

"You lie," Morwen reaffirms, though she sounds less certain than before.

Niamhara said she stayed in the Whispering Wilds because she was tired of searching, tired of following Morwen from realm to realm. I do not know her well enough to discern whether or not she is lying about abandoning us to our fate. Something tells me she is not the type to make idle threats.

"No," Niamhara says. "I am not lying."

Without warning, her body passes through the window, then she vanishes into thin air.

# 39

# VALERIA

*"I hate her, and I love her."*

**Morwen – Traveler**

"No!" I reach out a hand as Niamhara disappears, golden moonbeams illuminating the spot where she stood only moments before.

Her pale eyes wide and red-rimmed, her teeth bared, Morwen roars in anger, expelling a violent gust of wind. The window rattles, then breaks, shattering into a million pieces. Air spent from her lungs, she turns to face us.

Panic fills me. My ears ring from the sheer force of it. I take several steps back, dragging Korben with me. But where can we go?

"You ruined everything," she shouts, marching in my direction.

Korben blocks her path, but she sends him crashing against the wall with a flick of her wrist. His mother gasps and rushes to help him. I try to do the same, but Morwen's espiritu plucks me off my feet, an invisible hand wrapped tightly around me. My feet dangle several inches off the floor. I kick, trying to free myself.

"I could not see you on the other side, ruining everything I planned so carefully. Where did you come from, *human*?" she demands, shaking me. "What stupid creature decided to create *your* kind?"

"Let me go," I hiss between clenched teeth.

She squeezes harder.

I groan, then decide I'll go down fighting if she means to kill me. With merely a thought, I shift into Corvus form. Morwen's binding espiritu slackens, and I fly toward her face, claws aimed at her eyes. She puts a hand up, stopping my progress mere inches from contact. Her expression betrays surprise.

Unexpectedly, she begins to laugh. With a careless gesture, she releases me, unharmed.

"You have a spine," she says. "I like that."

Those pale eyes scan the room. Her unkind expression slowly degenerates into something unexpected . . . dejection.

Morwen glances toward the window as if searching for Niamhara, but her sister is truly gone. Suddenly looking panicked, she runs to the spot where Niamhara last stood.

"Has she truly left me?" she demands of no one in particular.

Korben's mother steps forward, hands clasped in front of her, posture regal. "Yes. She has. It was her plan all along. She was only waiting for The Eldrystone."

"No!" Morwen whirls, fists tight at her sides. "She cannot leave me. She cannot!" She sounds distraught now, the reality of her sister's departure sinking her claws deeper than I could have sunk mine.

Seeing the desperation on her face, I can't help but imagine suffering the same fate. At the thought of never seeing Amira again, my chest tightens with a desperate pang that promises a lifetime of pain.

"Niamhara, sister!" Morwen shouts into the night, then jumps out of the broken window.

I gasp, thinking she'll plummet to her death, but she is not human or fae, and instead, she floats in midair for an instant, then disappears the same way her sister did.

Everyone in the room is stunned into silence. Korben's mother presses a hand to her chest and sobs quietly. Her husband wraps an arm around her shoulders and pulls her close, the lines of his face drawing downward, his own sadness carved in his expression.

People trickle back into the room. Some sob, grieved by Niamhara's departure.

*Gods! Is she never coming back?*

Even though I've only been here mere hours, I think I understand these people's pain, their loss.

Some begin to pick up books and scrolls from the floor, tenderly cradling them in their arms. Then they glance into the distance through the window, their tears wetting the gilded covers of what I imagine were Niamhara's possessions—more precious than ever in her absence.

Korben, now standing, is the first one to speak. "You knew this would happen?"

Still in her husband's embrace, Shara Theric replies through her tears. "Niamhara told us that if . . . she got the opportunity to speak to her sister, she would do this. She thought it was the only way to stop Morwen's game, and it seems she was right. That creature's only aim is to mortify Niamhara."

"How can they be so different from each other?" Korben's father asks as if talking to himself. "Why could Morwen not let Niamhara be happy here? Instead, she drove her away, drove her back into the nothingness of the infinite realms. Her selfishness knows no match."

"I do not mean to be insensitive," Korben says, "but what does this mean for Tirnanog? For Castella?" His eyes rove over the floor as if he's searching for something. "My magic has returned, and I can still feel it despite Niamhara's absence, but will that change? If magic leaves us, regaining the throne will be harder. We will need to raise an army to fight Saethara."

"Her magic will remain," his mother replies. "She made sure of that. It runs strongly through Tirnanog once more."

Korben seems relieved, though not entirely. "Are you certain?"

"Yes, son," his father interjects. "As we speak, things should be back to normal in our realm. Without Morwen's intervention, the balance has been restored. Morwen was able to block magic and allow only a few to use it because Niamhara was weak. You see . . . Niamhara imbued Tirnanog *and* The Eldrystone with her power. Yet, she was still able to draw from both sources to remain strong. But when Morwen blocked our realm's magic and the veil between Tirnanog and Castella closed with The Eldrystone on the other side, Niamhara began growing weak. However, thanks to you, she is strong again. Everything is as it should be. Morwen's influence cannot travel past too many realms, and Niamhara promised to lead her far away. We are on our own now. All of us."

"You mean," Korben says carefully, "no more conduit. The Eldrystone will not be here to give us the edge against those who would use magic to do evil."

Faolan Theric nods knowingly. He once used The Eldrystone to keep a kingdom and its people safe from dark forces. He understands the challenge the task will pose without the amulet better than anyone else.

"I am sorry, Korben. You, of all the Theric kings, will need to be the strongest. I wish it were different, my son."

Korben sets his jaw, a muscle ticking as he clenches his teeth. "I will do whatever it takes to protect Tirnanog."

"I know you will. I am proud of you."

Shara Theric stands straighter, fully regaining her composure. "It has been quite the day. I think we should retire and rest. Tomorrow, you will need to return to Tirnanog to help our people. I will have food sent to your chambers." Her gaze goes out in a wider circle, making me realize that Jago, Esmeralda, Galen, and Calierin stand behind me. "I am sorry we could not enjoy the feast together."

"Yes, that was . . . unfortunate," Jago says, "but we forgive you."

"Jago!" I hiss through clenched teeth.

But Shara Theric laughs, and the tension in the room eases a little.

"You're incorrigible, Jago." I roll my eyes.

Korben and I lie in bed, both on our backs, staring at the ceiling. I'm not sure sleep will be possible this night. My mind goes round and round, replaying today's events and considering possibility after possibility—none of them good. And judging by Korben's restlessness, he's doing likewise.

We don't talk. We just lie there, too shaken for anything else.

Surprisingly, after an hour or so, Korben's breaths grow rhythmic.

I glance at him. His profile is stark against the deeper darkness at the edges of the room.

He's achingly handsome, as if made in an effort to attain perfection. In sleep, the worry lines on his face are smooth. He's always earnest, intense, like a well-tended fire.

I toss and turn for another hour. Frustrated, I get out of bed and pace the room. Empty plates sit on the table. Korben and I ate everything they brought us. The taste of the food barely registered, but I knew I needed to eat—if only sleep could be forced, too.

I leave the room and walk aimlessly through the grand palace. It's a place of wonder, large on a scale that dwarfs Nido and Elf-Dún combined. There are no guards anywhere, not even at the front door through which we entered. In fact, the doors are thrown open, providing a view of a star-studded sky stretching for infinity.

Without Niamhara here, will things change? Was it her power that kept everyone in check? Will weapons and guards become necessary now? The thought fills me with sadness.

I turn around and continue exploring the palace. My feet move of their own accord, though there seems to be a certain purpose to them, as if someone is guiding me. A moment later, I find myself in a circular room, a concave ceiling above me. A pedestal with a glass cover sits in the middle. Something glows inside it.

Slowly, I approach, feeling a strange pull toward whatever lies there. When I set eyes on the item, I gasp.

*The Eldrystone!*

The amulet shimmers under the soft glow of fairy lights attached to the corners of the glass case. Within, cradled on a bed of black velvet, lies the opal with its ornate frame. Its colors shift and change with every flicker of my eyes, a mix of blues, greens, and pinks dancing within the stone's depths. The lights catch the opal at its heart, sending rainbows of light cascading through the crystal cover.

*Gods!* So much contention over The Eldrystone, and now it's reduced to no more than a museum piece.

I raise a hand to the glass and gently press the tips of my fingers to the surface. A flash of light blinds me, and I stumble back. Taking deep breaths to calm my racing heart, I blink furiously. My vision clears by degrees, and I find I've been transported to a different place.

Clouds surround me. I'm back in that sky fortress where I first talked to Niamhara.

"Tell Korben to take the amulet back," Niamhara's kind voice says. "He will need help against any who try to use magic to do harm. Its power is . . . different now. I could not leave a part of me inside it as I would have liked, but it should still be of assistance when he needs additional strength. Tell him not to blame himself and to choose his allies wisely. It is more important than ever that he surrounds himself with people who do good with the skills they possess.

"There will always be those born with too much darkness within them. It is the nature of the universe. There is no light without its opposite. He must not fear his own nature. He is good, and Tirnanog needs him."

As quickly as I was transported away, I find myself back, except I'm sitting up in bed, panting, a hand to my chest where The Eldrystone hangs once more.

Korben is sitting up, too, his dark eyes wide as he stares at the amulet. "Valeria?"

"She . . . she didn't abandon us!"

# 40
## VALERIA

*"Fuck!"*

**Jago Plumanegra (Casa Plumanegra) – 3rd in line to Plumanegra throne**

We stand in the cave through which we first entered the Whispering Wilds. We have fresh supplies of clothes, water, and food for our journey, but most importantly, we have a measure of Niamhara's aid.

Korben embraces his parents, eyes wavering. "I will not see you again, will I?"

His question startles me, making me consider another consequence of Niamhara's departure. This must have been one of those things that plagued Korben's mind last night.

His mother presses a slender hand to his cheek and sadly shakes her head.

No one else will be called to the Glimmer anymore.

Korben inhales sharply and swallows thickly in a clear effort to shove his emotions down. "Well," he says in a strangled voice, "I never thought I would see you again, and I did. I count myself lucky."

Faolan Theric grabs Korben's shoulders. "Lucky indeed, son."

"I thought long and hard last night, thought I would ask you to come with me, but . . ." Korben pauses, scanning their faces. "But . . . you will not?" The last words are half question, half statement.

"We have had our time in Tirnanog," Faolan Theric says. "This is *your* time now. Though we may live forever, Niamhara was of the belief that everyone deserves an opportunity to make a difference. New generations bring new energy, new ideas. The young should not be burdened by the obstinacy of the old. Things need to be allowed to change. Otherwise, progress and betterment would be impossible."

Korben nods in understanding. "I could . . . come back," he adds tentatively.

His mother shakes her head. "When you walk back into Tirnanog, The Eldrystone, as it is now, will not help you cross the veil."

I gasp. Suddenly worried I won't be able to get home.

Understanding my reaction, Korben's mother turns her attention to me. "Do not fret, child. The veil between Tirnanog and Castella should remain as you left it."

Korben inclines his head, acknowledging my panic and looking as relieved as I feel. The veil between Tirnanog and Castella remains open.

Taking a step away from his parents, he bows. "Thank you." He lets his gaze rove around the alcove, regarding all of those who have come to say goodbye.

Following his lead, I do the same, and so do the others.

"I . . ." Calierin says, then cuts herself short.

"What is it, Calierin?" Korben says.

She hesitates.

"Speak."

"I do not want to appear ungrateful, but I thought I would get my magic back. King Korben says he did. Yet, I still feel empty." Her expression betrays a combination of anger and sorrow.

"Korben was touched by Niamhara," Shara Theric says. "That is why it is different for him. But everything will be as it should be when you cross back into Tirnanog."

Calierin straightens. "Truly?"

"Yes."

The Tuathacath warrior smiles broadly. Galen next to her only frowns. It seems to me he should be as relieved as Calierin—perhaps more, given how much he has complained about his lack of espiritu—but his serious expression reveals little emotion. Since that bookshelf fell on top of him, he has seemed shaken. But who can blame him? He probably stared death in the face last night.

"I have one last question," Korben says.

"Yes?" his parents say in unison.

He cocks his head to one side to indicate he wants to step aside to speak privately. They seem hesitant for a moment, then giving us an apologetic smile, step aside with their son.

I cross my arms and face Jago, turning my back on them to allow them privacy.

"Are you doing all right?" my cousin asks.

I nod, though I don't think I have felt *all right* for quite some time. I will have to redefine what that means for me.

"I'm glad she gave back The Eldrystone," he says, looking down at it where it hangs around my neck.

"Me, too."

Last night, after I explained my *dream* to Korben, I was close to telling him that Niamhara wanted him to have the amulet back. However, it didn't feel like the right time. He seemed so troubled, so lost in his own thoughts and worries that I feared he would reject it.

*"She said not to blame yourself,"* I told him, but he only twisted his mouth in displeasure, indicating he still does.

He has to forgive himself for what he did. But how does one do that? I know all too well what it's like to blame yourself for past events. Images of my parents' deaths and thoughts of how I could have saved them often haunt me, tired memories on an endless parade. Surely, Korben suffers the same affliction.

"Quite the conversationalist this morning." Jago pokes my stomach with a stiff finger.

I swat his hand away.

"There it is." He points at the smile appearing on my lips.

Esmeralda grins, looking lovingly at my cousin. She reaches for his hand and interlaces her fingers with his. He welcomes her touch, squeezing reassuringly, a reflex that appears so natural it makes me realize something deep has developed between them.

They love each other, and they both seem so comfortable in the feeling.

Why can't I feel the same way with Korben? Why is it so difficult to forgive?

Korben walks away from his parents and rejoins us. Steeling himself, he clenches his fists and says, "Farewell. You will always be in my thoughts."

"Farewell," everyone in the alcove echoes.

We turn and face the shimmering wall behind us. Korben takes a step forward, and we all follow in unison. In an instant, we find ourselves on top of the rock mound in the middle of the Mourning Moor.

The light behind us visibly shrinks as the veil is reduced to a near-invisible tear hovering in midair. It seems it was never fully open. We were only able to cross because Niamhara allowed it.

I've barely had time to register the change, when a group of ghostly shapes rises from below, their cadaverous faces grinning with flesh-less mandibles and rotted teeth.

"Witches!" Korben exclaims. "Get down!"

*Get down?*

I'm pondering what ducking is going to do to help when he erupts into an enormous black shape, long wings like giant windmills, beating and stirring the air into a vicious storm.

Jago pulls me down. I crash to the ground, hair flying into my face. I swat it aside, staring at Korben in awe. He's the size of a building, his talons as tall and thick as tree trunks. His wings span twenty feet to either side, their powerful lashings keeping the ghostly monsters at bay as they lean into the storm trying to reach us.

"What do we do?" Jago shouts.

Calierin and Galen are slow to react, but in the next instant, they both release bouts of espiritu, large orbs of energy that shoot from their outstretched hands toward the witches. I hold my breath. A cry of frustration escapes me as the espiritu passes through the phantoms leaving them unharmed.

Calierin lets out an angry growl and a curse.

"Wind!" I shout, taking hold of The Eldrystone at my chest.

"Create wind!" I extend a hand, and a gust of wind bursts from my fingers.

Calierin and Galen join in, and we manage to drive the ravenous-looking monsters further away, but they're still there, intent on stealing our bodies. There are at least a dozen of them, quite enough to devour us all.

*Gods! How did they get free?*

In unison, the witches begin to shriek with an ear-splitting force. We cover our ears, our espiritu disrupted. Korben shakes his head, huge round eyes narrowing. One of those eyes focuses on me as he jerks his head backward.

*He's trying to tell me something.*

Panic muddles my thoughts. I don't know what he wants me to do. He jerks his head again, that black eye determinedly aimed at his back.

"Of course!" I exclaim. "Climb. Climb onto Korben's back. Hurry!"

Galen is the first to react. He scrambles to his feet, approaching the huge raven tail. Using his espiritu, he latches what looks like a glowing red rope to the long feathers on Korben's back. The sorcerer tugs on it to ensure it's secure, then jumps. His foot lands on the raven's backside, but as Korben beats his wings buffeting the witches, Galen slips.

Calierin uses her own espiritu to give him a boost, and he regains his footing, pulling himself hand over hand on his glowing rope. When he reaches the top of Korben's back, he secures himself by tying more rope around his waist.

"Catch it," he shouts, throwing the slack down.

We all turn to Esmeralda. Everyone thinks she should go next. She shakes her head, clinging to Jago.

"You have to." Jago peels her tight grip from his arm and pushes her toward Korben.

She goes reluctantly, throwing backward glances toward Jago. With more agility than Galen displayed, she grabs the rope and jumps onto the raven. In moments, she's seated next to the sorcerer, the glowing red force encircling her waist.

"You go next." Jago places his hands flat on my back and pushes me forward.

I resist him. "No, you idiot! I can fly. *You* go!"

He hesitates for an instant, then shakes his head. "Your raven is too small. You may not be able to get away." He pushes me again.

I want to argue, but that will only waste time. Besides, he's right. I don't know if I would be able to outfly the witches.

Grabbing Galen's rope, I fling myself onto Korben's back. Anxiously, I glance around. The witches' faces are twisted into angry grimaces. Their shapes sway like flags in a storm of Korben's making. With every beat, the monsters are driven back, only to charge again with furious determination, gaining inches with each attempt.

*Gods!*

"Hurry up!" I shout, glancing back toward Jago, who has hold of the rope and is pushing off the ground.

Fast and agile, he reaches me, then Calierin is behind him, her own espiritu facilitating the maneuver.

"Go, Korben! Go!" I urge.

He wastes no time and flaps his wings faster and stronger. Our movement upward is painfully slow, our combined weight making the ascent difficult for Korben. The witches rise around us, some flying outward, away from Korben's wingbeats. Three of them climb to a greater height than ours, then plummet in our direction.

"Repel them!" I cry out, clenching The Eldrystone and aiming a torrent of wind at one of the witches.

Calierin and Galen take on the other two, and we manage to keep them at a safe distance as we gain altitude. If it weren't because the monsters surround us, Korben would be able to ascend without care, but he can't risk brushing one of them. We would all be lost.

Three more witches fly outward and come at us from above. Calierin and Galen shoot espiritu at them with their free hands. I try to do the same, but nothing happens. The Eldrystone seems to only provide a fraction of the power it used to.

"No!" I scream as the third witch lets out a gleeful cackle and dives for me.

Jago pushes me out of the way, taking my place. The witch crashes into him, her phantom shape molding to his body, then disappearing inside him.

"Jago!" As his eyes go wide and his body convulses, I reach for him, grabbing his hand.

*No no no!*

Esmeralda cries out in horror, her arms coming around me in a desperate attempt to reach him.

A horrifying cackle escapes my cousin's mouth.

"NO!" Reaching for The Eldrystone, I send espiritu into him, intent on shocking the witch out.

Nothing happens.

"Let go, Val!" Jago growls, batting me away. His eyes are suddenly bloodshot, his mouth open as he takes in air, wheezing.

I try to grab him again.

"V-Val, don't touch me!"

*Gods!* He's fighting. I need to help him, but how?!

We rock from side to side as Korben performs an evasive maneuver. We slide to one side. Galen's espiritu rope tightens around my waist. Jago looks down at the energy pulsing around his waist. He raises a trembling hand, slips a finger under the glowing rope, and makes a cutting motion. Galen's espiritu fizzles out, setting him loose.

Desperately, I send energy from the amulet to secure him in place once more, but he grins and shakes a finger at me. His honey-colored eyes are fully black, not his own.

"No, little girl," he says in a scratchy female voice. "I will not be bound again. Never."

He stands smoothly despite the lurching movements that jostle us about. Behind him, Calierin pushes away from him, espiritu still pouring from her hands as she keeps two witches at bay, slowly losing the battle against them.

"No, Jago!" Esmeralda cries as he lets out another cackle.

Suddenly, a guttural roar that rings with his own voice escapes him, and his eyes clear somewhat. He's still there! I have to try again.

*Release him!* I wish with all my might, aiming The Eldrystone's espiritu at his chest. Light hits, fully enveloping the rest of his body. His eyes clear entirely. He looks down at me, at Esmeralda. A sad smile stretches his lips.

"I love you," he mouths, then he jumps, plummeting to the ground as Korben breaks through the clouds, leaving the witches behind.

Esmeralda screams, a raw sound that joins the cry that rings inside my own head. She slumps against me, sobbing, her body shaking uncontrollably. Mechanically, my arms wrap around her, desperate incredulity washing over me.

"We have to go back. We have to go back!" I shout against the wind, my lips feeling frozen from the cold.

Calierin and Galen avoid my gaze.

"We have to go back!" I repeat. "Korben!"

He circles around. I push Esmeralda away, scramble to the edge of Korben's massive wing, and look down.

*Jago is all right. We will find him and . . . and drive the witch out of him . . . and . . . and . . .*

Tears spill down my cheeks as I attempt to search the ground through the phantom shapes of the remaining monsters. They circle and circle in an effort to rise higher and reach us, but something seems to stop them, either a barrier or their own limitations . . . I have no idea which.

We are too far, and I can't see past the whirling shapes. I can't spot him. I can't. I can't. I slump and clench Korben's feathers in my fists, pain sinking its claws into me, piercing all the way to my very soul.

*Jago, please. Please! I can't lose you. I can't lose you, too. Please, Niamhara. Please, saints! Don't take him.*

My pleas go unanswered.

*Jago!*

*I'm sorry. I should have never brought you here. This is my fault.*

I snatch The Eldrystone and yank it over my neck. With a cry of raw pain, I hurl it across the sky as hard as I can.

Calierin flings out a tendril of espiritu and catches it. Pulling the amulet back, she grabs it and slips it into her pocket, casting a wary glance at me. Galen, in turn, glares at her, murmuring something unintelligible under his breath.

But none of that matters. I don't care what they do with The Eldrystone. I don't ever want to see that damn thing again. If I hadn't taken it out of Mother's sewing box, Jago and I would be in Nido, talking to Nana, drinking wine in the cellar, sparring on the rooftop. He would be with me, living a careless life of parties, flings, and happy smiles.

Face buried in Korben's feathers, I scream, my soul breaking.

*This is my fault.*

*My fault.*

*My fault.*

*My fault.*

"Come, Valeria," Calierin says, her voice unusually soft. "Get down."

I lift my head to find that we're on the ground, and she's offering me a hand to help me off Korben's back. Numbly, I take it and slide off. The air is disturbed by a *whoosh* as Korben shifts, and in the next instant, I find myself in his arms.

The little strength I have left leaks out of me. He catches me, slides a hand under my legs, and lifts me up. Clutching me to his chest, he walks away from the others.

I don't see where we're going. I just bury my face in his chest, thinking of ways I can excise this horrible pain from my heart.

# 41

## KORBEN

*"I never told him how I felt."*

**Esmeralda Malla – Romani Healer**

Valeria sits, staring at the crackling fire, a warm cup of tea wrapped tightly between her hands, steam rising to her nose. Nighttime crept in, and I barely noticed, my worry for Valeria superseding any other.

Her previously pain-stricken face now displays a frightening glacier numbness. Esmeralda lies huddled on the ground, rocking gently, her green eyes locked on a faraway point. Calierin and Galen stand guard, peering through the trees of the small wood near the moor. Thankfully, the witches cannot cross the boundary, not unless they capture a flesh and bones body.

No one speaks, only the logs as they burn and snap.

"Ravógín, you should eat something." I offer her a piece of bread.

She takes it without objection, bites a piece off, and chews. She is doing exactly as I asked, but it does nothing for my peace of mind. She is in shock, and I fear what she may do.

Earlier, she flung The Eldrystone into the air, emotions overriding all concerns for the consequences. Calierin saved it and gave it to me shortly after we landed. The amulet now rests in my pocket, the onus returned to me. Valeria may take it back later. For now, I understand she blames it for her cousin's death.

Or more assuredly . . . she blames herself.

"We think it was the horses," I say, hoping to ease her mind. "Saethara's soldiers must have come back and released them into the moor along with some of their own mounts. We saw a couple of them trotting past the boundary. They carried Saethara's brand. It seems the beasts are immune to the witches, even though they release their spirits."

"Umm." It's all she says.

My gaze roves over her face. Flames from the fire dance in the depths of her brown eyes.

*Damn! Damn it all!* I want to help her, but I don't know how.

I pace from one end of our small camp to the other.

What she had with her cousin . . . it was a bond stronger than family, stronger than friendship—something no one can replace. To lose him like this, to have no chance to say goodbye, no closure . . .

I stop and walk to where Calierin stands. "I will be back in an hour."

"What?! Where are you going? I can—"

"No." I cut her off. "Guard Valeria with your life."

She thumps a fist to her chest. "Yes, my king."

I walk away, and when I reach the edge of the woods, leap into the air, morphing into Dreadwing form. Gaining altitude to the level the

351

witches cannot reach, I make my way back to the place where we lost him.

Gliding quietly through the currents, no wingbeats needed, I spot the rock mound below. Careless of the risk, I fold my wings and dive toward the ground, my keen vision piercing through the night.

The phantoms meander through the moor, seemingly aimless, dispersed. Committing to my dive, I keep scouring the ground until I spot Jago's broken body. Veering in that direction, I home in all my senses, intent on my goal. When I am about fifty feet from the ground, the witches notice me and, like hounds after the scent of blood, race toward me, shrieking in their hideous voices.

Spreading out my wing, I slow my descent and scoop Jago's broken body off the ground, cradling him gently in one talon. As soon as I have a good hold of him, I beat my wings with all my might. Dust flies into the air, obscuring my view of the charging monsters.

I ascend—bit by bit, at first, then faster. The shrieking witches ascend with me, quick at my talons, but every wingbeat takes me higher, and soon I am out of reach, soaring through the sky, headed back toward Valeria, the mourning cries of the ravenous Hexen Horde lost in the distance.

When I arrive at the edge of the woods, I gently deposit my charge on the ground. Using my talons, I dig a grave and place Jago in it. Shifting back to my fae shape, I carefully arrange his broken limbs, then remove my shirt and use it to clean the blood and dirt off his face. Mercifully, although battered, his face is unscathed. Mayhap the witch was able to use some magic to cushion the fall, though not enough to preserve the body and use it as her vessel.

Jago Plumanegra sacrificed himself to ensure we would escape, to protect Valeria and Esmeralda from the evil creature who fought to possess him.

"You were strong, Jago," I say as I clean the last of the blood from his forehead. "I wish it did not have to be this way."

Climbing out of the grave, I bundle my soiled shirt and cast it aside, out of view. I return to the camp, where I am met by Calierin's curious violet gaze. I ignore her, retrieve a new shirt from my pack, and slip it on.

For a moment, I hesitate, unsure of whether or not I have done the right thing. In the end, I decide that if I were in her place, I would choose to give my loved one a proper burial.

"Valeria," I say, crouching by her side. "I . . . I went back to the moor."

Her eyes snap to mine.

"I found him and brought him back. I thought he should get a farewell from you. From Esmeralda." I take her hand and help her stand. "Come with me."

She lets me lead her. Esmeralda stands, having heard my words. Tentatively, she joins us and takes Valeria's other hand. When we arrive, they edge closer to the grave and peer down. I stay behind, hands clasped in front of me.

Esmeralda lets out a disconsolate sob, which she quickly represses with a hand to her chest.

Valeria's shoulders shake, her soft sobs filling my ears. They are all I can hear despite their quiet nature. I feel her grief as if it were my own.

"You were my best friend," Valeria says. "You were a light in my life, in Nana's life. You always had a smile or a joke to lift our spirits no matter what. You were always strong, never selfish. I will miss you so much. Nothing will ever be the same without you." She gathers a fistful of loose earth in her hand and crumbles it over the grave. "Forgive me for bringing you here, Jago. I love you."

Tears stream down her cheeks, she whirls and walks away, in the opposite direction of the camp, while Esmeralda falls to her knees, all her strength gone.

I want to go after Valeria, but I understand she needs to be alone, so instead, I help Esmeralda to her feet and lead her away from the grave. I will cover it when they are back by the campfire to spare them further pain.

"I'll be all right," Esmeralda says, wiping away her tears. "Go with her." She points with her chin toward Valeria and heads back to the camp.

Calierin and Galen walk with Esmeralda. I peer toward Valeria, who stands with her back turned, moonlight casting a halo around her.

I wait, chest tight, anger against those responsible for what has happened building and building beyond what I ever believed possible.

They will pay. I will make sure of that.

# 42

## VALERIA

*"Do not weave your fate from the threads of another's undoing."*

**Old Castellan Proverb**

Morning light filters through the trees. The logs in the firepit smolder faintly, streaks of red glowing in the otherwise gray and ashen wood that remains.

Korben regards me with a concerned expression. He fears for me, for my mental stability. He would be right to worry if life hadn't dealt me too many similar blows already. Mother, Father, and now . . . Jago.

Pain surges, threatening to destroy the strength I've managed to gather through the night, but I shut all thoughts away, except for those that pertain to our immediate goal. Gathering my saddlebag, I walk to Korben.

"Are we ready to go? Do you have a plan?" I ask, stopping in front of him.

He straightens, blinking in surprise and searching my face.

The Eldrystone hangs around his neck, and I guess that's a good thing. Niamhara wanted him to have it, and I want nothing to do with it.

"We do not have to go yet," he says tentatively. "We can take as long as you need to—"

"I'm all right, Korben. I don't need time."

"I don't either." Esmeralda appears behind me, her satchel slung over her shoulder. "I want to go home."

I regard the dark circles under her eyes, and the dimness in her normally lively attitude. I bet, like me, she wishes we had never come here. I feel bad for her with no one here to console her, but I can't be strong for the both of us. It's taking all I have to be strong for myself alone.

"Are you sure, Valeria?" Korben insists. "We could talk and—"

I shake my head. "I don't need to talk, not right now. Later . . . perhaps."

He nods once, looking sad but understanding. He has seen his share of pain and knows me well enough to accept what I need.

"Then we are leaving." He raises his voice, attracting Calierin's and Galen's attention. The two come closer. "I will fly us to Riochtach," he says. "I will enter Elf-Dún at night, through the crown."

"Won't the protective dome stop you?" I ask.

He shakes his head. "No, over the crown, the barrier is designed to ignore anyone with Theric blood. What would be the point of such a grand *nest* if the palace's winged inhabitants could not fly straight into it?"

"True," I say, forcing a smile. I learned to perform early on.

"Could they have changed the way it functions?" I ask.

"Unlikely. It is ancient magic, and it has gone undisturbed for thousands of years."

After Orys killed my mother, Father told me she deserved all the dignity I could muster during her funeral. So I stood by his side in my black dress and slippers, holding his hand as well as my tears. Now, Jago deserves that I make sure Esmeralda gets back home safely, and he deserves for her to live in a place where no one is treated without respect because they're different. I will make sure to make those two things happen, no matter what it takes.

"They will be waiting," Calierin says. "Archers, for sure."

Korben smirks, exuding confidence. "I am extremely deft at avoiding arrows while in my Corvus form."

"You're planning to go in alone?" I ask. "That's unwise. I'm going with you."

"You have little experience flying, much less while being shot at," Korben says. "Who is being unwise?"

I narrow my eyes, angry at him for . . . for what? Facing a danger that can't be avoided? Making me fear losing him, too? I swallow my emotions and nod.

"You know best," I say. "Of course, we will follow your lead."

"What are *we* to do then?" Calierin asks. "Twirl our hair?"

"I have to cut the head off the snake," he says. "It is the only way. We cannot fight an army. I have to take back control from within."

I press a fist to my mouth, thinking. I might be able to follow after he goes in. I have Theric blood, too, don't I? Everyone will be distracted fighting, and I'll be able to—

"You could deactivate the dome," Galen says. "Then we can go in and help you."

Korben glares at Galen, as if livid he has dared mention this.

"The dome can be turned off?" I ask.

357

"Yes," Korben says grudgingly. "But what would you be able to do? Face a host of guards all by yourselves? No. I will not deactivate the dome."

"You can't do it all alone," I argue.

"But I must. *Everything* that has happened is my fault. It is my duty to repair the damage."

*Gods!* He blames himself the same way I do. Of course he does. His actions after Saethara's betrayal set in motion every event that has led us here . . . including Jago's death. But if guilt must be traced back to its source, isn't Niamhara responsible for creating The Eldrystone in the first place? If one must be entirely accurate, what about Morwen? She was the one who lured Niamhara away from their home, then abandoned her.

Yet, if none of those things had happened, the fae wouldn't exist, which means *I* wouldn't exist either. There would have been no Loreleia and Simón. No Amira. No Jago.

And that is infinitely worse than the alternative.

Morwen isn't to blame. Niamhara isn't to blame. Korben isn't to blame.

*I* am not to blame.

The people who released the horses, and the person who gave the order . . . *they* are to blame. The weight of an avalanche seems to slide off my shoulders.

I take a step forward and take Korben's hand, holding his gaze. The others meander away, leaving us alone.

"That isn't true," I say. "It's not your fault. Niamhara wanted me to tell you that. She wanted you to have the amulet back."

He frowns, his expression full of doubt.

"I didn't tell you last night because I didn't think you would listen."

He grunts but doesn't argue. He knows I'm right.

"I don't blame you either. Life is a series of events, good and bad. There's no way around that. Whether or not we want it, our actions ripple through time. The things we do may hurt someone in the future, but they may also be cause for joy. We mustn't judge ourselves too harshly. To live is to strive to do things well, but it is also to err."

An unexpected sense of peace washes over me as the words leave me and their meaning proves true in my heart. I lean forward and rest my head on Korben's chest.

His arms envelop me. "When did you grow so wise, Ravógín?"

Pulling away, I peer up at him and rest a hand on his cheek. "I forgive you."

His lips part.

"And I love you."

Eyes squeezed shut, he presses his forehead to mine and lets out a pent-up breath, as if he's been waiting to hear these words for some time, as if the uncertainty of my feelings were crushing his soul and my confession is a salve to his wounds . . . a peace to his inner war.

"I love you, too, Valeria."

"I know that."

"Never doubt it. I will spend the rest of my life doing whatever it takes to make you happy."

"Sounds like an amazing plan."

He kisses me gently, his lips a whisper over mine.

For a moment, I allow myself to find comfort in his embrace, then I pull away and say, "Let's go make sure our enemies don't ever steal anyone's joy ever again."

# 43

## KORBEN

*"I am not fuadach anymore. My magic has returned!"*

**Zylsa Bromin – Fae Sorcerer**

As we approach Riochtach from the west, I immediately know something is wrong. The city should be a tapestry of light, a perfect jewel against the twilight sky. Instead, a large section near the palace is a conflagration, a monstrous beast devouring itself. Black smoke billows into the heavens like an undulating ghost against the fading light. Flames, like hungry tongues, lick at the once-vibrant structures, reducing them to skeletal remains. The harmonious sounds of the city are replaced by a cacophony of crackling flames and terrified screams. Panic, like a tangible force, hangs heavy in the air. The sight is a mockery of who we are, of what we stand for.

I circle higher, heart pounding in my chest.

As we get closer to Elf-Dún, desperation claws at my heart as I search the roads and homes. Below, figures move like frantic ants, their silhouettes illuminated by the infernal glow. Some carry buckets of water, while others use their restored magic to douse the flames, a futile attempt to quench the powerful inferno. More flee, their faces etched with terror.

The chaos reaches for the palace, the nearby buildings spewing flames from their broken windows as if to claw away its taint.

*Damn Morwen!*

As my parents indicated, her sudden absence has lifted the barrier that stanched everyone's magic, and now, Riochtach fights for its liberation, unaware that I am here to eliminate the remaining blight on our realm.

The palace itself is yet untouched by the fire, but a torch-wielding crowd gathers around it, voices clamoring for the queen's head. Archers fill the parapets, but to my relief, no arrows fly. It seems the throng has not built up the courage to attack. Perhaps some respect for the ancient palace still lives in their memories. To my relief, Tirnanog's army has not been called to deal with the revolt. Not yet anyway.

I land away from the crowd, out of sight. Valeria and the others slide off my back and land on the ground. I shift from Dreadwing form back to fae form.

"What's happening here?" Calierin asks, attention fixed on a scorched tree, its leaves gone, its branches the color of charcoal.

"Everyone's magic *has* returned," I say, "and oppression only works against the weak. They are defending themselves against the chains Saethara cast around them. She and her allies may be expecting me, but I doubt they were expecting this. I believe I *will* disable the dome."

"Good," Calierin says with relish.

"Promise you will not harm anyone who stands down when you announce you fight in my name."

Calierin lets out a tired sigh.

"Promise, Calierin."

"I promise, my king."

I turn to Valeria and take her hands in mine. "Be careful."

"Me? You're the one going in there."

"I will be fine."

"How will we know the dome is down?"

"It will become visible for a moment, then it will retreat."

"Good."

"I know better than to ask you to sit this one out?" My tone, at the end, rises to form a question.

"Yes, you do."

I grunt in disapproval, rest my forehead to Valeria's for a few beats, then leap into the air. Shifting to my Corvus form, I fly straight toward the stars. Once I have gained enough altitude, I soar over Elf-Dún, positioning myself right above the crown. It rises one hundred feet from the center of the compound, its sight stirring countless memories of days past when I took to the skies, searching for respite from my duties.

Archers are positioned at regular intervals in the balcony that surrounds the structure. They search the dark sky but cannot see me. I am small and my black feathers blend with the velvet backdrop of the night.

I begin a sharp descent and wish for stealth from The Eldrystone, unsure of the extent of its power. To my relief, I sense the slight touch of magic around me.

When I am only twenty feet from the top of the tower, someone calls an alarm.

"He comes. There!" The words are accompanied by arrows and bouts of magic. Of course, sorcerers are on watch, using their skills to pierce any disguise, magical or not.

Still diving, I weave between arrows and orbs of energy and fire. They whiz past as I command The Eldrystone to abandon stealth for a shield. I dodge an arrow just to fly into the path of another. The air trembles before my eyes as the magic from the amulet halts the projectile.

Spreading my wings, I slow, make a circle around the crown, and gain a different angle, one that allows me to see the windows that lead inside, openings placed there for the easy entry of a winged creature of exactly my size.

A few more arrows *zip* by. I circumvent them, while my magical shield crackles. I feel it falter, but it holds. Folding my wings, I sweep through the small window and immediately dive once more, ready for anything. I stick close to the wall, a structure made of live branches that supports the copula. I am inside a shaft that travels downward toward the heart of the crown.

More archers stand at the bottom. Arrows shoot upward, some embedding themselves into the walls, others into the concave ceiling above.

As I continue my descent, I spot a sorceress preparing an attack, hands moving at a prodigious speed. Instinct taking over, I shift into my fae form and channel a spell of fire from The Eldrystone. Flames burst in front of me, shooting down the cylindrical enclosure. The guards and the sorceress cry out and leap out of the way just as the flames hit the floor.

Heat envelops me as I land, searing my skin. Growling in pain, I lunge out of the enclosure and roll, smothering the flames that eat at my clothes and skin. As momentum carries me forward, I take someone off their feet. They fall on top of me. I shove them off and scramble to my feet, layers of burnt skin peeling off my arms and falling to the glossy marble floor with a wet sound.

Teeth clenched against the pain, I jump over the railing of the spiral staircase leading to the bottom of the tower. I freefall for several seconds before I shift back into Corvus form. An instant later, I abandon the well hole for the safety of the staircase. Arrows and magic alike rain down the shaft just as I find cover. The pain of the burns is gone, the wounds healed by my shifting magic.

More guards await at the bottom of the stairs on each floor. They rush up to meet me, brandishing swords. I easily avoid them, flying in and out of the well hole and dropping down another level or two when the arrows from above pause.

I hit the bottom of the staircase running on booted feet. The tattered sleeves of my burnt shirt hang loosely. I tear them off and cast them aside.

A thick male, wearing a crown of mandible bones, pulls into my path. *Jaws*.

"Come to die, have you?" he says.

I unsheathe La Matadora and block the blow of his broadsword. The *ding* of metal fills the corridor.

"Stand down! I am your king," I order.

The male smirks, then lunges, driving his sword straight toward my stomach. I deflect the powerful blow with a sweep of my weapon, sidestep out of the way, and using Chimera form morph my hand into a talon. Viciously, I reach for his face, claws digging into his eyes. He crashes to his knees, hands to his face, sword clattering to the floor. His screams of agony echo in the corridor.

"I warned you," I say as I press forward to my first destination.

The dome's control room.

It's only in the next corridor. I round the corner at full pelt, then come to a sudden stop, boots skidding over the smooth floor. Six guards block the access door.

They all come at me with raised swords, except for one. He wears a black robe fastened at the waist by a belt made from golden links: a sorcerer. His long, gaunt face is that of a stranger. Quickly, I scan everyone else, but I do not recognize them.

"Stand down, soldiers. I am your king." I issue the same command once more.

A couple of them hesitate, exchanging glances.

"He's an impostor, responsible for the chaos beyond the walls," the sorcerer says, erasing any doubts.

"If I am an impostor, why do you guard that door? Only a Theric may enter, after all."

"No intruder will be allowed to soil Elf-Dún with their presence," the sorcerer sneers.

"Too late for that," I say, throwing a glance back. "I have left a trail of *garbage* behind." I straighten, sheathe La Matadora, and speak out the oath that only a Fae King can. "Let the whispers turn to screams if you dare defy me. My crown demands obedience. My blade demands respect. By the will of Niamhara and my people, I am your ruler! And in their name, you will stop."

One of the guards lowers his sword.

"Guard! Face this impostor or face me when this is done," the sorcerer growls, hand starting to weave a spell.

The guard raises his sword again.

"I gave you a chance," I say, exploding into a hundred ravens all bent on destruction.

Darkness swirls all around me, winged shape after winged shape melting from me and choking the passageway. I take a knee, eyes closed, awareness split into the many. Claws tear at fabric and skin. Swords cut me, killing me . . . or so they think.

At last, I stand, and my vassals return, rendering me whole again. Six bodies lie torn and bloodied on the floor, their eye sockets empty, their mouths twisted in horrible grimaces.

Steps firm, I weave through their ravaged shapes and reach the access door.

Cracking my neck, I rest a hand on the inscribed tablet to the side. The words are written in the ancient language, an enchantment created many generations back by a powerful sorceress of Theric blood.

"Open," I say.

The door vanishes. I step inside into a large room with a perfect replica of Elf-Dún. It is shaped from nothing but the light from the orbs attached to the walls. The representation is precise, except the dome—invisible over the real palace—shines with a tenuous white sheen.

I sweep a hand over the model, the way my father taught me the day he bestowed The Eldrystone upon me. It is all it takes for the dome and all its protections to disappear. With that done, I whirl to leave the room.

All the guards I left behind in my dash here wait outside, beyond the bodies of their fallen comrades. In front of them stands an enormous wolf with brilliant yellow eyes.

*Lirion Faolborn.*

I do not know where the knowledge comes from, but it is him. Morwen's and Saethara's ally—the first of the two who will taste my vengeance.

# 44

## VALERIA

*"I do not know where Morwen is, Saethara. Now, leave.*
*You should not be here."*

**Lirion Faolborn – Fae General**

My eyes are glued to the palace. Calierin, Galen, and Esmeralda also watch closely. We stand behind the crowd, which grows more restless by the moment, inching closer to the vine walls. They are still fearful of the protective enchantment that protects Elf-Dún, but their passions run high, making them progressively braver . . . or reckless.

The archers above hold their arrows. At least whoever commands them has the decency to not harm civilians. Captain Herendi, perhaps?

*Gods!* Shouldn't the dome be down already?

*He's all right. He's all right!*

My stomach roils with nerves. If something happens to Korben, I don't think I would—

The night sky above the palace seems to flicker, then the concave shape of a massive espiritu-shaped dome becomes visible. It remains in place for a couple of beats, then melts from the top to the bottom, going out with an audible pop.

Seeing this, people lose all control, rush toward the vine wall, and begin to climb. It takes a moment before arrows begin raining down, but they come regardless.

*This is wrong. So wrong!*

But there's only one way to stop this, so I must go and help Korben. Galen and Calierin dash forward and join the crowd.

"Stay here," I instruct Esmeralda, then run to join Korben, shifting mid-stride and taking to the sky.

I rise high over the palace, beyond the notice of the guards—not that many of them are watching for sky-bound threats at this point. Most are occupied with the people climbing the walls, and with two particular espiritu wielders, who are using their power to take down the main gate.

As I begin my descent, it is easy to avoid the few arrows that fly in my direction. No one seems too worried about a single raven when a horde of angry, long-repressed people are close to breaking into their fortress.

I quickly spot a group of palace ravens and veer toward them. A few more arrows fly toward me, spooking the ravens and scattering them in all directions. I follow the ones that fly toward the crown tower.

When I reach the structure, I search the ground for threats. I spot a couple of guards by the entrance, so I go around the back. No one is there. Wasting no time, I shift back to my human form. I imagine myself landing smoothly, but as my feet hit the ground, I stagger, arms windmilling. I nearly fall on my face, but manage to stay upright, if only barely.

I take a moment to catch my breath, heartbeats loud in my ears. The cries of the mob ring in the distance. Silently, I unsheathe my rapier and make my way around toward the entrance.

The tower looms, a dark shape against the night. I need to get inside. Korben is in there, but first, I must contend with the two hulking figures who block my way. They are armed with broadswords, and as they notice me, they advance, their movements heavy and deliberate, a stark contrast to the grace and speed I rely on. My rapier, a slender blade of tempered steel, sings in my hand as I slash it through the air.

The first strike comes from the left, a sweeping arc designed to cleave me in two. I parry, the rapier barely deflecting the blow with a sharp clang. As my attacker changes his stance, I lunge, my blade finding a gap in his defenses, stabbing his thigh. His companion charges, sword a blur of steel. I dance backwards, my feet moving fast, skillfully.

With a swift movement, I disarm him, his sword clattering to the ground. Rapier raised, I slash. He staggers back, a grunt of pain escaping his lips, his throat open, gushing blood.

My second opponent, seeing his comrade's fate, hesitates for a split second. I exploit this moment of indecision, driving my rapier into his exposed side. He collapses to his knees with a groan, the grip on his sword loosening. Eyes rolling into the back of his head, he falls forward and doesn't move again.

Whirling, I rush the carved wooden doors and march through the threshold. Gaze roving around, I try to decide which way to go.

There is a set of steps that leads downward, one that leads upward, and a passage that must give way to the rooms on this floor. I rush in that direction. Korben said the control room was on this level, didn't he? I cross through an area that appears to be some sort of museum display with paintings, sculptures, and artifacts inside glass cases. No one is here, so I keep going. I pick my way through another room just like the last, then run into the first sign of trouble.

Three people peer over their shoulders as they hear my steps. I freeze. They slowly turn to face me. Two guards dressed in shiny armor flank a blue-haired female. She wears a black leather suit that hugs her hips and breasts so tightly it must have been designed by an espiritu-blessed seamstress.

Saethara looks me up and down, focusing on my rounded ears.

"You," she says, her voice deep and dripping with contempt.

"Your powers of deduction are uncanny," I say, my sarcasm surpassing her contempt. "I hope you enjoyed your short stint as queen because today it comes to an end."

Her red-painted mouth twists, a slash that cuts through her beauty and reveals the truth behind the veil. Her dazzling appearance is nothing but a shell that hides a revolting spirit, rotted and crawling with maggots. I imagine she has known no love. I imagine everything she touches turns to ruin. I imagine she doesn't know what happiness is. For how could she notice when her own decay surrounds her?

"Kill her," Saethara orders her guards.

Without hesitation, they come at me, circling and twirling their large swords. Out of the corner of my eye, I watch Saethara, standing impassively, letting others do her dirty work.

I could take these two guards the same way I took the ones

outside, but I don't have time for that. Korben is somewhere in this building, and he needs my help. Ignoring the guards, I sheathe my rapier, face Saethara, and explode into Scatter form.

Saethara curses and attempts to run, but my ravens surround her, barring her way on all sides. I go for the guards first, their swords ineffective against the many claws and beaks that rip at their faces until they fall to the floor into puddles of their own blood.

"You are next," I say, the words formed by the snapping beaks of my ravens, the sound a series of choppy syllables that make Saethara shiver.

For a moment, I hesitate, thinking Korben should be given the satisfaction of ending her life, but after some thought, I decide it would be better if I spare him the sight of this hideous creature.

I aim all of my ravens in her direction and order then to attack. They obey.

A barrier stops them. I blink.

*What is this?!*

Wings flap desperately and ineffectually. Something holds my horde in place, an energy that suddenly wraps around every raven and pushes back.

Searing lines of pain cut across me as I'm pulled further away from Saethara. Through many pairs of rounded eyes, I watch her abandon her hunched-over position. She peers up with a mixture of surprise and satisfaction.

Growling in pain, I call my ravens back. They coalesce into one, into me. As my full awareness returns, I realize I'm crouching on the floor, a red glowing net cast over me, the mesh searing my flesh as easily as hot pokers.

I scream in pain, confused by what is happening. Is Saethara doing this? No, she has no espiritu. I lift my head, not without difficulty, and glance around.

Galen stands a few steps to the side, espiritu flowing from his fingers, pinning me in place.

"Worry not, Saethara," he says. "Morwen sent me."

# 45

## KORBEN

*"With Valeria and Jago gone, you're second in line to the throne, dear."*

**Duque Justo Ramiro Medrano – Grand Duke**

A wolf shifter. I was not expecting that.

Shifting is an uncommon skill, and wolf shifters haven't been seen in Tirnanog for a long time. In fact, the trait is thought extinct now. Did Morwen give Lirion this power when she decided to use him in her revenge toward Niamhara?

*Either way, I must be careful.*

The beast before me is immense, a wolf magnified to monstrous proportions. Its fur is a gray, impenetrable cloak, rippling with muscles beneath. His eyes burn yellow under the orb light, reflecting back hatred. A low growl vibrates through the air, a challenge.

I explode into Scatter form. My ravens dive in waves, a black tide against the threat. Beaks peck and claws rake, but their efforts are met with indifference. Each strike that finds purchase is met with a flash of healing light, the wounds closing as quickly as they appear. The wolf shakes himself, sending a shower of feathers flying.

I try once more, teeth clenched as the wolf snaps its maw right and left, destroying the ravens, sending stabs of pain through me. The wolf takes a few steps, then with a powerful leap, breaks free from the ravening horde. As he glides through the air, his eyes lock on to mine, a deadly glint of determination in their depths. His massive form is a blur. I hold my ground and send a host of ravens smashing into his side, but it is like hitting a wall. Lirion continues sailing in my direction.

I hold, hold, hold.

When he is a mere foot from me, I drop Scatter form and unsheathe my sword, slashing at the beast's chest. Impossibly, he changes course, as if the laws of physics do not apply to him.

La Matadora hisses through the air, while Lirion lands to my right, pivots, and attacks. A maw full of sharp teeth the size of daggers closes around my biceps. I growl in pain, pull the dagger from my belt with my free hand, and drive it into the wolf's side.

Lirion retreats in an instant, eyes wide, blood dripping from his wound. He has the look of someone who has never been bested, not even close.

"You have met your match," I sneer, circling.

La Matadora droops in my hand. My biceps throbs. I hold the dagger in front of me. He now knows he cannot overpower me. If he attacks, he will injure me, but he will not retreat unscathed.

"Where is she?" I demand, trying to delay him.

As the wound at his side knits, I retreat a step. I do not know how he can heal such a large wound without shifting. I cannot do that, but I am not totally at a disadvantage. Chimera form allows me to shift partially, so I can repair isolated parts of my body. Quickly, I put away the dagger and toss La Matadora into my left hand. At the same time, my right arm shifts into a wing, then immediately morphs back. I toss the sword back, the entire process taking only a second.

The wolf growls, a deep rumble in his chest.

"If you will not tell me where she is, I guess I will have to go through you first, then find her myself." I lunge, my grip around La Matadora strong, the strike powerful.

Lirion tries to dodge, but I am much faster. The sword strikes his chest, and as I follow through with the motion, the blade leaves behind a gash that yawns wide, revealing sinew and bone.

He lets out a bark that degenerates into a canine whine. As he falls with a *thud*, he swiftly shifts to his human form, a reflex that should allow his healing abilities to work faster.

I do not hesitate as I might have in the past. I never used to kill if it could be avoided, but deep in my bones, I feel this male's death is necessary.

Before he can heal and renew his attack, I position the sword over his heart and plunge it deeply.

His yellow eyes dim, leaving behind brown irises. He stares directly at me, still incredulous that someone exists who can best him. He was thoroughly unprepared for me. Perhaps he never expected to face me without Morwen's help.

"See you in the lowest of all hells," I say as his eyes close.

Freeing my sword, I stand and face the guards that still clog the corridor.

"Who is next?" I ask. "Who else dares defy Korben Theric, King of the Fae, Ruler of Tirnanog, Master of Elf-Dún?"

No one comes forth. Instead, everyone retreats, slowly disappearing from sight.

## VALERIA

As I writhe in pain kneeling on the floor and trapped by Galen's espiritu net, Saethara walks forward, the heels of her boots tapping the polished floor. She regards Galen from head to toe.

"Who are you?"

"Galen Síocháin."

"Korben's Master of Magic?"

"Yes." Galen's answer comes through clenched teeth. He seems to be under the control of some external force, acting against his will.

She frowns and cocks her head, silently asking for an explanation. I struggle, attempting to get free of the net that spreads over me, but I only manage to shift the threads, burning other areas of my body.

"Morwen met me in the Whispering Wilds," Galen says. "She . . . did something . . . to me before her departure."

"Departure? Where is she?!" Saethara demands, her voice panicked.

I understand her anxiety. We felt it dearly when we thought Niamhara would die. Saethara could have never gotten here without Morwen's help. Every step of the way, Saethara has had help and protection.

And now, she's alone.

I start laughing, unable to help myself. The shaking of my

shoulder causes the net's threads to dig deeper, burning me further. I hiss in pain.

Saethara's hateful eyes flick to me. She regards me as if I'm a stray dog come to soil her path.

"She is gone, gone, gone," I say, feeling a little crazy.

Pain ravages my mind, not only the physical wounds, also the sudden reminder that Jago is also gone.

"You're on your own, impostor queen," I go on, mockingly. "The only crown you'll wear from now on will be a death wreath."

Saethara kicks me, the point of her boot digging into my ribs. "Shut up."

I continue laughing through the pain.

She turns to Galen. "If Morwen sent you, I want you to kill this worthless human. Make sure it hurts."

"As . . . you . . . w-wish." Galen's face turns into a grimace, his green eyes vacant as he peers down at me.

It's not him, something else possesses him. Is he gone, like Jago? Will anyone mourn him?

He lifts an outstretched hand, palm up. Slowly, his fingers curl inwardly, forming a fist. The net around me tightens. I scream, curling into a ball on the floor, making myself smaller. Galen's espiritu constricts me further. The net forms a checked pattern over my face, cutting, cutting, cutting.

One of the threads sears my eyelid. Agony is a raw scream caught in my throat.

Instinct drives me to shift. Before I know it, I'm in my Corvus form, my wounds healing, the awful pain mercifully gone, though only for an instant.

It's Saethara's turn to laugh. She crouches, watching me with the interest of a child who has found a dying bug to poke.

"I suppose this means Niamhara is also gone, gone, gone," she says, her laugh far crueler than mine could ever be. She has practice and could be someone's maestra in the arts of malice.

The net shrinks in the blink of an eye, fully enveloping me once more, burning me anew. I claw at the espiritu-laden threads, attempting to tear them, but they cut through the black claws like a sword cuts through flesh. The tips of my claws clink to the floor. Galen's espiritu penetrates my flesh deeper and deeper, reaching bone.

In my agony, I vaguely wonder if there is a realm for human souls where our creator awaits us. I pray there is, so I can see Jago again and maybe Father. But never Mother. Never her.

The net tightens again, and I know this is it.

*I am dead.*

## KORBEN

I walk away from the bodies strewn on the floor. It is time to find Saethara. Surprisingly, it doesn't take long. She is past the doors at the end of the corridor.

The tableau that lies before me freezes me in place. Saethara stands next to Galen, her back turned. At first, I do not understand what is happening, then I see Valeria in her Corvus form at their feet. She is twitching on the floor under a net of red magic.

*Galen is hurting her!*

Reaching for The Eldrystone's power, I fling it at the sorcerer. The

379

amulet grants me just enough energy to restrain his magic and stay his arm. The red glow sputters out.

Saethara turns, dread radiating from her as she slowly faces me. Her expression falls as she realizes it is I who stands behind her.

I grapple with the many questions that rush through my mind. Why has Galen betrayed us? Is this some sort of twisted revenge for his exile? Does he hate me that much? I thought I could trust him, but it seems I never should have.

With deliberate steps, I move closer. Saethara sidesteps, meekly moving away from Valeria, keeping the distance between us equal.

A part of me wants to leap forward and strangle her, but Valeria's safety is my priority.

"Release her, Galen," I growl between clenched teeth.

He makes no effort to obey my command.

I tighten my grip around the hilt of The Matadora. His gaze remains glued on Valeria, even as I press the tip of the sword to his throat.

From the corner of my eye, I notice Saethara inching closer toward the door.

"I do not want to kill you, Galen," I say. "Release Valeria now, and I will spare your life."

He does not blink. Instead, his outstretched hand trembles with effort. Did his fingers just twitch? He is overriding The Eldrystone. The amulet is too weak to hold him. His red magic flashes to life.

*Fuck!*

"I am sorry, Galen. Valeria is my everything." With a quick flick of my wrist and a world of pain in my heart, I slash his throat.

There is no surprise or panic in his expression as he falls. His face is blank, features arranged in a mask of indifference. The magic around Valeria fizzles out. She lies broken, bits of claws and feathers strewn around her.

"Valeria!"

As I fall to my knees in front of Valeria, Saethara flees. I let her go. I doubt she will get far. I already hear the mob outside.

## VALERIA

The pain has pushed me to the edge of a deep abyss. If I fall, I know I will not return. I cling to life, even as heat cuts through my bones. Abruptly the constricting net disappears. Slowly, I'm led away from the precipice, the pain ebbing.

"Ravógín." Korben's voice is gentle, coaxing me further away from the edge. "Oh, Ravógín, I am so sorry. I would take your pain if I could."

He squeezes my hand. My hand? When did I shift back to my human form? I don't know. Profound instincts seem to rule me at times, a survival drive that supersedes all rational thought.

I open my eyes. My left eyelid remains half-closed, a stinging sensation cutting across it. Everything looks blurry.

"Shift again, Valeria," Korben says. "I know you are weak, but you have to. Some of your wounds have healed, but not all."

I gather my dwindling strength and do as he instructs. The pain in my remaining wounds disappears. Wearing Corvus form, I slump to the side, energy spent. Korben picks me up, his touch tender.

"You will be all right." He sheathes his weapon, stretches to his full height, and walks out of the tower, cradling me in his hands as if I'm the most precious thing he's ever held. He avoids looking at Galen's slumped shape. I understand why. He'll wear the blame of his death, and so will I.

Outside, it's chaos. Shouts and the clash of weapons reverberate in the air. A nearby building is on fire, choking the sky with gray smoke. Korben walks toward the main gate, in the direction of the noise.

I stir in his hands. I've gathered enough strength to shift back. Implicitly, he understands what I want and sets me on the ground. I morph into my human form, stretching upward in one smooth go, a far cry from the grueling transformations I endured in the beginning.

Korben takes my face in his hands. "Are you well?"

I nod. "I am, but she got away. And Galen . . ."

His eyes tighten at the mention of the sorcerer.

"She will not get far. Not in this." He gestures toward the chaos, choosing not to talk about his Master of Magic, his friend. I have a feeling Galen's death might haunt him for a long time.

We keep moving, walking side by side. Closer to the gate, we find guards clashing with civilians. I'm relieved to see the guards acting in a restrained fashion, using their swords and spears to keep Riochtach residents at bay, not to kill.

A group of weaponless guards wearing waist-long brown cloaks form a circle behind the armed guards. They stand with their hands held in front of them, as if ready to catch anyone who breaks through the first line of defense.

Suddenly, a ball of fire shoots upward from the center of the crowd, soaring over the guards' heads toward one of the majestic trees whose high branches connect buildings, acting as natural bridges.

One of the caped guards weaves his hands, releasing an orb of blue energy. It collides with the fireball and envelops it, disintegrating it to a shower of sparks that floats down harmlessly.

Korben walks forward, ready to intervene, but steps sound behind us. We turn to find Calierin, pushing Saethara along with the tip of her sword.

"Look what I found trying to escape," Calierin says. "I saw her run out of the tower and went after her. I would be honored if you let me take care of her." The Tuathacath warrior pokes Saethara with her weapon, making her flinch.

Next to me, Korben's features harden into a grim mask of hatred. When he was Bastien and Rífíor, I saw similar expressions on his face, but nothing quite like this.

He moves closer until he's only a foot from Saethara. His clenched fists tremble at his sides. Fearing he'll strangle her with his bare hands, I reach out and touch his shoulder. His gaze dashes to mine. In a split second, he reads my meaning.

*She's not worth it.*

Korben's attention returns to Saethara.

She tosses her hair and smiles a seductive smile. "Hello, Korben. You look . . ." her blue gaze rakes him up and down, ". . . *rugged*. That scar suits you."

He says nothing, only stares at her with that impassive expression he does so well.

Taking his silence as encouragement, she sticks out her chest, bosoms rising. "I have thought about you these past twenty years, about our . . . wedding night." She lifts a sinuous hand, long fingers reaching to touch Korben's scar.

He swats her hand away. Contempt dripping from his expression, he addresses her in a frigid tone. "Your ally, Lirion, is dead. I killed him."

Her face and bravado fall. In fact, her entire body seems to sag. A sob escapes her.

"Morwen is gone, too," Korben goes on. "She lost interest and is done causing petty squabbles. *You* are done."

Saethara's lower lip trembles as she recoils, fully understanding the magnitude of her defeat. She's alone now, all the support she has counted on to keep up the subterfuge eliminated. Though there might be others who have stood behind her, they're not here. Instead, there's only a bloodthirsty Tuathacath warrior, eager to lop her head off.

Eyes going wide, Calierin releases a warning. "Behind you!"

A cold smile stretches Saethara's lips.

Korben moves with the speed of the wind, unsheathing La Matadora as he whirls to face the danger. I've barely had time to turn my head, and he's slicing the weapon upward, cutting an espiritu attack in two.

The attacker—the same sorcerer who disabled the fireball—stands facing us. He's crouching, hands extended and ready to deliver another bout of espiritu.

Korben sidesteps, taking a protective stance in front of me. "Stand down, guard," he orders, his voice carrying through the ranks. "I am King Korben Theric."

Two of the other caped guards turn to join their companion.

"Kill them!" Saethara orders. "He is an impostor."

Korben tears The Eldrystone off his neck, the chain breaking. He holds it in his left hand, while his right positions the sword protectively across his body.

Three espiritu attacks unleash from the sorcerers. They act in unison, a tactic that is surely practiced. One of the attacks vanishes in midair while Korben slashes the other two with his sword, his movements fast and confident.

The sorcerer whose attack vanished stares at his hands with a frown. It seems The Eldrystone swallowed it up. The other two seem unable to believe Korben's speed. Their gazes dance between Korben and their supposed queen.

"Do something, idiots!" Saethara demands.

This time they appear uncertain.

Taking advantage of their hesitation, Korben says, "I am no impostor. The rumors you have heard . . . they are true. I am back to reclaim my throne from this usurper."

More guards turn to face us, including a few who were handling the crowd. The mood is changing, the denizens' shouts dying out slowly as news travels.

"I was not killed by humans," Korben goes on, his voice louder than natural, clearly enhanced by espiritu. The Eldrystone shines slightly, helping carry his message to the people in the back.

"I am alive and have returned from the human realm where I was trapped these last twenty years. I was betrayed on my wedding night, stabbed in the heart by the female I selected from the Royal Mate Rite."

Mutterings go through the crowd. People stand on their tiptoes and crane their necks to see better.

"She conspired with Morwen the Mistwraith and General Lirion Faolborn to murder me, but they failed. Their plans were thwarted by someone unexpected. Her name was Loreleia Elhice. She took The Eldrystone from my *wife*," the word sounds like a curse, "and took it across the veil to protect those she loved from my wrath, from my desire for retribution. I wanted the world to pay for the vile betrayal, but Loreleia Elhice acted wisely.

"When the veil collapsed, I was attempting to retrieve The Eldrystone, and instead, I was exiled. I have worked tirelessly to return, and what I found upon my reentry drove me to search for our Goddess, Niamhara. I found her, and she returned things to the way they have always been. Magic is restored, and we now can go back to the peace we used to know before this female's greed sought to steal what was rightfully ours."

The crowd is riveted now, hanging from Korben's every word. He lets out a relieved breath, then pronounces the oath of the Fae Kings.

"Let the whispers turn to screams if you dare defy me. My crown demands obedience. My blade demands respect. By the will of Niamhara, I am your ruler."

An eerie hush is left behind in the wake of Korben's pronouncement. The earth and the sky themselves seem to hold their breaths, Niamhara's power still coursing through Tirnanog, still empowering her children, including the leader she chose for them.

"Long live King Korben," someone says from the back.

The quiet returns, and I swear I can hear my agitated heart pounding.

Then another voice rises, followed by another and another and another . . .

"Long live King Korben. Long live King Korben. Long live King Korben."

The guards exchange glances, weapons still in hand. Despite Korben's words and the crowd's reaction, they appear unsure. Someone breaks ranks and comes forward.

Captain Herendi, the female who first arrested Korben. She sheathes her sword and approaches.

"You truly are King Korben?"

"I am."

"Prove it." She sounds desperate, as if her loyalty is wrestling with her desire to serve someone other than the ruler she knows.

Something tells me she isn't fond of Saethara.

"I just did," Korben replies.

"With something more than words."

Sensing an advantage, Saethara says, "Disobeying my orders will cost you your head, Captain Herendi. I gave you another chance after your failure. Do not disappoint me again," she threatens, dispensing fear the way someone else may dispense sweets to children. "Kill him!"

Captain Herendi's face betrays concern through a slight twitch of her eyes. Yet, she doesn't look in Saethara's direction.

Korben sheathes his sword and puts The Eldrystone in his pocket.

"I shall oblige," he says as two enormous black wings burst from his back, and he leaps into the sky.

My hair flies back with the powerful wingbeats. He looks majestic in his Chimera form, like a dark angel come to impart justice.

Everyone stares in awe, following Korben's progress as he circles above, his shape diving then rising back up, a sense of satisfaction in his movements.

Recognizing their king's gratification, the crowd erupts into cheers, their own contentment rising. For two decades, they have been oppressed, unable to express their views, their espiritu locked away.

I feel their joy as my own. My espiritu remained dormant for the same amount of time, and when it finally came to me, I felt whole for the first time in my life. I thoroughly understand them, though I suspect it was harder for them. No doubt, it's a far greater challenge to live with loss than with ignorance.

Captain Herendi's sword *zings* as she unsheathes it once more and walks to Saethara. Calierin grabs the traitor and pulls her back, distrustful of the captain.

Holding the sword straight up, the blade perpendicular to her nose, the captain says, "I hereby place you under arrest for treason, Saethara Orenthal. You will face a judge and the punishment they deem appropriate for your crimes."

"I will not do such a thing," she spits. "I am the Queen of Tirnanog."

Korben lands smoothly next to me, his enormous, glossy wings disappearing with a *whoosh*. "Take her," he says.

Two other guards come to assist the captain. They grab Saethara's arms and march her away toward the dungeons. Calierin lets her go reluctantly. She seems to want to follow, but in the end, she stays, likely deciding that protecting her king is more important.

The captain stands at attention, awaiting orders.

"Send out a message to all the ministers and heads of the guilds, captain," Korben says. "It is time to set Tirnanog to rights."

# 46

## KORBEN

*"Praise Niamhara! He was really the king, and he stayed in my inn."*

**Branwen Lazanar – Fae Innkeeper**

Valeria seems to be growing restless. Her gaze wanders east, her expression forlorn and detached. As the hours go by, I feel her thoughts stray further toward Castella and her sister, to those kept imprisoned for the crime of being fae.

This is only the third day since I retook the throne, but I sense her desire to leave already. I fear I will wake up one day, and she will be gone, her wings beating at the rhythm of her heart as it clamors to return home. That is why I am working tirelessly, meeting with all those who can help restore order to our broken realm.

Today, I have taken some time to assess the people Saethara condemned to prison without a trial. The list is long, and I have barely made it through the first set of names.

Not one of the first twenty-three I have interviewed deserved their imprisonment. Rolling my shoulders, I sit straighter and turn the next page of the extensive report. A wave of shock and relief hits me when I read the next name.

*Vonall Darawin!*

My eyes flick to Captain Herendi. "Bring the next person in. Right away!"

The captain is efficient, quickly becoming someone I trust. She leaves the room and returns with two more guards, who help her with the prisoner.

The male they assist can barely stand on his own two feet and is practically carried in. I stand, scanning his face, trying to recognize my good friend in this poor soul's features. Matted auburn hair tops his head, and a long graying beard hangs limp and food-stained on his chest. His frame is half the size of what I expect, the muscles depleted. He is starved, as evidenced by his sunken cheeks and eyes.

Rage burns in my veins once more, a common occurrence in the last seventy-two hours, as I have discovered all the awful things Saethara did in my absence. It is moments like this I would outright kill the harpy and deny the judges and denizens their right to condemn her themselves.

I move closer and, at last, discover my friend in the broken male before me.

Vonall's blue eyes dance around fearfully, giving him the appearance of a trapped animal who has been beaten one too many times. I meet him halfway in the large receiving hall. He shrinks into himself as I approach, head lowering, shoulders rising toward his ears. He stares at the floor, trembling, his once formidable spirit and presence not even phantoms of their former selves.

"What did they do to you, my dear friend?" I ask.

I wait for my words to register, but it is as if he has not heard me.

"Vonall?" I lift a hand, intending to place it on his shoulder, but he hisses, pulling back.

The captain and I exchange glances.

I try one last time, afraid to upset him too much. Only the gods know what he has been through, and he may need intensive treatment and time to recover.

"Vonall, it is I, Korben. I have returned, old friend."

Slowly, he looks up. At last, he meets my eyes, but only for an instant. I begin to think he is beyond my grasp, unreachable, but then he speaks.

"Korben?" His voice is nothing but a hoarse whisper, the rasp of a male much older than Vonall's years. "Is . . . th-that really y-you?"

I clasp one of his hands. "Yes, Vonall. It is I."

He shakes his head. "No. 'Tis a dream, a traitorous d-dream. Korben is . . . d-dead."

"I am not dead. You have been lied to. I was only . . . away. But I have returned, and I shall set everything right, the way it used to be."

His skeletal fingers squeeze mine, as if he is trying to make sure I am really here, and he is not confronted by an apparition.

"Y-you are truly here?" he asks.

"I am."

Vonall looks to Captain Herendi, searching for confirmation.

"This *is* King Korben, your friend. He is truly here, and now you are free," the captain says.

The last vestiges of strength leave Vonall, and he collapses, knees buckling. I catch him, indicating to the guards that they can leave. I need to take care of my friend. Whatever horrors he went through, I am to blame. He needs me, and I will not leave his side until he feels safe, and I make sure he has everything he needs. In honor of those who did not survive, I will do all I can for those who did.

## VALERIA

Cuervo sits next to me as I perch on a branch, legs swinging.

We watch people walk around Elf-Dún in a flurry of activity. Everyone is working hard to repair the damage done to the palace and the city. Improvements are happening quickly, the benefit of so many artisans with espiritu.

Korben has been busy. He tries to make time for me, but it's hard, which is fine. These last three days have allowed me to start processing Jago's loss. It has been good for me. Though I can't say the same for Esmeralda. She does nothing but sleep and ask when we're going back to Castella. I don't blame her. I've started growing restless, too. I bet she would be halfway there by now if not for the darkness that seems to come over her at the most unexpected times.

Cuervo hops excitedly as a female wearing a jeweled dress walks past.

"Treasure," he says, though his excitement dies quickly, as if remembering his fascination with treasure cost him a few days in a cage.

Soon after taking care of Saethara, I asked Korben to find Cuervo. He went with me to the aviary, and together, we freed our friend from his imprisonment. Thankfully, Cuervo was unharmed. Better yet, he doesn't seem to blame me for the ordeal, something I was worried might happen since I was the one who pointed him to Captain Herendi's medal.

One more thing Korben and I did . . . we returned the torn pages to the codex. Just as I hoped, The Eldrystone helped to reattach them. The large tome and the entire library seemed to sigh in relief as the pages melded seamlessly into place.

For the hundredth time, my thoughts stray to Galen. Korben and I have come to believe he was acting under Morwen's influence in the end. Since that night she appeared in the Whispering Wilds, the sorcerer didn't act like himself. In retrospect, there were small signs, but it all happened too quickly to notice them. Korben held an honorific funeral service in his name and declared him a hero of the fae, instrumental in defeating the usurper. He regrets his death but seems to find comfort in the fact that he saved my life . . . the most precious thing in all the realms—his words, not mine.

Looking east, I think of what awaits. I must confront Amira, must free the fae at any cost. I fear our friendship and familial connection will pay the price. Yet, I must act according to my convictions. We are all equal and must be treated accordingly.

It is time to return home and make Castella a better place.

## KORBEN

"I must go, Korben," Valeria says, pacing the length of my new bed chamber.

I have ordered the old one be torn down and remade into an inconsequential sitting area. It was the bedchamber where Saethara and I spent our wedding night, where she stabbed me through the chest and took The Eldrystone from me. I do not intend to step foot in that space ever again. Though it is not because the memories of that night are painful in relation to my once-wife (our contract has been thoroughly annulled). No, that is not what bothers me. What bothers me is the reminder of what I became, of what I allowed her actions to do to me.

It has now been two more days since I retook my position as king. In that time, I have seen to the creation of a cabinet charged with the task of restoring peace and normalcy across Tirnanog. I have met with all the guilds to reassure them I am truly back. I have retaken control of Elf-Dún's guard and ensured I am surrounded by trustworthy people. I have met with all the generals to test their loyalty and that of their soldiers. I have even fought a small group of Saethara's loyalists, who claimed she was the true ruler and I an impostor. (There were not many of them, and their efforts were half-hearted. Dismantling them was child's play.) I have issued a decree, forbidding Tirnanog citizens to cross the veil until further notice, citing a need to reestablish diplomatic relationships with the human monarch. Along with that, I have deployed troops to the border to prevent any desperate fae from going in search of their long-lost loved ones.

Most importantly—if somewhat selfishly—I have seen to Vonall's care. With pleasure, I have witnessed the slow improvement of his body and mind, his recovery from years of mistreatment at Saethara's hand. He seems stronger every hour, as if hope is his medicine and nourishment. At first, I feared he was entirely broken, but I underestimated his strength. In no time, he will be ready to retake his position as my closest adviser—something he insists will be the right salve for his mind and soul.

Now, seeing Valeria pace, charged with frantic energy, I can only be grateful for her patience while I repaired the damage that my twenty-year absence caused to my people. At last, I can give her what she needs.

"We will go, then," I say. "Tomorrow."

She stops, her brown gaze darting to meet mine. "Truly?"

I nod.

She seems to deflate. I walk to her and wrap my arms around her.

"I thought I would have to go by myself," she says. "I was ready to argue with you until you agreed to let me go."

I pull away and lock her gaze. "I would never try to stop you."

She seems skeptical, a frown line appearing on her forehead.

"It is true." I consider for a moment. "I understand how much you care for your people because I care for mine in the same way. I would never get in the way of that. In fact, these past couple of days have been difficult because I could see how hard it is for you to wait. I am grateful for your patience." I caress her cheek with the back of my hand. "I did not want you to go alone, but I would have understood if you had left without me. Thank you for waiting. I would have gone mad not knowing if you were well."

Tears waver in her eyes, and somehow, I know she is thinking of Jago, of a journey back to Castella without him.

I feel like a poor substitute. The love she felt for him was forged through years of shared happiness and struggles. I am glad she had someone like Jago in her life. I only hope that on her return to Nido, her home, she finds comfort in her sister. I refuse to think of any other alternative. Amira must be well, and beyond that, she must be willing to make amends for her mistakes.

Otherwise, I fear for Valeria's well-being.

# 47

## VALERIA

*"Can you teach my ravens to speak, Princess Valeria?"*

*Aimer Corvalur – Elf-Dún Ravenmaster*

We stand atop Elf-Dún's crown, outside on the balcony. There are only five of us when there should be seven. I inhale deeply, trying to control my emotions.

Galen is dead. And Jago . . .

I see the same forlornness I feel reflected in Esmeralda's face.

Jago should be with us, with the woman he loved, living his life to the fullest.

*Oh, gods! How will I tell Nana he is gone?*

Calierin puts a hand on my shoulder, offering me a smile. I compose my expression to hide the pain she must have seen. I fight the urge to shake her off. There is true regret in her eyes. She pulls back, her touch brief. I don't know how I feel about this show of sympathy. Will I ever forgive her for what she put me through? Maybe. I suppose we are on the same side now, and that has to count for something.

The sky above is clear, no clouds in sight. It will make for an easy flight, Korben assured me.

Pushing on one of the branches in the balcony's railing, Korben opens a gate, and a platform slides out, like a plank from a ship. With confident steps, he strides down its length, then leaps off, shifting into Dreadwing form.

Esmeralda and I both blink at the massive bird that appears in front of us, a creature so grand, it defies all imaginings.

The air displaced by his wings stirs our hair and clothes. With a few beats, he rises, then lands on top of the crown, which is now flat. Several guards climb up a spiral staircase, carrying bundles. We follow and watch them set to work, affixing a harness to Korben's back, straps going around his neck and chest. The harness has three seats and space for supplies. Everything fits perfectly, clearly designed to Korben's measurements.

Once the guards have secured all the straps and loaded the supplies, Esmeralda and I climb up a small ladder and take our seats. There are straps to keep us in place. I forgo mine, thinking of falling, falling, falling . . .

I shake my head and dismiss the awful memories that rise inside my mind, phantoms meant to drown me.

"Strap yourself, will you?" Esmeralda points at my unfastened belt.

"I can fly, remember?" I say.

She frowns, and I can almost read the thought careening through her mind: *Jago could not.*

For her peace of mind, I thread the strap and secure it in place. She seems satisfied.

I pat the stop in front of me, clucking my tongue. Cuervo comes reluctantly and positions himself on the harness, claws wrapping around a leather strap. Calierin takes the last seat.

Once everything is in place, the guards disappear down the stairs, and Korben leaps into the air, flying toward the sun. The city sprawls below, many of the buildings charred to black. It is a sad sight for such beauty to be marred in such a way, but it could have been worse. If we'd been even one day late, the entire city might be in ruins.

We glide above the clouds, the chilly air biting my skin, making me feel something other than the deep loss of my cousin, and how with every passing second, I get further away from him.

Instead, I try to think of what awaits us on the path ahead, of Castella and its people. Of my sister.

*Amira, do you hate me?*

She sent guards to arrest me for the charge of treason. Will she treat me as a traitor? Will she condemn me to death?

We will free the fae. Neither I, nor Korben, will allow innocent people to continue to suffer. We discussed our plan before leaving, and we're both in agreement about that. We also agreed that an army would be unnecessary. We want to avoid more bloodshed. We think a surprise attack will suffice. If that fails, we'll have to think of something else.

While still in Tirnanog, Korben flies low above each city and small town we pass. Calierin digs in a sack, pulls out handfuls of rolled up scrolls, and lets them fall. They sail downward to land on cobble paths and center plazas, imprinted with the news of their king's return.

Only two hours after leaving Riochtach, we spot the veil ahead, a shimmering curtain that seems to fall from the heavens down to the ground. It extends as far as the eye can see in both directions, north and south. I imagine it goes around the girth of the world, a gossamer skirt fashioned by a celestial seamstress.

Korben flies through the veil. I feel it as we pass like the cool touch of a damp cloth on my face.

I blink, and we are in Castella.

In my realm, we fly high, avoiding every settlement. In only three days, we arrive at the outskirts of Castellina, where Korben lands behind the cover of trees, unseen by anyone.

It is daytime, and we're tired, at least Esmeralda and me. For his part, Korben seems invigorated, as if flying were his life force. In Calierin's case, I doubt she would ever show any sign of weakness. Instead, she builds a small fire, using her espiritu, while Esmeralda and I spread sleeping mats over the ground and lay our weary heads down.

I fear I won't get any sleep, but the next thing I know, the scent of roasted meat is tickling my nose. I open my eyes to find that it's dark, the moon a waning sliver in the star-dotted sky. For a moment, I'm shocked by their number, their view unimpeded by the etherglow I've quickly become accustomed to.

Korben hands me a plate with food as soon as I sit up. Cuervo stands on a branch above. Esmeralda sleeps on, looking peaceful for the first time since . . . I lower my head and stare at the food.

"Would you rather something else to eat?" Korben asks.

"No, this is fine."

Roasted meat, flat bread, and a mixture of nuts and dry fruit . . . This is fine.

After a few quiet moments, Korben asks, "Are you certain of our plan?"

"I am," I reassure him.

"You would not prefer if I—"

"It's fine, Korben."

He exchanges a worried glance with Calierin.

I've had this conversation with him before. I won't have it again . . . lest I should falter in my resolve.

"How do you think things will go with your sister?" Calierin asks, pointing at me with her pocketknife, which she's using to spear her meat.

I shrug. "I've tried not to think about it."

She nods, looking as if this is a sensible thing to do.

"One way or another," I say to assuage any concerns she might have, "your people . . . we'll free them."

"I know," she replies in a tone that makes it sounds as if she truly was worried about my relationship with Amira and not the well-being of her kin. Is the Tuathacath warrior truly capable of caring about something like that? I thought she only cared about slitting throats, but she has surprised me again.

"It will be fine," Korben says. "Amira can have no objection to our kin's departure now that the veil is open."

I say nothing. He has no idea how affected Amira was after Orys supplanted her, and she woke up to find our father dead. She became paranoid, hateful, and ready to blame not only those who wronged her, but their entire kind.

I'm reminded of the evil sorcerer, and his vendetta against my family. When he first attacked, he seemed to only hunger for power and control. He, like Amira, was angry at an entire race, blaming us for the veil's collapse. He sought to kill the king, but instead killed the queen as she stepped in to defend her husband. Was that the only thing that drove him to attack? The question has been on my mind for many years.

"I've meant to ask you this before, but there never seemed to be time," I say.

Both Korben and Calierin look up and listen.

"Do you know who Orys Kelakian was?" I say. "Was he, perhaps, like Galen? Exiled for some reason?"

Korben shakes his head. "I never heard of him before."

"Orys Kelakian?" Calierin enquires, lifting an eyebrow.

"He was the sorcerer who killed Valeria's mother and father," Korben explains, sparing me the trouble, "and the same one who assumed Amira's identity as soon as she became queen."

"Oh, yes, him." Calierin appears indifferent to the information, making me doubt her ability to feel once more.

"*I swear a turnip has more heart than her,*" Jago's voice says in my head.

I nearly choke with emotion.

Calierin feels nothing, while I appear to feel too much.

Blinking, I shove meat into my mouth and chew. Korben glances at me sideways, missing nothing. Yet, he doesn't reach out to comfort me, understanding my mood perfectly. After all is said and done, there will be time to continue processing Jago's death. Right now, we still have much to do.

Oblivious to my subtle exchange with Korben, Calierin says, "I never heard of Orys before either."

I suppose the sorcerer's exact motives will remain a mystery like many other things in life.

Esmeralda wakes up some time later, the peaceful expression she wore in her sleep promptly slipping away.

She eats the food Korben saved for her, looking amused. "Imagine little old me, served by a king."

"A king that will always welcome you in his realm," he says, producing a pouch tied with a leather string. "I . . . want you to have this."

"What is it?" Esmeralda asks around a mouthful of food, not reaching for the pouch.

"Something for you and your family."

"Gold?"

"Jewels."

"I don't want them." She looks away, appearing offended.

Korben's jaw ticks in annoyance. He meets my gaze, his expression saying, *I tried*.

I narrow my eyes. *Not hard enough*.

He tries again. "Please, Esmeralda, take it. For your help."

"What help? I didn't help. I just sat there." Her green eyes reflect the dancing flames of our campfire, unshed tears pooling at the rims.

"You helped Valeria when she ran from Don Justo," Korben says.

I nod to encourage him.

He goes on. "Then you helped again when Valeria escaped Nido— in which instance, you also helped *me*. Without you and your troop, we might have never been able to reopen the veil, to save my people in Tirnanog. And now, those who are still stranded here."

Esmeralda shrugs dismissively. "Maybe, but I still don't want it."

Korben sighs, meeting my gaze once more.

I share his defeated expression. It would be useless to push. This Romani woman is hardheaded. Korben sets the pouch aside, and we finish the rest of our food in silence.

From our camp in the woods, we walk toward the edge of the city. The sliver of moon hangs directly above us, barely enough to see by, especially for Esmeralda. I have to warn her against tripping hazards several times lest she fall. My gaze roves around the thick trees, peering through their trunks and foliage. It's a marvel what has happened to my senses. I can see, hear, and smell so many things that would have gone unnoticed in the past.

When we exit the woods, we're faced with a row of small houses painted white, their red tile roofs speckled with dew. The drops look like small diamonds to my new eyes, painting a beautiful picture that feels ethereal.

In the distance, Nido rises above every other structure, flanked by the broken pieces of the Realta Observatory to the east. I ignore the sight of my home and focus on Esmeralda. She heaves a heavy sigh.

"Ma and Gaspar will be glad to see me." She sounds like someone trying to find a positive angle and discovering a poor substitute instead. She turns to me. "I can make it to the troop from here."

"Are you sure?" I ask.

She nods.

The troop moves around, keeping no permanent location. Some

of the troop members who are unable to travel settle for a time in small rented dwellings while the able members travel all over the realm. Esmeralda's mother, due to her ailments, normally remains in Castellina. However, by now, she has probably moved out of the little house where she was staying the day I met her. How will Esmeralda know where to look for her?

I'm about to ask, then press my lips together. Esmeralda is a grown woman with far more worldly experience than I'll ever have. She isn't always forthcoming about her troop's nomadic habits, but that doesn't mean she doesn't know what she's doing. Besides, the Romani know Castellina and many other areas of the realm better than anyone. It was thanks to them I was able to escape the catacombs after Ríffor abducted me from Nido, after all.

Esmeralda gives a curt nod and starts walking away. Without thinking, I grab her arm and pull her into a tight embrace. She stiffens, at first, but gradually relaxes, her arms wrapping around me.

"He loved you," I say.

She shakes her head.

"I knew him better than anyone, and I'm sure he was in love with you. I never saw him so taken with anyone."

"I . . . I loved him, too." She chokes on a small sob, then continues. "I never told him." She shakes as the tears pour out of her. "I . . . wish . . . I wish I had told him."

"He knew," I say with conviction. "He knew."

She pulls away. "Here you are, consoling me when you knew him your whole life."

A knot forms in my throat. It aches. I take a step back and stare at the ground.

"He was wonderful, wasn't he?"

"He . . . was," I manage.

"I know I'm going to miss him my entire life."

I smile, regarding her through blurry eyes. "We can miss him together. I'd like to . . . be your friend."

For an instant, I think she will balk at this, but she nods. "I'd like that, too. I'd love to hear all the stories you can tell me about him."

I half laugh, half sob. "That would be wonderful. I can see no better way to keep his memory alive. Our Nana—you'll love her— she can tell you a fair share of stories, too."

She takes several steps back, nodding. "Don't look for me. I'll find *you*, princess."

Remembering, I pull her kerchief out of my pocket and place it in her hand. "Thank you for letting me borrow it."

"Ah, yes. My ma embroidered it for me."

With her satchel slung over her shoulder, Esmeralda walks away. I swallow thickly, turning my back on her. Korben and Calierin have retreated behind the line of trees to give us privacy, but they join me soon after I wipe my tears away.

"Ready?" Korben asks.

I nod.

Taking several steps back, Korben shifts to Dreadwing form. The harness is still strapped to his back, retained and stored away by his shifting espiritu. After we climb and mount, Calierin secures our supplies, and Cuervo takes his place. With a powerful beat of wings, we rise toward the moon, until we're so high the frigid air sends shivers down my spine, and no one below would be able to spot us. The city is quiet. Too quiet, actually. It reminds me of Riochtach on that first night.

In only minutes, we circle above Nido. Korben surveys the ramparts, looking for guards that could raise the alarm. After a careful search, he banks to the side, moving away from the palace. This means he didn't find a place to land without being noticed. He warned me this would be the case, but I wanted to try anyway. All my life, the veil was closed and espiritu cut off from our realm. The skies never represented a threat to our fortified palace. This change means Amira fears an attack from the fae, a people who should be considered allies had she not decided to imprison our accidental guests.

Does she regret her actions? If she does, has she forgiven me for going against her will?

Korben alights on the other side of the same hill he and I climbed the day we escaped Nido through one of its many secret passages. As soon as Calierin and I jump off his back, he shifts to his fae shape.

"Are you sure this is how you want to do this?" He pulls me away from Calierin, grabbing my shoulders and staring pointedly into my eyes.

"It is." We have gone over this more than once, but he's still worried.

I press my lips to his, then hug him, enjoying his solidity, his warmth.

"Please be safe."

"I will. You, too." Reluctantly, I step back. "Don't let her hurt anyone," I remind him, gesturing toward the Tuathacath warrior.

"Do not worry. I will not."

His word is enough for me. Calierin is nothing if not obedient to her king.

"See you on the other side of this mess," I tell him, then shift into Corvus form and fly away with Cuervo at my side.

# 48

## KORBEN

*"Drocháin! I never thought a human would earn my respect."*

**Calierin Kelraek – Tuathacath Warrior and Veilfallen**

I watch Valeria's raven shape get smaller and smaller as she flies over the ridge of the hill. A moment later, she disappears. My heart constricts in fear for her, but I reassure myself she will be all right.

She is headed to her home, to a place she knows the way I know Elf-Dún, to her sister. Amira will not dare hurt her. The worst she can do is imprison Valeria, and if she does . . . well, Castella's queen will find out what it is to displease me.

Calierin stands ready, broadsword strapped to her back, violet eyes glinting with that coldness they seem to purposely breed into every Tuathacath warrior.

"I wish Kadewyn were here," she says. "For old times' sake."

"Yes," I reply, though I wish he were here for a different reason: to keep Calierin's blood lust in check.

I push this worry aside, too. Calierin's assigned task guarantees she will be too busy saving people to kill anyone.

Without another word, I shift and allow her to climb and secure the harness. Taking to the skies, I head toward the Monasterio de San Corvus de la Corona. It is time to free my kin.

As Valeria indicated, the monastery is impossible to miss. The place is only a fraction of Nido's size, but still a large edifice by Castellina's standards.

The structure sits atop a mountain, nestled in a plateau, amid sharp rocks and barren bushes. Its high walls are made of gray stone with watchtowers at each corner. Small fires flick in braziers, illuminating the indolent attitudes of the men on duty. It seems they have already grown comfortable and lax, something they will soon regret.

I land a safe distance away, unseen. Calierin jumps to the ground. Her movements lithe and silent, she scurries away into the night, immediately following her orders. I watch her cut through the terrain in bursts of speed that allow her to avoid the occasional prying eyes from above. It is easier than fooling a blind person.

She reaches the wall and, using her magic, begins to climb. She looks like a spider, slick and lethal. The guards in the nearest tower would have to peer straight down the length of the wall to spot her now. However, they are about to be too busy to bother doing any of that.

I shift into my unassuming Corvus form, circle once above the monastery, then land in its inner courtyard. A large gurgling fountain sits in the middle, while the rooms that used to host monks and now hold my kin go around the perimeter.

Flapping my wings noisily, I jump onto the rim of the fountain.

No one notices me. I flap my wings some more, then let out a loud *caw*. A guard standing by the front gate shakes his head, chasing off sleep, and moves closer to inspect. He is a young human with brown hair and a thin frame.

"Bruno, there's a raven on the fountain," he calls to his partner.

"So?" Bruno groans in a sleepy voice.

"We were told to keep an eye out for ravens."

"And we have. They're boring."

"This one is out at night," the young guard says.

"Perceptive, aren't you?" Bruno sounds annoyed, but he comes closer to inspect, anyway. He is older, his uniform jacket unbuttoned, his boots unpolished. Guardia Bastien would have words with him about his unkempt appearance.

I hop off the fountain onto the stone courtyard, cawing repeatedly.

"*Shoo! Shoo!*" Bruno makes a sweeping gesture with his hand.

I hop closer instead.

"That bird is acting strange," the young guard says.

"If you take all your orders so seriously, muchacho, you'll turn paranoid. Just feed the blasted thing some of those crackers you keep in your pocket, and it'll go away. It's probably hungry."

"I don't keep crackers in my pocket," the young man protests.

"Sure, and my wife's last name is Plumanegra," Bruno grunts. "Go on, Joaquin. Feed it."

"Fine." Joaquin rolls his eyes and reaches into the front pocket of his jacket. He produces a small round cracker and carefully throws it in my direction. It lands right in front of me.

I cock my head this way and that, inspecting it closely. As if I have decided it is not worth eating, I kick it back toward Joaquin, croaking in displeasure.

Bruno bursts out laughing. "I suspected those things were nasty."

"They're not nasty!" Joaquin protests. "My mother makes them." The man pulls out his rapier. It slides from its thin scabbard with a metallic song.

Bruno huffs. "What are you going to do? Kill it 'cause it doesn't like your mama's cooking?"

Curiosity aroused by the display, three more guards approach, appearing behind me.

Just as planned.

"What's going on?" one of them asks.

"Joaquin, here, is going to stab that bird because it turned down one of his mama's crackers." He laughs heartily, clearly in need of some sort of amusement.

Boredom is a problem guards deal with often. I had my share of it while standing outside Princess Valeria's door when I posed as her guard. That was until my desire for her took over, of course. After that, all I could do was grind my teeth as I fought the urge to barge into her room to make her mine.

"I'd like to see that." One of the newcomers grins.

"That's not what I'm doing," Joaquin growls, clearly mad at Bruno for making fun of him. "That raven's acting strange. Princess Valeria, the traitor, has a raven, a smart one. It could be this one."

"And what? He's here to escort her in?" Bruno glances over his shoulder toward the closed gate. "Maybe she's out there." He cranes his neck and shouts at the tower to the left. "Hey, you two up there!"

Two heads poke out of the tower, as well as two more from the one on the right.

"What?" a man shouts back.

"See anyone out there?"

One of the heads retreats for a moment, then reappears. "Um, no. There's no one out there."

"I guess that's not it then," Bruno tells Joaquin, who is slowly approaching me, the point of his rapier only three feet away from my beak.

A couple more guards appear, rounding the fountain. The others explain the situation, snickering. At this point, I am surrounded. I hop from talon to talon.

"The kid isn't wrong," one of the newcomers puts in, her tone steady, serious. "That bird is much too calm, considering he's flanked on all sides."

Bruno frowns but says nothing. It seems he has some level of respect for this stern-looking woman.

"Before you do anything, let me—" She does not get to finish her sentence because Joaquin leaps, slicing with his rapier, intent on cutting me in half.

I jump out of the way, fly straight up, and circle over their heads. I caw loudly, angrily. Some of the guards laugh, while others glance up warily, unsheathing their own rapiers.

"Idiots!" the woman exclaims. "May as well try to kill a fly with a quill. Get the nets and alert the archers to—"

Time to do more before the guards have time to organize.

Diving for the tall wooden gate, I shift into my massive Dreadwing form. The guards scream at the transformation, scrambling to get out of the way.

Beak first, I slam into the gate. It splinters and breaks apart, pieces flying in every direction. Cawing, I sweep upward, gaining altitude.

"Holy saints!" Bruno shouts. "Someone, shoot that thing!"

I veer toward the tower on the left, claws outstretched. The two men prepare arrows, but they are too slow. They duck as I sweep by and tear chunks of the wall with my claws. The brazier is knocked over, spilling hot coals and clattering loudly.

Sweeping around, I perch on the broken wall and screech at the guards. They drop their bows and arrows to cover their ears, then run down the stairs, terrified.

Arrows whistle in my direction from the other tower. I take flight once more, easily avoiding the projectiles. I take care of the second tower and its guards in the same fashion as the first.

More arrows whistle through the air, this time from below and the other towers. Turning away, I fly a short distance down the path that leads away from the gate. Circling to face the monastery once more, I shift into my fae form and hit the ground running. I unsheathe La Matadora and run toward the stupefied soldiers, who stand framed by the building's entryway.

Faced with a different, less formidable foe, they gain courage and charge, their battle cries rending the night. I face them full on.

The dim moon casts an eerie glow over the path, a pale wash of light that reminds me of battles past. Though this one is different. I am not here to kill them, only to distract them. A dozen rapiers gleam in the moonlight, their wielders wearing the terrified expressions of men who fear this will be their last night alive, a stark contrast to the cool calm that courses through me. Yet, their eyes burn with determination. They are good men, brave men.

As our weapons clash, I toy with them, feinting and dodging, drawing them backward, away from the monastery.

Their attacks are predictable. I parry, riposte, disarm. Though I allow a few victories to keep them coming. Still, their fear seems to grow. Their frustration at their inability to stop me is palpable. They press harder, their movements frantic and wild. I let them come, their aggression a fuel for my performance. I dance in a blur of steel and shadow. My opponents' weapons clatter to the ground. I knock several guards unconscious, striking at their heads when there is a chance.

More guards run out of the monastery and join the fray. I fight them in the same fashion, panting as I retreat to make sure they do not surround me.

A loud blast sounds in the distance. The guards turn toward the monastery. A few attempt to run back, but I block their path and re-engage them. Soon, all they can think about is blocking my attacks.

One by one, they fall, their weapons discarded. At last, the last man stands, his eyes wide with terror. It is Joaquin, the young soldier. I approach him slowly, my sword held low. In a final act of defiance, he raises his rapier. I disarm him with a single, fluid motion, the rapier flying from his grasp and sinking into the earth.

I step aside and, extending my arm, invite him to trek down the mountain. He does not wait to be invited twice and runs away, headed toward the city below, where he will, perhaps, find comfort in his mother's arms. I would not blame him.

I have won, not through bloodshed, but through the sheer artistry of combat. It pleases me.

Men lie strewn at my feet, some groaning in a semi-conscious stupor. I sheathe my sword and stroll into the monastery, eyes roving in every direction. I walk along the length of the cells on the right side of the courtyard, observing the doors and the way each one is opened a crack. I smile as I enter one of the small, austere rooms. It is empty.

I keep walking, moving further back. Across the courtyard, a man scurries away in the shadows, crouching low and pretending I do not see him, though he knows well I do. I watch him until he runs past the broken gate, then continues walking.

One of the cell doors in the back is thrown wide open. A man lies on his stomach in front of it. I approach and notice blood glinting on the ground.

I wince. *Oh, Calierin, you couldn't keep your promise, could you?*

Stepping over the man, I enter the room. It is also empty but with one distinction. A large hole pierces the back wall, revealing the night and the rocky mountain terrain beyond. I smile as I imagine Calierin leading our kin away, promising them a return to their true homes. Our job is now to ensure their travels are safe, that no one pursues them. Valeria will accomplish that by talking to her sister. If she does not, I will soon join them to protect their passage.

The man on the ground groans.

I turn. Not dead, after all. Maybe there is hope for Calierin yet.

Dazed, he sits up and looks around. Blood seeps from a gash in his forehead. When he spots me, he tries to scramble to his feet but falls back down.

"I will not harm you," I say.

He stills, eyes wide. "Who . . . who are you?"

"I am Korben Theric, King of the Fae."

A sharp inhalation has him sitting up straighter.

"I came to free my people," I say. "They were unfairly imprisoned."

The man thinks for a moment, then says, "I'm glad you have done so, King . . . Korben."

I frown, surprised by his words.

"The queen wanted them all hanged. Tomorrow."

Rage blazes through my chest. "Queen Amira would have faced my sword had she dared."

"No," he shakes his head. "Not Queen Amira. She's dead. Queen Sara Plumanegra rules Castella."

"Who?!"

"The late queen's cousin. She and her husband . . . they roost in Nido now."

*Gods! No!*

Valeria's sister is dead. She cannot take another blow like that. Whirling, I run out the hole in the wall and leap into the sky, shifting to Dreadwing form.

I have to get to Valeria.

# 49

## VALERIA

*"I will take care of her. We have a score to settle."*

**Gran Duquesa Sara Plumanegra (Casa Plumanegra) – 3rd in line to Plumanegra throne**

In the shape of a lonely raven, I go unnoticed. Floating on outstretched wings, I land on the sparring terrace that saw Amira and I practice a thousand times. There are no cries of alarm, no guards coming after me. I made sure to swoop down when no one was looking. Cuervo does the same and lands a distance away.

I shift back into my human form, heart knocking as fear of what's to come unfurls in my chest. I pat my shoulder and Cuervo jumps to perch on it.

"You have to be quiet." I press a finger to his lips. He bobs his head.

Bracing myself for the worst, I make my way up the stairs that lead to the armory. Unsurprisingly, the door is open. It doesn't lock from the outside, and there are guards out here who will need to go back in.

Padding silently, I walk inside and ease the door shut behind me.

An oil lamp sits on a stand, illuminating the many rapiers, shields, and other sparring gear hanging on the wall.

Like a ghost who doesn't belong in her own home anymore, I make my way toward Amira's bedchamber. On my way, I notice more guards than usual. They're stationed throughout the palace, but I avoid them with ease. No one knows this place the way I do.

When I peek around the corner into the corridor that leads to my sister's quarters, I'm surprised to find no guards posted at the door. This signifies she isn't there. After Rífíor held her at dagger point demanding The Eldrystone be returned, her paranoia grew to new levels, and she began stationing people outside every room she entered.

Regardless, I approach her door and listen. Nothing. I quietly open the door and step inside. The curtains are thrown open, letting in a wash of dim moonlight. The bed is untouched, the hearth unlit, the desk barren. I frown. Amira can't sleep unless her room is completely dark, and her desk has never been so bare. Perhaps, after all that happened here, she decided to move to a different bedchamber. I wouldn't blame her. But where did she go? There are literally dozens of possible rooms she could have chosen.

*Damn!*

Maybe she's in her study. Looking for her there would be more fruitful than searching countless bedchambers on different floors. I head in that direction.

In her study, I find a similar situation: no guards, the door unlocked, and a clean desk inside.

A gnawing feeling starts at the pit of my stomach. I ignore it and try to think of the next best place to look for my sister. Perhaps one of the libraries. She enjoys epic novels, though it's been some time since I found her curled up with one of them on one of the comfortable settees.

Cursing inwardly, I head toward the east wing to one of her favorite spots to read. It never occurred to me I wouldn't be able to find her. When I get to the library, I find it desolate, the books standing like silent tombstones. My disquiet grows.

"What now, Cuervo? Where should I look next?"

He makes a purring sound in the back of his throat.

I could spend all night wandering Nido's corridors and never find her. Maybe I should ask someone, but who? I wouldn't dare disturb Nana, and there's no one else I really trust. It is sad to realize how disconnected from Nido's residents I've always been. If I'm able to return—if Amira doesn't throw me in a dungeon—I will fix that.

I leave the library, my steps somewhat aimless. I consider holding one of the guardias at dagger point and demanding where to find the queen, but they may be as clueless as I am. I stop at a fork with three other corridors leading in different directions. I have no idea which way to go.

A faint sound comes from my left. I cock my head and listen. A woman's laughter. I veer in that direction, following the noise. After a moment, I find myself on the path toward the throne room. Maybe Amira is holding some sort of gathering there. She hates late-night parties, but such things are often part of a monarch's duty.

When I get close, I observe two guards standing by the side door. There are four entrances to the grand room, one at each cardinal point, the one in the south side is the main one, consisting of tall doors with intricate carvings, designed to impress visitors with their grandeur. There are two side doors on the east and west flanks, and a back door on the north side, which leads to a dressing room and subsequently to the dais. This entrance allows the reigning monarch to go about unseen. Only Amira's Plumanegra key opens that door, which means I need to use one of the others, all likely guarded the same as this one.

The female laughter issues from the room once more. It's high-pitched and overly excited, not one I recognize. The rumble of a man's voice, faintly familiar, accompanies it. I listen a while longer, growing certain that only two people are in the room, and they're occupied in some sort of sexual diversion or game. The playful patter of feet, the woman's shrieks of delight, the man's lascivious tone . . .

But who could they be? Certainly not Amira—not unless she's drunk or out of her mind. I can't even imagine who she would engage in such activity. Besides, she would never behave that way in the proximity of her Guardia Real or . . . anyone.

That feeling in the pit of my stomach fully unfurls. Something isn't right. Obeying only my instincts, I march toward the guards. When they notice me, they peel away from the door and face me.

"Who goes there?" one of them asks.

As I get closer, I see no recognition in their expressions.

"Stop and identify yourself." The guards take hold of their rapiers, ready to draw them.

I come to a halt several paces away from them. "If you must know, I am Valeria Plumanegra, daughter of Simón Plumanegra and Loreleia Plumanegra."

Their eyes go wide, and they immediately unsheathe their swords and lunge. Cuervo leaps into the air, and I move out of the way, easily sidestepping them. Gliding past them, I burst into the room to find a revolting, unexpected tableau.

Bent over the dais with her elbows propping her up, my second cousin, Sara Plumanegra, stands in front of none other than Don Justo Medrano. Her skirts are gathered around her waist, and his pants hang around his knees as he services her, pounding repeatedly into her, skin slapping against skin. The crown that father wore only on official events rests on his head.

At the intrusion, Sara shrieks, pushing back her skirts to cover her nudity, attempting to get away from the disgusting man. For his part, he doesn't release her. Instead, he holds her in place and turns to look in the direction of the interruption.

"How dare you . . .?" He trails off as he recognizes me, and at last releases Sara, quickly pulling up his pants.

The guards who I left behind scramble into the room. This time I unsheathe my rapier and back away from them, still trying to process what I've just seen. Cuervo flies into the room, cawing loudly, and circles over our heads.

"What are you two doing here?!" I demand. "How dare you disrespect this place?"

Sara's face is bright red with shame and agitation as she quickly rearranges her dress. Her eyes are downcast for a moment, but her usual gall quickly finds its way back.

"You are the only *disrespect* here. Guards!" she exclaims. "Arrest her."

More guards burst in through the other two doors to join the ones already in the room. I stand my ground, not the least bit intimidated by their presence.

"What are you waiting for?" Don Justo demands. "Do as my wife, *the queen*, ordered." He smirks, triumph stamped all over his face.

*My wife. The queen.*

*My wife. The queen.*

*My wife. The queen.*

The message he so eagerly delivered reverberates loudly inside my head like the overwrought clanging of a bell.

"Where is Amira?" I demand. "Where is my sister?" The images of her abandoned-looking bedchamber and study flash before my eyes. "Where. Is. My. Sister?" I repeat, my voice a raw staccato of anger.

Don Justo's triumphant smirk deepens. "She is dead."

I shake my head. "No. No!"

Amira can't be dead. She is the only family I have left.

*She can't be. She can't be. She can't be!*

My hands tremble. The rapier falls from my grip and clatters to the floor. I stare between the spots where Mother and Father exhaled their last breaths. They both died in this very room, and now, in the same place, I learned that Amira . . .

No!

I look up. Don Justo is still smirking. Sara wears an undecipherable expression.

"Arrest this pathetic woman." Don Justo flicks a hand in my direction, affecting a tired expression, as if the past minute in my presence has already been too much.

The guards move closer, cautious but confident as I'm not armed anymore. In their regard, I'm only a harmless, distraught woman they would have no trouble handling.

Something quakes inside of me, something that starts like pain but quickly morphs into fury. My blood boils, a furnace of rage igniting within me. Sara shakes herself, her eyes suddenly glittering with cruel satisfaction as she moves closer to Don Justo, both looking proud of their heinous crime.

"Amira was a terrible excuse for a queen," Sara says in her haughty voice. "She needed to be . . . removed. You shouldn't have returned, Valeria. You and Jago were always a disgrace, and now you are traitors."

"Get Jago's name out of your filthy mouth!"

"Oh, please, don't make a spectacle. You have already soiled the Plumanegra name enough."

I clench my fists, nails biting into my palms. My sister, the untried queen, sacrificed on the altar of their twisted ambition.

"You monsters," I spit, the words laced with venom. "How could you? She was . . . she was . . ." I falter, unable to complete the sentence. Tears, hot and stinging, blur my vision.

I'm a volcano erupting, a tempest unleashed. Shifting magic surges through me, a torrent of raw power. The room shimmers, the air crackling and igniting. My form begins to change, beak sprouting, bones reshaping. Feathers erupt from my back, a dark, iridescent shroud. My fingers transform into talons, sharp and deadly.

Then I grow and grow and grow.

I hold Dreadwing form, a raven of magnificent size, a creature made to deliver vengeance.

The approaching guards retreat, their rapiers nothing but useless sticks. Sara screams in horror and tries to run. I block her path at the same time that I stretch out my wings and send the guards flying against the walls. I stoop under the tall ceiling, rage searing my veins.

The space feels small, a stifling prison unable to contain the extent of my anger. I kick the balcony door open, thrashing, wanting to tear everything in sight. A gust of cold wind sweeps into the throne room.

With a deafening *caw*, I leap, beating wings a blur against the stone walls. My monstrous shape blots out the light from the gas sconces on the walls.

Sara and Don Justo cry out, their voices lost in the cacophony of my wings. With a powerful grasp, I snatch them up, their bodies dangling helplessly from my talons, and jump out through the balcony. Wind whips through my feathers. Cuervo follows but can't keep up.

Nido falls away as I climb. I squeeze my talons, eliciting cries of pain that are lost in the wind. I rise higher, the moon a shard in the vast night sky. The city lights twinkle like distant stars, and I'm reminded of everything I've lost. Why were we cursed with being Plumanegras?

Numbness replacing my fury, I release my grip. Sara and Don Justo plummet toward the earth, the sound of their screams growing dim.

"Amira, she's still alive!" Sara's voice, a desperate plea, reaches my ears.

She lies, the viper.

A flicker of doubt crosses my mind. But what if Sara isn't lying? What if Amira isn't truly dead? I dive, tucking my wings. I catch the bastardos just before they hit the ground. With a grunt of effort, I carry them to a desolate expanse of shadows and whispering trees.

I drop them, their bodies hitting the ground with a sickening *thud*. They lie still, their faces contorted in pain. Shifting back to my human shape, I stalk closer.

My hand still a talon, I dig my claws into Sara's shoulder. Two new forms in one night, but it barely registers.

She cries out, her eyes wide with fear.

"Where is she?" I demand.

"The dungeon," she whispers, her voice barely audible. "The deepest one."

"Tell me the truth," I growl, tightening my grip. "Or I'll send you back to the heavens as food for the vultures."

Don Justo, his face a mask of panic and cowardice, intervenes. "It's . . . it's true! W-we didn't kill her." He tries to reassure me, except he doesn't seem as skillful a liar as Sara. "Um, she's guarded by my most loyal subjects."

"You lie!" My other hand shifts into a talon, and I grip his throat.

His blue eyes—once so cold and full of bravado—waver. They flick toward Sara, begging for some sort of mercy.

"Yes. Yes! Justo is lying," Sara squeaks as blood stains her dress where my claw punctures her shoulder.

This gives me pause.

Sara rushes to add a breathless explanation. "It was his plan to . . . to kill her, and I told Justo I would get it done, but in the end, I couldn't. I'm not a murderer like him."

"You bitch!" Don Justo lifts his hands as if to strangle her, but I squeeze his neck more fiercely.

A bud of hope blooms in my chest.

"If you're lying, Sara, I will kill you," I say, digging my claws deeper into her flesh.

She screams in pain. "No, I'm not lying. I swear."

Suddenly feeling as if my hands are in contact with refuse, I release the couple, two harpies made for each other. My hands shift back, claws turning to fingers, the taint of blood disappearing.

The urge to kill them assaults me, but that would make me no better than they are. Besides, death is too easy. I can think of a much better punishment to make them suffer.

"You can go," I say.

They seem surprised and exchange incredulous glances. Don Justo stumbles to his feet and straightens his clothes, trying to appear dignified. A muscle in his chiseled jaw stiffens and twitches. He seems to be holding back words.

I take a step back, ready to leave.

He straightens his spine further, making himself as tall as he can while Sara still kneels on the ground, wiping away tears.

The words Don Justo is holding back finally make their way out. "You and your sister don't have what it takes to rule."

"And what is that?" I say.

"Ruthlessness," he replies.

"Oh, you're mistaken. I can be ruthless. Except, it takes much more than a cold heart to be a leader."

He huffs. "Really?"

"Yes. It takes . . . gold," I say and pause to let my message sink in.

He's slow to catch my meaning, but in the end, he does. "No! You wouldn't dare take what is mine," he barks, face turning red with anger.

"But I would because *I am* ruthless. All your property will be seized by the monarchy."

"No!" He makes as if to lunge for me, but the reappearance of a clawed hand makes him stay in place, trembling with fury.

I look down at Sara. "And you . . . never set foot in Nido again. Your stolen title of *queen* means nothing, and if you were once a duchess, you are one no more."

"No, please, Valeria, have mercy," she begs.

I laugh because letting her live would be considered a mercy by most, but not by Sara. That is how I know I've chosen the perfect punishment. She would rather die than miss an appointment with her seamstress.

"Enjoy washing each other's undergarments," I say, retreating into the shadows.

Shifting, I take to the sky once more.

*Amira, I'm coming.*

Below, I hear Sara scream at Don Justo. "This is all your fault."

"She will not get away with this," he roars.

"And how are you going to stop her? What are you going to do now that you've lost us *everything*? Where are we going to live? What are we going to wear? Oh, saints! All my beautiful dresses and jewelry."

"Shut up, woman!" He slaps her.

Sara shrieks in outrage.

*Good, they really deserve each other.*

Their voices fade away as I fly back home to find my sister.

---

"*The dungeon. The deepest one,*" Sara had said.

No one is sent there—not even Father could remember the last time someone was sentenced to rot in the bowels of Nido, a place the sun has never reached.

Cuervo stands on my shoulder as I march down a labyrinth of darkness, a place where the very air seems to decay and only a few torches light the way. A weird stench, a corruption I can't identify, hangs heavy, making me wonder what horrors once lurked within these walls.

I navigate the twisting corridors, my rapier held high, ready to face the guards assigned to watch over Amira, but I find no one. She's down here utterly alone.

A faint glimmer of light by one of the cells leads me to a heavy iron door. Cuervo jumps off my shoulder and lands on a ledge in the wall. I force the door open, the hinges groaning in protest.

Before me, the sight chills my blood. Amira lies on the cold stone floor, chained to the wall, her body gaunt and frail. Her eyes, once bright with life, stare vacantly. Her skin is pale as parchment, her hair matted and tangled. Heavy manacles circle her wrists, embedded into her flesh. Her face is contorted in pain.

A white-hot fury boils within me, threatening to consume me.

*I should have killed them!*

Setting the rapier aside, I approach my sister, my heart aching with sorrow. I kneel beside her. My hands tremble as I reach out to touch her face. She flinches, eyes wide with fear. I speak softly, reassuringly.

"It's over, Amira. I'm home."

She stares at me. Hope flickers in her gaze.

"Valeria?" she whispers in a quiet breath. "Is that really you?" A single tear tracks down her cheek, a silent plea for help.

I gently stroke her hair. "You're safe now. I won't let anyone hurt you ever again."

Weakly, she pushes away from me. Eyes shut tightly, she recoils from my touch.

*Oh, gods!* She's still mad at me. She'll never forgive me.

"I'm sorry I went against you," I say. "I—"

She groans, waving a filthy hand at my face. She doesn't want to hear my apologies.

"Please, Amira, let me explain."

My sister shakes her head.

"At least let me get you out of here." I try to help her up, but she shies away. "You can't stay in this cell." Nothing. "I'll get someone then. You trust Renata, right?" I start to stand, but Amira protests.

"No." Her voice is a low croak.

"I promise I'll leave you alone, but let me help you right now," I plead.

"F-forgive me, Valeria."

*What?! Forgive* her?

"You were right. I . . . should have listened to you."

"Oh, Amira. I don't care. I'm only glad—"

"Let me talk. I *have* to do this before I die."

I shake my head. "Nobody's dying. You're fine."

"No. No one is coming. I'll die here."

She must think I'm a hallucination. I really should have killed Sara and Don Justo! *Bastardos!* I'm starting to regret my decision to let them live.

I pull out my dagger and work it into the locking mechanism of one of the manacles. In a moment, it pops open, and I attack the next one. When her arms are free, Amira brings them together. Groaning as if it pains her, she hugs herself.

Grabbing her shoulders, I help her sit up, then take off my cloak and drape it over her chest, tucking it around her. She slumps against the wall, head hanging.

I exit the cell. "Cuervo, find help. Find help!" I point down the dark corridor.

He wastes no time and flies the way we came. I run back to Amira's side.

"I'm really here, Amira," I say, pushing matted hair out of her face.

She blinks in surprise as if she'd forgotten me. Swallowing thickly, she seems to struggle with her thoughts but manages to find the thread she let fall.

"I've had time . . . to think," she says. "There's nothing but time down here. That and an ache in my bones."

"Please, let me take you away from this awful place."

She rolls her head from side to side against the wall, a clear refusal. "They killed our mother and our father," she continues in an absent, delirious tone. "Then they turned my sister against me."

"I have never been against you. I only wanted to help you find a different way."

Ignoring me, she goes on. "They invaded my mind."

*It was only Orys, one evil male*, I want to say, but I don't dare speak his name for fear of causing her further distress. She seems to be . . . mad, caught in the past and all the terrible things that happened to us.

*Gods! What will become of Castella without her?*

She looks at me sidelong, perhaps accepting the *unreality* of talking to her hallucination.

"What happened to me, Valeria?" she asks. "You knew what I wanted to do was wrong, but in my mind, I saw no other alternative. Because . . . Because I wanted someone to pay. I wanted someone to suffer the way I have."

Tears fall freely down her face, carving trails in the filth that soils her cheeks. The admission pains her deeply. It's clear to tell. Amira has never been the type to admit when she's wrong. In that respect, she's much like our father.

I consider her question, making me doubt my initial assessment of her state of mind. A mad person doesn't self-examine, does she?

She goes on, "But I gained no satisfaction from what I did. I only felt . . . shame. Deep shame, the kind Father warned me about. He said . . .

*"My child, when you take the throne, you will make countless decisions. Some will be right, and some will be wrong. That is unavoidable. But remember this, the decisions that leave a nagging doubt, that stir unease in your heart and later bring you shame . . . those are the ones where you went wrong."*

She sobs, hugging herself tighter. "I was going to undo it, Val. I was going to take it all back, but . . ." She trails off.

"But then Sara and Don Justo threw you in here," I finish for her.

Closing her eyes, she slumps further against the wall. "Oh, that I could stay in this dream with you."

I clasp her hand and squeeze tightly. "It's *not* a dream, Amira. I'm truly here."

When Gaspar rescued me from the catacombs, I felt exactly the way Amira does at this moment. I kept thinking that I wasn't free, that none of it was real. It took hours for me to believe I was safe from Calierin and her torturous espíritu.

So I don't press Amira further. Instead, I hug her and rock her gently, humming the same tune she hummed for me that day, the one Mother taught us.

I don't know how long we stay that way, but the sound of hurried steps makes me jump to my feet and retrieve my rapier. A familiar flap of wings accompanies the noise. Cuervo! Has he found someone? I step out of the cell, peering into the dark.

Immediately, I recognize the silhouette of the male headed my way. Korben. I set aside the rapier and wrap my arms around him as he crashes into me. The crush of his strong embrace leaves me breathless. I sense his relief as if it were a current of energy washing over me.

After a moment, he pulls away and holds me at arm's length. "Valeria, your sister . . . she . . ." He can't finish. He must have heard the same lie Sara and Don Justo told me.

"She's here." I peer into the dark cell. "She's alive."

"Oh, thank the gods!"

The exclamation is genuine. He's glad I have not suffered another loss. I doubt he's ready to forgive Amira for what she did to his kin, no matter what my sister has gone through, but at the moment, he's truly relieved.

"Let us take her out of here." With firm steps, he marches into the cell, picks Amira off the floor, and carries her out. "This is no place for a queen."

# 50

## VALERIA

*"I never thought I would see its grandeur again. The Realta Observatory will host our astronomy eruditos once more!"*

**Diego Fontana XI – Erudito de la Academia Alada**

### ONE YEAR LATER

I stand on top of Nido, my home, in my favorite sparring rooftop courtyard. Castellina shines below, looking like a dark sky dotted by winking stars. Night has descended, and it seems the capital's residents have brought every fairy light to life, refusing to end the celebration. For three days, the denizens have reveled in commemoration of The Revival of the Veil.

Instituting the holiday has been a labor of love that required months of work, but most of all . . . patience. My job as Ambassador to the Fae is far from over, but I think we are headed in the right direction.

I'm aware that one festival will hardly begin to erase years of the animosity we showed toward our fae neighbors. Many more years of concerted efforts will be needed to establish a positive alliance between humans and fae, efforts that must have their roots in education. Children must be taught to love and help. Not to hate and hinder. If we succeed, within one generation, Castella will be an entirely different realm.

With a satisfied sigh, I turn east and regard the Realta Observatory. King Korben Theric sent his best sorcerers and sorceresses to reconstruct its previous grandeur. Now, its crystal towers jut toward the night sky, glowing with inner light, spearing the firmament with the promise of many astrological discoveries.

Every time I look at it, I can't help but marvel. As many times as I tried to imagine its broken pieces weaved back together, I failed to envision its true magnificence.

*Saints and feathers! It's beautiful!*

A sound makes me turn and face west. A small dark shape approaches, flying at top speed in my direction.

*Cuervo!* He caws repeatedly in warning. I sent him on a quest, and it seems he has news for me. My heart leaps.

With a grace I'm yet to accomplish when I land, Cuervo alights on the battlements, his entire body quivering with excitement.

"Korben! Korben! Korben!" he croaks, flapping his wings and hopping from talon to talon.

My heart leaps again, his excitement ratcheting up my own. I haven't seen Korben in over two months, and since his last visit, I've been counting the hours until his return.

Eyes roving all over the black sky, I search for him. I hear the *thump, thump, thump* of his large wings before I spot him, his massive Dreadwing form flying at top velocity.

435

My breaths grow fast. My hands tingle. I have been reduced to a mass of expectation, the half of a whole that yearns and yearns to be complete again.

As soon as Korben reaches the end of the courtyard, he shifts to his fae form and hits the ground running. He comes at me so fast that I barely have time to take a good look at him. Instead, I find myself wrapped in his strong arms, the scent of an east-bound wind and an otherworldly forest overwhelming my senses.

Squeezing me tightly, he lifts me off my feet and twirls, chest rumbling with laughter. "My little raven! I have missed you so."

His deep voice is like the touch of many feathers. My skin pebbles, and the next thing I know I'm pulling back to find his mouth and kiss him the way I've been wanting to do every day since he left. He responds in kind, threading his fingers through my hair and slipping his tongue into my mouth. A burst of desire spirals down to my core, and I want to take him right here and now. *Damn everyone who's waiting for us!*

We break our kiss reluctantly and pull away from each other. He looks me up and down, his tailored eyebrows drawing up to his hairline. Taking my hand, he raises it and makes me twirl. My gown flares out, its silky layers ballooning with the motion.

He whistles admiringly. "A dress," he says. "A dress!" he repeats incredulously. "You look stunning."

"You don't look so bad yourself."

He wears fitted black pants stuffed into tall boots and a waist-long burgundy jacket that molds to his torso, accentuating his massive chest and tapering to his narrow midsection. Gold embroidery trims the collar and cuffs, lending him a regal air.

Smiling, he interlaces his fingers through mine and turns to face the city. "How go the celebrations?"

"I believe the festival is a success," I say with pride because it was my idea and my tireless work that made it possible—not that I could have done it all by myself. I had plenty of help, and most importantly, Amira's support.

"I had no doubt it would be." He nods with satisfaction.

"The fairy lights are functioning again." I point at some of the lights in front of the palace, then make a sweeping gesture toward the city beyond. "One of the sorceresses you sent to work on the observatory offered to fix them."

Before the veil collapsed, lamp posts that housed fairy lights illuminated Castellina's streets. For two decades, they shed no glow, but now they're back, and I have begun to get a glimpse of the capital city Father grew up in.

"How are things in Riochtach?" I ask.

"Better every day. All trade routes to Castella have been reestablished. The Human Council has had a few productive meetings and a census is underway. Most of those who got stranded on our side have decided to stay."

"That's good," I say, though I don't manage to keep a tinge of bitterness from entering my words.

"But?" Korben asks, missing nothing.

"No buts, just . . . shame."

"Shame? What do you mean?"

This past year, shame has been an emotion that has tainted my contentment more than I'd like to admit. This is the first time I have mentioned it to anyone.

"I wish that we had treated your people better. I wish our hearts were kinder. Many times, I find myself wondering if we're simply not capable of more, that our nature is corrupt somehow."

He shakes his head and turns to face me. "There is nothing corrupt about any part of you, Ravógín."

"But I'm half-fae, so . . ." I shrug.

"Yes, but you are also half-human." He caresses my cheek. "Worry not, Valeria. Your people will be fine. What you have achieved this past year is proof of that. Besides, mistakes were made on both sides."

I bat a hand in front of him. "You're right. Don't listen to me. We're supposed to be celebrating all our accomplishments. Come on, everyone's waiting for you."

Taking his hand, I guide him in through the armory, and the many labyrinthine corridors that lead to Nana's favorite dining hall—a small, cozy room close to the main kitchen. It has a large fireplace that is kept lit all through the year for Nana's comfort.

Just before we enter the dining hall, Korben stops and rolls his shoulder as if trying to dispel tension.

"Are you all right?" I ask.

"Sure."

I cock an eyebrow.

"Well, to be honest, I am . . . I do not think your nana likes me," he blurts out.

Biting my lower lip, I repress a smile. "Um, I didn't know you felt that way."

"You are not denying it."

"Korben Theric, the mighty raven shifter, afraid of an old lady?"

It's taking all my strength not to lose my composure and start laughing.

"After the fae healer treated her, she still kept that walking stick even though she did not need it. I believe she wanted to whack me with it."

That does it. I start laughing, the picture of Nana chasing Korben with her stick is too much.

He crosses his arms, looking entirely unamused.

I clear my throat and sober up. "I promise you she has no stick today, and she doesn't *not* like you. She's just very protective of me and wants to make sure you're an honorable male deserving of all of this." I slide my hands down the length of my body.

He nods in a slow, deliberate way. "That is what worries me."

I take a step closer to him. "You're really worried about this?"

"Of course I am. The way I entered your life was not exactly noble."

"It's all right, Korben. I promise you. She has no other alternative but to like you. Eventually."

"I knew it," he grinds between clenched teeth. He makes a fist and squeezes it with his opposite hand.

I narrow my eyes, hands on hips. "So what are you going to do about it?"

He sobers up at the challenge. "I . . . I am going to charm her. Yes." He nods repeatedly. "I will use all my guiles on her and charm her. Thoroughly."

"Good plan," I say.

He gives one final, emphatic nod.

I walk into the room and as we cross the threshold I whisper under my breath, "Good luck with that."

Behind me, Korben sputters. I glance over my shoulder, throwing a mischievous smile at him. He glares back. His expression is sharp and seems to say, *You will pay for that, Valeria Plumanegra.*

And suddenly, all I think about is how he plans to make me pay. I can't wait to find out.

"It's about time, Chavé," Esmeralda exclaims when we enter.

She sits next to Nana, surely coaxing more stories about Jago out of her. They have been a salve to each other, talking about my cousin is their favorite pastime whenever Esmeralda visits. I think Nana would not be doing so well if not for keeping Jago close to her heart by reliving memories of him.

Amira gets up from her chair and greets Korben with a formal bow. "King Korben, it is an honor and pleasure to see you again."

"Likewise, Queen Amira." He inclines his head, arms held tightly at his sides—the perfect picture of royal proprietary.

This is the way they interact with each other all the time, no matter the circumstances. I think Amira keeps things stiffly diplomatic because she's ashamed of her actions against faekind, while Korben follows along because he carries a certain amount of shame as well. He was the leader of the veilfallen after all—not to mention he held Amira at dagger-point in her own bedchamber.

Talk about emotional baggage. I only hope one day they'll be able to dine without so many introductory genuflections. It's tiring to watch. Though, I can't say I'm not glad for my sister's poise. She has come a long way since that day I found her in the dungeons. It wasn't a quick recovery. It took many weeks for her to regain her physical strength—not to mention her emotional strength. At first, she doubted her every decision, and even suggested she should abdicate in my favor.

*"You are strong and a true Plumanegra,"* she said. *"I didn't even inherit Father's espiritu."*

Obviously, I had to quickly disabuse her of that stupid notion.

*"Would you say Jago wasn't a true Plumanegra?"* I demanded.

*"Of course not!"* she replied with conviction.

*"Then stop talking nonsense."*

Jago didn't inherit espiritu either, but he was a Plumanegra through and through.

As time went by, and Amira returned to her queenly duties, every success helped her gain confidence. Nonetheless, I had to remind her of Father's advice more than once. She seemed to want to focus on the first part alone: *"My child, when you take the throne, you will make countless decisions. Some will be right, and some will be wrong. That is unavoidable. But remember this, the decisions that leave a nagging doubt, that stir unease in your heart and later bring you shame . . . those are the ones where you went wrong."*

Except he also said . . .

*"Making the wrong decision is inevitable. To err is to learn and grow. So in the end, it's all about how you rise above your mistakes that truly defines who you are."*

I would definitely say she has risen very high. I'm proud of her, and I think Mother and Father would be, too.

After greeting Amira, Korben shakes Gaspar's hand. "It is good to see you again, El Gran Místico. Do you have any foretellings for me? Anything I should keep a close eye on?"

Gaspar strokes his braided beard, green eyes twinkling. "In fact, there is something, but I'd best keep it to myself." He raises an eyebrow and gives Korben a pointed look.

Korben frowns, then seems to catch his meaning. "Oh, yes. Please do."

"What are you ... ?" I begin to ask, but Korben turns sharply toward Nana, giving her his full attention.

"Señora Serena Aguila." He bows even more deeply than he bowed to Amira. "I am delighted to see you and to find that you are in good health."

Nana wears a cream-colored dress with a high neck, her gray hair arranged in a perfect chignon. She sits as straight-backed as she used to do fifteen years ago while she made Jago and I mind our lessons. She doesn't stoop or complain about pain in her bones any longer, and it's a wonderful thing, a relief to my soul.

"King Korben." Nana nods, her brown eyes assessing the male from head to toe.

He practically squirms inside his polished boots, his charms all forgotten. I wish Jago were here to see this. He would derive endless enjoyment out of it.

Without ceremony, Nana rings a tiny silver bell. A battalion of people enter from every direction, carrying trays laden with food. Korben and I hurry to take a seat.

He blushes a deep crimson and whispers in my ears, "I was not late, was I? I flew as fast as I could."

"No, Korben, you were not late. Nana just likes to preside and be in control."

He arranges his napkin on his lap, frowning at it as if it's a puzzle.

I take his hand. "It's all right, Korben. It's just a family dinner. Nothing to stress out about."

"If you say so."

We eat one course after another. The food is delicious. Nana made sure they prepared all of my favorites, including suckling pig and Tarta de Santiago. It's the best meal I've had in a long time. Esmeralda and Gaspar keep the conversation lively, relating their troop's adventures during their last journey to Alsur.

During the entire meal, Korben fidgets and stares at his napkin, never seeming to solve the puzzle it represents.

"Something troubling you?" I ask, as he picks at his dessert.

He only shakes his head. What is wrong with him? He seemed fine on the rooftop. Is my family too much for him? Does he not feel at ease among humans? Maybe coming to Castella brings back too many bad memories of his time as a veilfallen. Maybe now that he has spent time in Elf-Dún, he only visits Nido for my sake and would rather not have to.

*Saints and feathers!* Now, I'm the one frowning at my napkin.

Suddenly, he takes a deep breath and dumps the napkin on top of his Tarta de Santiago. The chair scraping behind him, he stands and stretches to his full height. He throws his shoulders back and holds his chin high, a look of unwavering determination in his onyx gaze. In that moment, he is a king, fully in control. It appears he has come to some sort of decision.

Conversation around the table ceases. All eyes turn to him. Nana's are full of distrust, and as they dart in my direction they seem to say, *I knew we shouldn't trust him.*

For some reason, my heart thumps fast. Is he about to announce some terrible decision he's made? The silence is deafening. An attendant starts to enter the room, then whirls and walks right back out, upon noticing the imposing fae male presiding over the table with the look of someone ready to go to war.

"Queen Amira," he says, his voice strong and full of conviction, none of the worries that seemed to plague him only a moment ago evident in his tone or demeanor.

"King Korben?" Amira frowns up at him and begins to stand.

He puts a hand up. "No need to stand." He clears his throat. "I wish to make a request of you."

My sister holds his gaze, a queen also in control. "And I hope I am able to grant it."

"Queen Amira, I request your sister's hand in marriage."

Everyone gasps in unison, except for Amira and Gaspar. The former only tightens her eyes slightly, and the latter nods knowingly.

What in all the gods' names does he think he's doing?

My sister shakes her head. "I am sorry, King Korben, but I cannot grant you this wish."

Korben flinches as if struck by an arrow.

"That's right!" I stand, glaring at Korben.

"Only Valeria can," Amira adds with finality.

He seems to recover somehow and slowly turns to face me. He is met by the force of my disapproval. I know it's tradition to ask the reigning monarch for the hand of any of their relatives, but he knows better than this.

A smile stretches Korben's mouth. He's not the least bit intimidated by me. In fact, he seems to have regained all his cocky confidence. Dark eyes never leaving mine, he drops to one knee.

"No," I say, pointing a shaking finger at him.

"But I have not asked you anything yet," he says.

I open my mouth and close it again. My heart thumps hard, then seems to stop as I hold my breath.

Korben takes my hand. The world around us seems to disappear.

"Will you be my wife, Princess Valeria Plumanegra?"

I inhale sharply and shake my head.

He frowns, his confidence slipping. I stop shaking my head. I wasn't saying no. I just can't believe he's doing this, springing it on me in front of everyone.

"Will you not let me love you for as long as I live, Ravógín?"

"No," I say, this time with conviction.

"What?!" Esmeralda exclaims from the other end of the table.

The air in the room congeals.

Nana rises. "We will take tea in the Iris Room."

As Nana waves them out with impatient hand gestures, the others file from the room, throwing glances over their shoulders. Korben stands, straightening his jacket and staring at the floor. Nana walks with her hands interlaced in front of her. Before crossing the threshold, she meets my gaze.

"You might be making a mistake, child," she says, then she leaves.

Korben's head jerks up, and he watches her go, surprise etched in his features. "And I thought she would be the one to reject me." Shaking his head, he takes several steps back, putting some distance between us.

"You shouldn't have . . . asked me in front of everyone," I say.

"If I had asked on the rooftop, would your answer have been different?"

I hesitate.

He nods. "I thought so." He rubs his chest and turns, presenting his profile as if to hide the bulk of his emotions.

"Korben, I can't marry you."

"You have made that abundantly clear. I should . . . leave?" It's a hesitant question, even though he begins a retreat from the room, turning his back on me.

I swallow the aching lump in my throat. "You should marry someone who will live a long life by your side. There, I said it."

He stops and, bit by bit, turns to face me again. His expression softens, something like hope flickering in the depths of his bottomless eyes.

"Is that the reason for your rejection?" he asks.

I can't answer. I'm too busy fighting back tears.

He comes closer, so close that I want to melt into his arms and weep. "You deserve someone who will love you for as long as *you* live."

Korben takes my face in his hands, his touch as gentle as the caress of a wing. "Silly little raven, don't you know that one day with you is much more than a lifetime with anyone else? I love you, Valeria. It is you who my heart has been searching for all these years."

"It wouldn't be fair, and I won't do that to you," I say firmly, trying to break contact.

Except he holds me in place, gaze drilling into mine. "Just one thing, Valeria . . . your truthful answer. That is all I want. Will you give it?"

"Of course."

"If you knew that you had inherited your mother's fae longevity, would you marry me then?"

I turn my head away, but he gently brings it back, so I'm facing him again. "Your truthful answer, Valeria."

The word bubbles up, searing my chest and leaving a trail of pain behind. "Yes, of course."

With an exhalation of relief, Korben falls to his knees, wraps his arms around my waist, and rests his head on my stomach.

His chest spasms. Is he crying?

*Gods! My heart can't take this.*

I immediately want to take back my answer. I will not marry him. This hypothetical is just that. I will not be the old lady he has to cart around while he remains young and vibrant. I will not give him children whose lifespans might be a fraction of his own.

My fingers thread through his silky hair. I love him so much, and that is why I can't stand the idea of bringing him more pain. He has endured enough.

"Please, Korben, get up."

He pulls back and swiftly slips a ring onto my finger.

"What are you doing? No." I try to take it off, but he holds my hands and stands, tears pooling in his eyes.

"How does Queen Valeria Plumanegra Theric sound to you?" he asks.

"Korben, that's not—"

"Before we left the Whispering Wilds, I told my parents you were the one, that I was going to ask you to marry me."

I remember he stepped aside and talked to them in private. I didn't ask about the conversation because I didn't think it had anything to do with me.

"They gave me their blessing," he adds, "and then my mother said that she knew you were the one and was happy for us. She told me that Niamhara saw in you the queen Tirnanog needed, and that it was fortunate you had inherited your mother's longevity."

"What?"

He nods.

"Niamhara said that?"

"Yes."

"And you didn't tell me." I pound a fist on his chest. "You idiot."

He picks me off my feet, laughing and turning in slow circles. "You nearly killed me, Ravógín."

"You nearly killed *me*," I protest. "You could have saved us all this . . . torture if you'd told me. I love you, you fool, and I absolutely want to be your wife."

I kiss him, the vision of a boundless future stretching before me, a future full of peace and prosperity for Castella and Tirnanog.

DON'T MISS THE BEGINNING OF VALERIA
AND RIVER'S STORY . . .

Available now!

THE PRINCE WOULD CHOOSE
TO SAVE HIS REALM.
BUT THE BEAST WOULD FOLLOW
HIS HEART . . . TO ME.

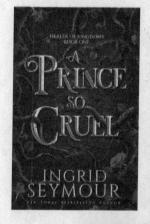
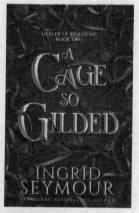

Available now!